ZANE PRESENTS
PASSION Island

Dear Reader:

Cairo always brings the heat, along with drama, and *Passion Island* delivers it.

Readers are exposed to the lives of three couples—Krista and Kendall Evans; Brenda and Roselle Woods; and LaQuandra and Isaiah Lewis—as they explore the ups and downs of their relationships on a private island off the coast of Tahiti in the South Pacific.

This adventure offers the best and worst from this trio of couples under the direction of Dr. Gretchen Dangerfield, a sexologist and therapist with actions and thoughts off the planet when it comes to her clients. She's cool, savvy, seductive and practices a no-holds-barred theory where anything and everything goes in this lush paradise. The couples, who've arrived for a six-week session to reignite their relationships, get more than they bargained for, including the revelation of dark secrets and desires.

While the novel is entertaining and loaded with Cairo-style erotica, there is another side of the journey: the doctor's tactics are engaging with her consultation style, and readers may feel as if they too are in a therapeutic chair. Her messages are realistic and provide challenging techniques on relationship advice. Whether the characters decide to heed it or not, they must face their own realities.

Sit back and become immersed in tropical temptation on this wild ride.

As always, thanks for supporting myself and the Strebor Books family. We strive to bring you the most cutting-edge, out-of-the-box material on the market. You can find me on Facebook @AuthorZane.

Blessings,

Zane

Publisher
Strebor Books
www.simonandschuster.com

ALSO BY CAIRO

Prison Snatch
The Pleasure Zone
Dirty Heat
Between the Sheets
Ruthless: Deep Throat Diva 3
Retribution: Deep Throat Diva 2
Slippery When Wet
The Stud Palace
Big Booty
Man Swappers
Kitty-Kitty, Bang-Bang
Deep Throat Diva
Daddy Long Stroke
The Man Handler
The Kat Trap

WITH ALLISON HOBBS

Sexual Healing

ZANE PRESENTS

A NOVEL BY

CAIRO

SBI

STREBOR BOOKS

NEW YORK LONDON TORONTO SYDNEY

Strebor Books
P.O. Box 55471
Atlanta, GA 30308
www.simonandschuster.com

This book is a work of fiction. Names, characters, places and incidents are products of the author's imagination or are used fictitiously. Any resemblance to actual events or locales or persons, living or dead, is entirely coincidental.

ISBN 978-1-59309-698-4
ISBN 978-1-50111-736-7 (ebook)
LCCN 2017941829

First Strebor Books trade paperback edition November 2017

Cover design: www.mariondesigns.com
Cover photograph: © Keith Saunders/Keith Saunders Photos

10 9 8 7 6 5 4 3 2 1

Manufactured in the United States of America

For information regarding special discounts for bulk purchases, please contact Simon & Schuster Special Sales at 1-866-506-1949

The Simon & Schuster Speakers Bureau can bring authors to your live event. For more information or to book an event, contact the Simon & Schuster Speakers Bureau at 1-866-248-3049 or visit our website at www.simonspeakers.com.

Dedication

For you, the readers . . .

Step into your own sexuality, embrace sensuality,
and allow passion to guide you.
Keep waving those freak flags!

Acknowledgments

What's good, my freaky peeps? It's been a minute since I've written one of these. I mean, after seventeen books in, whom else should I have to acknowledge? You all know you're my motherfuckin' peeps. You all know how thankful and blessed I am to have you riding on this literary journey with me. You all know how much I appreciate you waving your freak flags and spreading the heat with ya own peeps.

So, again . . . whom else do I need to say thanks to?

But, uh, for the hypersensitive—I say, thank you, thank you, thank you!

Enough said.

So moving on. *Passion Island* was supposed to be a story of three couples seeking sexual freedom, welcoming hidden desires, and embracing unbridled passion like never before; it was supposed to be a mush love story with a happy-ever-after ending.

But somehow the story evolved into something much bigger than I had any control of. The voices, the characters, their personalities—all had influence over how the tale should be told. With that being said, this is their story. Not mine. And, hopefully, you will enjoy their journeys as lies are uncovered, truths are exposed, and loads of drama unfolds.

Now open wide, you nasty heathens. And step into the heat. ☺

One luv—

Cairo

Prologue

Rope looped around each wrist and tied to the headboard, her cunt tightened up like a vise, her slick walls clutching, as her six-foot-three, two-hundred-and thirty-five pound anonymous lover pummeled his thick, long dick into her wet valley.

Skin the color of mahogany, stretched over rippled abs and miles of muscled back, glistened from sweat as Mr. Anonymous stroked her walls and slid his dick back and forth over her G-spot; the head of his dick nudging her cervix.

The woman arched her back, her eyes slowly rolling back in her head. Her anonymous lover was fucking her . . . *down*. And yet he methodically stroked the core of her soul. Sweetly. He was fucking her pussy. Loving her pussy.

How could that be?

How could a man, a stranger, dig so deeply into her guts, stretch her cunt, and ravish her walls and then so gently caress every fiber of her being at the very same moment?

How could this man burn the essence of her skin with just his touch?

A man she could not see. Or touch.

The woman couldn't make sense of it, even though she knew there had to be some rational reason for this exquisite man being able to—

"Aaah. *Oooh.* God, yessss . . ."

The air heated and sweetened from her musk. And she audibly inhaled. Her pussy smelled . . . intoxicating. She—*unh, ooh, yes*—tried desperately to remember the last time she'd had an orgasm—one not manipulated by her own hand or by some ridiculously expensive sex toy.

She couldn't.

And, and . . . oh, God, yes . . .

This was what she'd asked for, wasn't it? Yes, yes, yes. Oh, God, yes.

She croaked out a half-grunt, half-groan as a tear—a mixture of pleasure and heartache—slid down her cheek.

Oh God, oh God . . . yes, goddammit, yes . . .

Her pussy rippled over her secret lover's cock. Smooth velvet wrapped around thick, hard dick. This, this—oh God, yes . . . this anonymous fucking, felt so d-d-damn good. She needed this—God knows she did. But it wasn't the man she loved. It wasn't her husband. And yet her body defied the confusion swimming around in her mind. She couldn't get her husband out of her head, wondering what he was doing at this very moment. Was he somewhere fucking some island whore behind her back? Was he somewhere with his dick stuffed down in some other bitch's neck?

Still . . .

She cried out, her hands tightly gripping the restraints. She felt so helpless. So trapped. And, yet, so liberated.

"Oh God," she heard herself murmur as she felt soft fingers rolling lazily around her clit, making her skin erupt with goose bumps.

This wasn't cheating. It was therapy. Sexual healing. Wasn't this why she'd come to Passion Island, for passion and therapeutic healing?

"God, God, God . . . yes, yes, *yessss,*" she chanted as another woman's delicate hand drew slow, deliciously sweet circles over her clit.

"*Mm. Ja, mijn liefde,*" the other woman whispered in her ear. "*Geniet van zijn grote pik met uw natte kutje* (Mm, yes my love. Soak his big cock with your wet pussy)."

Tears gathered behind the woman's eyelids as she tried to imagine what her lover looked like, while fighting through the hurt and betrayal she felt so consumed with. Her husband had hurt her over and over and over again—with his lies and infidelity. Yet she was too weak to leave him. She didn't want to abandon their marriage the way he had abandoned her, leaving her heart aching and her cunt empty.

However, through everything, she still summoned the fortitude from somewhere deep within to forgive him for his indiscretions, his moments of weakness. After all, what man didn't cheat, at least once? It was in their DNA. Men were born to be dogs. They were bred to be unfaithful. They had to be *trained* to be faithful and loyal.

So why hadn't he been faithful and loyal to her? She fought to understand, nearly driving herself crazy, trying to figure out what it was those other bitches had that she didn't?

Still, in spite of her husband's faults, he was a good man. But she was simply tired of his shit. She was tired of being in her marriage by herself. She was tired of begging—for attention, for love, and now, most recently, his dick.

She was a woman with wants and needs and desires, too.

And what she wanted most was for her husband to love her again, to want her again. And she was willing to do whatever it took to win him back.

The woman tethered to the bed cried out as her clandestine lover began thrusting furiously. The steady pounding of his body into hers made her toes curl. He was fucking her like a wild, rabid animal as he rammed in and out, pounding her into the maelstrom of a third orgasm.

"*Yessss, yessss, yesssssss . . .*"

She gasped for breath, her body arching, welcoming the rippling waves of ecstasy. She heard him growl, and then it dawned on her that she hadn't heard him say one word the whole evening; only grunts, groans, and garbled sounds of pleasure.

"*Ja*, my love," she heard the woman with the seductive drawl murmur near her ear. The thick accent warmed her skin, causing prickly heat to coat her flesh. "Let yourself go, my darling. *Geven uw natte kut.*" The woman's native tongue whispering in her ear, urging her to give into her wet pussy made her walls clench. She moaned as she felt the fluttering of fingertips over her nipples. She'd never had another woman touch her breasts, her clit—or any other part of her body before and the sensation, the knowing, was startling. Her nipples suddenly became turgid, chocolate peaks of arousal, swollen and painfully tight.

Heat splintered through her.

Behind the blindfold, her eyeballs rolled around in their sockets, and her lids struggled to flutter open against the silky material. But there was nothing but a blanket of blackness over her eyes. More heat danced over her skin as her mystery lover's dick—

"Oh God, oh God . . . *ohhhh* . . . *unh* . . ."

The curve of his dick swept around her cunt, brushing her walls causing vibrations to ricochet through her womb.

"Please God, yes, yes, *yessss!*" the woman cried out and grew wetter, her lips swelling between her legs.

The scent of sex and sin and unbridled lust filled her nose. She breathed in, and swallowed as her lover's gaze dipped to the swell of the other woman's own breasts, her nipples and chocolate-colored areolas visible through her sheer gown. He growled over the red gag ball strapped in his mouth at the erotic image.

Everything about the exotic beauty standing before them was breathtaking. She'd been one of his many fantasies. He'd fucked her in all of his fantasies, his dreams, many times over the years.

As he eyed the exotic goddess, he imagined it was her cunt his dick was in. He wanted nothing more than to feel his thick organ snuggled deeply inside her heated walls. He imagined her pussy being hot silk.

The striking enchantress licked her lips and slid a hand through the thigh-high slit of her dress and pulled it back like a curtain, unveiling her heavenly cunt. With eager fingers, she opened herself to him, pulling open her petals, giving him a glimpse of her glistening pink flesh.

Transfixed on the magnificent view of her cunt, her labia, her beautiful clit, he drew in a breath and slammed his dick in and out of his bounded lover's quaking body; his dick knocking against her cervix with a ravening hunger.

His fantasy woman leaned forward and licked over the ball stuffed in his mouth, and—*holy shit*—he nearly came on the spot.

He grunted again, sweat dripping from his face, sliding down the center of his chest. He gripped the edge of an orgasm, and fought to contain himself.

The seductress watching him watch her undid him. She wet her lips again, the pink tip of her tongue seductively darting out, teasing him. He nearly groaned. And then she leaned forward. Her mouth brushed against the woman's ear beneath him, and he felt her pussy quiver around his dick. "*Je wilt je kut gevuld met lul, mijn liefde* (You like your cunt stuffed with cock, my love)?"

His mystery lover had no idea what the sexy siren was saying, but it made her toes curl again. And she mewled out and writhed as her lover's hips rocked forward, thrusting hard and urgently into her body—his dick sliding against the walls of her cunt.

The masked woman moaned. "Yes, yes, *yessss* . . ."

She felt herself being tossed around in a sea of sexual pleasure and emotional pain as sensual heat washed over her as she became swept up into the blaze of another orgasm.

"Welcome to Passion Island, my darling," was all the woman heard before the room went blurry around her and she grew hotter, wetter, and then . . .

She felt herself getting swept up in the firestorm.

One

Brenda Woods stepped on the gas and ran through the red light, not caring about the posted speed limit or potentially getting a speeding ticket. She was going seventy in a forty-mile zone and still running late. She had a plane to catch. And she didn't give a damn how fast she was going. She had no intentions of missing her flight.

The thick-hipped, curvy diva with the butterscotch complexion and almond-shaped eyes was on a mission. Come hell or high water, she would be boarding that plane. And nothing but death would stand in her way from climbing aboard the luxury private jet.

She needed this six-week, all-expense-paid getaway, like she needed the air she breathed. She needed her *whole* life back. And she needed it back, fast, before she became unglued.

Professionally, she had it going on. Her trendy hair salon, Scissor Happy, was finally pulling in the clientele and the coins that would set her apart from her competitors. No, no. She had no competition. She considered her salon one of *the* best.

Shit. Who was she kidding? She knew as did the rest of the hair industry that until she crushed out her only real rival—the highly successful Nappy No More hair salon—she would *still* be second best. The salon's owner had several locations in Jersey, New York, and California. Now *that* bitch was getting paid. And Brenda wanted that same level of high-profile success. She'd never openly admit it, but she secretly admired, idolized, and envied its owner, Pasha.

Still, Nappy No More—aside from numerous locations—didn't have anything that her salon, Scissor Happy, couldn't have. It was in a class all by itself. And it had the potential to be one of the world's premier hair salons. And it was well on its way to being just that. And she was happy. Finally living the good life.

Now her personal life . . . *ugh*. Well, it was part good, and part bad, with a mixture of bullshit stirred somewhere in the middle, thanks to her philandering husband. Roselle.

Simply put, she was tired of his cheating . . .

Her stiletto-clad foot pressed down on the pedal and the car flew through another light as it turned from yellow to red.

Roselle—red-skinned with jet-black wavy hair and dark, long lashes (a pretty boy)—cut his eye over at his wife, then flicked his gaze to the speedometer. What the fuck? She was flying. And he had to wonder if she was trying to kill them—*him*, intentionally.

It wouldn't have been the first time she'd tried some crazy shit like that. But he wasn't going to let himself think about her crazy-ass antics. It was too early in the morning for this shit.

The bitch was crazy.

But the pussy was good.

Real good. Wet and juicy good; he had to keep reminding himself of that. Hell, yeah, she had good pussy. And she sucked dick and swallowed. It didn't get any better than that, crazy or not. Still, she had multiple screws loose.

However, two kids and eleven years later, he had no intentions of leaving her. Like the saying went, it was cheaper to keep her. So fuck a divorce. He'd ride it out with her nutty-ass until she'd had enough and wanted out of the marriage on her own. Until then, he'd be stuck with her evil ass. And he'd keep slinging his dick whenever his salacious urges heated through his veins.

That didn't mean he didn't love her. He did. She had his heart in a way that no other woman ever had, or would. But he loved himself more. And—in no particular order, he loved fucking, getting head, and busting a heavy load. Yeah, he was a selfish motherfucker, and a very horny bastard.

And?

Shit. She knew what it was before she'd married him. She'd played the sidepiece for almost two years, was willing to share the dick, before she'd finally made her way to MVP—Most Valued Pussy.

So what the fuck was her problem now?

She knew he loved her crazy ass. Knew that them hoes in the streets didn't mean shit. They were just a piece of wet ass and a nut.

Roselle sighed inwardly, glancing over at Brenda. She was pretty as fuck. He allowed his gaze to linger over her breasts—oh hell yeah, those big, bouncy tits with the big areolas and thick nipples. He felt his dick thicken as he imagined sliding his meat between the folds of her breasts. A nice titty-fuck was what his dick needed.

Brenda felt his gaze on her, and shot him a hot glare that said, "Why the fuck are you staring at me?" She rolled her eyes for emphasis and sped through another light.

Roselle shook his head. *Evil ass.*

Truth be told, he hated what his cheating ways did to his wife. And he hated even more having to apologize for shit he wasn't necessarily sorry for. And he hated making promises he knew, *she* knew, he most likely wouldn't keep. He'd try, like now, to not fuck another woman.

And, so far, for the last two months, he'd managed to keep his dick home. Well, shit, wait—head didn't count, right? Nah, head definitely wasn't cheating. And it was that mindset that told him it was okay for him to let some young booster chick suck his dick in the backseat of his truck in exchange for a pair of woman's Gucci shades she'd managed to swipe out of Neiman Marcus for him.

The same oversized sunglasses his wife currently had wrapped around her face, his gift to her for her birthday. It was fair trade. He got superb head, and his wife got a banging pair of shades.

"Don't you think you should slow it down?" he asked calmly as she made a sharp right, then sped down the street.

She sucked her teeth, cutting her eyes at him. "I got this," she grumbled. "But if it wasn't for *you*, I wouldn't have to run red lights 'n' shit. So don't start."

They were running late, once again, because of his ass. Red-skinned fucker. She felt like backhanding him. He'd been dragging his heels all goddamn morning, being his usual passive-aggressive self. And all she knew was, if they missed this flight, she was going to jail because she was going to slice open his face with her six-inch acrylics.

"All I'm saying, Bren, is slow down. Damn." He shook his head. "I know I was dragging my ass this morning, but that doesn't mean you gotta be reckless behind the wheel."

"Don't tell me how to drive," she snapped. She felt like slamming on the brakes and watching his head go through the windshield. God, he made her so fucking sick, just looking at him or hearing his voice made her want to claw his face open. And if she thought she could get away with it without him beating her ass—not that he'd ever put his hands on her, but there was a first time for everything. Shit. She knew her man—pretty boy or not—was no punk, and she knew just how far to go with him; even though he allowed her to get away with more than she knew any other man would.

Roselle was a mixture of men—a little street, a little hood with a splash of sophistication and lots of education (yes, she'd snatched herself a man with a college degree!). And those were some of the things that had drawn her to him.

"Yo, I'm not telling you how to drive," Roselle said, trying his damnedest to keep from snatching the steering wheel from her. "I'm telling you to slow the fuck down. Period."

She blinked him back into view and said, "I said I got this." She clenched her teeth, gripping the steering wheel tighter. "So don't start your shit with me."

Roselle gritted his teeth. *This disrespectful bitch!* Anger splintered through his mind. He was really getting tired of her calling him out his name. Her slick-ass mouth would be the reason he'd conveniently forget real men didn't put their hands on women, and crack her motherfucking jaw open. Shit. She was lucky he'd never beat her ass, like the last motherfucker she was with. He didn't agree with a man putting his hands on a woman, but he definitely understood why some motherfuckers knocked a bitch's eye socket in, and punched all of her teeth out.

That mouth.

Sweat trickled down Roselle's back. Brenda picked a ninety-eight-degree day to decide she wanted to have the goddamn windows down instead of pumping the AC.

All for spite, he was sure.

She was spiteful as hell, he admitted inwardly. *I knew I should have driven my own shit*, he thought to himself as he took several moments to keep his attitude in check. He glanced over at the speedometer again.

"Slow the fuck down," he ground out, giving her a hot stare. "Or pull this motherfucker over."

She took her eyes from the road for a moment to throw a glare in his direction. Opened her mouth to say something, but closed it just as quickly. She faced forward before speeding through the intersection. They were only a few blocks from the ramp that led toward the Garden State Parkway, and twenty minutes from the airport.

Her SUV bounced as she hit a deep pothole.

"*Shit*," she hissed. The last thing she needed was another bent rim or her front end tore up again. She'd just gotten her truck back a few weeks ago after damaging her suspension system.

Fucking potholes!

Roselle's head hit the roof as the car jolted them. "Fuck, yo," he snapped. "So what you gonna do, tear this motherfucker up?"

She sped through another intersection, then veered onto the ramp for the Parkway, ignoring him. Several painfully long seconds passed before she shot him another look, and then her eyes narrowed slightly. Her gaze caught his masculine jawline, and she felt herself fighting the urge to slap the shit out of him and then lean over and kiss him.

She wondered how one man could have such an effect on her. Love him one minute, then hate him the next. Want to kill him one second, then fuck him dry the next.

"If you wanna live to see another day, I'd advise you to not say another fucking word, Roselle. And I mean it."

She stepped on the accelerator.

Roselle shifted in his seat and frowned.

But he kept his mouth shut.

This fuckin' crazy bitch!

Two

I WISH I COULDA LICKED UR ASS N SUCKED UR DICK ONE LAST TIME B4 U LEFT 4 UR TRIP. I LUV THE TASTE OF UR ASS N THAT SWEET NUT ON MY TONGUE

Kendall grinned as he read the text message, before looking up from his iPhone to see if his wife, Krista, was anywhere in sight. She'd walked off to use the bathroom before they boarded their flight, and the last thing he wanted to do was get caught texting another woman.

Yeah, it was a No-Strings-Attached situation, but—*shit*—damned if she didn't make his dick stir every time he thought about her, or every time she sent him a dirty text. And though he loved his wife, she wasn't sexually adventurous. She wasn't open-minded. And she damn sure wasn't freaky.

If only she were . . .

Shit. Quite frankly, Kendall found his wife's ignorance to sex and sexuality repressive and emotionally stifling. And he blamed her, partially, for his infidelity. Although he knew his cheating was a choice. Still, he believed he wouldn't have had to seek fulfillment of his baser needs outside of his marriage if she were the type of woman who was more open to explore a wilder side. But, no—*hell* no—Krista was satisfied with missionary, doggy-style (every few weeks) and, maybe, the occasional cowgirl, where she got on top and *rode his dick wet and wild.*

But even that was a stretch.

Give her a good, old-fashioned missionary dick down and she'd mewl like a kitten, and then sleep like a baby when the deed was done.

Shit. Krista didn't even suck dick, except for maybe his birthday and Christmas. She didn't like having all that *leaky shit*—referring to his precum—in her mouth, and the thought of his nut busting in her mouth made her stomach queasy.

Who the fuck didn't give head? What woman didn't suck dick in her relationship and expected her man to be okay with that?

Fuck if he knew.

Kendall shook his head. The shit disgusted and bored him. And it confused him even more, because he loved his wife. Truly he did. And he loved fucking her. He loved the feel of her pussy rippling along the length of his dick; he loved losing himself inside the warmth of her silken valley. And he loved when she gave into his desire to see her facedown, ass up, her ass cheeks pulled apart and her asshole puckering while he fucked her from the back.

If only she'd let him spit into her asshole and slide a finger inside, or pull his dick out of her pussy so that he could dip his head in between those soft ass cheeks of hers and tongue that sweet-looking brown hole.

Fuck yeah. Kendall would love nothing more than to lick all in his wife's ass. He loved eating ass, almost more than he loved eating pussy. It was still considered so taboo, so dirty . . . and the idea of going against the grain of what society considered sexually acceptable gave him a hard-on. He opened and fanned his legs again. Precum was already coating the head of his dick. It was only a matter of time before there'd be one big-ass wet spot in his Calvin Klein's.

DAMN, BABY. WOULDA LUV'D THAT, he quickly texted back.

Seconds later, his phone buzzed. MMM. ME 2! ☺WHILE UR AWAY WITH UR WIFE, HOPE YOU'LL BE THINKING OF MY TONGUE WEDGED IN BETWEEN THE MANLY GLOBES OF UR ASS AS I'M STROKING UR DICK IN MY SOFT HANDS. MY PUSSY IS SO WET THINKING ABOUT IT

"*Fuck*," he hissed, pressing his legs shut, then spreading them open; he fanned his legs a few more times, the inner part of his muscular thighs pressing into the thick width of his dick; cramped up in his boxer briefs, like a caged beast desperate for release.

Kendall felt his scrotum swelling with lust. He hadn't nutted in almost—he glanced down at his Tag Heuer watch—*eleven* hours. He knew if he didn't end these sordid text messages soon, he'd wind up having to slip into one of the stalls in the men's bathroom and rub out a quick nut, before they were shuttled to their plane, just to ease the pressure.

His balls were heavy and tender and begging for release.

That's what sexting with her did to him. Wet his drawers with his arousal, with his hungry need and freaky want for *her*.

Persia.

He didn't necessarily consider her a sidepiece, although they hooked up at least once or twice a month over the last two years, but they were definitely friends, of sort, with benefits. Though he didn't have feelings for her (other than having a fondness and mutual respect and admiration for her sexual confidence)—or at least he didn't think it was any more than that—they shared a special connection. Their sexual chemistry was intense. She was sexy as fuck, freaky as fuck, and chill as fuck.

Everything his wife wasn't.

He'd met Persia nearly three years ago when she'd replied to an sex ad he'd posted on a sex site called Nastyfreaks4u.com looking for an open-minded woman for no-strings, stress-free freaky fun that included sucking his dick, licking his ass, and stroking his prostate—*yes*, he was a *hetero*sexual man who enjoyed having his asshole licked. What was the problem with that?

Nothing, he thought.

But his wife, and so many other closed-minded women like her, didn't share that same sentiment. They saw a man enjoying ass play as being either gay or on some down-low shit. That was some straight-up bullshit. He couldn't speak for anyone else, but he was neither. And, he learned that he wasn't alone in his desires. There were other *straight* women-loving men out there, like himself, who enjoyed having their assholes licked and their prostates stroked.

So he would post ads from time to time—not anymore, though, since he and Persia connected. But, in the past, when his dark desires crept up in him and they needed to be indulged, he'd post an ad; like the one he'd posted the day he'd met Persia.

And out of all the responses he'd received, she'd been the only one who captured his attention. And held his interest.

And she'd kept it since.

NO DOUBT, he finally replied back. DEF GONNA KEEP THAT WET TONGUE N THEM SEXY LIPS ON THE BRAIN

"Who is that you're texting?"

Shit.

"It's work," Kendall lied, glancing up at his wife, who was wearing a frown on her smooth brown face. Krista wasn't the prettiest woman, but she wasn't butt-ugly either. She was simply unassuming. Plain-looking. However, what she lacked in the looks department, she made up for in other areas.

Krista huffed. "Don't they know you're on vacation?"

He looked over at his wife, sheepishly, as she plopped down beside him. "I'm not officially on vacation—if that's what you wanna call it—until we board the plane."

Krista rolled her eyes. "Well, you need to *officially* let them know that you're off duty for the next six weeks, starting right now. And I mean it, Ken."

Krista snatched open her pocketbook, and pulled out her own cell to check for any missed calls or messages. There were none. "*You're* the one who convinced me to go on this couple's retreat for *six* damn weeks—having me use up all of my time at work." She shook her head, trying to bite back her annoyance.

This whole idea of Kendall telling her he wanted more intimacy, more excitement, between them was a bunch of foolishness. As far as Krista was concerned, Kendall got more sex than most married men, so what more did he want from her?

How more intimate did he want her to be? Did he want her to fuck him upside down from a chandelier? Swing from a damn stripper pole? Invite another woman into their sacred bed? Suck and swallow his damn dick?

No.

She was not about to ratchet up her sex life to appease some selfish-ass man, who couldn't appreciate all the good loving she'd been giving him. Letting him use her body up. Fuck her pussy inside out whenever he wanted. Hell no. And she knew good and goddamn well—even though he'd hinted around the subject several times over the course of their marriage—Kendall wasn't even thinking she was going to consider letting him stick his fingers in her butt, or lick her *there*. It was nasty. And unnatural for a man to want his tongue wedged in the crack of some woman's ass. And she wasn't even about to go there with him.

Her asshole was off limits.

Krista looked over at Kendall. "The least you can do is disconnect from work and *that* damn phone."

Krista was right. He had been the one who broached the subject of taking part in a couple's retreat with two other couples on a remote, private island in the middle of the South Pacific Ocean. Krista had been reluctant, more like resistant. But he was persistent, and still very patient, presenting it like a chance of an opportunity to take a long-needed vacation. But secretly, he hoped that working with a sex therapist/relationship coach might help loosen the screws on his wife's prudish ways.

"I don't need no damn therapy," she'd said to him when he'd approached her with the idea of doing couples work. "Are you unhappy? Because if so, then you're the one who needs the therapist."

He quickly texted: WIFE. GOTTA GO. TTYL

Persia would know not to reply back. They understood each other's boundaries and relationships. She too was involved—*happily* as she would say. In fact, she was due to be married sometime next year.

Krista tossed her phone back into her purse, then shot Kendall an evil eye.

"Okay, baby," he finally said to his wife. And then he quickly deleted the entire text, before powering off his cell and sliding it down into his front pocket. He leaned over and kissed his wife on her pouty lips. "Whatever you say."

Three

"Why the hell are you on the phone with *that* bitch right now, Isaiah, huh?" LaQuandra hissed as she dragged her carry-on onto the luxurious aircraft, The Pleasure Chest. A ninety-foot-long Gulfstream G500, with enough space to accommodate twenty passengers.

"She doesn't need to know shit about . . ."

Isaiah ignored his wife. She stayed tripping and talking dumb shit. Fuck what she was talking, his *BM*—baby mother—needed to know he'd be out of the country for a minute, and that he'd only be accessible via email (one of the rules for couples taking part in the retreat) if something popped off regarding his teenaged son, Isaiah Jr.

So fuck what she was popping shit about.

He caught the eye of a brown-skinned woman who looked up from her book, *The Wait*, and nearly frowned as LaQuandra breezed by her seat. LaQuandra gave the woman the evil eye as she proceeded to an empty set of seats on the other side of the spacious cabin.

Good, Krista thought as the loudmouthed woman walked by. She didn't want *that* in back of her, all up in her ear with all that negative energy the whole flight. She cursed herself for not bringing her Essential oils to ward off negative energy; that one there needed an exorcism, Krista mused, before catching the eye of Isaiah.

Isaiah offered her an apologetic smile as he strolled behind LaQuandra, while he listened to his BM on the other end of the phone run her mouth nonstop. LaQuandra and his BM were more alike than not when it came to not knowing when to shut the fuck up.

Krista shifted in her seat. Isaiah was handsome, Krista thought as she returned a smile of her own, one meant to be more sympathetic than friendly.

She decided she'd seen enough and returned to the page in her book.

"And why is you gonna be gone for so long with that dogged-face bitch, anyway?" Isaiah's BM asked. "I know that flat-ass ho ain't ever gonna clap her ass cheeks around that big thick dick the way I do."

Isaiah shook his head. "Cass, chill with that shit," he whispered. "You always tryna . . ."

"Isaiah, did you hear what the fuck I said?" LaQuandra said in a staged-whisper as she slung her carry-on into the overhead compartment. She waited for Isaiah to come closer and then snatched his cell phone from his hand. "My husband has to go. Don't call. Don't text. Don't fucking bother him, or *us*, unless it's an emergency."

Isaiah didn't even try to take the phone from her. It was useless. He simply repositioned his wife's carry-on in the overhead bin, then slid his carry-on inside, before closing it shut.

"Coon bitch, *boom!*" his BM snapped loud enough for Isaiah to hear through the phone. "Eat my ass, LaQuandra. He might be off with you, but he'll still be thinking about all this big fluffy ass I shook in his—"

LaQuandra removed the phone from her ear and ended the

call. Then she threw Isaiah's cell phone at him. "I know you did *not* fuck that bitch last night when you dropped little Isaiah off."

He sucked his teeth. "Quandra, chill with the dumb shit, a'ight. No we didn't *fuck*. Damn." He'd only eaten her pussy, then tongued out her ass. So technically he wasn't lying. And lying by omission didn't count.

Did it?

"Well, you sure as hell haven't been fucking *me*," she said nastily.

Isaiah cringed, glancing around the aircraft's cabin. The last thing he wanted was for the two other couples to hear LaQuandra's big-ass mouth. Too late. They'd heard it all.

He shot her a hot glare. "Bring the volume down."

LaQuandra sucked her teeth. "My volume *is* down. But if you want me to turn it all the way up, you know I will."

"Yeah, okay," Isaiah said, taking a seat across from his wife. "Whatever you say, Quandra. Just sit the fuck down and use your damn quiet voice." *Before I punch your fucking teeth out.*

Roselle glanced over at Isaiah, and smirked, giving him a head nod. Isaiah did the same, then shook his head, causing Roselle to chuckle. Roselle's wife, Brenda, gave him a look, then made a face, before dipping her gaze back down to the *Ebony* magazine article she was reading on her iPad.

Isaiah spotted a sleek bar near the back of the aircraft and swallowed the cotton swelling in the back of his mouth. Shit. He needed a drink.

He sighed. "Look, Quandra. I'm not tryna beef with you."

"Neither am I," LaQuandra admitted, finally taking her seat.

"A'ight then. 'Cause I'm not flying halfway around the country to hear you bitching and complaining the whole time because if that's what you're about to do, I can get my shit and step." He raised a brow, then pinned her with a hard stare.

LaQuandra stared back, feeling the urge to reach over and slap the shit out of him for treating her so damn shitty. *This cocky bastard!*

She was cranky. Evil. And she needed a good fucking.

It'd been months since she and Isaiah had been intimate; let alone, shared the same bed. He'd moved out of their master bedroom nearly two months ago, and she'd been stricken with anxiety ever since. She loved him. Her love, however, sometimes—okay most times, bordered along the fringes of obsession, but—oh well.

So what if she stalked his text messages and calls, or rifled through the clothes hamper and sniffed his dirty drawers every night? So what if she stood at the door, arms folded, foot tapping, and waited for him. Then fought to snatch down his pants and drawers to smell his dick? Daring him to have another bitch's dried-up pussy juice on his dick.

What woman hadn't done so once or twice in her lifetime?

Sniffed her man's drawers and smelled his dick?

Real love, she reasoned, made a bitch do some crazy things. So crazy or not, LaQuandra had no intentions of searching for someone else to call her own when she already had whom she wanted.

He wasn't perfect—hell, neither was she, but he'd been her perfect love story.

She hadn't snagged Isaiah sixteen years ago, only to lose him now. He was hers. And she'd do whatever she had to do to keep him. Bottom line, she missed what they'd once shared. And she missed him fucking her. Oh God how she missed the stretch of her pussy melting over his powerful dick.

That's what she'd fallen in love with, *first*. His dick.

Long, thick (oh so *very* thick) and curved.

And, now, selfishly, the bastard denied her it. What kind of man denied his wife dick? That was so goddamn thoughtless, cruel, and unusual torture. She was so fucking angry with him for being such a selfish prick.

Sure, she'd sneak into the guestroom where he'd taken up residence and slip between the covers and take his dick into her lush, greedy mouth. She'd suck him hungrily (and, with no words spoken, he'd fuck her mouth with an urgent need), until he'd explode his warm seed down into her throat. Tears streamed down her face every time she swallowed him. She'd drink him, empty him, until he had nothing left to give her while she rubbed her pussy and shuddered. Then after she'd cleaned his dick with her tongue, she'd tiptoe back into her big, empty bed with her wet, lonely pussy weeping as she cried herself to sleep.

Sadly, *that* had become the soundtrack of her now failing marriage.

She was goddamn miserable.

And yet she didn't want to lose Isaiah. He was a good provider. And, as painful as it was to admit—he was a damn good father to his fourteen-year-old bastard son. Isaiah Jr. The lovechild he'd conceived with some hoodrat bitch he'd been fucking almost a year into their marriage.

Cassandra Simms.

She hated that bitch with a burning passion.

She was everything unholy and foul. And she was the cause of LaQuandra's grief. Cassandra just couldn't stay the fuck out of *her* life, *his* life . . . and their marriage. And their bastard child—a spitting image of the man she loved—was a constant reminder of how deeply he'd sliced open her heart with his sordid affair. That bitch, Cassandra, had given him the son she couldn't. And every time she looked into his handsomely chocolate face, that painful fact was smeared in her face.

Her marriage was in shambles. And she felt as if she were hanging on by a thin thread—no, no . . . a cobweb. Yes. That's what she'd been hanging onto. But this couple's retreat, she hoped, would be what they needed to relight the flame in their marriage, a start to a new beginning.

LaQuandra breathed through her mouth, then exhaled. The fact that Isaiah had even agreed to participate in this once-in-a-lifetime experience had to mean something.

Didn't it?

"All I know is," LaQuandra said as she eyed him, "shit is gonna have to change, Isaiah. I can't keep going through this shit with you and that ghetto bitch. What kind of man lets some bitch disrespect his wife, huh, Isaiah? I'm your *wife*. Not some dirty piece of ass you found on some street corner. I deserve respect from that ratchet bitch."

Isaiah swallowed, then blew out a frustrated breath. He was royally fed up with LaQuandra's bullshit. However, deep down, he knew she was right. His BM needed to respect her more. Nevertheless, respect went both ways, and LaQuandra needed to figure out a way to respect the mother of his son regardless if she despised the woman or not.

Yeah, his BM was ghetto. But, shit, so was she. The only difference was, LaQuandra had a college degree and his BM had a bunch of kids. Ten.

With *eight* baby daddies, he just so happened to fall into the lucky number seven spot. And, yeah, he admitted that when he'd first met her, he'd thought with his twenty-year-old hard dick when he'd seen all that ass his BM had bouncing in the back of her the day he'd spotted her fifteen years ago, strutting across Essex County Community College in some skimpy-ass outfit with an infant son already propped up on her thick hip.

What he hadn't known before he'd fucked her sexy-ass raw was that, at twenty-five, she already had seven kids. Shit. Had he known she was so damn fertile, he would have probably pulled out. Then again, on second thought, he would have still busted inside of her. The pussy had been too damn good to pull out.

Hell. It still was.

"Are you hearing me, Isaiah," LaQuandra badgered, reaching over and slapping his arm. "Shit's gotta change. I refuse to . . ."

Isaiah opened his mouth to say something, anything, to get her to shut the fuck up, but a beautiful dark chocolate angel, with long sculpted legs appeared from out of nowhere—wearing a dangerously short, very fitted, black skirt and a pair of killer gladiator heels. A mouthwatering amount of cleavage spilled out over the top of a black corset, and her thick black hair was braided and coiffed in an elegant knot.

Isaiah caught himself admiring the way the gold straps wrapped seductively around her toned calves, then swirled up and around her shapely thighs.

"Hello," the chocolate beauty greeted, clasping her hands together in front of her. Her full lips were spackled to perfection in gold lipstick "On behalf of Captain Daniels, welcome aboard The Pleasure Chest. I am LaLani. And this is"—she gestured toward a lighter-skinned, more voluptuous woman donned in the same outfit as she stepped beside her—"Mocha . . ."

Next appeared two tall, dark, and very chiseled men, who stood bare-chested and oiled on either side of the two women, wearing nothing but a pair of black slacks.

"And to the right of me is Sin." He gave a slight head nod, his dreads brushed over his chest. "And to my left," the strikingly beautiful woman continued, "is Saint." He also gave a head nod—his smoothly shaven head gleaming under the cabin's lights. He ran a hand down over his neatly trimmed goatee. "And we're here, along with the rest of The Pleasure Chest crew, to cater to your every need. So, as we prepare for departure, please, get comfortable. And enjoy the experience."

LaQuandra shot Isaiah a nasty look. "I mean it, Isaiah." Her voice rose in frustration. "I refuse to continue to be disrespected by that bitch. I deserve . . ."

Isaiah sighed, waving over his Chocolate Angel.

She smiled. "Yes, Mr. Lewis. What can I get you?"

"Let me get a shot of Henny. Please."

She gave him a slight nod. "Coming right up." She looked over at LaQuandra. "Ma'am, can I bring you anything?"

"No. I'm fine," she said tersely, sizing the sexy vixen up. Another bitch with a big, voluptuous ass, she thought as she glanced at her cantaloupe-sized breasts that were practically spilling out of her corset.

Isaiah eyed LaQuandra and shook his head. This was going to be one long-ass flight. "Um. On second thought," he said to the flight attendant. "Make that a double."

Four

Four hours, and fifty one-thousand feet of altitude later, the magnificent aircraft was somewhere high above puffs of sunlit clouds. The start had been rocky due to a significant amount of turbulence that had kept Brenda and the rest of the passengers confined to their plush cream leather seats.

But now that the ride had smoothed and the captain had given the okay to move about the cabin, Brenda peeled her gaze from the breathtaking window view and quickly unlatched her seat belt to stretch. She had never ridden in a private jet before, but she'd experienced the comforts of first-class travel several times. However, this right here was how real ballers traveled—in sophisticated comfort and endless luxury.

And she loved every second of it.

She glanced over at Roselle, who was reclining in his seat, sipping a Hendrick's gin and tonic. He seemed to be enjoying the velvety smooth drink as he peered out the window. Drink number three, of course. But she promised herself not to keep count.

When he drank gin, his dick stayed hard and he could fuck literally all night long. Cum. Then want to fuck again. A blessing and a curse, for her, her pussy, and the bitches he made time to cheat on her with. But Brenda wasn't going there. Not now.

She eyed Roselle as he pressed his forehead against the portal glass and peered downward into the thick cloudbanks beneath the plane as if he were looking for something. Probably some damn pussy, she thought, narrowing her eyes.

She simply couldn't trust his ass. Not even when he sat across from her, and she had her eyes trained on him.

His ass was sneaky.

Roselle smiled. He knew Brenda was staring at him as he attempted to get a glimpse at the terrain below, but all he got so far was a foretaste of the sun slicing through the clouds. And he was cool with that. The view was awe-inspiring nonetheless.

He took another sip of his drink, then glanced over at his wife and winked.

Damn, she was fine. He sensually licked his lips at her. Against her will, she smiled. Damn him.

The flight attendant, LaLani, came to Roselle's seat. "Can I get you *any*thing else, Roselle?" she asked in almost a breathy whisper, bending at the waist, her face mere inches from his.

Roselle smiled, then licked at his bottom lip, trying like hell not to ogle her cleavage nearly spilling out of her dress. "Nah, baby. I'm good. But thanks."

"How about something to *eat*? I can have the chef whip you up something really delicious, if you'd like."

Roselle felt his dick stir, but then he caught Brenda's glare and it went limp again. "Nah. Not right now."

"Okay then," she said with a wink.

Brenda tilted her head and raised a questioning brow. Oh, so this bitch was on a first-name basis with her husband. When did that happen?

Most likely, she guessed, when she'd dozed off about two hours into their flight.

Still . . .

I know this messy bitch is not *trying to flirt with my man knowing I'm standing right here.*

LaLani turned to Brenda. "Can I get you anything?"

"No. You can't," Brenda said nastily. "But you can make a note that *Roselle* over there is a very married man. Please and thank you."

LaLani smiled. "That fact is duly-noted." She matched Brenda's stare. "Will there be anything else, ma'am?"

Brenda gave a fake smile. "No, sweetie. Not at the moment."

"Very well."

As LaLani moved back toward the galley, Brenda sneered at her, and Roselle shook his head, but said nothing.

"*Baby*, huh? So that's how we're doing it, Roselle. Huh? *Baby?* Since when?"

"It's a figure of speech. Damn. It meant nothing," Roselle said nonchalantly. "Why you always tripping, Bren? All she was doing is her job."

Brenda rolled her eyes. "And I doubt anywhere in her job description does it say for her to fall into your lap and suck your damn dick."

Roselle laughed. But the imagery made him shudder inwardly. He'd love nothing more than to see her fine-ass on her knees, her mouth wet and open, and his dick pressed to the back of her throat. He'd fuck her mouth dry. Knock her tonsils loose. Skull-fuck the shit out of her.

He looked at his wife. "Stop being so melodramatic, Bren. You're always looking for shit to fight about." He shook his ahead again. "But you know I love your crazy ass, right?"

She sucked her teeth. "Maybe." She stepped out into the aisle. "I'm going to walk around. See what's going on. Don't have me come back and find you grinning in that ho's face again."

"Yeah, a'ight," he said over a chuckle. And then he reached out and grabbed her by the forearm, pulling her to him. "C'mere."

He pulled her closer.

"What?"

He gestured for her to lean in.

She huffed, bending at the waist. "What is it, Roselle?"

"This Hendrick's got me feeling some type of way."

Brenda raised a brow. "So."

"You know what it is, baby."

She frowned. "And?"

He reached around and cupped her ass. "You wanna earn your points into the mile-high club tonight?"

She saw heat flash through his eyes, and she knew that look very well. She slid her hand over his crotch, and smirked. As she'd thought, he was aroused. She squeezed the bulge under the button fly and teasingly licked her lips and squeezed his dick over his Robin's jeans. Then she leaned in a little closer and kissed him softly on the lips. Mm, yes. Fucking in the friendly skies would be a delicious thrill. She'd love nothing more than to get fucked in the cockpit. Getting fucked on a plane had always been one of the things she wanted to cross off her sex bucket list.

She and Roselle had experienced a little hand play under a blanket in their seats on a flight to Jamaica once. And another time, she'd given him some wet sloppy head, while the other passengers slept on their flight to Hong Kong last summer. But fucking on this aircraft would take their sex life to another height. And yet she pushed out, "No," before slapping Roselle's hand off her ass and then mushing him in the head. She walked off, leaving him sitting in his chair, sipping the rest of his drink and stroking a hand over his jeans.

Roselle went back to dazing out of the window, smirking. He was going to get a nut off tonight, with or without her, even if that meant using his damn hand.

Brenda headed toward one of the three bathrooms. As she walked through the cabin, she glanced over and smiled at Krista and Kendall. They seemed nice enough. They were in their seats, swiveled to face each other, playing a game of Scrabble. While Isaiah was on the sofa near the bar drinking a beer. And then there was LaQuandra seated across the aisle talking loudly on one of the sky phones that were mounted beside each chair.

She hadn't officially met the woman with the braids cascading down her back, but so far what she was noticing, she didn't like. Yet, she knew better than anyone to never judge a book by its cover. She reminded herself to keep that in mind.

Brenda finally reached one of the bathrooms at the far end of the aircraft. Once inside, she locked the door and took in the exquisite space. The walls were white marble, veined with gold. There was a glass shower stall with multiple showerheads. A white leather swivel chair faced a white marble vanity that held gold baskets of top-of-the-line hair-and skin-care products. On a shelf rested a tower of fluffy white towels.

Brenda ran her fingers over the gold embroidered lettering: THE PLEASURE CHEST. This was the kind of wealth she'd dreamed of her entire life. And she wanted it.

One day.

She relieved herself and then washed her hands. And when she stepped out of the bathroom to head back to her seat, she was greeted by one of the two deliciously sculpted male attendants—the dark-skinned one with the shoulder-length dreads.

Her breath caught in her chest at the up-close-and-personal sight of him. He had his locks pulled back. Damn, he was fine. And God knew she loved herself some dark chocolate, every now and again.

He met her eyes with a sexy grin. "How are you enjoying the flight so far, beautiful?"

She blushed, and a quick rush of heat splintered through her. She hadn't expected that. She hadn't expected to feel her cunt pulsing between her legs, either. And she hadn't expected to have this overwhelming desire to reach out and touch him, slide her hands over the stretch of rippled muscle over his dark, chocolaty skin.

She swallowed. "So far, so good," she said. And then she swallowed again.

"Cool." He grinned again. "If there is *any*thing I can do to help make your flight an even greater experience, don't hesitate to call on me. I'm at your service. For as long as you need me to be."

Brenda's mouth went dry, but her pussy got wetter as she drank in the sight of him, her eyes taking snapshots of his rippled abs and chiseled pecs; the way his dark nipples reminded her of two chocolate-covered raisins.

Raisinettes. *Mm, yes.*

Finally, the valves to her saliva glands opened, and her mouth watered. And, instead of swallowing, she allowed her lust to pool inside her mouth until she almost drowned in it.

Lord, help me . . .

"By the way," he said. "I'm Sin."

Oh yes you are.

Brenda was sure this fine black man, this Adonis, this Pussy Slayer, was full of just that. Sin. And if she didn't hurry up and get back to her seat, she'd be tempted to pull him into the bathroom and yank down his pants. Yes, God. She'd drop to her knees and cup his balls and then spit-shine his dick.

Thick and veiny, she imagined. Dear God. Adding him to her sexual scrapbook of naughty deeds (and, yes, there'd be a few salacious moments) would be an exhilarating experience for sure, but not worth the risk of getting caught.

Or was it?

She finally swallowed. "I'm Mrs. . . . uh, Brenda."

He smiled. "I already know who you are, *Mrs.* Woods."

Wait. How did he know who she was?

Then it dawned on her before she could ask the question. From the portfolio each couple had been required to submit with a very lengthy application. Included in that packet were photos of her and Roselle. Yes. That was it. He had to have seen the photo of her to know who she was.

"Anyway," Sin went on, "I'll let you get back to your husband."

Oh. Right. Him. Her husband.

Of course.

Sin's eyes lingered on her face, her lips, and then traveled over the curve of her hips. He pulled in his bottom lip. Then he said, "I bet you taste like honey," before licking his lips.

And then he winked, before disappearing behind a wall of frosted glass, leaving Brenda nearly panting and her panties sopping wet.

Tonight, she'd have to give Roselle some pussy after all.

Maybe.

Five

It was nearly two a.m. when Krista heard what sounded like whimpers as she stepped out of the bathroom. She thought her ears might have been playing tricks on her. But then she heard the whimpers again. Someone had to be in the other bathroom across from the one she'd used, crying.

There went the muffled sounds again.

Krista thought to knock on the door, but stopped herself.

No. Whatever was going on behind that door was none of her business. But then she heard grunting and what sounded like a low groan. So, the nosey part of who she was got the best of her and she quietly placed her ear flush to the door, and listened.

No, no. They were cries of pleasure emanating from behind the door.

Her eyes widened. And a hand went up to her chest.

Lord Jesus . . .

Nasty-ass heathens.

"Ooh, yes. Fuck me. Mmm. Oh, yes. God yes . . . your dick is so big . . . yes, yes, yessss . . ."

Krista blinked.

Those nasty fools were in there fucking. But who could it be, she wondered. She flipped through her memory. When she'd gotten up to use the bathroom and freshen up, she'd walked by that loudmouth woman (she'd introduced herself earlier in the flight, but Krista couldn't remember for the life of her, her name. All she knew was, it was ghetto!), stretched out beneath a quilt; her chair-turned-bed now the resting place for her snore-fest.

Krista was glad someone could sleep on this aircraft. Luxurious or not, she was so over this flying shit. Sixteen hours and twenty-three minutes on somebody's jet was a whole lot more than she imagined it to be. She'd traded in the book she'd been reading for the first few hours of the flight for her Bible, clutching it most of time, praying that she'd be able to make it through the remaining hours. Yes. They'd been in the air for more than ten hours already. And, although the accommodations were plush and the service was phenomenal, she was over it all already.

So, when she sat up from her bed and decided to shower and use the bathroom before everyone else awoke, she hadn't expected there to be much activity at this time of the night. Aside from Isaiah sitting up on the sofa (still awake!) watching some racy Showtime movie, she'd imagined everyone else would be asleep.

So it had to be that thick-hipped woman, Brenda, who sat up closer toward the cockpit, with that light-skinned husband of hers. With his long lashes and all that pretty hair, he was simply too fine for Krista's taste. She liked her men handsome, but they had to have rugged, manly features. But that one there was a pretty boy in every sense of the word. And obviously a real nasty one judging by what she was overhearing, although muffled.

"Yeah, baby. This dick feels so fucking good in that deep, wet pussy . . . aaah, shit. That's right . . . throw that pussy up on this dick . . . aaah, yeah, baby . . . just like that. Fuck this dick . . . make that shit disappear. I knew you had some good pussy . . ."

Krista pressed the whole side of her face against the crack of the door to get a better listen. She squinted an eye and concentrated.

"Mmm, yes. You like this pussy, daddy?"

"Fuck yeah. It's so fuckin' creamy, baby . . . mmm, fuck . . ." He began pumping into her hard, nearly frantic. He felt his nut building, yet he was determined to hold out until her she came again.

"Ooh, yes, yes, yes . . . you're gonna make my pussy cum . . . ooh, yes . . ."

"Yeah, baby. Cum all over this hard dick, so I can bust this nut before my wife wakes up . . ."

Krista's lashes rapidly fluttered. And then her jaw dropped again.

Wait.

What the . . .?

On the other side of the bathroom door, LaLani was holding onto the handholds over the toilet with her skimpy black dress bunched up over her hips and her black lacy thong pulled to the side as Roselle's condom-covered dick slid in and out of the back of her wet, pink hole. Her pussy lips flared open and sucked at his shaft with each pulsing thrust.

Ooh, he had some good damn dick.

If he fucked his wife's cunt as good as he was fucking hers—whew, yes, God. Have mercy on her horny soul—then LaLani knew his wife was one happy, well-fucked woman.

She arched her back and reached in back of her, pulling open one ass cheek, giving Roselle more access, his dick slicing in and out of her wetness. She loved fucking the men who boarded The Pleasure Chest. Horny men, unhappily fucked men, cheating men all en route, with their partners, to Passion Island to work on their failing relationships/marriages.

There was always one on every flight. And her pussy stayed ready. After all, that's what she was here for. Pleasure. That's what she got paid to do. To feed their passions. To cater to the whims of passengers. To quench their thirst for sordid, uninhibited pleasure.

Roselle grabbed her hips, and watched his dick disappear inside the depths of LaLani's silken valley. Fuck yeah. The pussy was good.

"Aaah, yes, yes," Lalani murmured. "Give it to me, harder, harder . . ."

Krista couldn't believe what she was hearing on the other side of the door. Lord, that man was a hot mess. Cheating-ass dog. She was so glad she wasn't married to *that*.

She wondered if his wife knew about his scandalous ass. *Mmph. She probably did.* She shook her head in disgust. *Dumb-ass women staying with a cheating-ass man!*

There was no way she'd ever tolerate Kendall cheating on her. She'd leave his ass in a heartbeat. This plane was filled with negative energy, she thought as she kept her ear pressed to the door. Lord God. She needed to burn some sage to purify the air.

"Oh shit, oh shit, baby . . ." Roselle was on the verge of an orgasm. "Here it comes . . . aaaah, yeah . . ." And then a guttural sound escaped him as the walls of LaLani's velvety cunt clutched his dick, massaging his condom-sheathed shaft as his semen, hot and thick, shot out of his body like lava.

Krista's breath hitched.

"Can I help you find something—or some*one*?" asked a sultry voice in back of her.

Krista jumped, startled.

It was Mocha.

Krista's face flushed, embarrassment spreading through her like a bacterial infection. She suddenly felt sick. She hadn't expected to be listening for as long as she had been. And now she'd been caught with her ear pressed up against the bathroom door. Caught lurking like some, some, uh, well . . . she couldn't think what to call it. But she was sure there was some twisted word for what she'd been caught doing, something dirtier than eavesdropping.

Pervert. Deviant.

"No, no. I, um," Krista stammered. She averted Mocha's curious gaze and the sly smirk that curled her luscious lips. Brenda straightened her body. Smoothed a hand down the front of her shirt. Then she simply stated, "I thought I'd heard someone crying."

Mocha's brow furrowed, and then she smiled like a woman with a secret. "Does it still sound like crying?"

Love cries. That's what they'd been.

Krista's stomach tightened.

"No. I was mistaken."

"Would you like something to calm your nerves?" Mocha asked, feigning concern. "You seem a bit shaken." She stifled a giggle. "Shall I bring you some Advil? A sedative? A shot of something wet?"

The way the words *something wet* rolled off Mocha's lips made Krista feel dirty.

"I'm fine. Thank you."

Mocha smiled as Krista quickly made a beeline back to the front of the private aircraft. When she returned to her bed, Krista quickly crawled back under the thousand-count Egyptian sheets woven with 22k gold thread. She couldn't even enjoy the way the exquisite linen felt against her skin.

Fucking, fucking, fucking. She was surrounded by sexual energy. From the soft porn that played on the large flat-screen to the half-naked attendants, this plane was a den of iniquity. It was the breeding ground for sin.

Krista shuddered. She could only imagine what lied in wait for her once they landed. She reached for her Bible beneath the pillow, and closed her eyes.

My Father who art in heaven . . .

Six

LaQuandra rewarded her palate with a long swallow of some of the best champagne she'd ever tasted and pulled up the window shade.

It was eight a.m., and the sun's rays were already slicing through the clouds. The captain had finally announced that the plane was preparing for its descent.

Thank God.

This shit was almost over. It hadn't been a bad flight. In fact, LaQuandra had found it quite exciting, being surrounded by so much lavishness. Still, she was ready to land already. The farthest she'd ever been was the Bahamas. And she'd been there twice.

She'd always wanted to travel more. See more. But Isaiah seemed to always have an excuse as to why they couldn't afford getaways. They both made good damn money. Between her salary as a principal for a private boys school and Isaiah's job as an IT manager, combined they grossed close to a hundred-and-fifty grand.

So there was no reason why they couldn't travel more. She didn't expect anything lavish, just a yearly trip—somewhere. Anywhere. But Isaiah's cheap-penny-pinching-ass would rather drive down to Baltimore harbor or Busch Gardens with his bastard son—Lord, help her—in tow rather than spend any quality time with her—*alone*.

But she wasn't going to let her mind take her there. She was grateful for this all-expenses-paid trip, and the fact that Isaiah and her would finally be *alone*, away from distractions, like his son and his ghetto-ass baby mother.

Goddamn it.

She'd promised herself she wouldn't give thought to that bitch while she was away, and already that trashy whore was invading her headspace. She couldn't get away from her. Everywhere she turned, that bitch was there.

Haunting her. Stalking her. Tormenting her. Stealing what was hers.

Her man.

His dick.

And probably his heart, too.

Isaiah always vehemently denied being in love with that trifling bitch, and LaQuandra wanted so desperately to believe him. But Cassandra had given him a child—a son—something she still had been unable to do.

And there was no way she could ever compete with that.

She sighed, shaking the thought from her mind before she ended up throwing her flute across the aircraft. She'd gulp down the rest of her drink, first, though.

Wasting good liquor was a no-no.

She took another sip of her drink as she forced her attention back to the panoramic window view. She caught a teasing glimpse of the most beautiful turquoise water she'd ever seen. It nearly stole her breath as she soaked it in.

She sighed, then glanced over her shoulder and caught a glimpse of Isaiah as he sat on the sofa in the same spot she'd seen him sitting last night before she'd finally dozed off.

She'd already showered and had had her breakfast in the dining area with Brenda way before the sun's rays pierced through the sky. The two of them had been able to get acquainted. Brenda seemed nice enough. A bit braggadocious for her liking, though. My salon this, my salon that, but LaQuandra had managed to smile and nod and push through breakfast while Brenda prattled on about her ambitions to open more salons across the Tri-State Area. She'd been kind enough to invite her to her salon for a free mani-and-pedi when they returned to the States.

LaQuandra, however, didn't have the heart to tell her that she was loyal to Nappy No More body and hair salon, so she most likely wouldn't see the inside of Brenda's salon to get her hands and feet done. Still, LaQuandra had thanked her for the kind invitation.

Isaiah walked over, pulling LaQuandra from her thoughts. Mmph. He'd finally made his way back to his seat after staying up all goddamned night doing only God knew what. LaQuandra rolled her eyes.

"Were you on the phone with that bitch all night?" LaQuandra said to him.

"Good morning to you, too," Isaiah said, glaring at her. No. He hadn't called Cassandra. In fact, he hadn't even touched his phone. He'd sat up most of the night indulging himself on the continuous porn movies that had been showing on the television. Soft porn. However, it was still capable of making his dick hard.

He'd been tempted several times through the night to walk back here and brush the head of his dick over LaQuandra's lips until she opened her mouth for a feeding. But his pride and the fact that he wasn't sure if he wanted to remain married to her had stopped him from busting his nut in her throat. So he'd bust a quick round in the bathroom, then eventually fell asleep on the sofa.

When he'd awaken this morning, he found himself under a blanket someone had covered him with sometime in the middle of the night. Surprisingly, with only a few hours of sleep, he'd slept like a baby.

"I've been over here not even four seconds, and you're already on your shit." Isaiah shook his head. His first thought was to snap on her. She wanted confrontation, then motherfuck, he was going to give it to her ass. But then he glanced around the aircraft's cabin and decided to let it go.

He leaned in, and then took her drink from her hand. "You've had enough." She opened her mouth to say something and he shot her a hot glare. "You heard what the fuck I said."

She stared at Isaiah as he raised *her* flute to his lips and guzzled down the rest of *her* champagne. *Bastard!* She felt her cold pussy suddenly heating. She needed some attention given to the slow-throb pulsing between her legs. Right now. Her thirsty, wilting pussy needed a burst of Isaiah's man cream to coat its walls. God, yes, she needed her pussy stuffed with his dick. This was so goddamn ridiculous—him not fucking her.

"Please take your seat, Mr. Lewis," LaLani said, interrupting LaQuandra's sordid thoughts. The color of her hip-hugging dress was now a crimson red. And her shade of lipstick matched perfectly. "And secure your seatbelt. We're preparing for landing."

Isaiah couldn't help but smile at the flight attendant as he complied. She was a stunner, for sure. Aside from fucking his BM from time to time, he'd never cheated on LaQuandra with any other woman. But if the opportunity presented itself, he thought, he'd slide his dick deep in her cunt and fuck her lights out.

LaQuandra eyed Isaiah. Then LaLani. Then Isaiah again.

She noticed the gleam in his eyes as he grinned at LaLani. And suddenly the slow throb in her pussy went still. She bit her tongue from going off on him. She felt hurt and disrespected. Again. But right now wasn't the time to dredge all that up. That didn't mean she didn't want to curse him the hell out, maybe even lay hands on him, for treating her so fucked up. That's exactly what he needed, she reasoned. Her nails slicing open his goddamn skin.

She sighed.

Yes. Shit definitely needed to change between her and Isaiah or she was sure she'd be going to jail for murdering him in his sleep.

Frustrated, she pressed her legs shut and turned her attention back to the window. All she saw was miles and miles of clear blue water. And right in the center of it all was a heart-shaped island—three-thousand acres of languorously leaning palms and powder-soft sands, but she couldn't even enjoy the view.

Her mind was on Isaiah.

And her aching cunt.

Seven

"Welcome to Passion Island," said a long-lashed woman with doe-shaped eyes and skin the color of rich creamy fudge as she took the circular stage. She was dressed in a long, chic white dress with billowy sleeves and scalloped neckline. Her hair was cropped stylishly short and framed her oval-shaped face perfectly.

Red lipstick made her sumptuous lips pop.

She was obnoxiously pretty. Effortlessly.

Her gaze swept over the couples. "I am Dr. Gretchen Dangerfield. And for the next six weeks, you will embark on a journey like no other. One that will, hopefully, tantalize your senses, tempt your libidos. Indulge your desires. And stretch your imaginations to newer heights."

Brenda grinned. She was all for trying new things, and she was so looking forward to the experience.

"During your stay, you will be tested, challenged, and dared," Dr. Dangerfield continued. "As your packets stated, you will be put through a series of relationship building exercises and be required to participate in individual, couples, and even group sessions." She paused.

"Are there any questions so far?" Dr. Dangerfield asked the couples.

Roselle's gaze roamed all over her body, trying to imagine what was underneath her dress. Thong or G-string? That was his question.

Yeah, baby, Roselle thought, *can I kiss your pussy lips?* He licked his lips as he imagined her sweet chocolate pussy opened, wet and ready for the taking. He could almost see its pretty pink center glistening. Fuck, yeah. He'd siphon the juices out of her cunt, swirl his tongue all up in her. *I bet she tastes good as fuck.* He felt his dick thicken and had to force himself to look away, before he ended up with a full erection.

As if on cue, Brenda glanced over at Roselle. He glanced back and winked, then placed his hand on the inside of her thigh.

Sneaky bastard was probably thinking about fucking her, Brenda thought, peering down at his lap. She thought to grab his crotch to verify if his dick was hard or not, but decided against it. Let him fantasize. Brenda had a few fantasies of her own. None of which included *him* or *her*.

Brenda turned her attention back to Dr. Dangerfield just as Krista raised her hand.

"Yes. I have a question." Kendall looked over at his wife, and braced himself. "Why exactly do we need six weeks here? I mean, six weeks seems like an awful long time."

Hadn't this bitch read the pamphlets?

It clearly stated that it took about six weeks to strip down most couples' defenses, to chip through their denial, make honest personal assessments of their relationships, and finally get to the crux of their marital discord. And, in doing so, it eventually raised many thorny questions. Should couples stay? Can trust be rebuilt? Can passion be reignited? Can they forgive and move on? Or should they throw in the towel and head for divorce court?

Although couples were removed from their families and careers and the daily routines of their lives, they gained so much more—

a deeper understanding of themselves and their relationships with one another, while on a beautiful tropical island.

Oh. And lest she forgets . . . they would be paid a substantial lump sum of money (a hundred grand, to be exact!) once they successfully completed the six weeks.

The caveat was this: There was one flight in, and one flight out. In order to leave the island, unless it was an emergency, both partners had to be in agreement about leaving.

If not, they stayed.

Stuck.

Forced to make the best of a failed situation.

Dr. Dangerfield ran her tongue over her teeth, and then forced a smile.

"Liken your stay on Paradise Island," she suggested, "to an intensive boot camp experience, minus the drill sergeants shouting in your face. However, as in any boot camp, there will be obstacles that you all must face, some as a couple, others done individually. And it is my hope that each of you will afford me a glimpse into your relationships, so that I might be able to help you maximize your emotional and sexual experiences."

Krista nearly frowned as she shifted in her seat and gripped her purse.

It was all nonsense. But coming home with a hundred grand in her hand made it that much easier to keep her mouth shut. Besides, she wanted to prove to Kendall that whatever marital issue he thought they were having was all in his damn head, thank you very much.

Krista was as sexually free with him as she was going to be. However, she'd be damned to hell if Kendall thought for one minute that she was going to discuss the most intimate, the most private, details of their sex life with some stranger. Therapist or not, she didn't need therapy—or coaching in how to be a good wife and lover.

She was both.

Krista glanced over at LaQuandra, and then Brenda. *Mmph.* Now those two heifers, they needed it, coaching and mentoring, more than she ever would. No judgment, though.

She then cut her eye over at Roselle and bit back a sneer.

Ooh, he was a dirty son-of-a-bitch, that one there.

Cheating-ass bastard. No-good motherfucker.

She made a quick mental note to pray a few extra minutes tonight. She'd already prayed while on the ride from the landing strip, and had asked her Savior to bridle her tongue, to keep profanity at a minimum. No more than two to three curse words a day. Yet, so far, she'd already managed to exceed her limit.

She shifted in her chair as Dr. Dangerfield's voice reeled her attention back into the room.

"The goal," Dr. Dangerfield continued, "is that you leave Passion Island after your six-week stay empowered. That you leave here more passionate, more attentive, more loving to one another. That you prioritize passion back into your lives, and be more creative in pleasuring your partners . . ."

Brenda cut an eye over at Roselle. Being creative wasn't the problem. It was his damn cheating.

Roselle squeezed the inside of Brenda's thigh as if he knew what was running through her mind, while he kept his gaze on Dr. Dangerfield. She was sexy as shit. And, although the dress she was wearing wasn't clingy or tight-fitting, he could tell that underneath the gauzy fabric, she was hiding a bad-ass body.

"We all crave passion," Dr. Dangerfield continued, meeting the gaze of everyone in the room. "Brenda and Roselle Woods, LaQuandra and Isaiah Lewis, Krista and Kendall Evans . . . each of you want to be desired, to feel special and needed, by your respective partners . . ."

The three couples, subconsciously, were in agreement with her. They wanted to be appreciated, to be respected, and, goddammit, be—with the exception of Krista, who thought all was good in her bedroom—sexually fulfilled.

Dr. Dangerfield noticed the way Krista was staring at her, sizing her up almost, or maybe she was simply sitting there daydreaming. She decided to call Krista out. "Mrs. Evans, is there something you would like to say?"

Krista blinked, caught off guard by her directed question. *What the hell?* When she finally spoke, there was a crack in her voice. "No. Not at the moment."

Dr. Dangerfield smiled. "Very well. Now, as I was saying . . . for some of your relationships, the passion you once felt for your partner has since waned. That is a natural course of any relationship. Life and the careers and the kids and family all happen. The fire dies down. You become complacent. You start to take one another for granted. And, somehow, you have forgotten about those things that drew you to your partners in the first place . . ."

LaQuandra swallowed. *You better preach!* She felt as if Dr. Dangerfield was speaking directly about her miserable-ass marriage. It pained her to be so unhappy. To feel so damn neglected. If Isaiah just fucked her, beat her pussy up, all night long, she could think clearer. Maybe not be so on edge.

LaQuandra believed she could eventually find a way to forgive Isaiah for fucking his baby mother, Cassandra—that trashy-bitch. What LaQuandra knew she couldn't forgive was his disregard for her needs as a woman and his wife. She felt anger rising up within her like bile. She could almost taste it. And it made her sick.

She shot a look over at Isaiah as he pulled his iPhone from his front pants pocket and glanced at the screen, more out of habit than anything else. There was no signal, so he slid it back down into his pocket.

LaQuandra's nose flared. "*Really*, Isaiah?" she hissed. "You really had to check your phone *now?* Who the hell you expecting a call from?"

He shot her a side-eye glance. And then decided to ignore her.

LaQuandra clenched her jaw, but then she closed her eyes and took several deep breaths before she forgot her manners and set it off up in here. Oblivious to the glances of Krista and Brenda, LaQuandra reopened her eyes when she heard the silky sound of Dr. Dangerfield's voice again.

"Passion is an important component of a relationship," Dr. Dangerfield stated, running a slender hand through her hair. "But do not be fooled for it is not the glue that will keep your relationships, your marriages, intact. It will not sustain your relationships. Some of you have altered your commitments to your partners and to your marriages and have forgotten to alert your partners of those changes. You have forgotten to inform them that you are no longer committed to being dedicated and loyal to them. And that within itself can make it more difficult to stoke the fires of passion in your marriages."

She paused, purposefully. Allowed what she'd already said to linger in the room a beat, before she continued. "Remember this: the heart wants what the heart wants, even when that which it wants is hurting us the most."

LaQuandra gritted her teeth, and looked over at Isaiah again. She felt like backhanding him.

Dr. Dangerfield caught the scathing look that LaQuandra had given her husband and surmised their relationship was probably in the most trouble, just judging by the way they were sitting.

Isaiah sat wide-legged with his arms folded, while LaQuandra sat, legs crossed, with her back to him. There was clearly no passion between the two of them.

Passion was energy. It was intense. It was powerful. It was the essence of desire.

And Passion Island was about cultivating those feelings. It was about reigniting—or igniting, in some cases—that spark. It was about renewing sexual energy.

Every hosted couple's retreat (and so far there'd been sixteen over the last three years) was all about teaching couples how to give and take, how to be more open, more receptive, more pleasing to one another, more passionate.

Yes. That was always the plan.

And yet the saying about the best-laid plans going awry held painfully true. Dr. Dangerfield had seen her share of unexpected breakups and divorces over the course of her career, but she'd also seen some of the most damaged couples heal and grow in forgiveness, in love, and in lust for one another.

Yes. There was hope.

Always.

"Tonight you rest, ladies and gentlemen. But tomorrow, the journey begins. I'll see you all at breakfast." With that, Dr. Dangerfield sashayed off the stage, a grin sliding over her lips. She loved her work on Passion Island. It afforded her a bird's-eye view, a front-row screening, of a couple's indulgences as well as their indifferences in regards to sex and sexuality. So far, it had been a rewarding, sexually exhilarating experience. To inspire and arouse and challenge couples, to push their sexual boundaries, to test their commitments, and to dare them to be more open, more daring, and more sexual.

And she was allowed a voyeuristic view inside their private sex lives. She loved working with the ones who had kinky, secret fetishes that they'd kept hidden from their partners. Delicious scandal, that's what she called it. She'd been a sex therapist with a booming private practice in L.A., for nearly fifteen years, but had been working with couples on the remote island since the concept of helping couples in unhappy marriages find their way back to loving and lusting one another came about three years ago.

Her soror, confidante, and closest friend, who owned the island nestled eleven miles between Mo'orea and Tahiti, had approached her with the idea of turning this paradise into a tropical sex haven for couples whose relationships had become boring and mundane, where the lovemaking had somehow turned into a tedious task. Fucking had somehow become a chore. And couples allowed conflict and life's problems to consume them, suffocate them, and snuff out the flames of passion needed to keep them sexually charged, hungry and eager to please one another.

But Passion Island (somewhat like a long-stay hedonism resort but with therapy and lots of fucking—or *not*) was the fuel needed to reignite their fires, to reclaim lost desires—in each other and within themselves. Or it was the last stop before calling it quits. The choice was up to each and every one of the couples that made the sixteen-hour trek across the globe in search of truth and light.

And, hopefully, find their way back to passionate love.

Only time would tell.

And Dr. Gretchen Dangerfield would be watching closely.

Eight

It was an hour before sunrise. And a full moon was still glowing midsky, slowly waning to give way to dawn. Yet, there was a thick blanket of fog still covering the island. Outside the villa, the melodic sound of birds chirping and the ocean's waves crashing at the shore could be heard from the opened windows.

Kendall pressed a soft kiss on Krista's pubis and then licked over her clit, and she writhed against the budding arousal, against the burning need to have her husband inside her. All this kissing on her pussy was ridiculous. All she wanted was his dick.

He'd wanted her last night. But Krista had been too tired and simply wanted to take a long, relaxing bath, then turn in for the night. And so she did, leaving Kendall up until God knew what time. And now here he was snacking between her legs, like she was some damn breakfast burrito.

Goddamn him.

Why did he have to make sex complicated?

She didn't need all this extra shit, all this teasing and playing.

Kissing her passionately, brushing his lips along the column of her neck, caressing her body, and sucking her nipples, that was all that she really ever needed.

It made her wet. It made her ready.

Just his touch alone made her pussy churn.

But Kendall trying to pleasure her with his mouth only frustrated her.

And yet she grunted as his tongue flicked over the hood of her clit, and then he had it rolling around on his tongue like a Jolly Rancher, swiping it from top to bottom, side to side.

"Mm, baby," Kendall rasped, gazing up at her, his mouth wet from her juices. "Your pussy tastes so ... good; so sweet ..." He licked his lips and stroked his fingers down her glistening folds, before sliding his fingers into her pink center.

Krista felt a scream bubbling up from the back of her throat. This unwelcomed invasion, this ... this intrusion ... of his fingers and tongue should have been met with more enthusiasm, more excitement. Instead, all it brought was a coiling frustration, a splintering need, to be stretched and filled.

Why couldn't he just fuck her? Stroke her pussy deep with his dick, instead of all this goddamn licking? She couldn't understand Kendall's (any man's, for that matter) obsession with eating pussy, just like she couldn't wrap her brain around women who loved sucking dick.

But ...

God. It felt so dirty. And, and, and so—

"Come in my mouth, baby," Kendall murmured. "Fill my mouth with your sweet pussy." His eyes were dark, glimmering in lust, as he looked up at her, his gaze heavy, filled with heat and hunger.

Krista drew a gulp of air into her lungs. She wanted to take her hand and push Kendall's head from between her legs and then slam her thighs shut.

Fuck her already!

Krista knew any other woman would probably be taking dirty delight in Kendall's magnificent tongue work, the way he used his tongue to skillfully lave every nerve ending, every single nook and cranny of her pussy, every inch of her aching flesh. But all it did, this licking and teasing, was cause a hint of revulsion, no matter how slight, to swirl to life inside her.

But then Kendall whispered, "Squeeze your titties, baby," as he thrust his fingers firmly into her wetness, and her disgust quickly morphed into a tiny ball of tension.

She drew in a ragged breath as Kendall's fingers moved methodically through her slickness, plunging in and out of her body, over and over, as he licked and then sucked her clit into his mouth.

Her eyes had fallen shut. And all Krista could think to do was ball her hands into tight fists, and then open them wide, her fingers spreading out, before clawing at the sheets.

"Put it in me," she pushed out impatiently, her eyes flashing open. "Give me the dick, Kendall . . . *now*."

He bit back a curse. Why the fuck couldn't she just chill, just lie back and give into the pleasure? Why couldn't she simply find a way to sink into the lust and allow him to love her with his mouth and lips and tongue? Why couldn't she let him pleasure her in a way that pleasured him? Tasting her turned him on. Wedging his tongue in between her opened slit aroused him.

So why couldn't she allow her man to love her *there*—he licked over her slit? And right *here*—he flicked his tongue over her clit?

Krista squirmed. She fought off the sensations, and pressed her thighs together, squeezing him there, and then trying to push his head away.

Kendall caught her hands with his and held them. "Stop fighting it. Give me what I want, baby." It sounded almost like a plea than a request. "Open your legs," Kendall prodded gently, gazing up at her. His voice was deep and smooth and dark with desire. "Let me have you, baby."

Yes, she had a choice to stop this right now, or lie here and be devoured like some early morning buffet. She chose to open her legs. And still she didn't appreciate him subtly forcing her to submit, because all he was doing was filling her body with more and more heated frustration.

She was wet enough, and still Kendall kept licking and sucking, licking and sucking . . . licking, licking, and licking, over and over, until Krista felt herself going limp.

"Fuck me," Krista whispered, her voice barely audible. She squirmed her body as the already hard pebbles of her nipples tightened more.

Fuck.

He wasn't done drinking in her juices, but he eased up and covered her body with his, and held himself on his elbows, careful not to crush her. Positioning his semi-erect dick at her juicy entrance, Kendall pressed himself there and then leaned in and attempted to kiss her, to share the taste of her on his tongue with her, but Krista quickly jerked her head away and his cunt-drenched lips caught the side of her jaw instead.

Kendall frowned and cursed inwardly again. Krista knew how to fuck up a man's wet dream with her frigid-ass bullshit. Fuck it. If she wanted the dick, then he'd fucking give it to her.

She lifted her hips, inviting him, silently welcoming him where she'd wanted him to be in the first place—inside her. But Kendall pulled back from between her legs and sat back on his calves. "Get up and turn over," he said, no demanded. "Get up on your knees."

Finally. What she'd been waiting for. Hard dick. Krista scrambled, eagerly willing to assume the position. Doggy-style wasn't her favorite position, but she'd take it. She'd let him hit it from the back as long as he was giving her the dick.

"Arch your back," Kendall instructed. She did. And then she felt Kendall ease behind her. He pulled open her ass cheeks and thrust forward in one big surge, stuffing the entire length of his dick inside her, not caring that he was being forceful as he impaled her.

Krista gasped as she felt him stretching her wide and she dug her fingernails into the sheets. "Oh! Oh . . ."

Kendall glanced down, drawn by the sight of his dick gliding in and out of Krista's pussy as he rapidly thrust in and out, pounding into her, making her ass bounce. And staring back at him, nearly winking at him, was her puckering asshole; all brown and tight and moist from the mixture of her juices and his spit that had slid down into her crack while he'd been eating her out.

He swallowed. Gritted his teeth, and tamped down the tugging urge to lick her there.

"Unh, unh, unh . . . oh, yes," Krista moaned, feeling her orgasm quickly tighten in the pit of her stomach. "Mm. Yes, yes . . ." She could feel his dick hitting the mouth of her cervix and she groaned. Cried out his name.

Ooh, it felt so good. His dick. The pounding. God, yes . . . Kendall slammed in and out of her with a fury that shocked and aroused her.

Then Kendall's hand came down across her ass. And Krista shrieked, the sting causing her pussy to clench.

"Aaah, *fuck*," Kendall hissed. "Throw that ass back on this dick," he urged. And then he slapped her ass again, this time harder, causing Krista to yelp.

"Oww. Don't do that shit," she snapped, tossing him a hot glare from over her shoulder. He ignored her. And then she groaned again, more pleasure taking over her, as he slammed harder, faster, into her body.

Kendall glanced down again, taking in the way Krista's cunt sucked him in, slurping at his dick, coating him with her juices. And there was that sweet hole again, waiting and winking. Kendall swallowed again, steeling himself against the sight.

He wanted some of that. Wanted it on his tongue, and then clamped around his dick, but he knew his wife wouldn't go for that. So he pulled her ass cheeks apart as far as they would go without hurting her, opening her to him. And then he spit down into her little brown hole as Krista humped and pumped and slammed her pelvis back at him.

And then, and then . . .

Krista felt something, a feathery-like touch—the brush of a finger in the center of her ass, lightly grazing along her seam. And then she felt it—that finger, flirting around the rim of her asshole. But she knew that Kendall knew better than to go there.

She felt his dick twitching inside her and that gave cause to fuck him back faster and harder the way he'd been fucking her. Kendall waited, eyeing her sweet chocolate hole—so tight, so lickable—admiring it, lusting it.

"Uh, yeah . . . aaah, shit . . . give me that pussy, baby," he murmured, feeling his nut ratcheting up through his balls.

Krista cried out again. And at the same time—*oh hell no!*—he pushed the tip of his finger into her anus, fingered her there with the tip. And then he sunk it in deeper, feeling Krista's pussy spasm around him as she grew wetter and hotter.

Kendall pounded his dick inside her harder, faster, his thumb going deeper into her asshole. And she arched into the stretching, the burning sensation suddenly making her pussy turn into raw heat. His digit was fully inside now and Krista's body grew taut, trembled, as she held her breath.

No, no, no, no, Krista's head screamed, but her body defied her as it screamed *yes, yes, yes, oh God, yes* and then she braced herself for an orgasm that crashed through her like a tornado. She cried out an incoherent "oh God, no, no, no," as this new sensation, so forbidden, so, so dirty took over her body.

"Aw fuck, baby. I'm gonna nut," Kendall muttered, jolting her with his thrust again, again, again, ramming into her wetness. "Come again, baby. Come with me."

Moments later, he growled out his orgasm. She cried out hers. And his thumb stayed there, in her ass, until her body stopped thrashing. And then she gasped when he slowly pulled his dick *and* his finger out of her body simultaneously.

Eyes wide. Heart pounding. Skin damp.

Krista finally caught her breath, and looked over at Kendall, who was lying on his back. His eyes were closed and his breathing had slowed, but he wasn't asleep. Because if he'd been, she would have heard light snores coming from him.

"I didn't appreciate you stuffing your fingers in my ass. I told you about that nasty shit. You know how I feel about all that ass play shit. And you know I don't like you trying to kiss me in my mouth after you've been licking down . . . *there.*"

Kendall slowly opened his eyes and turned to look at her. He met her eyes, his full of disappointment, and then he scowled.

Was she serious right now? Hadn't he just fucked her down real good? And hadn't she come hard, multiple times no less?

"What the fuck, Kris." Kendall eased up on his elbows. "You're my wife, damn. It's your body. You clean your pussy, right?"

She gave him an incredulous look. "You know I keep it clean down there."

"Okay, then what's the problem?"

She huffed. "It's nasty. All that bacteria down there, and all them juices are not meant to be mingling inside my mouth. Period. And I told you, I don't like that shit."

Kendall shook his head, and kept from rolling his eyes at her crazy-ass thinking. "Well, it tastes good," he said, trying to make light of the situation. "And I enjoy tasting you."

Krista cringed.

"Look. If I want to spend all night between your legs licking you out," Kendall said, "then that's what I should be able to do."

Krista huffed. "And you know I don't like it, and still I *let* you do it because it's what *you* like."

"Oh don't even talk like you're doing *me* some favor, by letting me do shit to you, Krista. If you don't want me to please you orally, then fuck it. I won't."

"Oh God, Kendall. Stop. Why are you getting mad about me not liking oral sex?"

Kendall blew out a frustrated breath. "And why exactly don't you like it, Krista, huh? What is so horrible about me giving *you*—my wife—head?"

"Nothing," she said, trying to keep her anger in check. "I just don't like it; that's all. And I don't like the fact that you disrespected me by shoving your fingers in my ass."

Kendall scoffed. "*Fingers?* Krista, I had my damn thumb there. Not fingers."

Well, it felt like fingers to her; big thick fingers stretching the inner ring of her ass. But before she could speak, Kendall was firing more words at her.

"So what is the real issue here, Krista? Me giving you head or pressing a thumb in your ass?"

Her eyes narrowed. "Both."

Kendall stared at his wife, long and hard. "My bad for sticking my thumb in the beautiful ass that I love watching so much. And my bad for loving the way you taste, for loving my tongue inside of you; I got carried away. It won't happen again," Kendall said, tossing the covers off his body and swinging his toned legs over the edge of the bed. "But mighty funny that didn't stop you," he said over his shoulder at her as he stood, "from arching your back and getting wetter. And it didn't stop you from coming all over my dick with *my* thumb in *your* ass."

Krista frowned. "That doesn't mean I wanted your damn fingers—no, excuse me, your *thumb*—there. I'm not with all that nasty, freaky shit."

Freaky shit?

What the hell was so freaky about thumbing his wife's ass?

Krista waited; obviously expecting him to say something, perhaps offer her an apology. Kendall didn't respond. Hell, he couldn't. He had to be seriously missing something. But he didn't have the strength to question her for clarity, for understanding.

He'd heard enough. So there was nothing left for him to do except stare at Krista like he was finally seeing her for the first time, and he found himself wondering how the hell he'd be able to survive in this marriage the way things were between them, sexually, for another five, ten—hell, fifteen—years.

He couldn't.

He wouldn't.

And with that conclusion, came a rise of anger he hadn't known lived inside him. He needed to get out, to get away from her, before he said something he'd regret later.

He loved Krista. God, he loved her. But he was slowly beginning to think, to feel, that *that*—love—might not be enough.

Krista stared at his bare back and eyed him as he moved toward the dresser and yanked out a pair of red and white swim trunks and then slipped them on, his bare ass and sticky dick suddenly disappearing.

"Where are you going?" she asked, stunned by the tension hovering in the air between them.

"For a swim?" His tone was sharp, and to the point. He grabbed a white wife beater and pulled it on over his head. "I need to clear my head."

She blinked. "*Now?* Aren't you going to shower, first?"

Kendall turned to face her. He clenched his jaw and looked his wife square in the eyes. He knew if he said something it wouldn't be anything nice. And yet he didn't want to walk out on her angry, either.

So he simply walked over, leaned forward, and since she didn't want his pussy-scented lips anywhere near hers, he planted a quick kiss on her forehead.

And then he walked out.

Krista stared at the bedroom door. Then with a sigh, she pressed her back against the headboard, the sheet wrapped tight around her. She stole a glance over at the now empty space where Kendall had been, the imprint of his body still freshly dented in the sheet.

What the hell?

Why was he so mad at her? It was her body. And her right to say what she liked and didn't like. This wasn't anything new. So why was that man acting like he was all of a sudden put off by it?

Krista didn't realize that she had been tensed up until she heard the outer door slam shut and Kendall was gone. She breathed in and out and told herself that Kendall was overreacting, being a damn drama king—as usual, because he couldn't have his damn way.

Still, she shoved her hands through her weave, trying to make sense of it all. And when she couldn't come up with anything that made sense, she looked over at the window and pushed out a deep sigh.

The sun had finally risen and replaced the illuminated moon from the night before with the promise of bright skies and lots of sunshine, but, so far, Krista's first day on Passion Island was starting off on the wrong damn foot.

Nine

The cuisine on the beautiful coral island was a hodgepodge of Tahitian and Fijian and French influences. And LaQuandra was sadly disappointed to see that there wasn't a pancake or waffle in sight. She'd had her mind set on a buttery flapjack with a side of scrambled eggs—cooked hard, hash browns or home fries and some turkey bacon.

Instead, she'd been greeted with banana puree (bananas covered in sugar and coconut milk and then baked), Firi Firi (fritters made from flour and coconut milk), tuna marinated in line juice and coconut milk (a famous, must-eat Tahitian-style raw fish); mahi mahi prepared with a vanilla sauce; platters full of local fruits—bananas, papaya, pineapple and mangoes; a smorgasbord of French salami and cheeses; crunchy baguettes; and a variety of freshly baked muffins and croissants. So LaQuandra settled on two banana muffins and a scoop of pineapples with lemon grass tea.

While everyone else ate, Kendall stole a moment and tilted his head back and took in the beauty of the sky. He inhaled, deeply, then exhaled as his gaze latched onto the pink sandy beach ahead of him. The sound of Egyptian music played lowly in the background. It was soothing. Sensual. And hypnotic.

The couples ate in near silence save from the occasional grunt or groan, or the click of silverware against their plates.

"Mr. and Mrs. Evans, how did the two of you enjoy your first night on the island?" Dr. Dangerfield asked the couple as she eyed them over the rim of her teacup.

She was casually dressed in a white embroidered tunic dress; her skin glowed.

"It was fine," Krista said as she dabbed at the corners of her mouth with her linen napkin. Although she and Kendall had since made up from their early morning quarrel, she was *still* annoyed at him for getting mad at *her*, but she had no intentions of letting the other couples in on her annoyance with her husband. That was private business.

Dr. Dangerfield nodded. "And your meal, how is it?"

"Very good," Krista admitted. She tried the raw fish in coconut milk. And, to her amazement, it was surprisingly delicious and melted in her mouth. She nearly moaned in between bites.

"And yours, Mr. Evans?" Dr. Dangerfield asked.

"Huh?" Kendall's mind was elsewhere. He hadn't wanted to come to breakfast, but Krista had insisted, demanded, that he not embarrass her with his absence the first day of their stay on the island. So here he sat, trying to push past his resentment toward his wife.

Compromise. That's all he did. Compromising with Krista was one-sided—with him somehow getting slighted sexually—and it was slowly becoming exhausting. And yet he'd come to his senses from earlier and knew he wasn't going to leave her—not over a lackluster sex life, but—fuck if the shit didn't piss him off. Kendall, however, resigned himself to the fact that he would continue to indulge his sexual desires, secretly, with Persia—or with someone else, if things between the two of them managed to change.

Life happened. People changed. Minds changed. And Kendall was okay with that. He'd go back online and seek out another freaky woman, if he had to, to give him what his wife wouldn't.

Nevertheless, Krista was a good woman. A bit moody—and bitchy at times, but what woman wasn't?

"She asked you how your meal is," Krista said, cutting into Kendall's reverie, while trying to tamp down the bite in her tone.

Kendall let out a chuckle, placing an arm over the back of Krista's chair. "Oh, my bad. I got caught up in the view," he said, gesturing toward the panoramic sight of the ocean. "Everything's really good." He'd opted for bonito fish cut into cubes, marinated in lemon juice, sliced onion, tomatoes, cucumber, and homemade coconut milk.

Dr. Dangerfield smiled at Kendall. "I'm glad you are enjoying it. Here on Passion Island you must eat like a king, which is why every meal is a feast. Like our libidos, we must feed our appetites. Nourish our minds, bodies, and loins."

LaQuandra grunted. "Well, someone needs to tell my husband *that* since he doesn't seem to think my loins need a feeding. Isn't that right, Isaiah?"

Isaiah lifted his gaze from his plate, a forkful of fish midway to his mouth, and gave her a hard stare. He then slid the fork into his mouth and shook his head. He wasn't about to get lured into LaQuandra's bullshit. Not this morning. And still every line in his body strained with tension.

He needed to fuck—just not her.

Smirking, LaQuandra reached for her third muffin, then took her knife and sliced it in half, before spreading coconut butter over it.

"Ooh, this is so damn good," she said over a moan as she bit into it. She chewed, swallowed, and then licked her fingers. "I can just taste all the sugar and fat."

Brenda chuckled. "And feel it already clinging to my hips."

"Yes, girl, yes," LaQuandra said, before she took another bite of her muffin.

Roselle leaned over and kissed Brenda on the cheek. "I love them sweet, sexy hips, baby. The more the merrier."

"Lies," Brenda said playfully.

Roselle leaned back in his chair and eyed her ass. "My baby got back."

Krista fought to keep a frown from forming on her face.

Brenda giggled. "I sure do. But I don't need any more than what I already have."

"Well, how about donating some of that butt right on over here," LaQuandra said over a laugh. "I'll gladly take it. And put it to good use, too."

Isaiah shook his head again. More ass would be nice, but quite frankly, he'd prefer to have her jaw wired shut.

"Nah, I need all my baby's cushion," Roselle stated.

Krista made a face that hadn't gone unnoticed by Dr. Dangerfield or LaQuandra. LaQuandra had thought to call Krista out on it, but decided some things were better left unsaid—for now.

"Sooooo, Doctor," Brenda said, lifting her flute from the table. "When does the 'journey' begin?"

Dr. Dangerfield took a sip of her black tea, then set her cup back on its saucer. "Oh, the journey has already begun. The moment you opened your eyes this morning, the clock started. From this point forward, everything you do, everything you say, will be defining moments. And I promise you"—she swept her eyes around the table at the couples—"by the time this is all over, your relationships will feel very different. You will look at your partners through a new set of eyes, with a new set of expectations—or not. And none of you will ever be the same again."

Dr. Dangerfield stood to her feet. "Today, go out and explore some of the wonders of the island. If you'd like a tour guide, that can be arranged for you; but for the daring—the many trails on the island have colored markers that will guide you, should you wish to venture out on your own." Her gaze landed on the men. "Gentlemen, I will see the three of you at two p.m. in Passion Hall."

Passion Hall was where most of Dr. Dangerfield's therapy sessions were held. It was where truths and dirty secrets were told and sordid confessions were made.

"Oh, before I forget," Dr. Dangerfield said, before leaving the table. "Later tonight, you are expected in The Garden for game night."

A sly smile slid over her lips, and then she was gone, leaving the hint of seduction lingering in the light morning breeze.

Ten

Infidelity . . .

It was the breaking of a promise, or uttered agreement between lovers, to remain faithful—in what one person viewed as a mutually monogamous sexual relationship.

Cheating.

It was all around us. It permeated the universe like a plague. It destroyed relationships. Broke hearts. Weakened trust. It crushed hopes. Shattered dreams. Created bitterness. And caused resentments to fester. It hurt people. Ripped the fabric of a relationship apart.

Oh, yes, infidelity was an insidious threat that could crack the foundation of even some of the most stable relationships. And yet people cheated. And people still stayed. Still believed. Still hoped. Still held on.

And they only saw what they wanted to see, like the Lewises and the Evanses and the Woodses. These three couples were affected by it, infidelity, in some form. Be it emotionally or physically, someone (or perhaps both) had crossed the line at some time or another—whether they knew it or not.

Still, Dr. Dangerfield believed that there was hope for couples to reconcile, to reconnect, to rebuild, and recreate a stronger union. With work, with transparency, and with honesty, there was always hope.

Always.

But, first, couples had to want the same relationship goals before the healing and repairing could begin. She knew what had been written on paper. But things always looked good on paper—or sometimes worse.

Face-to-face was always better. Things began to always look different when you stared into the window of someone's soul. The eyes never lied, even when the lies clung to their tongues. So Dr. Dangerfield had decided to engage the men today—first, to assess their level of commitment to their marriages; and, second, to gauge at what level of transparency they were willing to give. Afterward, she'd see the women and determine how honest they could be in their personal assessments of their marriages. Men were less likely to express themselves openly, especially in a room with other men. Men simply weren't expressive. Counseling of any form went against everything men were taught as boys about masculinity, about being strong, about not ever showing emotion.

Consequently, she didn't have any high expectations that the men would be completely honest today. Most times they weren't. Not at first. A man expressing his deepest fears, his darkest desires, or his insecurities went against his socialization.

Dr. Dangerfield enjoyed the challenge, however. She enjoyed the cat-and-mouse game they played. And the fun in it all was trying to crack open their shells, just to see how big the nut was inside.

Subconsciously, she licked over her lips.

"Have any of you ever cheated on your wives?"

Crickets.

Isaiah folded his arms and pulled at his chin hairs, doing his own assessment of the doctor. Five seven without her heels on—almost six feet with 'em on; smooth, flawless skin; she weighed about a buck thirty-five, shapely in all the right places. Real sophisticated.

He took in the two-carat diamonds in her ears, then the five-carat tennis bracelet on her wrist, before his gaze traveled down her legs and landed on the soles of heels.

Red bottoms.

High-end pussy.

Probably a real live freak, he mused, not sure he wanted to flat-out admit that he was still fucking—on occasion—his son's mother.

Kendall glanced over at the life-like statue of a man standing with his legs parted; behind him was a woman on her knees, her breasts large, her face wedged between his white-marbled ass cheeks, her hands wrapped around the man's thick erection.

Damn.

Kendall thought the piece erotic.

It made him think of Persia. His very own cock-sucking, ass licker.

And it made him want—

Dr. Dangerfield cleared her voice. "Well, don't all answer at once," she said lightly. "How about you, Mr. Woods . . ."

Roselle sat in his chair wondering what color her panties were, and—most importantly—what style they were. She looked like a lace and silk kind of woman.

Nice bare pussy.

I bet that shit's pretty as fuck, he thought. He was glad to be sitting down—just the thought of her pussy made him start to get hard.

She probably can't take dick, though.

Or maybe that shit had teeth.

"Mr. Woods . . .?"

Isaiah reached over and tapped Roselle on the knee.

"Huh?" Roselle said as he shifted in his seat, his mind back in the moment, his semi-erect dick now deflated at the vision of her cunt gnashing its razor-sharp shark teeth at his dick. "Oh, damn. My bad. What was the question?"

Dr. Dangerfield smiled, and then repeated herself. "I asked you if you've ever cheated on your wife?"

"Yeah," he said in a matter-of-fact tone. "It's really the only thing we ever fight about."

Kendall tore his attention away from the statue and looked at Roselle.

Dr. Dangerfield nodded. "How many times have you cheated on your wife?" she asked Roselle.

Roselle laughed. "You mean, how many times have I gotten caught?"

"Damn, bruh," Kendall said over a laugh of his own, "it's like that?"

"Man, what can I say . . . I'm addicted to sex."

"So you are saying, you're a sex addict?" Dr. Dangerfield asked.

Roselle nodded. "Yes. My name is Roselle Woods. And I confess: I'm addicted to sex."

Dr. Dangerfield shifted in her seat and then crossed her feet at her ankles. "So you're saying sex consumes you, which is why you cheat?"

Roselle shrugged. "Yeah, something like that. It's like them panties be calling for me. I can see a fine woman and, before she speaks, I'm already undressing her. In my head, the way she's walking, it's like she's thrusting her pelvis at me, throwing the cookie at me, wanting me to beat it up. And, nine times outta ten, if I step to her, I'ma get them drawz. Maybe not that same day, but if I get them digits, I'm definitely getting a sample of that cookie, too."

Dr. Dangerfield almost rolled her eyes up in her head. Being not only a psychologist and a certified sex addiction therapist, Dr. Dangerfield knew the difference between an addict and a pathological cheater. Yet, it seemed that every time a man (most) got caught cheating multiple times, the easy way out, the way to be absolved of any accountability, was to proclaim being a sex addict as if waving some colorful banner that said "I can't control my dick" would make it all okay.

When, in fact, the majority of cheaters were far from addicts. And they didn't always meet the clinical criteria for sex addiction. They didn't use sex to cope with feelings or with life in general. Sex wasn't used as a drug. And a cheater wasn't obsessed with sex. Nor were they riddled with shame and/or guilt for their behaviors the way a sex addict was.

Many of them were simply thrill seekers. Pussy chasers.

Dr. Dangerfield believed they were simply self-indulgent, irresponsible and/or amoral. Fucking multiple partners was simply one of many forms of manipulation and opportunistic self-gratification. They cheated because they wanted to. Cheaters genuinely believed their cheating was justified. They didn't want to stop because it disrupted some moral compass. No. In their minds, they cheated because they could, because they could get away with it. Because they knew more likely than not there would be no real consequences, not any that would be detrimental to them. The women in their lives would curse and scream and fight and, more than likely, toss him out. But the cheater knew, she'd eventually—with some work on his part—take him back.

Sadly, over and over again.

So, no, Roselle Woods wasn't a sex addict as far as Dr. Dangerfield was concerned. What he was, was a self-absorbed, selfish-ass bastard. Period.

"So how many times have you cheated or gotten caught, Mr. Woods?" she asked.

Roselle shrugged again, shaking his head. "Damned if I know. I've lost count." And that was the truth. His dick had been buried inside more wet holes than his memory allowed him to remember.

Shit. He couldn't remember what half those bitches looked like. He nutted on 'em. Then bounced on 'em.

"Tell the truth. It's them long lashes and that wavy hair," Isaiah said jokingly.

Roselle chuckled. "Nah, nah. It's the swag." And the good dick he put on 'em. Yet, he didn't feel the need to mention that part. All pretty boys didn't have small-ass dicks, and they all weren't minutemen. And Roselle was walking, talking, *fucking*, proof of that. And he had a string of well-fucked bitches to prove it.

Dr. Dangerfield's gaze landed on Isaiah. "What about you, have you cheated on your wife?"

"Nah—I mean, does oral count?"

Kendall chuckled.

She nodded. "Yes. Oral sex is *still* sex."

Roselle shook his head. "Nah, Doc. Sorry. Eating ain't cheating."

Roselle and Isaiah laughed, while Kendall pretty much stayed quiet.

Dr. Dangerfield tilted her head. "Oh, is that so?"

"No doubt," Roselle said confidently.

"Okay then," Dr. Dangerfield challenged. "Tell me this, are you letting your wife know every time your penis slips into another woman's mouth? Or the number of times your face finds its way between another woman's thighs? Are any of you?"

Roselle and Isaiah said in unison, "Hell nah."

"Damn, Doc," Roselle added, "you tryna get me killed."

Dr. Dangerfield pursed her lips. "Mm. Then it's cheating. Anything that *you* do with someone other than your wife—*without* permission—is cheating. Anything you do that you keep secret from your spouse *is* cheating. Anything that may have dire consequences in your marriage is cheating. There's no way around it."

She looked over at Kendall. "What is your view on cheating, Mr. Evans?"

Kendall stretched his neck from one side to the other, then looked at her. He wasn't about to make a confession. But he still wanted to know, "What if you don't wanna cheat; what if every part of your marriage is everything you want it to be, except for in the sex? Then what are you supposed do? Be sexually unfilled?"

Dr. Dangerfield crossed her legs. "No. You talk to your spouse. You share with him or her what your desires are, what you would like for your partner to bring to the bedroom. But it has to be done thoughtfully, with tact, and with love."

"And if she isn't open to that?" Kendall asked, pinning her with a penetrating stare. "Then what?"

"Then you seek counseling." Dr. Dangerfield studied him, her gaze lingering longer than it probably should. "Is that your story, Mr. Evans?"

Kendall shook his head. "I love my wife, okay?"

"But . . .?" Dr. Dangerfield prodded.

But she isn't everything I need in the bedroom. "There is no but," he said instead.

"Does she satisfy you?"

Kendall's lip twitched. He wasn't comfortable putting his business out there like that, especially in front of other men. He didn't know them. And he didn't trust them.

What was he supposed to tell her? That he wanted his wife to suck his dick and lick his balls and then, every so often, tongue his ass? He wasn't about to share any of that to her, and definitely not in front of these jokers.

Motherfuckers pillow-talked and gossiped more than females at times. So he wasn't going to put his wife out there like that. He had too much respect for Krista. Maybe he'd be more open with the Doc in private. Maybe.

"She's a good woman," was all Kendall offered for now.

"That wasn't exactly the question, whether or not your wife was a *good* woman."

Kendall quickly glanced over at the sculpture again, then looked back at Dr. Dangerfield. But he only replied with a shrug, as if to say, *Oh well.*

"We're good."

Dr. Dangerfield smiled. Less was sometimes more. She'd read between the lines. And so she moved on. "What about you, Mr. Lewis? Does your wife satisfy you?"

Isaiah grunted. "Yeah. When she can keep her mouth shut. I wish she knew when to use it for more than eating and talking shit."

Kendall and Roselle chuckled.

At that, Dr. Dangerfield simply gave Isaiah a sympathetic look as if to say, *Poor thing.* "I understand you've had a child with another woman during your marriage to your wife, and that seems to be a source of contention for her. Why?"

Isaiah shook his head. "Hell if I know."

Roselle looked over at him. "Yeah, right. You know you still hitting that. Aren't you? We won't tell." He laughed again.

"Quandra thinks I am," Isaiah said flatly. "That's all we beef about—my son's mother. I'm like, damn already—give it a rest. That shit stresses me out."

"She's hurting," Dr. Dangerfield said thoughtfully.

Isaiah grunted, his face drawn into a scowl. "Hell, I'm hurting too. You see who I'm chained to?"

Roselle shook his head. "I feel your pain, bruh." He was thankful he didn't have to wake up to a loudmouth bitch like Isaiah's wife.

"Try to see it from her perspective," Dr. Dangerfield encouraged.

"You not only at some point had an affair on her, Mr. Lewis, but you brought another life into the equation. A child is a constant reminder of the deceit. And *that*, for many women, is oftentimes more hurtful than the actual affair itself."

Isaiah sighed. "I can't change that. My son is everything to me."

Dr. Dangerfield nodded. "I'm sure he is. And I'm sure your wife doesn't expect you to choose her over him."

He shrugged. "I don't care what she thinks. There'd be nothing to think about. I'd be out."

"Yo, keep it a hunnid," Roselle goaded, "you still gotta thing for your BM, don't you?"

Isaiah shook his head. "Nah. It's not even like that. She and I—"

"Still fuckin'," Roselle interjected over a laugh. He looked over at Dr. Dangerfield. "No disrespect, Doc."

She nodded, appreciative of his mindfulness. "None taken, Mr. Woods. So, Mr. Lewis, what you're saying is, your wife's accusations of sleeping with your son's mother holds no merit?"

"Only in her head," Isaiah lied. "I don't know what else to tell you. I'm gonna always have to deal with Cass. At least until my son is old enough to be out on his own. Until then, I'm stuck with her. And so is Quandra—if she wants this marriage. My son and his mother are a package deal, whether I want it to be or not."

Dr. Dangerfield said, "Okay. So it's a package deal. But what exactly do you do to make sure your wife feels supported and comfortable with the situation?"

Isaiah shrugged. "When Cass—my son's mother—gets on her bullshit, I tell Quandra to ignore her ass. Of course she doesn't listen." He shook his head. "They both like keeping shit stirred up. They both crazy."

Dr. Dangerfield's facial expression was neutral when she said, "You don't end up with crazy because you're the normal one.

There's usually some form of energy that someone gives off that attracts crazy."

He shrugged. "Then I guess I'm crazy for putting up with it."

Dr. Dangerfield sighed. Clearly, he'd missed the point. She glanced up at the time. "Well, gentlemen. That's it for today. Time's up."

Eleven

Later that evening, as the three couples took their positions, the sun dipped low, giving way to a reddish-orange sky—the perfect magical backdrop for starry-eyed lovers.

The gated-entrance to The Garden greeted its guests with colossal erotic sculptures situated atop enormous pedestals, marbled columns, and the sounds of hummingbirds. Surrounded by lush foliage, coconut palms, waterfalls, orchids, birds-of-paradise, and tropical hibiscus, there was also a lagoon with its azure-colored water and a nine-hundred-square-foot infinity pool.

But the couples weren't out here to enjoy the landscape. Nor were they here for the sunset. They'd been summoned to The Garden for a game of "I Know You Best." The game was designed to see exactly how well couples knew their respective partners.

Dr. Dangerfield believed that real intimacy began with not only knowing oneself, but also knowing one's partners. What she'd learned over the years of working with couples was that many times than not—most couples simply didn't know their partners as well as they'd thought or believed. Sadly, but horridly true.

So, this evening, she—and each couple—would see who knew whom the best. The men were in partitioned booths, while the women sat up on stools facing their respective husbands on the other side of the garden.

And Dr. Dangerfield—who was wearing a white off-the-shoulder blouse that crisscrossed in the front and then tied in the back paired with white fitted jeans and a pair of seven-inch, salmon-colored red bottoms—was looking as flawless as ever as she stood at the podium.

Waiting.

Watching.

That bitch gives me my whole life, Brenda thought as she glanced over at the therapist, before pulling at the hem of her white mini-skirt and then crossing her thick shapely legs.

Brenda then glanced over at LaQuandra, who was sitting to the left of her. She was wearing a yellow romper and a pair of sandals. She looked cute. But her face was puffy-looking, and the way she was guzzling down bottle after bottle of Passion water—yes, the island had its own brand of water bottled straight from its springs—she was either profoundly hung over from all of her heavy drinking from the night before or somewhat still drunk from earlier today.

Either way, she looked like shit in the face.

The next stool over from LaQuandra was Krista, who was wearing a blue lotus-pattern fringed-trim skirt and long tank shirt with a wide floppy hat on her head and a pair of Birkenstock-type slides on her feet. She looked like an Amish woman gone rogue.

Brenda shook her head and then glanced back over at Dr. Dangerfield.

"Okay, ladies and gentlemen," Dr. Dangerfield said, leaning into the microphone. "Who's ready to play *I. Know. You. Best . . .?*"

The women clapped.

"*Yassss*, baby," Brenda said as she clapped. "We got this!"

"Woo-whooo!" Roselle pumped a fist in the air. And then he whistled as he, Isaiah, and Kendall clapped.

First up were the husbands.

Dr. Dangerfield would ask a series of very simple questions that the husbands were expected to know about their wives. For every correct response, that couple received two points in the first round. Round two, another set of questions would shift to the wives to see how well they knew their husbands and each correct response would be worth three points.

At the end of each round, the couple with the highest score would win a ten thousand dollar cash prize along with a seven-day, all-expenses-paid trip to the French Riviera.

The music faded.

"All right then, "Dr. Dangerfield said enthusiastically. "You know the rules. And you know what's at stake. So. Let's play—*I. Know. You. Best.* First question, gentlemen: What is your wife's middle name?"

As the theme-music—an instrumental version of "If You Don't Know Me By Now"—played through the speakers, each person wrote their answers on a medium-sized white erase board.

Each couple had thirty seconds to answer.

"Um. Mr. Lewis. Please. Jot down your answer, please."

Isaiah grunted something inaudible, scribbling something down in red marker.

"Okay, gentlemen. Reveal your answers."

The men turned their boards to face the women.

Isaiah: CHARDONNAY

Roselle: MONIQUE

Kendall: NICOLE

LaQuandra, Brenda, and Krista were then instructed to show their answers.

All three men answered correctly, and the women clapped.

"Okay, next question"—Dr. Dangerfield paused, giving everyone a chance to wipe their dry boards—"What is the name of your wife's favorite love song, with name of its artist?"

Roselle and Kendall didn't have to give much thought to the question. They'd heard the songs enough times to know the words to it.

"Mr. Lewis, answer, please," Dr. Dangerfield prompted.

Hell if he knew. They rarely played music when they fucked. But he knew enough to know LaQuandra was strung-out on freaky-ass R. Kelly.

So he wrote his answer.

"Okay, gentlemen. Reveal your answers, please."

Isaiah: HONEY LOVE R. KELLY

Roselle: XSCAPE WHO CAN I RUN TO

Kendall: SWEET LOVE ANITA BAKER

"Okay, ladies," Dr. Dangerfield said, "answers, please."

Roselle and Kendall were correct.

LaQuandra slammed her board back on its easel. "Isaiah, you know Keyshia Cole's 'Love' is my favorite song. Not '*Honey* Love.'"

He shrugged. "Thought you was big on him."

She huffed. "I am. But that wasn't the question, *Isaaaaiah*."

Dr. Dangerfield kept from shaking her head. "Next question, gentlemen: what is your wife's favorite television show?"

"Baby, you got this," Brenda stated, and a buzzer blared out.

"Sorry, Mrs. Woods. That'll cost you one point," Dr. Dangerfield said. "There's no talking across the Garden."

"Shit," she hissed.

"Okay, ladies and gentlemen. Write out your answers, please."

The music played again and LaQuandra found herself slowly rocking side-to-side as she hummed along. At this point, she didn't give a damn if Isaiah knew her or not.

When the music faded again, that was everyone's cue to show their answers.

Isaiah: The Housewives of Atlanta

Roselle: Being Mary Jane

Kendall: Rich in Faith

Roselle and Kendall both answered correctly.

LaQuandra scoffed, revealing her answer: *Little Women: Atlanta*. "Isaiah, you know I don't watch that trifling shit."

He frowned. *And Little Women: Atlanta* wasn't trifling? Whatever.

Brenda and Krista clapped.

The next question was, "What is your wife's favorite color?"

The music faded again, and seconds later, each man was turning over his board.

Isaiah: Burgundy

Roselle: Pink

Kendall: Navy blue

Roselle and Kendall were right yet again.

LaQuandra scoffed. "Ohmygod, Isaiah. How do you not know that one? You know I love purple."

"Okay, gentlemen. Those were warm-ups. Now here come the real questions. Y'all ready?"

"Yeah!" Roselle said over a loud grunt. "Let's do this!"

Dr. Dangerfield smiled. "Okay. Next question: what is the month and day of your wedding anniversary?"

Roselle and Kendall had their answers written in less than a minute.

"Mr. Lewis. Please. Your answer," Dr. Dangerfield urged after the music had faded.

Isaiah scribbled his answer.

"Okay, gentlemen. Please turn your boards."

Isaiah: 11/7

Roselle: 2/14

Kendall: 11/14

The women turned their boards around. Once again, Roselle and

Kendall were correct. LaQuandra stamped her foot. "Mother*fu*—Isaiah, how you not gonna know this? It's the *seventeenth*. Not the damn *seventh*."

"I was close," he said nonchalantly. What the fuck more did she want. At least he remembered the damn month. He took a long swig of his beer.

"Okay. So far we have the Evanses in the lead with ten. Followed by the Woodses with nine. And, finally, the Lewises with two."

The next question was, "When is your wife's birthday?"

Easy question, you would think. But Dr. Dangerfield knew many men who simply didn't remember their wives' birthdays.

Isaiah: JANUARY 1

Roselle: Nov 3

Kendall: APRIL 3

Once again, Roselle and Kendall had answered correctly.

LaQuandra was too through. Her birthday was December 31st . "C'mon, Isaiah. Get your head in the game, nigga!"

"Mrs. Lewis, please," Dr. Dangerfield warned, pinning her with a raised brow. "I'm going to need you to refrain from using the *N*-word or any other derogatory language during the game. Please and thank you."

LaQuandra rolled her eyes.

The next question was, "What is the most sensitive spot on your wife's body?"

Brenda shimmied her shoulders. She knew her baby knew.

Several seconds later, the men were turning their boards.

Isaiah: BEHIND THE EARS

Roselle: CLITORIS

Kendall: NIPPLES

All three men answered correctly.

LaQuandra grunted. *Finally, his ass got another one right*. This motherfucker is gonna need to follow the yellow brick road in search of the Wizard for a new goddamn brain if he doesn't step up his game, she mused as she shifted in her seat. She was still stuck on the fact that he hadn't gotten their anniversary date right—or her goddamn birthday.

The last question for the men was, "At what age did your wife lose her virginity?"

Fuck if I know, Isaiah thought as he held the red marker in his hand and stared at the blank board.

Roselle and Kendall quickly wrote their answers.

"Mr. Lewis," Dr. Dangerfield called out. "Answer, please."

Isaiah: 11

Roselle: 14

Krista: 20

Roselle and Kendall were once again correct. LaQuandra nearly fell off her stool when she saw what Isaiah had written. The goddamn nerve of him! She hadn't started fucking until she was twelve.

There was a brief intermission, giving the couples a chance to use the restrooms, saunter over toward the wet bar for a cocktail, or—in LaQuandra's case—to curse Isaiah out.

"After all these years and you *still* don't even know who I am, Isaiah," she hissed. "How dare you embarrass *us* out here like that?"

Isaiah stared at her, hard. "So you think you can do better?"

LaQuandra grunted. "Nigga, I know I can."

"Yeah, a'ight. We'll see." And then he walked off toward the bar. He needed something stronger than beer.

Several moments later, "If You Don't Know Me By Now" played again and the men switched positions with the women.

Dr. Dangerfield shuffled her cards, and then spoke into the microphone as she glanced around the beautiful garden, before landing her gaze over at the women. "Okay, ladies. It's time for one of you to bring it on home for the win. Each correct answer is now worth three points. Right now, we have the Evanses in the lead with sixteen points, followed by the Woodses with fifteen, and the Lewises with four."

Everyone else clapped except LaQuandra and Isaiah. He'd utterly embarrassed her and now she would have to fight to carry them to a win. She wanted that trip.

"Okay, ladies," Dr. Dangerfield said as the music faded. "What is your husband's favorite sport?"

The men wrote down their answers, and waited for the women.

LaQuandra: FOOTBALL

Brenda: BOXING

Krista: BASKETBALL

"Gentlemen, reveal your answers."

Brenda and Krista were correct.

Isaiah smirked at LaQuandra, and then shook his head. Basketball was his thing.

The next question was, "What is your husband's blood type?"

LaQuandra: HIV NEG?

Brenda: AB-

Krista: O+

Again, Brenda and Krista were correct.

Dr. Dangerfield blinked at LaQuandra's answer. "Mrs. Lewis, the question was, what is your husband's blood type, not his status."

"I know," LaQuandra stated flatly. "But *are* you, Isaiah?"

Roselle and Kendall slowly shook their heads, while Isaiah's jaw twitched. *This punk-ass bitch stays tryna play me*, he thought as he gulped back his drink.

"Next question," he snapped. *Ignorant-ass.* She knew he was O+.

"Okay, ladies," Dr. Dangerfield said. "What is your husband's favorite sexual position?"

LaQuandra: DOGGY STYLE

Brenda: REVERSE COWGIRL

Krista: MISSIONARY

Dr. Dangerfield glanced over at the men. "Gentlemen, reveal your answers, please."

Roselle's tongue hung out of the side of his mouth, and then he rapidly moved it up and down at Brenda. She was the only one who'd gotten it right.

Isaiah preferred *her* to ride him, but he loved hitting his BM from the back. He loved watching all that ass bounce.

Kendall loved it doggy-style. He loved seeing his dick move in and out, while watching Krista's asshole clench.

"*Yasss,*" Brenda said excitedly. "We're in the lead, baby. Ha!"

Roselle rubbed his hands together. "French Riviera, here we come! Let's do this, baby."

"Okay, ladies. Next question: How often does your husband want sex with *you*?"

LaQuandra scoffed as she wrote her answer.

"Ladies, please turn your boards around."

LaQuandra: NONE

Brenda: 3-4X A DAY

Krista: 4X A WEEK

All three women were correct. And now the score was twenty-five for the Woodses, twenty-three for the Evanses and the Lewises at seven.

"Next question: does your husband prefer to wear boxers or boxer briefs?"

Of course the women knew this one since they were the ones buying their husbands' underwear.

LaQuandra: BOTH

Brenda: BOTH

Krista: BOTH

The next question was, "When giving your husband oral, does he prefer you to swallow or spit?"

Krista frowned as she wrote her answer.

"Your answers, ladies."

LaQuandra: SWALLOW

Brenda: SWALLOW

Krista: NEITHER

LaQuandra and Brenda answered correctly. Krista narrowed her eyes at Kendall's board, taking in his response in big red letters. SWALLOW

Oh, he must have had one drink too many to even think some shit like that, Krista thought, raising a brow, then erasing her answer.

Brenda hopped up and down and squealed. She felt like doing a happy dance. Unless she got the rest of her answers wrong (she'd be damned if she would, thank you very much!), there was no way Krista and Kendall would catch up to her and Roselle.

The next question was, "Does your husband have a fetish?"

While Dr. Dangerfield waited for the couples to write on their boards, she glanced over at the men, wondering what those fetishes might be. She imagined Roselle secretly enjoying bondage or the feel of women's panties on under his True Religions; Isaiah was probably a pygophilia—sexually fixated on a woman's ass; and, Kendall—well, Dr. Dangerfield imagined him either being a voyeur or lusting over women's feet.

The music faded, pulling Dr. Dangerfield from her naughty thoughts. She licked her lips, then swallowed. "Okay, ladies. Your answers, please."

The three women revealed their answers.

LaQuandra: NO

Brenda: YES

Krista: No

When the men revealed their answers, LaQuandra frowned. Krista grimaced—she felt blindsided. Exactly what type of *fetish* did Kendall have? And why hadn't she gotten the memo? And Brenda screamed excitedly as she hopped up and down.

LaQuandra blurted out, "What fetish do you have, Isaiah, huh? You just full of goddamn surprises tonight, nigga?"

Dr. Dangerfield cringed inwardly. "Mrs. Lewis, unfortunately, due to your blatant disregard of my request to refrain from using the *N*-word, that outburst will cost you six points, bringing your score back down to seven."

"*Womp*, *womp*, *womp*," came from out of the speakers.

LaQuandra scowled. *Bitch, bye. Fuck a score. Fuck this shit.*

Isaiah shook his head. She stayed doing the most.

"I don't know what you over there shaking your head for, I*saaaaaiah*. I wanna know who the fuck you out there having fetishes with?"

Dr. Dangerfield tapped on the microphone. "Um, hello. Mrs. Lewis. Do you need a moment?"

"No," LaQuandra snapped, looking over at her. "I don't need a moment." She glared back over at Isaiah. "I need an answer, I*saaaaaaiah*."

"Mrs. Lewis, I'm going to have to ask you to refrain from any further outburst. Your concerns can be discussed further after the game—in private."

LaQuandra took a deep breath, then blew it out. "Next question," she snapped.

"Great. Okay, ladies. Right now we have the Woodses in the lead with thirty-six points, followed by the Evanses with twenty-eight points. And Mr. and Mrs. Lewis with seven points . . ."

Brenda rolled her eyes up in her head at the Lewises' score. It was real telling. And a damn shame, she thought.

“This next and final question,” Dr. Dangerfield continued, “is for the win. Ladies, does your husband masturbate?”

Brenda and Krista were the first to write their answers on their respective boards.

“Mrs. Lewis. Your answer, please.”

The bastard probably is jacking his dick, LaQuandra thought as she wrote her answer, *since he ain’t jacking it inside of me.*

“Okay, ladies. Turn your boards.”

LaQuandra: YES

Brenda: YES

Krista: NO

The men revealed their answers. LaQuandra and Brenda were correct. Krista had a surprised look on her face at Kendall’s answer—yes. She wondered why the hell he would be playing with himself when she kept him fucked. Krista stood there dumbfounded as Brenda screamed and Roselle ran around from his booth and swept her in his arms, swinging her around.

Bells and horns blared out. Confetti burst out of trumpets.

“Congratulations, Mr. and Mrs. Woods,” Dr. Dangerfield said over the hoopla. “You are the winners of . . .”

LaQuandra half-clapped.

“I . . .”

Isaiah headed for the bar.

“Know . . .”

Krista stared Kendall down.

“You . . .”

Kendall sighed.

“Best . . .”

Twelve

Roselle's dick was hard. And if he were embarrassed by that fact, he wouldn't have stood up in his Speedo swim trunks with his thick bulge on display. Fact was, he wasn't ashamed of his dick, erect or flaccid. Shit. He was a man. All man. And men got aroused.

So what was there to be ashamed of?

He was proud of his smooth, golden-brown dick. Back when he was in high school, it'd been given the name "Beauty" because it was just that—beautiful. And because of the beauty mole on the front of his shaft, just over the thick vein. The name stuck with him all through high school, college, and even now.

Horny bitches loved his dick.

They loved *Beauty*.

So if a chick—or another motherfucker—was bold enough to stare at it, oh fucking well. He'd proudly give them a full view.

Roselle, Isaiah, and Kendall were ushered off to one of the private beaches without their wives and, so far, it was a day of peaceful bliss. There were about thirty half-naked women of different shapes and sizes (who all had one thing in common—they were stunningly beautiful) on the beach with them. Eye candy was everywhere, and none of the men could stop eyeballing all of the bouncing ass and jiggling breasts.

Arabian belly dance music played through the speakers, while the men were being waited on hand and foot. It wasn't the type of music any of them would ordinarily listen to. But, then again, there was nothing ordinary about this island, or its inhabitants. So the men sat back and drank their respective drinks and watched as a group of women sensually danced for their viewing pleasure.

"Damn, that dark chocolate one gotta nice, fat ass," Roselle said. "I'd like to bend her over while she holds open them ass cheeks and I push this meat up in her."

Isaiah shook his head. "Bruh, you crazy."

"Nah. I'm dead-ass. Tell me you wouldn't go guts deep in that?"

Isaiah looked over at the thick-hipped, D-cup Antiguan with the dark chocolate nipples and an ass that would put most porn stars to shame. Yeah, he'd definitely fuck her. She slowly turned, bent at the waist, placing her hands on her knees and then making each ass cheek bounce in sync to the music.

Isaiah's eyes stayed glued on her, and when he didn't respond, Roselle laughed. "Bruh, you can't even take your eyes off that ass. So don't front. You'd fuck that. Shit. We all would."

Kendall laughed as well, but said nothing. She was nice to look at, and he'd definitely be down to peek inside them cheeks and look at her butthole, maybe even lick over it. But fucking her—nah.

Roselle rubbed a hand over the front of his skimpy swimwear. "You think her pussy stink?" he asked, no one in particular.

"Fuck if I know," Isaiah stated. He took a swig of his beer. "I would hope not. She too bad to be walking around with a stink-hole."

Roselle gulped back his drink. "You'll be surprised how many dimes look like they got that good-good until that shit gets wet 'n' starts smelling like a septic tank."

Isaiah made a face. "*Eww.* Fuck."

"Damn, man. That was some random shit," Kendall said. "Where do you come up with this shit?"

"Can I get you gentlemen anything else to drink?" asked the young woman wearing a multicolored bikini top and matching sarong, walking up on them. She had smooth, deep-brown skin and slightly slanted brown eyes. She'd been serving the three men one of the island's specialty drinks, Passion Drops, which consisted of part Grand Marnier, Chambord, Malibu Coconut Rum, cranberry and pineapple juices. And at the bottom of a chilled glass were layered chunks of pineapples that had been soaking in Jim Beam Honey whiskey.

Roselle was on his fourth drink. And he was lit. Two more and he'd be near drunk. While Isaiah and Roselle drank the island special, Kendall stuck with bottles of Vonu Pure Lager—a local beer.

The young woman smiled. "I'll be right back with your orders."

But before she could walk off, Roselle was closing a hand around her left wrist. "What's your name, beautiful?"

"Aurora," she said sweetly.

"Aurora. I like," Roselle said. And before the shy, twenty-something knew what was happening, he'd spun her so that her back was to him and slid an arm around her waist. His other arm wrapped around her shoulder. Roselle drew her back against him, so that his arousal pressed into her lower back.

"You sexy as fuck, *mami*." He spoke low in her ear. "How many strokes does it take to get you to squirt?" Who said the word *tact* was in his vocabulary? Roselle was known to be bold, after a few drinks, and especially when Brenda was out of sight. He knew what he was here on the island for, but—hell—if he could get himself a dose of some island pussy while working on his marital issues, then it was a win-win.

The sex ep on the plane with LaLani in the bathroom should

have been it for Roselle. He knew it. But—shit, he was surrounded by too many fine-ass women to not sample as many as he could without getting caught.

Temptation was a motherfucker.

But the chase was so much better.

Roselle ground his erection in the young woman's back, and she blushed as his hand rose sensually up her left side until it was cupping the outer curve of her breast.

Isaiah eyed him. *This muhfucka wildin' for real*, he thought as he slowly shook his head. "Yo, man, chill," he said. "Let her go get my drink—*first*, before you start molesting her."

Roselle extended his long tongue and slowly licked the side of her face. "Yeah, go on 'n' get my man's drink, baby. I got something for you when you get back." He lightly smacked her on the ass just as she scurried away, then sat back down on his double-chaise lounge. "Man. I'm tryna freak," he boldly stated. "You muhfuckas can sit around and look at ass all day, but I'm tryna stick this dick in something wet."

"Man, sit ya drunk-ass down somewhere," Isaiah joked. "You better go stick that shit in that big-ass ocean out there."

Roselle laughed. "Fuck that. I want it in something tight and wet *and* exotic."

"You better use ya damn hand, bruh," Isaiah warned. "You wanna be out here fuckin' random ass. Ya ass fuck around 'n' catch some exotic shit you can't get rid of."

"No doubt," Kendall added. "What would your wife say if she found out you were out here mauling the help?"

Roselle finished off his drink. "Man, what my wife doesn't know won't hurt her. What you think they're over there doing on the other side of the island, crocheting?"

"Probably talking shit about us," Isaiah admitted over a laugh.

"Yeah, that too," Roselle stated emphatically. "But they're also over there looking at another muhfucka's dick, and probably letting him feel all up on her. All in jest."

"Shit. Then I need to go shake his hand," Isaiah said. "And then hand him over my marriage license, so he can take over the headaches."

Kendall laughed. "Both y'all crazy, man. I can't speak for anyone else's wife, but . . ." He paused when Aurora returned with their drinks. He waited for her to set them down on their individual tables, and then eyed her as she walked off.

Roselle had since moved on from her, his attention back on the big-assed beauty twirling her hips, watching him watch her.

"I know for a fact Krista isn't letting another man touch her," Kendall continued once the young woman was out of earshot. "And she's damn sure not dick watching."

Roselle pulled his gaze away from the women dancing and gave Kendall a questioning look. "You sure about that?"

Kendall nodded. "Yup. There's not a doubt in my mind." He sipped his beer.

"That's what's up, if you have it like that," Roselle said. "But I know for a fact Brenda's freaky-ass is licking her lips and talking shit and—"

Kendall gave him an incredulous look. "You're cool with that?"

"Hell yeah," Roselle admitted. "She can let him get her all hot 'n' bothered and then bring that sweet kitty home so Daddy can beat it up for her."

Isaiah shook his head. "So you're cool with your wife cheating on you?"

Roselle frowned. "Hell nah. I'm cool with her flirting. Big difference. My baby's a big flirt, but she's definitely not giving up the cookie to any other muhfucka. She's too in love with this quarter-pounder to play herself like that."

Roselle took a long swallow of his drink, before standing and facing Isaiah and Kendall. "I'ma tell you cats this—you ready?" He took another large swig from his cup, then wiped his mouth with the back of his hand. "Wait for it . . .?"

He belched.

"Man, will you get on with it," Isaiah said, "or sit ya drunk-ass down. You blocking my view."

"Fuck a view, bruh. Know this," Roselle continued, "a wet pussy has no conscience. And neither does a dick when it's hard and has no one watching it. Now you mofos can sip on that, while I go get me some ass."

He stripped out of his swimwear and then headed toward the group of dancing women, while Isaiah and Kendall looked on in wide-eyed amazement as Roselle hoisted the object of his desires up over his shoulder and then ran into the ocean with her, leaving his Speedos and his footprints in the sand behind him.

"Damn," was all either of them could say as they watched Roselle whisper something in her ear, and then watch her disappear under the water and Roselle's head roll back.

Thirteen

"What is love . . . to *you*?"

Dr. Dangerfield asked the question moments ago, looking over at Isaiah, but the question was meant for LaQuandra. And she still had yet to respond. She was pondering the concept, its abstraction. These days, the word *love* was elusive to her.

Had she'd been asked the question this time last year, hell seven months ago (when Isaiah was still sharing a bed with her and fucking her down three times a week!), she would have said something goofy like, "Love is dancing naked in the rain."

Then again, she might have gotten all poetic and said, "Love is the beat of my heart, the nourishment to my soul." Or she might have said, "Love is tattooed across my lower back centered over a red heart."

Oh. Wait. Maybe she would say some ridiculously dumb shit like, "Love is running through fire while having multiple orgasms."

Ironically, her horny pussy was hot and on fire. And she didn't know how much longer she could go on without the feel of hands slowly roaming her body, while a hard dick was thrusting into her, burning with her, melting into her.

She had yet to explore her secret fantasy of being fucked by a stranger, because, although it was a fantasy, it still felt wrong simply thinking about it.

Passion Island was supposed to be about rekindling the romance in her marriage, to get Isaiah to see his wrongdoings (i.e., fucking that bitch, Cassandra!); that's what she'd signed up for. Not this extra shit. The focus should not be on *her*.

It was like this therapist bitch was trying to make *her* out to be the problem in their marriage, when Isaiah was clearly the one with the problem.

Dr. Dangerfield kept her eye trained on LaQuandra, while Isaiah sat silent, the both of them watching her, waiting.

LaQuandra drew in a breath and considered. *What is love to me?*

The hell if she knew anymore.

All she knew was, she wanted Isaiah to want her, to have naughty thoughts of her. She wanted her marriage. And she wanted her man.

Because he was the best thing that had ever happened to her.

Because she accepted him for the man he was, flaws and all.

Because—more importantly, if she were going to be completely honest with herself—she didn't want to lose him to that bitch, Cassandra, or make it any easier than Isaiah had already made it for her to sink her cruddy acrylics into him.

"*The heart wants what it wants*," she heard Dr. Dangerfield saying, and she nearly rolled her eyes up in her head.

She replayed the question in her head: *What's love to me?*

"I . . ." LaQuandra swallowed, overwhelmed with emotions—anger, confusion, fear, love. She felt like her heart was being crushed in someone's fist.

Isaiah was her everything, her entire world.

She loved him desperately. Maybe that was the goddamn problem. She loved him more than she loved herself.

God. What the hell was wrong with this picture?

And what the hell was wrong with her?

She dreaded her answer.

"I don't know," LaQuandra finally responded. "I spent the first part of my life not knowing what love felt like. And then, as I became a woman and met Isaiah, I thought I had finally figured it out. Thought I knew exactly what it was." LaQuandra looked over at Isaiah, and felt her mouth go dry as she tried to control the beat of her heart. She was hurt, plain and simple.

Isaiah met her eyes, but said nothing. He felt beads of sweat glide down the center of his back, though, and his hands went clammy.

Dr. Dangerfield gently said, "LaQuandra, why don't you share what you're feeling right now with your husband. Look at him and tell him how the lack of intimacy in your marriage has affected you."

Isaiah shifted in his seat, unsure if he really wanted to know. He wasn't beat for a lot of talking, or listening to it. And yet he knew he owed it, his ear, to her.

Isaiah calmly said, "I'm listening."

LaQuandra *tsked*. "Oh really? Now you're going to listen? Why weren't you listening when—?"

Dr. Dangerfield cut her off. "LaQuandra, let's stay in the here and now. You have your husband's ear and his attention now, so talk to him."

LaQuandra felt her nostrils flaring. "Why don't you fuck me, huh, Isaiah?" The word *fuck* came out harsh and dirty. That was what she wanted. To be fucked, hard and dirty by him, fucked in the same way she knew he fucked Cassandra. Obviously, the slutty-bitch was a good fuck for him to keep running back to her.

She shifted her body, so that she was turned in Isaiah's direction. "Why do I have to practically beg you, just to suck your goddamn dick?" she continued. She bit her lip to keep it from quivering. "Did you stop fucking me, so you could have an excuse to go over and fuck Cassandra whenever that whore spread her legs open to you?"

Isaiah scowled. "Why do you have to always call her names, LaQuandra? She's the mother of my child."

LaQuandra huffed. "And she's still a goddamn *whore*."

Isaiah shook his head and then looked over at Dr. Dangerfield. "You see what I have to put up with? *This* shit?"

"Oh really, Isaiah?" LaQuandra snapped incredulously. The fucking nerve of him! "What about all the shit I've been putting up with, huh? After everything that *bitch* put me through, disrespecting *me*. Coming to my job and attacking *me*, and you still take up for that ignorant, ghetto-ass bitch!" LaQuandra looked over at Dr. Dangerfield. "And you see he *still* didn't answer the question, right?"

Dr. Dangerfield decided to stay quiet and see how things played out between the two of them. The couple clearly had different communication styles. LaQuandra yelled and cursed. And Isaiah withdrew and became silent. Neither ever heard the other. But Dr. Dangerfield decided to wait it out. She wouldn't play referee. And she wasn't going to hold up a scorecard as to who raised the most valid points. But she would address them both as needed.

Isaiah frowned. "What question, LaQuandra?"

"I *asked* are you fucking that *bitch?*"

Isaiah knew that wasn't what he'd heard her ask him, but whatever. Deny. Deny. Deny.

"No, I'm not fucking Cass." He saw the doubt on LaQuandra's face as her eyes stayed firmly on him, but she was talking to Dr. Dangerfield when she said, very softly (a stark contrast to the anger etched on her face), "He's a fucking liar."

Isaiah went tense. Tight. And he was chanting in his head:

Deny, deny, deny . . .

"I have no reason to lie to you, Quandra," he stated flatly. And yet he had every reason to stretch the truth, for no other reason than not wanting to hear her damn mouth.

This motherfucker must really think I'm some stupid bitch. LaQuandra tilted her head and gave him an "oh really" look.

"*Mmph.* Well, if you're not screwing *her*," she said disbelievingly, "then you must be out there giving that dick to somebody else because you sure in hell haven't been giving it to *me*."

"There's no one else, Quandra, damn," Isaiah said, frustration lacing his tone.

"You're so full of shit, Isaiah," LaQuandra snapped, and Isaiah saw her jaw tighten as fury marred her face.

"How long has it been since you've been intimate with your wife?" Dr. Dangerfield asked Isaiah.

He shrugged. "I don't know. It's been a minute."

LaQuandra scowled. "It hasn't been no damn *minute*," she snapped. "Try *months*." She looked at Dr. Dangerfield, who saw the hurt in LaQuandra's eyes. "Who does that? Not fuck his wife? And I know his ass isn't somewhere jacking his shit because he doesn't like it. Ain't no real man not fucking something."

Isaiah shook his head. "And you're wrong. I do jerk off when I feel the need to. But you're right, I don't like to. I'd rather have it done for me."

LaQuandra sneered at him. "Yeah, I bet you do." She huffed. "I'm stuck with a battery-operated playmate and my goddamn fingers, while you go off and fuck your trifling-ass baby mother."

"I don't run off and fuck her," Isaiah countered over his frustration. "Damn. Why the fuck are you so damn obsessed with Cass, huh, Quandra?"

LaQuandra blinked. "I'm not obsessed with that bitch. What I am is pissed that you keep choosing that bitch over me."

"Listen. Stop that dumb shit," he warned. "I haven't chosen Cass over you. I'm with *you*, ain't I?"

Barely.

And the question meant nothing to LaQuandra when he hardly ever made her feel like he was present in their marriage the way he used to.

She huffed. "Isaiah, kiss my fucking ass. Okay? Don't even try to play that shit with me."

"What shit, Quandra?" Isaiah felt himself becoming increasingly agitated. Perhaps it was the guilt getting to him. "Damn. What the fuck you want from me, huh?"

LaQuandra blinked. She couldn't believe his ass needed to ask. Wasn't it obvious what she needed, wanted, from him? Hadn't she been clear all these months and even now?

Dr. Dangerfield slid her glasses up over her head and crossed her legs at the ankles. "Isaiah, can you tell me why you've withheld sex from your wife?"

He shrugged one shoulder. "I'm not beat for the bullshit."

LaQuandra's eyes widened. "You're not *beat?* You're not beat for what, huh, motherfucker? I've been nothing but good to you, nigga. And time and time again, all you do is give me your motherfucking ass to kiss."

Isaiah frowned. "Then why the fuck are you still with me, huh, Quandra?"

Good question. But goddamn him . . . this wasn't about her.

"Motherfucker, don't you dare flip this shit on me. How about I ask you why the hell you're still with *me?* Answer *that*, nigga!"

Dr. Dangerfield cleared her throat. "LaQuandra, can you tell me how Isaiah not being intimate with you makes you feel?"

LaQuandra blinked. Why was this bitch making the session about *her? LaQuandra* this. *LaQuandra* that. The bitch had yet to confront Isaiah's ass on his bullshit and it was getting on her last damn nerve.

She shot the therapist a scathing look. "Excuse *you?*"

Dr. Dangerfield ignored the attitude, and rephrased her question.

"Can you please put into words how Isaiah moving out of the marital bed has made you feel?"

"Like I'm not shit," she hissed. "Like I'm some fucking sidepiece he fucked at will, then discarded once he'd had enough. I feel like he's more in love with that ghetto-trash bitch than he is with me. He treats me like *I'm* his problem. And not *that* bitch. She has been nothing but trouble from the moment he slid his goddamn dick in her. Not once has he ever checked that bitch anytime she said some slick shit about me. Not once. But the minute I call her out of her name, he's quick to remind me that *that* bitch is his son's mother and that I need to respect her." She sucked her teeth. "Fuck that. *I'm* his wife. Not that whore! And she needs to respect *me.* The woman who puts up with all of his shit!"

Isaiah bit his bottom lip, letting the truth of LaQuandra's words slice into his guilt. She was right. He hadn't really stood by her, or checked Cassandra's ass whenever she disrespected his wife, which was usually any chance she could.

"That EBT-having, Section-8 bitch calls my home and talks down to me, like she's some boss-bitch, when all she is . . ." LaQuandra paused and shook her head. She felt the beginnings of a pounding headache pushing its way to the front of her head.

"LaQuandra," Dr. Dangerfield said gently. "I see how upsetting it is for you every time you mention Isaiah's child's mother. Why is that?"

LaQuandra momentarily closed her eyes in an attempt to compose herself. When she reopened them, her pupils appeared wide and full of disdain.

"I hate—" She drew in a breath. "I hate that woman. And I hate the fact that Isaiah lets her disrespect me and does nothing about it."

Truth was, she was jealous. But she would never openly admit that.

Dr. Dangerfield could see Isaiah's body tense, his muscles tightening as if he were a caged animal, searching for an escape.

He was drained. And he had a splitting headache. He wasn't built for all this back-and-forth shit. He wanted this session over, so he could get back to the villa, slip into his swim trunks and take a long swim.

"Isaiah, what are you hearing your wife saying to you at this moment?" Dr. Dangerfield asked him as she observed his aloof demeanor.

LaQuandra speared Isaiah with an impatient glare when he didn't answer right away. "See this is the shit I'm talking about, Isaiah. You never fucking listen to shit I have to say."

"I heard you, damn."

"But, motherfucker, are you *listening* to me?!"

He started to say no, then stopped himself. "Of course I'm listening. *Fuck*," he added, as he stretched his long legs out and ran his palms over the top of his head.

Dr. Dangerfield decided to intervene. "LaQuandra, please try to refrain from name-calling."

LaQuandra rolled her eyes. She'd had enough of this uppity black bitch. "I'll call him what the hell I want. I have a right to after all the shit he's put me through. I'm his wife, so if I want to call him a mother*fucker*, then that's what the hell I'll call him. Because, quite frankly, that's exactly what the fuck he is. A. Mother. *Fucker.*"

Well, all right then.

Honestly, Dr. Dangerfield hadn't expected any other response. LaQuandra might have held a college degree, but she was still just as ghetto as she claimed Isaiah's child's mother was as far as she was concerned. No amount of education was going to ever change that, no matter how proper she tried to present herself. Somehow, some way, the ghetto part of who she was would eventually find a way to rear its ugly head.

"What your wife is saying, Isaiah," Dr. Dangerfield simply said, thoughtfully, "is that she misses you. Her husband, her life partner;

the man she committed herself to. And she's frightened. She's afraid that the two of you are growing apart, and that she is losing you. She feels alone in this marriage. She's married to you, but feeling single and that in itself can be very frightening."

LaQuandra felt herself becoming overwhelmed with emotions. But she wasn't about to give this motherfucker the satisfaction of seeing her fall apart.

"I hate you, Isaiah. Do you hear me? I fucking *hate* your black ass."

It was a boldfaced lie. But still she said it. She couldn't hate him. She wanted to. Oh, God, how she wanted to. But she loved him too much and that hurt her the most.

Loving him.

Isaiah said, "I'm sorry you feel that way. I don't want to hurt you, LaQuandra. But . . ." He trailed off as he measured his words. "I . . ."

LaQuandra shook her head, unwilling to hear him out. "But you don't want to keep me either, do you?"

He didn't know what to say to that, and LaQuandra saw it written all over his face. She felt the tears prick at her eyes. Goddamn him—goddamn him for being responsible for causing her all this anguish. Pain she hadn't realized ran so deep.

"Fuck. You."

LaQuandra stood up. She had to get out of here.

Isaiah caught the eye of Dr. Dangerfield, who gestured with her own eyes for him to go after his wife.

"LaQuandra, wait," Isaiah called out, standing to his feet.

She turned back, her finger held up, her eyes fiery slits, her expression pained so vividly that he could feel his own heart pounding in his chest. He knew LaQuandra was fighting an explosion. She was keeping a tight rein on a temper he'd seen before.

"I'm—"

"No. Don't say *shit*," she warned, cutting him off. And then she turned away again and stalked off.

Fourteen

Surrender . . .

Letting go of the parts of yourself that no one else could see. Peeling back the petals of your soul and allowing room for vulnerability. That's what surrendering was all about.

That was the lesson. Correction. That would be the lesson. One day.

Surrendering.

For each couple to give into their desires unapologetically (and respectfully—of course) without shame or regret. But each couple had work to do before they could ever cross that proverbial bridge.

What Dr. Dangerfield had come to learn about most of the couples she counseled and coached over the years was that they were afraid of letting go, afraid of giving into pleasure with one another. They held on to their fears, their resentments, the past, and, most importantly, their control. And it limited them in their relationships. It stifled their emotional and sexual growth. It blocked their ability to be more open-minded.

And it kept *many* of them stuck.

Stuck in mediocre sex. Stuck in sexless marriages. Stuck in sexual misery.

Yes. Surrender. That was the lesson. But, first, Dr. Dangerfield had to start from the bottom, then fight her way up to liberating the couples. She had to dig deep, and pull even deeper, to get some of them to feel safe enough to eventually step into their own truths.

She didn't doubt that the couples didn't love one another. Sadly, love wasn't enough. Not in a society where everyone, everything, was easily replaced by the next best thing—good or not.

But the question was: how much was each partner willing to invest in (and commit to) in the process? How emotionally transparent were they willing to become for the sake of their relationships?

She looked forward to finding out. For the next several weeks, she had her work cut out for her. She would push and probe. And they would either break or bend. Fight or flee. The choice would be theirs.

And she'd be right there along the way to guide them. But, first, in order for the couples to surrender, to let go, to free their inner sexual beasts, they would need to learn to trust in not only their partners, but, also—most importantly—themselves.

Dr. Dangerfield shook her head as she thought of the couples. She definitely had her work cut out for her, especially with that loudmouthed ghetto one.

La*Quandra.*

She was clearly a walking billboard for what an angry black woman looked like. Her mouth was filthy. And her disposition was shitty. But Dr. Dangerfield knew that behind her roar was a hurting woman, a damaged one. And she looked forward to peeling back LaQuandra's very thick skin, one layer at a time. And Isaiah—*mmph*—with his detached self. Hood dick, that's what he was. Probably a real good fuck, too, Dr. Dangerfield thought as she slowly kneaded her nipples.

She nearly died out there in The Garden when they'd both answered nearly every damn question wrong. What a damn mess.

Clearly, neither had ever taken the time out to talk, to really get to know one another.

Her thoughts then shifted to Brenda. Brenda, Brenda, Brenda. Brenda with the big bouncy ass, she mused. Oh she was a wild one, Dr. Dangerfield realized. But she needed to learn ways to not emasculate her husband, Roselle. *Whew.* He was a fine one, Dr. Dangerfield thought, sliding the tip of her tongue over her top lip. Not her type, though. He didn't wet her pussy, but he was definitely nice to look at.

And then her mind went back to Krista. *Jesus.* She was clearly the most sexually repressed of them all. Bless her heart. She didn't love fellatio—giving or getting.

She couldn't imagine life without head. She simply couldn't wrap her mind around women not giving their men oral pleasure, especially when he eagerly tongued and laved her sex. She couldn't fathom the thought of not having a man's turgid shaft sliding over her tongue, or her tongue catching his precum, or her succulent lips being painted with his milk.

However, this wasn't about her dick-sucking eps or her sexual liberation; this was about the three couples that awaited her in The Aquarium, where tonight's festivities were being held, a tank full of pleasure, sort to speak.

Janet Jackson's *Damito Jo* album played low in the background.

She pinched her nipples, and a low moan escaped her.

Dr. Dangerfield suspected Krista—and, maybe even, LaQuandra—would be the most difficult to engage. Hell. Krista appeared to be the least creative in the bedroom out of the three women. So Dr. Dangerfield already made it up in her mind that getting *her* to let go of her sexual inhibitions was truly going to be the most challenging. But she lived for moments like this. *Oh yes.*

Dr. Dangerfield spread her thighs open and her freshly waxed pussy greeted her. She smiled as she imagined one of her secret Island lovers kneeling before her, tonguing the slit of her cunt, brushing his tongue over the hood of skin that covered her clit . . . *God, yes* . . . and then sucking one of her swollen labium into his hot, juicy mouth; the taste of her rippling over his tongue.

Mm. How decadent.

Her pussy throbbed. And yet, somehow, she managed to peel herself away from her salacious thoughts, her mind momentarily drifting back to LaQuandra Lewis.

Dr. Dangerfield believed she was the saddest, most hurt, of them all. Not solely from her strained marriage, but more so from her past. A past she was certain scarred her deeply. *Mmph.* At least *she* gave oral pleasure, Dr. Dangerfield mused. It was the least she could do with that mouth of hers. She shook her head, reaching for her bottle of Rogue by Rihanna.

She sprayed it over her body, its scent filling the room.

She inhaled, and smiled.

She had a vast collection of very high-end bottles of perfume, but this scent here was most fitting for tonight. She felt naughty, and playfully mischievous.

Roguish.

That's what these couples were in their own way—deceptive and deceitful.

Defiant.

Destructive.

Dr. Dangerfield sighed. *Same story, different set of couples.*

She set the bottle back atop her vanity and then stood naked in front of her mirror and slid her diamond studs into each earlobe, before clasping her diamond choker around her slender neck. A large teardrop diamond lay perfectly in the center of her bosom.

She loved diamonds. Loved the way they came alive under the lights.

Although she was mostly business conservative in her dress during the day, she had a wild side. Bold and daring. And, tonight, she planned on showing the couples that other side of her—in her dress, that was. There was nothing wrong with being sexy, feeling sexy. There was nothing wrong with exuding sex appeal.

Being naughty.

And, on occasion, being slutty.

Dr. Dangerfield stared at herself through the mirror, and then a sly grin eased over her lips as she slid into a red silk, backless halter dress with a plunging V-neckline and side slits. The short dress was bold and daring and dangerously sexy.

Exactly like her alter ego.

Oh yes. She knew how to be slutty. Knew how to fuck and suck and pleasure herself.

And a man.

Or a woman.

Or both.

Anonymously or not, she knew how to be nasty, and take what she wanted. But she also knew how to be submissive. She knew how to give as well as she could take. Mutual pleasure. Reciprocity. That's what lovemaking and fucking were all about—giving and taking gratification.

Dr. Dangerfield admired her lithe body, cupping her taut breasts. She plucked at her nipples until they tightened and her cunt clenched. Then she raised her arms up over her head and began a slow sensual roll of her hips as Janet sang, in her whispery voice, about getting moist. Her gaze locked on the reflection staring back at her as she drew her tongue over her upper lip and slipped a finger inside her pussy.

Oh, yes, she was very moist.

And the night had yet to begin.

Fifteen

They'd followed a lighted stone pathway toward a three-story, stoned elliptical structure landscaped with coconut palms and large pink hibiscus flowers. The main entrance, which was flanked by marbled pillars and life-like statues of nude lovers that sat atop enormous pedestals, faced a garden of exotic flora.

LaQuandra and Isaiah were the first to cross the opulent threshold, followed by Krista and Kendall, and then Brenda and Roselle—who were holding hands and strolling like young, horny lovers. LaQuandra found the couple disgustingly happy. Miss Brick House and her wavy-haired stallion, always pawing and kissing on one another.

Yes. She was hating. Hard.

They seemed too damned perfect.

So, why the hell were they—?

"Welcome to The Aquarium," said a woman with skin the color of brown sugar. A hint of a smile pulled at her tangerine-glossed lips. She was beautiful, LaQuandra decided. Like every other woman she'd seen on the island thus far. Her lithe, youthful body could have easily belonged to a Victoria's Secret model. Her beautiful breasts, with their dark chocolate nipples, swayed slightly as she swept an arm back, welcoming them inside.

Isaiah tried not to stare, but he found his gaze dipping down over her flat belly and then over the slight curve of her hips, then at the strip of silk that covered her sex.

He found himself imagining her bent over with him behind her, pulling open her cheeks, licking the inside of her ass, over her brown hole, over the thin string of her panties, before pulling the string with his teeth.

LaQuandra caught the way Isaiah was looking at the little tight-bodied bitch and rolled her eyes. A hand closed around Isaiah's arm, and he found himself being dragged away.

"Oh hell no," LaQuandra hissed as she pulled Isaiah by the arm.

Tinashe's "Bet" seeped down over the massive atrium through Bose in-ceiling speakers, her voice raining a melody that almost made LaQuandra want to use one hand to snap her fingers, and the other to slap the shit out of Isaiah.

She was so over him.

The sexy door greeter gave a quick glance in their direction as a smile shadowed her mouth as if she'd known why LaQuandra had stomped off angrily. It wasn't the first, nor would it be the last, time a wife trudged off with her ogling hubby in tow. They—the insecure ones—always managed to see her as a threat to their already fucked-up marriages.

"Damn," said Isaiah once they were out of earshot. He yanked his arm from her grasp. "What's up with you now, Quandra, huh?"

"You eye-fucking that bitch; *that's* what's up now." LaQuandra slammed a hand up on her hip. "I'm sick of you disrespecting me, Isaiah. What, you wanna fuck her now, too?"

Isaiah frowned, but *damn* . . . he'd been busted. "Ain't nobody thinking about that lil-ass girl," he lied.

LaQuandra scoffed. "Yeah, right, motherfucker. I saw how you were looking at her."

Isaiah shook his head, and *tsked* her. "You stay on your bullshit. You know that, right?"

"Whatever, Isaiah. If you think you're gonna be sticking your dick in her or any other island bitch, you have another thing coming. If *I'm* not fucking, neither are *you*, nigga."

All eyes turned to LaQuandra and the spectacle she was making of herself, while Isaiah stayed silent, impassive almost. He wasn't about to argue with her, not here. Not in front of all these nosey-ass onlookers.

"Whatever, man. Go get our seats. I'm going to the bar." Isaiah walked off, leaving LaQuandra looking like a crazed woman. *I'm sick of this motherfucker disrespecting me. Eyeballing some other bitch right in front of me.* She quickly slid a hand up along the side of her dreadlock bun updo, thankful that Brenda approached her. She desperately needed the distraction, before she really showed her ass.

"Girl, you okay?" Brenda wanted to know as her gaze skittered from LaQuandra, then over toward the direction of the oval-shaped bar, where Roselle meandered over to. She trusted him enough to know he wouldn't blatantly do any dumb shit that would get him fucked up out in public, but still . . . she had to be on the lookout.

Krista had made her way to the ladies room to freshen up, bypassing the two other women. She didn't particularly care for females. And she only had one good girlfriend, and that was her older sister, Latrice. Out of her four sisters, Latrice was the one whom she confided in, and trusted the most. Sure, she had female acquaintances and colleagues that she'd be friendly with—or perhaps *cordial* was a better suited-word, but she'd never consider any of them a friend.

LaQuandra gave Brenda a dismissive wave. "It's nothing, girl. Just Isaiah being a man, eyes gawking everywhere."

Brenda chuckled, smoothing a hand down the front of her dress. "Tell me about it. I've been keeping my good eye on Roselle, because I know how he can get. Acting like some horny adolescent boy."

LaQuandra glanced around the opulent atrium with its mammoth crystal chandeliers and Fazioli Brunei centered in the middle of the room. The four hundred thousand-dollar grand piano was a spectacular sight to behold for any piano enthusiast.

"Girl, my motto is," Brenda said, causing LaQuandra to focus her attention back on her, "let them look. As long as they don't touch, who gives a damn? I know I don't. Hell, even I look. And if Roselle's a good boy, I might even bring him home a sexy treat for us *both* to enjoy."

"Wait," LaQuandra said, giving her a baffled look. "You go both ways?"

"Girl, I go whatever way my mood is." Brenda glanced back over toward the bar and spotted Roselle grinning in the face of a tall woman wearing a red, bullet-cone bra corset with a matching thong. She shook her head. "Anyway, look on the bright side," Brenda continued. "At least your husband isn't eyeing another man. Now *that* might cause a problem." She tooted her lips as she fingered the triple strand of Tahitian pearls dangling from her neck. "Well, not unless you're into that kind of stuff." She eyed LaQuandra, waiting for her reaction. Personally, Brenda loved bisexual men. In fact, one of her exes, Franklin, was bisexual. And he had been upfront with her about his sexuality, which Brenda had found refreshing and oh so very sexy. Franklin had oozed masculinity and sexuality, and he fucked real good. She also had him to thank for turning her on to the world of bisexuality.

Of course, she was more open-minded than most women, and a whole lot more daring sexually than many, especially black women, she believed. They were simply too uptight about sex and sexuality, unlike her Latina sisters, and—of course, the Beckys of the world.

LaQuandra frowned. "Hell no. I'm not down with that nasty

shit. Bisexual and down-low niggas can't do shit for me; except for show me where the straight men are."

"I heard you on that," was all Brenda said over a laugh.

LaQuandra sighed, and then she scanned the bar area. Perhaps she'd overreacted, she mused. Brenda was right. What was the harm in Isaiah looking at that little perky-tit bitch? As long as he was nowhere near Cassandra's ass, there shouldn't be any pause for concern.

No other woman, besides that bitch, was the problem.

Brenda glanced down at her Gucci timepiece. "Ooh, the show is about to start," she said to LaQuandra. "Let me go grab Roselle, so we can get our seats."

"Oh, okay," LaQuandra said. "If you see my husband over there, tell him I'll be inside."

"I'm sorry," LaQuandra said, low enough for only Isaiah to hear the moment he took his seat beside her. He had two drinks in his hand. He'd already tossed back a shot of Cuevos, while at the bar, with Roselle. These two drinks would do him right.

Isaiah gave her a look. He was sick of her shit. And he was really starting to get sick of looking at her. He took a long gulp from one of the drinks.

"You're sorry for what, Quandra?"

"For carrying on out in the lobby like that. It was stupid of me."

"You can't help yourself," he said. She acted like a stupid bitch sometimes.

LaQuandra gave him a look, and he stared back. He was really trying to bite back his temper. He wanted to light into her, but this was neither the time nor the place to check her ass. So he finished off his first drink in another large gulp.

"I don't wanna fight tonight, Isaiah," she stated. "Truce? Please."

"Yeah, a'ight. Whatever you say, Quandra."

She eyed the tumbler resting in the cup holder and then asked, "Is that drink for me?" She reached over for the glass and Isaiah grabbed her hand.

"You don't need a drink," he said sternly. "Ya ass don't know how to act." And then he lifted the glass to his lips, tipped his head back, and drained it.

Isaiah was certain that if he was going to get through the rest of the night, then he needed to be fucked up, or damned near close to it.

Before LaQuandra could open her mouth to say something slick, of course, a very feminine, very seductive voice floated out through the speakers, quickly quieting the theater.

"Good evening, my beautiful people. Welcome to The Aquarium. Filled with raw sensuality, tonight's show will tantalize and entice you. It will be an experience . . ."

LaQuandra looked around the amphitheater-type setting, and for the life of her, she couldn't understand why it had been called an aquarium when there wasn't a tank or any amphibian life in sight.

The oval room reminded LaQuandra of a Roman coliseum without the concrete and sand.

There was stadium-style seating. And in the center of the amphitheater was an enormous circular stage that was surrounded by a thick velvet curtain, the same black curtain that covered the length of the walls around them.

The way the space was quickly filling—many of the exotic-looking, scantily dressed women were on the arm of casually dressed men, while others had come alone or with other women, who wore nearly nothing—something was definitely about to go down. And, whatever it was, LaQuandra Lewis was excited, almost too excited (to the point that her pussy tingled) to have a front-row seat.

She sighed. She was so tired of wondering, tired of fantasizing, tired of wanting and fighting and being denied.

She needed a hard dick. She needed a man with large hands and long fingers to smack her on the ass and finger her cunt. But she wouldn't cheat. No matter how many times she'd considered it. Cheating was out.

Suddenly, LaQuandra dragged in a frustrated breath, aware that Isaiah was looking over at her. Deep-set eyes glowering at her.

"What you over there grunting about?"

She swallowed, then obliged him with a scowl of her own. *This motherfucker really knows how to fuck up a wet dream.* "Nothing."

Isaiah cocked a brow. "Oh a'ight. For a minute there, it sounded like you were taking a shit," he stage-whispered.

LaQuandra rolled her eyes. Although she knew Isaiah was half-joking, she found no humor in his remark. Smart-ass. Before she had a chance to respond back, the lights dimmed and the circular stage wrapped in thick velvet began to slowly spin.

". . . so sit back, relax," the sultry MC continued over the music, "and indulge your senses in the underwater world of erotica."

Krista shifted in her seat as her gaze swept around the mini-arena. She found herself surrounded by half-naked women—they were everywhere; suddenly, she felt like she'd been the only one who'd gotten the memo on how to dress appropriately.

She rolled her eyes up in her head, but then smiled when Kendall reached for her hand. He leaned in to her, and then he whispered, "You know I can't wait to get you back to our villa, right?" He took her hand and discreetly placed it over the lump in his pants.

Krista swallowed. She was tempted to squeeze him there, but she couldn't bring herself to do it. Not here.

FKA twigs' "Ache" eased out of the speakers and then the curtains along the walls slowly slid open.

Gasps could be heard as the entire room transformed into one enormous aquarium filled with some of the South Pacific's most beautiful coral reefs and fish.

They were surrounded by water.

Inside the massive glass walls were six large glass-like boxes equally spaced a part suspended in the water in front of them, giving the illusion that they were floating beneath the sea.

Within each box were human statues.

Sculpted.

Voluptuous.

An erotic assortment of chocolate bodies airbrushed in shimmering gold paint.

All in various tantric poses.

Naked.

Wearing elaborate facemasks.

Krista's body stiffened. She clutched the armrests on either side of her seat, and nearly hyperventilated, while Brenda leaned forward, her gaze filled with hunger.

LaQuandra pressed her legs together.

Suddenly, she wished she'd worn a panty liner.

Sixteen

"Mm. Pacify . . . clarify our love . . ."

Brenda found herself becoming entranced by the sensual melody seeping through the speakers. She wasn't familiar with the artist, but she was enjoying the vibe. FKA twigs was once again luring listeners in with her sultry beats and seductive voice as she moaned and asked for *papi* to pacify their love, to tell her she was the only one.

As she moaned out *mm* . . . *mm* . . . *mm* . . . the curtain covering the ginormous glass cylinder in the middle of the room slowly retracted.

The already dimmed lights went dimmer; leaving the room alit by only the fluorescent lights inside the large aquarium. The encased human statues suspended in the water nearly glowed. And then slowly they moved, changing positions, hard dicks sliding out of clenching slits, then sliding back in. And then they froze again.

Brenda bit her bottom lip as she glanced up at the erotic sight. She didn't know whether to look up at one of the large LED monitors that captured everything or keep staring straight ahead.

So she did both, her gaze going from the monitors to the glass wall, wondering how the hell they—those human statues—could stay in that position, dicks wedged inside wet pussy—and *not* thrust.

How could they not fuck?

She'd be crazy, wild with lust, raking her nails over the globes of his ass as she ground her pelvis, trying to fuck herself on his impaled dick.

No, God. That couldn't be her.

"Damn, baby," Roselle whispered as he leaned into her, "this shit got me right. Dick harder than a muhfucka. Take your panties off," he said in a seductive whisper.

"Right now?" she asked, glancing around her.

"Yeah. Let me get them panties."

"Nasty ass," Brenda murmured, before quickly glancing over her shoulder. It was dark enough. She slowly lifted her hips up from her seat and discreetly slid her pink Stella McCartney lace-trim bikini briefs down over her curvy hips.

She stifled a giggle as she eased her panties down to her ankles and stepped out of them. Roselle licked his lips as she reached down and then placed the lace and nylon/spandex undergarment in his hand.

He placed her panties up to his nose, as if they were a handkerchief, and inhaled.

Brenda felt her nipples tighten, and she—

"Kendall," Krista whispered, "why exactly are *we*—?"

"*Ssh*," he whispered, cutting her off. "Looks like the show is about to start. We'll leave in a few—if *you* want." He reached for her hand. Krista's body stiffened, then relaxed as he lightly stroked his thumb over the top of her hand.

LaQuandra wished—whatever the show was—that it would start already. The waiting was a sweet torture, one that had her cunt aching in anticipation. Staring at those human statues—*Lord-Jesus*—made her skin heat. Isaiah had better fuck me tonight, she thought as she cut an eye over at him.

Synchronously, the male statues moved again; hips retreating, the tips of their dicks barely touching their female counterpart's slits. In. Out. In. Out. And then they froze again.

Living, breathing, erotic art . . . that was what this was.

Colorful fish swam around the glass encasements.

The females threw their heads back. Then slowly thrust their pelvises forward, sliding their pussies over the dicks, then sliding back in slow motion, just to the tips of each dick.

How did they do that? Not shiver and whimper?

"*Mm . . . pacify . . .*"

Self-control, that's all it was.

But damn if Isaiah would have any. He pressed his legs together, feeling his arousal bubbling up to the tip of his hard dick. Three drinks in, and he was horny as fuck.

He leaned into LaQuandra, and then, with his warm lips, flush to her ear, he whispered, "You wanna suck this dick, tonight?"

His breath heated LaQuandra's skin and she felt her legs closing as if to stop the sensations she was suddenly feeling. Yes, she would suck his dick. But she wanted, needed, much more than his dick wedged between her lips. She needed him embedded deep inside her body.

"Are you gonna fuck me?" she hissed; her tone louder than Isaiah would have preferred. "I need some *dick*, Isaiah—inside me. *Tonight.*"

"Yeah, maybe," was all he said, before his attention got lost on what was rising up from the glass cylinder's floor on a huge glass pedestal.

A woman.

Bronze-dusted.

Goddess-like.

Nude.

A dangerous mixture of . . . seduction and sin.

Her head thrown back, her arms up over her head, right hand clasped over her right wrist. She stood motionless as the pedestal slowly rotated.

Kneeling in front of her was a man—and woman.

Both naked.

Still.

Mannequin-like.

Their eyes closed.

Their tongues touching, positioned, angling for her clit, for her opening.

Sheets of aqua-blue water began sliding down the sides of the cylinder, giving the illusions of a waterfall, as it slowly spun around.

Suddenly, the men in the encasements began thrusting simultaneously in sync to the slow, seductive beat of the music. They slow-fucked.

"*Mm . . . mm . . . mm . . .*"

The mesmerizing beauty on the pedestal captivated the audience.

Her two lovers, precipitously, began stroking her clit with their tongues and then sucking her like she was a sweet juicy fruit.

The rotating pedestal slowed.

Large green sea turtles could be seen gracefully swimming around the large glass encasements, as the human statues got lost in the throes of passion.

In. Out. In. Out.

Slow, deep thrusts in rhythmic motion.

In. Out. In. Out.

And then they froze, again.

Now the females began thrusting, slowly sliding their pussies back and forth over each man's shaft, as he stood motionless. Up. Back. Up. Back. Up. Back.

The female statues froze again as the exotic beauty's face suddenly appeared on the large screens, ensnaring her audience.

Applause erupted. Men whistled.

And LaQuandra looked around trying to understand what the hell they were all clapping for. The woman's face was vaguely familiar to her, yet she couldn't place where'd she'd seen it. And, honestly, she didn't care. What she cared about was how this show of sorts had somehow managed to have her panties a soggy mess.

"Goddamn she's fine," Roselle murmured.

Yes, God, she was, Brenda admitted inwardly. She felt her inner walls tighten and a tiny drop of warm heat trickle out of her.

She'd seen that face before. That body. That ass. Those beautiful breasts.

She and Roselle . . . they both had. And they had the videos—every last one of them.

Krista shifted in her seat. A hand went up to her neck. She felt herself growing warm. This is getting ridiculous, Krista thought as she glanced over at Kendall who seemed to be spellbound.

The music looped to the beginning again.

"*Mm . . . mm . . . mm . . .*"

And the men in the background, with their hard-bodies, chiseled pecs, and ridged six-packs began thrusting again.

Slowly.

In.

Out.

Push.

Pull.

Deep.

Deeper.

The exotic beauty's eyes finally flashed open on the monitors.

And staring out into the audience were gray eyes.

Sultry.

Alluring.

Every man's wet dream.

Seventeen

Eleven a.m.

The three couples were down on the beach, sitting across from their respective partners on extra-large white leather pillows—its cushions covered with red rose petals.

Beside each cushion was a huge gift basket. Inside the respective baskets were a collection of male and female sex toys, edible creams and lubes, and an autographed hardcopy of *Good Pussy.*

Champagne sat on ice in metal buckets. Silver platters of strawberries, mangoes, grapes, and kiwi were picked over.

Each couple had been tasked with feeding the other.

With the exception of LaQuandra and Isaiah (he struggled with pretending), everyone else had rose to the occasion, happily licking one another's fingers clean. Surprisingly, even Krista—although she'd held back some—had enjoyed being fed by Kendall.

Now Dr. Dangerfield was greeting the couples.

"Good morning," she said. The morning breeze coming from off the ocean blew strands of her hair every which way. She swiped her bang from her eye and then placed the large white floppy hat she'd been holding in her hand on top her head.

"I hope everyone has enjoyed the shows and nightlife the island has to offer."

"Yes, girl, yes," Brenda said, waving a hand up in the air. She leaned in and planted a soft kiss on Roselle's lips and then added, "My baby and I love it."

Of course they did. They'd gone back to their villa after The Aquarium show and practically tore the sheets off their mattress.

Sex—or the lack of it—would never be their issue.

Roselle had ravished her body. And she had given it back as roughly as she had taken it.

She still felt the throb between her thighs.

Krista pursed her lips. That so-called show was nothing short of a damn porn video. Tastefully done or not, it was simply too damn much. And then that damn night—no, *sex*—club. There hadn't been an electric slide in sight. And the only thing wobbling were the men and women who'd been getting fucked.

Why was everything on this island tied to sex in some form or fashion?

She hadn't come way out here for all that.

Her gaze snared on Dr. Dangerfield's body beneath the sheer white cover-up she wore over her white halter-top jumper. It clung to her body in all the right places. The gap between her legs gave anyone who was at eye-level a sneak peek of her twat print.

She was classy, sure. But something about Dr. Dangerfield made Krista think she was a bit . . . *hoish.* She didn't want to judge her. Lord knew she was anything *but* judgmental. Or at least she tried *not* to be. Still, her God wasn't through with her yet.

So it was okay if she judged a little.

Dr. Dangerfield caught the frown on Krista's face. She ignored it for a brief second. "Mr. Evans, how did you enjoy the show the other night?"

Kendall's gaze soaked in the therapist's body, before he looked up at her. "I enjoyed it," he said honestly. It had turned him on. In turn, he handled his business in the bedroom with Krista. Some light foreplay—rubbing her pussy while they kissed. And then right to fucking. Because that's what she'd wanted. He'd wanted to see her facedown, ass up.

But he'd settled for her favorite position.

Missionary.

Very vanilla sex, but the pussy was still good.

It always was.

Dr. Dangerfield smiled. "I'm glad you enjoyed yourself. What about you, Mrs. Evans," she said, her eyes landing on Krista, "how'd you enjoy the show?"

Krista shrugged. "It was okay. I guess. But I need for you to explain to me why everything on this island is about sex? So far, that's all I see."

Kendall stared at his wife. In his mind's eye, he saw himself shaking his head at her ass. Because you need to step it up in the sheets, he thought.

Brenda rolled her eyes up in her head.

Dr. Dangerfield smiled, her gaze raking over Krista's billowy tank dress and then her painted toes. Her white sandals were lying beside her cushion on the sand. Everyone had received an embossed note with instructions to dress in beachwear. And yet this bitch had come down to the beach wearing a . . . flowered *dress*. She hoped a bathing suit was hidden beneath.

"This island is about passion," Dr. Dangerfield said. "Not sex. Sex can be meaningless for many. It can become almost a mechanical act of copulating for the sake of getting off. But passion on the other hand"—she shook her head—"it's a powerful, emotional experience. Sex and sexuality are a part of human nature. But passion and sensuality are lost on many. So here at Passion Island we seek to infuse the two into each and every one of your sex lives. It is my hope that we'll be able to help you—for those of you who need it—revive your sexual imagination."

"I love it," Brenda said. "I think couples should always want to keep it spicy in the bedroom. And as women we should always embrace our sensual sides."

LaQuandra grunted, and then glared at Isaiah. He hadn't fucked her yet. But last night, he'd haphazardly fingered her pussy, while she'd sucked his dick.

She'd sucked him as if she were sucking him for her life. And there were parts of her that felt like she had been, sap sucking him for dear life, suckling on a dick that her body needed so desperately.

When she tried to straddle him, he'd grabbed her, stopped her.

What kind of fuckery was that . . .?

Isaiah reached for the magnum of Dom, then poured himself another drink. He'd been drinking since they'd arrived on the beach at eight this morning.

"I invited you all down here," Dr. Dangerfield continued, "to help you tap into each other's sexual energy."

Through observation, she hoped to gauge each couple's intimate connection through their touch and the way their bodies responded to their partners. With the help of the island's owner, she'd be able to do exactly that.

It was all about helping couples find a spiritual connection.

Ideally, she'd prefer the couples were naked. But she suspected most of them weren't ready (or comfortable enough) for that. So she'd settled for bathing suits.

"Everyone, please, strip down to your swimwear," Dr. Dangerfield instructed, "and then resume your positions back on the cushions, facing each other."

Dr. Dangerfield waited.

To the left of her, in back of the couples, she caught the sight of her soror sitting up on the broad shoulders of Sin.

Yes, *him*.

Sin.

He was long dreads; six foot, three inches of dark chocolate masculinity. Bare-chested. His dick swinging proudly in his white drawstring pants.

Dr. Dangerfield's breath nearly hitched as she eyed him crossing the white sand. He stopped and lowered *her* to the sand, and then led her the rest of the way by the arm toward the group.

Donned in a white ankle-length dress, her cleavage on full display—thanks to a devilishly low neckline, her side slits daringly high up to her curvaceous hips, she glided over the sand.

Her porn star body was mouthwatering.

Dr. Dangerfield couldn't help but notice her areolas and thick nipples peeking through the sheer fabric of her dress, taunting, teasing.

Work, girl, weeerk!

LaQuandra spotted Sin and the woman walking toward them, but pretended not to see them, since no one else seemed to have noticed them approaching. She brushed the back of her bathing suit—a red strapless one-piece—and then took her seat.

And stared over at Brenda and Roselle.

Brenda had boldly worn an orange two-piece bikini, her thick body smooth and glowing from her recent tan. Roselle had topped that wearing what looked like a jockstrap, his muscular ass out, the thick bulge of his dick all on display.

And here was Krista, face twisted in disgust. She nearly threw up in the back of her mouth at the sight of Roselle. *What in the hell?* Men in thongs? *A hot damn mess.*

However, LaQuandra couldn't stop staring at the couple.

Oooh, they some freaky-asses, she thought. But if she had been blessed with an ass like Brenda's, she probably would have had hers hanging *all* out too. But, ooh, her man—*mm, yes*—that pretty motherfucker . . . he was too many things.

Behind her designer Bumblebee shades, even Dr. Dangerfield allowed her gaze to creep over Roselle's body, then linger over his very impressive dick print.

She cleared her throat. "Now that everyone has gotten comfortable, I'd like to turn the rest of the morning over to the woman of the hour . . ."

And there *she* appeared—the woman from last night, her gray eyes staring into the faces of the couples.

She prowled closer.

Known for her exquisite beauty and hedonistic lifestyle, she was an icon, a sex goddess. Once known to her legions of fans as Pleasure, she was an author, a model and the recipient of a slew of awards. She was a woman who'd graced the covers of *Playboy* and *Penthouse*. She owned two very successful upscale For Adults Only clubs, one on Passion Island and the other back in New York, with a third opening in Vegas soon—The Pleasure Chest. She was the CEO of her own production company, and had built a multimillion-dollar empire with her exclusive adult toy line.

"Without further ado," Dr. Dangerfield said over a smile. "I introduce to you, my soror, my friend, and the owner of this beautiful island, Nairobia Jansen . . ."

The two women hugged, and then air-kissed.

"Thank you, my darling," Nairobia said in her sultry voice, a hint of her Dutch and Nigerian ancestry lingering over her words. She faced the couples, one foot in front of the other; a hip thrust forward, a hand on her hip. At five feet ten, she commanded attention wherever she went.

"I welcome you to my island, my darlings. And I do hope you will find your stay full of sensual adventure. Passion Island is more than sordid sex, my loves. It is a journey into the unknown, a voyage to toe-curling pleasure. It is, my darlings, testing your limits and pushing you to complete surrender."

The wind blew the slits of her dress up, exposing the sides of her luscious ass cheeks, and a flash of her sweet pussy. She was beautifully flawless, that's what she was.

Sweet seduction.

Nairobia licked over her perfectly painted lips. She was known for being shameless, fearlessly exploring her sexuality and expressing her sensuality through her scandalous dress. And she lived to make the world around her uncomfortable in all that she was.

God, she was mesmerizing.

"Today, my darlings, we touch. We explore . . ."

Brenda and Roselle both licked their lips. They'd watched all of her porn videos, even reenacted many of the sex scenes.

Kendall and Isaiah found it nearly impossible to keep from staring at her, her nipples, the treacherous curves of her hips, and the silhouette of her body beneath the sheer fabric of her dress enticing them. Both men had masturbated to many of her videos.

Kendall's favorite—*Ass Licker*—was still in his browser on his iPad.

LaQuandra feigned not knowing who the seductress was, but she'd bought her book, *Good Pussy*, on release day two years ago and had read it cover to cover the same day. She kept it hidden in her lingerie drawer, under silk thongs, boy shorts, and garter belts. Shit she'd not worn in months.

Krista, on the other hand, sat tight-lipped, feeling the urge to reach down into her straw beach bag and pull out her scriptures. All she saw, while looking at Nairobia, was immorality. She was sin in its highest form. Temptation. Forbidden fruit. She could be nothing but trouble.

"The seat of your sexuality lies in your erogenous zones," Nairobia said. "My darling, men, close your eyes. Ladies, reach out and touch your men. Caress his face. Allow a finger to trace the curve of his lips. Let it linger there for a bit . . ."

Isaiah frowned. He was not about to close his eyes. LaQuandra would fuck around and do some dumb shit and he'd have to beat her ass out here on this sand.

LaQuandra was surprised the bastard sat still, so that she could feel on him. Her hands slid over his shoulders, then across his chest. She felt her inner walls clench.

"Mm. *Ja . . . ja*," Nairobia purred. "Love over your husband's skin. Allow the palms of your hands to breathe in his heartbeat." Nairobia paused, waited for everyone to get on board.

Dr. Dangerfield sat in back of Nairobia, facing the couples on a white cushion, where Sin had joined her, to observe the couples. So far, the only person who had her attention was Sin.

Damn him.

Krista's hands slid over Kendall's chocolate skin. She was thankful for having such a good man, a loving man—a monogamous man.

LaQuandra, although mad, welcomed the contact with Isaiah's flesh; even if he did keep his eyes open the entire time.

Brenda, always the eager one, had no problem laying hands on Roselle, be it passionately or aggressively.

Nairobia continued, "Now, my darlings, gently graze a fingertip over his nipples. Twirl. Tease. Lightly tweak until it tightens, until it pebbles into tiny balls of pleasure."

"Oww! Shit," Isaiah snapped, slapping LaQuandra's hand away when she pinched and twisted his nipples.

LaQuandra smirked. *Bastard.* "Oops. My bad."

He scowled at her. "Whatever, Quandra. Don't have me break your face out here."

LaQuandra rolled her eyes. "Nigga, I dare you."

Dr. Dangerfield eyed the two. The tension between them was thicker than she'd imagined. She'd have to really—

"You're looking sexier and sexier every time I see you," Sin whispered, cutting into Dr. Dangerfield's thoughts. He kept his gaze on Nairobia's mouthwatering ass, before landing his eyes back on Dr. Dangerfield.

She waved him on dismissively. She'd seen how he looked at Nairobia. Entranced by the enchantress. They all were. Always lusting for the infamous sex goddess.

"I bet you say that to all the girls," Dr. Dangerfield teased.

Sin grinned. "Only to the pretty ones."

Dr. Dangerfield playfully rolled her eyes. "Stop trying to distract me."

He leaned in closer, and then licked his lips. "How am I doing so far?"

She imagined him devouring her cunt right here, out in full view for all to see.

"You'll have to try a little harder," she lied.

"Yeah, okay," was all he said, before his eyes drifted back over to Nairobia, and then over at Brenda. He'd caught her eyeing him, so he winked, causing her to blush, then quickly turn away.

"Ladies," Nairobia said. "Look at your husbands. Stare into his eyes, and repeat after me: I am good pussy."

Brenda was the first to comply, proudly boasting, loudly, "*I* AM GOOD PUSSY."

LaQuandra glared at Isaiah. "You already know this pussy is good. So no announcement needed."

Isaiah rolled his eyes. "Yeah, but I ain't fucking it—now what," he felt clinging on the tip of his tongue. But he settled for, "Yeah, a'ight. Say it anyway."

LaQuandra sucked her teeth. "I *am* good pussy, nigga."

He smirked.

Krista sat and looked at Kendall as if she were a deer caught in headlights. Kendall smiled, reaching for her hand. "Baby, I know you're good pussy," he stated warmly. "But let me hear you say it." He leaned forward and kissed her softly on the lips. A little dirty talk was what Kendall needed. He'd love to hear Krista talk shit in the bedroom, just once—damn. Was that too much to wish for? "Tell me how good it is."

He grinned.

Krista scoffed. "I'm not saying that shit out here."

"Don't be shy, my darlings," Nairobia said, as if sensing Krista's resistance. "You are your pussies, my loves. Love it. Embrace it. Allow your husbands to know how you celebrate in that knowing." Nairobia glanced over at Krista. *Mmph.* Resistance was key to disaster.

She walked over to Krista and then squatted, her legs spread, her heavenly scent wafting up around the three of them. Fresh floral pussy.

Enticing. Intoxicating.

Kendall tried not to inhale too deeply.

"Are you not good pussy, *mijn liefde* (my love*)*?" she asked Krista.

Krista gave her an incredulous look that bordered on indignation for trying to embarrass her. "No—I mean, yes. I mean, of course I am."

Nairobia gazed into Krista's eyes. She saw it—her sexual limitations.

So, so pitiful.

"Then look into your husband's eyes, *mijn lieveling*, and tell him—*u bent goed kut*."

Neither Krista nor Kendall knew what she'd said in her native tongue, but Krista felt her face flush. And Kendall's dick stirred in his swim trunks.

"Say it," Nairobia urged. "You are good pussy."

Krista looked at Kendall and reluctantly said it. "I am good pussy." There, satisfied?

It was a mediocre attempt that made Nairobia want to extend her arm back and slap Krista's pitiful-ass face.

Nairobia sighed inwardly. "My darling, you can't expect your husband to believe you are good pussy—if *you* do not believe it." She stood, leaving her scent swirling up around the two of them.

"If you are not good pussy, my darlings, then you are *not* good loving," Nairobia stated in a matter-of-fact tone, "and if you are not good loving, then you can never be *unforgettable* fucking."

"I know that's right," Brenda said, snapping her fingers.

The wind blew the slits of Nairobia's dress up again, this time higher than before, causing Roselle's gaze to latch on to a glimpse of her sunbaked cunt.

Unfazed, Nairobia smiled.

"Good pussy, ladies, is more than a state of mind. It's a state of being. Good pussy, my loves, speaks to the dick . . ."

Isaiah pressed the palm of his hand in his lap to tamp down the swelling in his trunks. He wanted to ask her what it was saying—the pussy, but Roselle had beaten him to it.

"Tell us what it's saying," he said over a laugh. But what he really wanted to know was what *hers* would say to the dick.

Nairobia's eyes bore into him, heating over his skin in a way the sun overhead had not.

"Lean into your wife's *kut*," she said seductively. "And ask it. The next time you find yourself deep inside it, listen to what it is saying to you."

Roselle grinned. "Got you."

"Now, my darling men," Nairobia said. "Your turn . . ."

Sin leaned into Dr. Dangerfield and then whispered, "My dick wants you."

Dr. Dangerfield slid the tip of her tongue over her top lip, remembering their last heated encounter. He'd fucked her so deep she could feel him lingering inside her for days afterward.

Oh, yes, Sin never disappointed.

"Then bring *it* with you tonight," she whispered back. "Nine o'clock."

"Look into your wife's eyes," Nairobia instructed the men. "And tell her *you* are good dick."

"I am good dick," the three men said in unison, loud and proud.

"Tell her," Nairobia continued, "you are good loving, good fucking . . ."

"I am good loving, good fucking," Roselle, Isaiah, and Kendall repeated.

Nairobia glanced over her shoulder, catching the eye of Dr. Dangerfield.

Dr. Dangerfield smiled knowingly.

Nairobia Jansen (if she felt compelled to) would sample one, if not all, of them.

And they would surrender to her desires.

And then . . .

She would fuck their souls loose.

Eighteen

The head of Sin's thick meaty dick pushed inward, peeling open Dr. Dangerfield's pussy, and then he glided in, deeply, smoothly, to the hilt.

He stayed like that. Balls deep. Buried within her slickness, for a long moment, while she watched him, their gazes full of want and desire, their bodies burning from the pleasure.

Her pussy clamped around his shaft, wrapping him in a sheath of delicious heat as her orgasm fluttered around his condom-covered dick.

Magnum-sized goodness.

Ah God, she loved the stretch of her cunt over the width of him.

He grunted.

And she moaned.

No words had been spoken between the two lovers from the moment she'd opened the door to her luxurious villa an hour ago, greeting him in nothing but her six-inch heels, their leather straps sexily wrapping around her calves, then up around her thighs.

He'd simply smiled, pulling her into him, his mouth capturing hers, while kicking the door shut with his foot.

And now they were in her bed—him on top, her shuddering beneath him, his smoldering gaze scanning her face.

Fuck me, she pleaded with her eyes. *Oh God, please . . .*

Sin sucked in one side of his bottom lip; easing his thick shaft halfway out of her body and then thrusting it back in.

He did it three more times, her juices soaking him, *his* condom. Sin pulled back slowly and thrust forward again, watching her closely, gauging her responses to his strokes—his rhythm relentless and so, so, perfect. His deep strokes were neither too slow, nor too fast. Dear God—they were just right.

Deep.

Deep.

Deeper.

Dr. Dangerfield gasped.

Sin dusted kisses along her jaw, over her neck, then down to her breasts—left one first, then her right one.

Scootie's "One" played low in the background. Not her choice of music. She preferred something a bit more sensual, something with a more erotic vibe. But it was Sin's song choice. And what Sin wanted, Sin got—or he took.

He repeated what he'd done—pulling out of her body in a slow, wet glide, then plunging back into her wetness, and she nearly cried out. An orgasm danced along the edges of her cunt, sweeping tiny sparks of pleasure along her walls.

Sin repeated his movements twice more and then he stopped going slow—his dick strokes becoming more driven, deeper, piston-like, his strokes echoing over the music. Each stroke reminding her of how good his dick was, of how much she needed *this* . . . this good loving.

No talking. No promises.

Just strokes and moans and the swish-swish of her pussy, wet fire spreading through her—almost infinitely—as she thrust upward, greeting his movements with her own hungry need.

He fucked her orgasm loose, and she arched her body up into the vortex of exquisite heat.

Dr. Dangerfield hissed, her eyes rolling up and around in her head.

A deep groan left Sin's throat as he drove up into her harder, deeper, his mouth covering hers as she twined her arms around his neck.

She was spread wide for him, her thighs, her cunt, her mouth, capturing every inch of his flexing flesh, his thrusting cock, and his sumptuous lips. She sucked on them with tender abandon, her tongue sweeping inside his mouth every so often.

Sin's hips moved languidly, lingering in her juicy heat, before he wrapped his arms around the backs of her thighs and folded her body in half, tenderly loving her in that position, stroking over her G-spot.

Yes, yes, yes—oh sweet Lord, yes . . .

Sin was definitely the one you called for good loving, Dr. Dangerfield decided as she felt him everywhere—in her, on top of her, all around her.

She circled her legs around his waist, giving him as much of her as he'd given her of him, her flaring lips suckling his shaft with every stroke.

Swish, swish, swish . . .

Wet pussy.

Clutching walls.

Sin moving in and out of her, stroking *that* spot deep inside her.

Dr. Dangerfield moaned.

Sin was an enigma, one that Dr. Dangerfield admitted not having quite figured out. But she knew enough about the man with the good dick to know whenever she was with him, she never had to worry about not being pleasured.

The man was consistent.

Dr. Dangerfield gasped again.

She whimpered.

She writhed.

Her pussy, opened and stuffed, throbbed around him.

Sin.

Sin.

Sin.

He was good dick.

He was good loving.

He was unforgettable fucking . . .

Sin pulled out, then slammed deep. A hard, sharp thrust. Another. Another. And then he was stroking her slowly again, sweetly, teasing her, the stretch of his dick inciting a wave of heat as it swelled even more.

Dr. Dangerfield groaned.

Sin moaned. And then his lips moved over her jaw to her neck. He sucked her there, behind her earlobe.

He was loving her, slowly, loving her purposefully, loving her rhythmically, and oh yes, oh yes, oh yes, she was loving every minute of it.

"Mind Fucking" eased from the speakers and the sound of Trey Songz's voice upped Dr. Dangerfield's desire as her cunt swallowed Sin's cock, whole, greedily, filling her body with delicious thrusts. Sin's dick nudged her cervix and she felt another wave of heat wash over her, within her.

She mewled out as Sin used a hand to grip one of her breasts, leaning down to suck it between his lips. He nipped at it, causing heated sparks to shoot through her belly, and then he twirled his tongue wetly over its stiffened tip.

More tension coiled low in Dr. Dangerfield's belly and she heard herself humming along as Asiahn sang about waiting, waiting, waiting . . .

"I'll let you take the lead...oh baby take . . ."

Sin kissed her neck again, and Dr. Dangerfield closed her eyes and effortlessly gave her power over to him.

By the time her fourth orgasm spiraled out of her body, she was creaming all over his dick, her warm creamy juices sluicing out of her body, soaking the sheets beneath her. Sin bit down on her neck and Dr. Dangerfield dug her nails into his ass, her cunt wetly clutching around him, sucking him.

"Ah shit," he muttered, breaking their code of silence. "Pussy so fuckin' creamy."

He was on the verge of coming. Finally.

"Ah fuck," he ground out. "Where you want this nut?"

Her eyes opened and he was looking at her. Lids half-mast and full of lust, burning into her.

"All over my pussy," she murmured.

"Oh, yeah," he breathed. "Ah, fuck."

And then he was pulling out of her body, yanking off the condom, then stroking his dick, grunting, his gaze never leaving hers. His eyes darkened, his stare intensified and Dr. Dangerfield cupped her left breast in one hand and licked over her nipple as she lowered her fingers to her clit, sensually stroking; her clit slippery and swollen.

"Goddammit. Fuck," Sin growled, his orgasm spurting out, warming Dr. Dangerfield's flesh. His body jerked, and another rope of semen shot out of his dick, coating her slit and splashing over her clit, and her still-stroking fingers.

Dr. Dangerfield moaned.

And then Sin's mouth was over hers again, kissing her, tonguing her, before trailing wet kisses along her neck, over her breasts, down her quivering belly.

And then—oh God, oh God . . .

Sin licked over her hot, aching flesh. He licked one labium and then the other.

"Yes, yes, yes!" she cried out as he slid his wicked tongue over her slit and then her fingers and then over her clit, causing her hips to buck.

He sucked her fingers into his mouth, one by one, as he took a finger of his own and smeared her pussy juices and his nut over her asshole. He slid the tip of his finger in her ass as he licked her pussy again and then fucked her with his tongue.

Thrusting and withdrawing, then thrusting again, over and over.

"God, yes, Sin . . ." Dr. Dangerfield thrust her hands into his locs, her undulating hips meeting his lips, fucking his tongue, fucking his face.

He licked her clean, sucked her clit back into his mouth, his finger writhing inside her heated asshole, and then abruptly pulled away. His finger, his tongue . . . *gone.* Leaving her body empty and quaking.

Dr. Dangerfield gasped as Sin moved back up her body, then lowered his head and kissed her.

"*Mmmmm, mmmm* . . ." He tasted of heat and pussy and nut, the mixture of their orgasms causing her to kiss him, forcefully, in hungry need, the taste driving her wild.

Dr. Dangerfield, her eyes closed—so caught up in the kiss, his lips, his mouth, his cum-soaked tongue—hadn't noticed Sin reaching beneath her pillow for another condom, skillfully tearing open its wrapper and then rolling it onto his hard dick until her legs were up over his shoulders and he was thrusting inside of her all over again.

Oh God . . .

Sin.

Sin.

Sin.

Nineteen

There was something magical about this landmass of tropical rainforest and waterfalls, Brenda thought as she untied her sarong and let it flutter down around her ankles. Maybe it was the different colors of greenery in the lush jungle or the colorful reefs, or the whimsical sounds of some of the most exotic birds on the island; or perhaps it was the soothing sound of the waves lapping at the shore; all Brenda knew was, this was a paradise like no other.

And she and Roselle wanted to explore every square inch of island before the end of their stay. Consequently, over the week-and-a-half, she and Roselle had taken it upon themselves to venture out on their own.

Today, they had decided to leave their villa after lunch and meander along one of the island's many trails. Somehow, three hours later, they'd stumbled upon one of the most breathtaking sights: a watery wonderland.

There were three waterfalls—two small ones on either side of a larger one, while several crystalline lakes tumbled into each other by a series of waterfalls and cascades.

The larger waterfall was shaped like a horseshoe and water fell three-hundred-and-fifty feet down in a straight line, spilling into a pool of turquoise water.

Tiny rainbows could be spotted all around in the mist.

It nearly stole Brenda's breath.

Almost.

Roselle, being ever so bold, had trumped the view. He'd decided to strip out of his swim trunks and sandals and run around the back of the larger waterfall, instructing her not to move.

And so she didn't.

Instead, Brenda slowly unhooked her bikini top. And then that too was on the ground.

There was so much sensuality around the exotic island that it was hard *not* to be aroused. It was difficult not getting caught up in all the sexual energy that floated around them.

And it was even more challenging for Brenda to stand here and watch Roselle stroke himself and not run through the veil of water that separated her from him and leap up on his dick.

But Roselle had insisted she stand there.

Watch.

Play the voyeur while he pleasured himself.

Everything in Brenda ached as Roselle leaned into the wall of rock in back of him and eyed her as she struggled to watch him from the other side of the waterfall, her pussy moistening with every stroke.

Goddamn him.

Brenda didn't know what was more erotic: watching her naked husband jack off while beads of water slid off his body, or standing out in open view in nothing but her black thong, knowing there was a chance she, no *they*, could be caught. A chance she was willing to take, knowing how much it turned her, and Roselle, on.

Roselle felt himself becoming more aroused.

He loved masturbating. Loved the way his dick swelled in his hand. Loved the way his veiny shaft throbbed every time his hand slid up from the base of his dick and then glided over its mushroom-shaped head.

Sometimes he enjoyed playing with his dick more than having someone else play with it. There was something empowering in the art of self-pleasure.

And he loved being watched.

His sex drive was high. He could bust big loads and come multiple times. He had a strong, sturdy dick. And Roselle took pride in knowing his stroke game was superb. Yeah, he knew he had good pipe. And so did his wife and every other woman he blessed with his stamina and the stretch of his dick.

Good dick made the pussy weep, and it made the soul weak.

Brenda let out a low moan.

The sight of him—with his long, wavy hair, curled wetly over his cheeks, brushing over his shoulders as he fucked his hand—incited Brenda to orgasm. Clenching bliss. She shoved a hand between her thighs and hungrily used her fingers to draw out her juices, wringing out more of her orgasm.

Roselle grunted; his eyes locked on his wife as she shifted her weight from one sandaled-foot to the other, and then slipped her cum-stained fingers into her mouth and sucked them clean.

Roselle grinned, and stroked his dick harder, faster.

Brenda licked her lips, loving the taste of herself. She pulled at her nipples as she strained to see her husband through the magnificent sheets of water cascading overhead. The muscles in his arms and shoulders rippled as he slowly fucked his fist.

"Mmm, yes," Brenda moaned as she watched. Her pussy began with another slow, throbbing pulse that was now nearing a steady, rhythmic thump.

Thump-thump-thump.

Thump-thump-thump.

She would come again. Soon. God, yes, she would explode all over herself.

Brenda drank in the sight of Roselle, her gaze climbing its way up his taut body, stopping at his face, then crawling back down to the heated steel in his fist.

The motherfucker knew he had a beautiful, rock-hard body.

It was so masculine.

It was so, so, goddamn sexual.

And that dick—Lord Jesus, *yesssss* . . .

Her smoldering eyes latched onto Roselle's half-closed fist as it stroked his engorged shaft. Yes, God, yes. His dick looked impossibly larger, corded with veins as she envisioned a shining bead of precum welling from the crown.

Brenda licked her lips again; her right hand slipping down over her body and then in between her slightly parted thighs, again. The erotic view before her admittedly transfixed her.

She knew her marriage needed work. That was the whole point of being on the island in the first place. But, so far, she'd found solace in knowing that her marriage wasn't in shambles. She believed that what she and Roselle shared was special, even though he could be a self-absorbed, egotistical pain in the ass.

But he was her self-absorbed, egotistical pain in the ass. And she didn't want to ever change that part of who he was—just his goddamn cheating.

So, yes, she and Roselle had their marital issues, but as far as Brenda was concerned, they were in a much better place than that LaQuandra woman. Bless her heart, she thought. Brenda couldn't imagine Roselle moving out of their bedroom and not serving her up a dose of his good loving on a weekly basis.

Even when he went out and cheated, he still made it his business to take care of home *first*. He made her and the kids his priority. And he made it his duty to keep her well fucked.

Cheating or not.

Brenda gazed at Roselle's twisting fist and rippling muscles as she lightly pinched her clit. She couldn't believe she was out here in the nearly dusk evening stoking her lust with greedy fingers, while watching her husband masturbate. Her eyes followed Roselle's fist as it moved languidly up and down, up and down, and she wanted to cry out. She was slowly becoming fevered with need.

She needed to have her cunt impaled by the meaty girth of his manhood. Needed the mouth of her cervix plugged with the broad head of his cock. She needed to feel his dusky sac slapping the back of her pussy as he pounded himself into her quaking body.

She needed, craved, all of this in the same way she depended on air to breathe.

Desperately.

Roselle's knees dipped. Oh God. Oh God. Pressure built. Heat coiled. His balls clenched. His thighs tightened.

He was on the verge of an orgasm.

He stroked faster, swiping his thumb across the engorged head. He hissed in pleasure, and then he clenched his jaw as need clawed its way from his balls, up his dick, the swelling of his nut right below the crown.

He could hold out, if he wanted. Could hold back the thick, creamy heat before it jetted out of the slit of his dick.

And he would. Long enough for his wife to come to him, so he could sink his dick into the plushness of her mouth, and coat the back of her throat.

Wild with wicked desire, Brenda bit down on her lip, trying to stave it off. She wanted to reach out, stick her arm through the curtain of water and touch her husband. Feel the hard ridges of his chest and abdomen . . . along with that mouthwatering dick he held in his hand.

Brenda caught her husband's darkened gaze and she grew wetter.

The hunger on his face was unmistakable. A bone-deep yearning that matched her own.

"Come suck this dick," he ordered in a voice so thick and rough that she barely recognized it.

And she went to him. Eagerly. Trekked through the roiling river. Stepped into the cascading water and squealed as it drenched her, causing her nipples to tighten.

The water was warm and surprisingly steamy, a cascade of sensuality.

God, this was so, so, arousing—sucking Roselle's dick. Brenda never imagined how tantalizing the experience would be. And here she was. Squatting, fingers in her pussy, her mouth stretched wide as her husband's hands slid into her hair.

"Yeah, baby," he breathed. "Oh. Yeah."

Brenda anchored her free hand on the outside of his thigh and let her head bobble back and forth, her mouth wetly gliding over the length of him. She licked him over and over, from the base of his shaft to his tip, her tongue brushing him in long, wet strokes, painting him with streaks of her own hungry need. Languorously. Lightly. Sweetly.

Roselle hissed out a sibilant curse as he threw his head back and shut his eyes. Brenda was sucking the shit out of his dick, loving it, milking it, the way he liked it. She drew her mouth back slowly, suckled on the head for several moments, then took him back in her mouth, this time all the way to her throat.

"Goddamn. Shit, baby. This shit . . ." Roselle groaned, and his hands tightened in her hair. "Feels so fucking . . . *good*."

Brenda moaned, her tongue catching a hint of cum. She tongued him, laved him, peering up at him to only find his face an exquisite mask of ecstasy. She reached around and clenched a hand to his ass, her nails digging into his flesh.

Roselle began thrusting furiously. "Suck that dick, baby. That's right. Get that nut, baby. Uh. I'm"—thrust—"cummmmmming"—thrust—"*uh . . . uhhhhh . . .*"

Thick cream hit the back of Brenda's throat. And before she could finish swallowing all of him, Roselle had managed to spin her around without causing her to slip and topple over into the pooling water, his dick still rock-hard.

Bent forward with her ass cheeks splayed open, Roselle gripped around her waist as he grabbed his dick and pressed it into her, wetting himself with her juices, teasing her there. Yes, yes. Right there. At the center of her cunt, poking the head of his dick in and out of her slit. She wanted to slam her ass into his groin to claim the dick, *her* dick.

It belonged to her, no matter how many times he loaned it out to those other bitches. She wanted to feel it inside her, all of it. But Roselle used his hand to control how much of it he would give her, would let her have.

"You want this dick?" he asked, taunting her, teasing her. He kissed the back of her neck. The kiss turned into a bite.

"Roselle," she gasped. Goose bumps pebbled her skin. And Roselle bit her harder, only to soothe it with his tongue. Brenda cried out in pain even as her pussy tightened and became wetter.

He lunged forward and drove himself inside her, stretching her entrance, her slickened walls, pummeling himself deeper inside of her.

"Oh yes, yes, yes," she breathed as pleasure radiated out from her core. She arched back. And then her mouth fell open, and her eyes drifted closed. "*Mmmmmm*, yes, yes, *yesssss!* Oh, God, yes. Fuck me, baby!"

Roselle slapped her wet, jiggling ass, and the sting sent shivers along her spine as his deep, steady strokes kept her suspended on the brink of another orgasm.

Brenda moaned, right before she screamed with unexpected release. And Roselle slapped her ass again. The wet-smacking sound echoed as her ass cheek turned a bright red. When his wife's moaning reached a crescendo, he slammed his dick in and out of her pussy, increasing his tempo, fast, faster, faster. Pounding, pounding, pounding, Roselle held Brenda's body in place by anchoring an arm tightly around her waist as his quick hard thrusts lifted her up on the balls of her feet.

"Uh, uh, uh . . . ooh, ooh, ooooh . . ."

Brenda's breasts bounced and swayed as her husband fucked her, mercilessly. Her pleasure built quickly and within seconds, her cunt was clutching Roselle's dick, and she was shuddering with another release.

"That's right, baby," Roselle whispered at the back of her earlobe. "Come for me. Wet up this dick . . ." And then he thrust harder. "Give me that nut, baby."

Her cunt spasmed, and then her body shuddered, her breaths coming in trembling gasps as Roselle continued stroking inside of her.

"Ohgodohgodohgod," she deliriously muttered.

And then Roselle brushed her spot and Brenda mewled like an alley cat, heat splintering through the walls of her cunt. Pleasure soared between them, in between the whimsical splatter made by the waterfall, in between her *oohs* and his *aahs*; desire heightened within them as he filled her insides and made her come, come, come—hard and steady and fast, over and over and over.

Brenda's eyes fluttered. She blinked. Then blinked again.

A large rainbow emerged as flaming, white-hot need erupted around them.

In between her moans and his groans, Brenda's vision blurred. She'd lost count of the number of times she'd already come. And here she was—on the verge of another rippling orgasm.

"Oh God, yes. I'm coming," she said in between heavy breaths.

"Come, then, baby." Roselle pushed his middle finger into her ass, twisted his finger inside her warm tunnel. "I'm right there with you, baby." His tempo increased, his breath hitching in the back of his throat.

His loud growl matched her mewling, sending both of their arousal spiraling.

Brenda came.

Roselle came.

Slowly, the world around them changed colors.

And then disappeared.

Twenty

FKA twigs' "How's That" played softly in the background. Candles of varying sizes flickered around the room. The sultry aroma of lavender scented the air.

And there, behind a sliding wall, was a private suite. Surrounded by plush white leather and erotic sculptures made of alabaster and marble, it was where hidden truths and untold desires unfolded.

It was where Dr. Dangerfield had been for more than an hour.

With eager fingers and a buzzing clit wand.

Teasing herself.

Pleasuring herself.

Stroking through her folds.

Peeling back the silken petals of her cunt and loving herself.

She was so wet.

Her body was so hot.

It felt so . . . *good*—her hands, her fingers—touching herself.

Her pussy clenched and nipples tingled.

Her painted toes curled into the silken fibers of the rug beneath her feet.

Blood red.

Seductively, Dr. Dangerfield pulled in her bottom lip as she glanced up at the bank of monitors that covered a long wall on one side of the room.

Spying on the private lives of the couples that came to the island seeking love and light and reignited passion. That's what she was doing.

That was what had her veins pooling with heat.

Oh sure it was unorthodox. Illegal. Scandalous. And, maybe, even a bit creepy.

But it was also more telling than any session could ever be. It showed, at times, couples at their most naked, most vulnerable.

Alone.

Behind closed doors.

When no one else was looking.

Dr. Dangerfield believed she couldn't always trust that couples would bear their souls freely. So she needed to see that secret part of them, the part of whom they were that they didn't always want her to see. She needed to keep her eyes on the couples, and her fingers on the pulse of the island; hence, the reason why every part of the island had hidden cameras, including each couple's villa.

Each surveillance camera offered an overhead and eye-level view of everything happening around her.

The debauchery. The drama.

Each monitor displayed some part of the island. There were small surveillance cameras hidden up in coconut trees, along the trails, along the beaches, in the gardens. From every angle imaginable, nothing on Passion Island went unnoticed.

All caught on camera, every couple's precious, private moments, all available for her viewing pleasure. There were even night-vision cameras to ensure everything, enticing or not, was captured.

The only room that was off-limits was the couples' bathrooms. She didn't need to see *that* part of them.

Dr. Dangerfield sighed and sat up from the sofa, reaching over and grabbing a remote from off a white marble table. She then leaned back again; her legs spread, and looked over at a Zone three monitor.

LaQuandra and Isaiah.

She was already in bed, her hands between her thighs; the top sheet twisted around one of her legs; her mouth open in what appeared to be a silent scream; her fingers driving deep inside her body.

And *he* was stretched out across the sofa asleep. Well, drunk—judging by the six empty beer bottles and bottle of Jack Daniel's on the coffee table.

Dr. Dangerfield feigned a yawn.

No excitement there.

She switched to Zone four.

Krista and Kendall.

She was in the bathroom, the door shut tight.

He—

Dr. Dangerfield blinked.

Mm. Yes.

Kendall was out on the balcony in his boxers, his dick in hand, masturbating. His jaw was set firm, as if his teeth were set hard, as if he were on the verge of an orgasm.

What—no, who*—are you thinking about Mr. Kendall Evans?*

She watched the way Kendall's hand moved fluidly up and down and around the thick curve of his dick. Why wasn't Krista out there with him, sucking him, fucking him?

Why wasn't that dumb bitch down on her knees, making wet-sucking sounds as she bobbed her head, her mouth, back and forth over the length of him?

Dr. Dangerfield nearly laughed aloud, but then she mentally scolded herself for asking such an asinine question. She's probably sitting on the porcelain throne, while reading scriptures, she thought as she switched the camera from the balcony to the living room and then the bedroom. Krista was still in the bathroom.

Mmph.

With the door probably locked, Dr. Dangerfield mused.

She shook her head, switching the camera back to the balcony, back to Kendall.

"Yes," she murmured as her gaze locked on his hand. "Stroke it, baby."

And then her hand was back between her thighs, her fingers moving in sync to Kendall's.

"Yes. Come for me," she whispered. "Give me that sweet nut. Coat my pussy. Come all over my breasts."

Dr. Dangerfield took her free hand and caressed her breasts, alternating between them. And then she used the same hand to finger her clit as she rotated her hips, grinding her ass into the sofa, her juices sliding over the leather.

She watched as Kendall glanced over his shoulder at the closed sliding door, before sliding a hand down into his boxers as he fisted his dick.

He threw his head back.

And Dr. Dangerfield's eyes went wide.

Oooh, Is he playing in his ass?

She zoomed the other hidden camera for the balcony in on his ass, and watched his hand move there, too.

My God! He is playing with his . . . hole.

Now this newfound information was just too juicy.

Dr. Dangerfield licked her lips. She loved ass play. Loved a man comfortable enough in his masculinity, in his sexuality, bold enough to go there.

She thought it sexy.

She went wetter than she already was around her fingers.

Her orgasm rose.

But she held out.

Fought back the sweet ache that slowly spread through her loins.

And waited.

—For Kendall.

To come for her, come with her.

Dr. Dangerfield's lips curled into a sly grin as Kendall slid the tip of his finger in his ass. Threw his head back.

And came.

Finally . . .

So did she.

Mm. This was better than porn. Well, scripted porn, that was. She kept her gaze trained on Kendall as his body jerked one last time, and then his hand came from out of his underwear. He glanced over his shoulder, again. Flung the nut from his fingers and hand over the balcony. He reached for the towel draped over the railing and then wiped his hands on it.

Dr. Dangerfield screamed in her head *no*, *no*, *noooooo*, and then cursed Krista for not being out there with him to lick up, to enjoy, to savor, the creamy fruits of his labor.

Damn that silly bitch.

Dr. Dangerfield sighed. Oh well.

Languorously, she lifted herself up from the sofa and—not before kneeling and sliding her tongue over the leather, licking her pussy juice from the sofa—sauntered over to a barstool positioned in front of the bank of monitors.

Strapped in the center of the stool was a thick black silicone dildo.

Dr. Dangerfield reached for another remote, a longer, much sleeker, one, and then pressed PLAY.

It was the recording of Brenda and Roselle at the waterfall earlier in the day.

Videos were kept for no more than forty-eight hours from the time they were replayed, before they were destroyed. Any evidence of her salacious invasion of privacy erased.

Dr. Dangerfield fast-forwarded to the part where Brenda had finally joined Roselle behind the veil of water. Droplets of water had been splattered on the hidden camera's lens, but the erotic sight was still worthy of first, second, *and* third viewings.

Dr. Dangerfield eased up on the stool, positioned her juicy pussy over the protruding phallus, and then lowered her body down on it, its bulbous head sinking its way into the pink, fleshy part of her quaking orifice.

Dr. Dangerfield heard H.E.R professing how she said it, her sultry voice blanketing her like warm silk. She moaned softly and twisted her pelvis, adjusting her position, so that she took the ten-inch dildo all the way in.

"All you gotta do is say yes . . ." Dr. Dangerfield sang softly as she reached for another remote. With the press of a button, she zoomed in on Brenda's face. Her gaze suddenly drawn to Brenda's mouth, the tip of her tongue—wet, its tip pressed to the underside of her upper lip.

Dr. Dangerfield watched Brenda's eyes, the way they swarmed with desire; the way pleasure swirled in her pupils.

Those two seemed to fit perfectly together. They had great sexual chemistry. Dr. Dangerfield had seen it, sensed it, felt it, the moment she'd laid eyes on them.

She studied the way Roselle took Brenda from behind, the back of her cunt capturing his dick in a wet, tight grip.

"Ohhh, yesss," she murmured as Roselle's hands reached around and grabbed Brenda's breasts as he drove himself into her pussy. "Fuck her good."

Roselle pinched Brenda's nipples between his thumbs and forefingers and Dr. Dangerfield cried out for her as if it were her very own nipples being tweaked.

She gripped the sides of the stool; her nails digging into its leather, and rapidly rode the harnessed dildo.

Her cunt clutching, her walls slick with arousal, as she stared into the face of Roselle as he bit the side of Brenda's neck, his teeth sinking into her skin, marking her.

"Pretty motherfucker."

Dr. Dangerfield rose up and then slid back down on her dildo, so long, so black, so . . . *mmm* . . . oh-God-yes thick.

She rotated her hips. Her blood pounded.

She went wild atop the stool, head swinging side-to-side, breasts bouncing, nipples tightening, her orgasm coiling around her uterus.

The scent of her sweet, tangy sex filtered through her nose.

The sound of her wet pussy—sloshing along the length of her dildo as she rode it, bounced on it, swirled on it—filled her ears.

Enjoying the sensuous slide of the dildo in and out of her body, Dr. Dangerfield bit her lip. Her gaze went dreamy, falling from the monitor, from Brenda, from Roselle.

She shuddered.

And came.

And all she saw in that moment were stars glittering behind her lids.

Twenty-One

Erotic passion . . .

The deliberate seeking of pleasure; it was unpredictable and defiant. It elicited curiosity and intrigue. It consisted of sexual desires and fantasies. Sadly, not many men and women paid attention to their sexual desires, their erotic needs, and sexual fantasies.

It always amazed Dr. Dangerfield how much people were willing to experiment sexually outside of their relationships, yet they willingly denied themselves the freedom to explore sexually with the one they professed to love. Instead, they went through the motions of having sex—emotionless, uncreative fucking at best—devoid of excitement and eroticism with their significant others.

So they'd rather immerse themselves in anonymous bar sex, cybersex, scouring illicit online sex sites for one night—or more—of hot dirty sex. Filthy fucking. Taboo acts.

Blah, blah, blah . . . They consumed their sexual energies on porn, and masturbation instead of having open and honest conversations with their lovers.

There was something almost pathological, almost masochistic, for someone to stay in a sexually unfulfilling relationship, for someone to deny his/her own desires.

Yes. Lord. It took a special kind of person to be okay with

mediocrity, with settling. Although sex wasn't *the* most important part of a healthy relationship, good sex—good fucking, good loving—was (or should be) *one* of the most important things.

As far as Dr. Dangerfield was concerned, nothing should be forbidden between equally yoked lovers. Nothing.

The explicitness of sex, the voyeuristic pleasures . . .

Dr. Dangerfield's attention drifted over to the three curvaceous women over on the circular stage, the erotic sway of their hips as they stepped through the fog, their naked bodies moving seductively to "Thoughts" by Naji.

Their arms up over their heads, their arms slowing moving through the air as their hips winded, undulated, their pelvises thrusting as they inched closer to the three men swathed in ropes of muscle and dark chocolate skin, seated front and center in folded chairs—leaning back, one arm up over the back of their chairs, their legs spread wide, their dicks hanging downward over big round chocolate balls, smooth and mouthwatering.

As the women neared, synchronously, the men licked their lips, each one eyeing a dancer as she taunted them with her sultry moves, slowly prowling, slowly luring, then working their way backward again.

Twirling their hips, then slowly turning, their hips rolling.

Suddenly, the three women dropped down, then pumped the air around them, their asses facing the men, their waxed pussies facing out toward the crowd.

Slowly, their bodies turned. The women moved like snake charmers, their arms and bodies moving in sync. When their bodies were completely facing in the opposite direction, the women slowly cupped their breasts and licked over their nipples, eyeing the male dancers as they grabbed the edges of their seats and thrust upward, downward, upward—their dicks flopping up and down with every move.

One after the other—the female dancers twirled back up, then thrust their pelvises at the male dancers, taunting them. Then they simultaneously glanced over their shoulders, glancing out at the mostly male audience, before bending over and grabbing their ankles. Their ass cheeks shook, their fat pussy lips peeking out at the audience.

Kendall pressed his legs together.

Roselle rubbed a hand over his hard dick, then over the head of it, every so often squeezing. This shit was bananas. All of this seduction, it was torturous pleasure.

It made no damn sense to be surrounded by so much sexiness, so many sexy-ass women, and not be able to reach out and touch any of them. Squeeze their tits, smack their asses, finger their cunts—something. Shit.

Isaiah leaned forward in his seat, his eye trained on the mocha-skinned beauty with the elaborate butterfly tattoo in the center of her lower back, its colorful wings spreading over the cheeks of her ass.

All three women were sexy in their own way. But *she* had the biggest ass of them all. And fuck if Isaiah wasn't an ass man. Yet he still couldn't understand how the fuck he ended up with LaQuandra's flat-ass.

She was a freak, he inwardly admitted, shaking his head as his eyes followed the butterfly as it sensually flitted around the stage. He'd fuck her too, he mused. Bust that ass wide open.

Hell yeah.

Dr. Dangerfield scanned the small audience of men, most of them with their wives or mistresses, vacationing on the other side of the island.

The couples were already in their second week on the island, and there still hadn't been any real exciting breakthroughs made. Dr. Dangerfield was hoping to change that, hopefully today.

Kendall, Roselle, and Isaiah were here at the request of Dr. Dangerfield—without their wives. She wanted to have them alone. Get them mentally aroused. Then probe their imaginations. Assess the landscape of their erotic intelligence.

Amiah sang about having a thing for a real nigga as each female dancer straddled a respective male dancer and grinded up on him, before lifting up, reaching between their legs and in chorus, sliding their dicks inside their bodies, making them disappear.

In sync, the male dancers slapped each female's ass.

Smack!

The sound echoing over the music, and then came the ass clapping over the dicks.

Goddamn. Fuck yeah.

Kendall thought he'd bust on the spot. His balls were painfully swollen with arousal. He needed to bust a nut. Soon.

The three women lifted up, releasing each man's dick from their wet clutches.

Dr. Dangerfield's gaze danced over at the male dancers, latching on to the hard wet dicks, pointing upward, as they seductively moved in sync with the female dancers.

Erotic passion . . .

Sexual expression.

Sensual bliss.

Dr. Dangerfield caught herself thrusting her own hips and quickly stopped herself, before she forgot she wasn't on holiday, before she forgot her role on the island, what her purpose was here, and stripped out of her dress.

She shook the erotic images of stepping out of her thong and twirling the silky undergarment around her finger, before tossing it out into the crowd from her thoughts.

She swallowed back her dirty thoughts and glanced over at

Kendall, Roselle, and Isaiah. Dr. Dangerfield believed couples who were able to talk openly about their sexual desires with another created room to grow together in emotional and intimate bonds. If couples wanted more passion in their relationships, they would need to learn ways to be more sexually expressive; they'd need to learn how to balance gestures and words with those rich nuances of sexuality and exploration.

She was looking forward to digging through their sexual repertoires and uncovering their deepest, darkest desires.

An hour later, Dr. Dangerfield sat in her plush leather chair; her shapely legs crossed at the ankles, her cunt still throbbing from where Sin had been the night before.

She took in the three men sitting before her.

"The beautiful thing about sexual fantasies," she said, "is that we get to imagine things we would never say or do in reality. Fantasies give us license to be as dirty, as sexually carefree, as we want to be."

Roselle nodded his head in agreement. "Word. Because I know some of my fantasies be way out there sometimes." He laughed. "I be on some real-live freak shit."

Dr. Dangerfield raised a questioning brow. "Oh? Would you like to elaborate?"

Roselle cut his eyes over at Isaiah and then Kendall, unsure if he wanted to divulge too much about the way his mind was set up sexually.

Although most of his fantasies included Brenda, there were those that didn't. Like being in a room full of midget *bit*—uh, um, little women. They had all that fat puffy ass and he fantasized about fucking them, spinning them around on his hard dick. He secretly wondered just how deep the pussy really was, if their bodies were built for a good dicking.

Another fantasy was fucking someone's granny—sixty-plus years old or better, preferably with removable dentures. And if she wore those adult pampers, he'd remove her pamper and wash her pussy and ass, then dick her down real good, before strapping her up in another one. In his fantasies, he'd fuck her gums and cunt raw.

And then there was his fantasy of being blindfolded and strapped down, being sucked and fucked by a group of big, beautiful women with thick hips, thick pussy lips, and fat asses. And then there was his darkest desire, one he knew he'd never share out loud—not even to Brenda. He fantasized about fucking a Transsexual. Not one of those big, burly ones either with the fucked-up weaves and razor bumps. Nah. A soft, feminine, passable one, like those he'd seen in Brazil three years ago, was what crept in his fantasies at times.

Some of them with all that big bouncy ass and full breasts were bad as fuck.

Facts. The few he'd met in Brazil he'd thought they were straight-up females—born that way. Someone like *that*—that's what he'd slide his dick up into, just once—for the experience. He wanted to know how that manmade pussy felt. If it got wet, if it gripped a dick, the way a real pussy did.

But, nah, Roselle wasn't about to share that shit. He'd have to take that one to the grave with him. He didn't care about being judged, per se. He was strong in his spot as a man. But he didn't want to have to knock a muhfucka in his mouth if he thought to say some slick shit.

So he settled on sharing his little women fantasy instead.

Isaiah laughed. "Damn, bruh, you wild as shit."

"Man, some of them look like they have some real juicy puss-puss."

Kendall shook his head. But he didn't judge. Hell, he fantasized about having a woman strap on a dildo and slowly fucking him in the ass. Pegging him, that was the term for it. He'd already graduated from a finger to having a slender vibrator stroking his prostate. Persia, his—shit, he didn't really know what she was to him—side-piece for a lack of a better term, wanted to give him the experience, but he hadn't really gotten up the nerve to go all the way. Tongue and fingers and a vibrator were one thing. But having a whole silicone dick inside of him, he really didn't know if he'd go that far. Not that he thought it would take away his manhood. He simply didn't like the idea of having his asshole stretched open. What if Krista decided to—he nearly laughed at the ridiculous notion of her ever wanting to go anywhere near his ass. Still, although he fantasized about it—a dildo stroking his P-spot, he'd decided some fantasies weren't meant to live out.

But fuck if sex with Persia didn't make him want to do shit he never imagined he'd do. She made it easy to be free. Made it easy to have those types of desires and *still* be a man—and feel like one, most importantly. Because that was what he was—a man. All man. He didn't second-guess his masculinity or his manhood. He embraced who he was as a man. He didn't think it was wrong to enjoy having a tongue licking his ass or a finger stroking over his prostate.

Persia indulged his desires without judgment. And he trusted her with his secret—something he was certain he could never do with Krista. He sighed inwardly. It was what it was.

"If you can understand your sexual fantasies and desires," Dr. Dangerfield said, as if she were reading Kendall's thoughts. "You'll begin to learn a lot about yourself as a sexual being. Mr. Evans, what do you fantasize about?"

"Nothing much," Kendall said absently.

Roselle cocked an eyebrow at him. "*Nothing?* Man, we grown men. We're always fantasizing about a piece of ass." He gave Dr. Dangerfield an apologetic look.

She shrugged it off. Language was the least of her worries. "Mr. Evans, fantasies are a healthy part of our sexuality."

Kendall glanced down at her feet. Shit. She had pretty-ass toes peeking out through her peep-toes on top of every-*fucking*-thing else that was sexy about her.

Truth be told, he had a thing for pretty feet and toes. But Krista's feet were—well, uh, flat and wide and not worthy of being anywhere near his mouth or tongue.

Kendall sucked in a breath and cursed himself for imagining her soft feet massaging his dick, and then him licking over her soles.

"I have a foot fetish," he admitted, but that wasn't the damn question. So he added, "I sometimes fantasize about masturbating and then coming on a strange woman's feet."

Not quite true. But it would need to do.

That's it? How damn boring, Dr. Dangerfield thought as she kept her face from frowning. She had hoped to hear something a bit more exciting.

Roselle gave Kendall a blank stare. "Damn, bruh. You can't do any better than that?"

Kendall laughed, and so did Roselle and Isaiah.

"It's all I got," Kendall said, feigning embarrassment.

How uninspiring. "Oh. Okay," Dr. Dangerfield said. Moving along. "What about you, Mr. Lewis?" she asked. "Would you care to share one of your sexual fantasies?"

Isaiah ran a hand over the top of his waves, then slid it over his mouth, before smoothing it over his goatee. "Man . . ." He scratched the top of his head, his nails raking along the deep ripple of a wave. "I'm not gonna hold you. Pleasure. She's wifey in my head. Word is bond." And she could get the dick raw.

"Yo, fam," Roselle said over a laugh. "I got next. She bad. I had a woody the whole time she was standing there talking."

Dr. Dangerfield smiled knowingly.

"Facts," Isaiah said. And then he laughed. "I didn't wanna look thirsty, but when she showed up down at the beach, I was tempted as fuck to ask for a flick with her."

"You should have," Dr. Dangerfield said. "Nairobia's very down-to-earth."

"Man, I'm glad you didn't," Roselle said. "Your wife woulda tried to choke you out. She seems like the type to body a muhfucka over you."

All three men laughed at that.

"Yeah, you probably right." Isaiah shook his head. "She'd fuck up a wet dream in a heartbeat."

Dr. Dangerfield studied Isaiah, trying to figure out how in sweet hell he ended up with *her*. Sure he had a hood edge, but he wasn't ratchet with it. He might have been from the hood, but he wasn't ghetto. Or maybe he hid it well.

She shifted in her seat. Cleared her throat. And then asked, "And what if your fantasy were able to become a reality, Mr. Lewis? Would you still want it?"

Isaiah's mouth turned to a lopsided grin.

Sexy. Real sexy, Dr. Dangerfield thought as she waited for his answer.

"If I could have one night with Pleasure," he said, "hell yeah, I'd take it. No questions asked."

"And what of your marriage?" Dr. Dangerfield asked. "Would you be willing to risk one night of passion with a fantasy woman?"

Wait. Was that supposed to be some trick question or some shit? Hell yeah, he'd risk it. Shit, it wasn't like he was happily married any-damn-way, so he'd might as well go out with some good pussy.

His son's mother was a freak. His wife was a freak. But

Pleasure . . . Pleasure was the cream of the crop. She was the filling and icing and the cherry on top of the cake.

"Without a doubt," Isaiah said, pinning Dr. Dangerfield with a look, one full of certainty and conviction. "One night—*all* night. That's all I'd want."

Twenty-Two

Enabling . . .

Losing one's sense of self for the sake of maintaining a relationship. Over the years, Dr. Dangerfield had witnessed, more often than not, exactly that. Men and women losing themselves to the behaviors of others—their partners, family members, and even their children—allowing themselves to become absorbed in the life and behaviors of everyone else, fighting who they were against who they believed they should be in order to coexist in a world as they saw it. A world that was oftentimes full of drama and disorder, replete with a slew of lies and distrust.

And that's what Dr. Dangerfield saw in LaQuandra. She was an enabler in the worst way, and in being so, she engendered a shitload of resentment and a loss of personal joy.

No human being, Dr. Dangerfield believed, should have that level of control over someone else's thoughts, feelings, or actions. Accepting behaviors or not, was merely a choice. And LaQuandra Lewis chose to linger in misery, Dr. Dangerfield decided, because she didn't truly believe she deserved anything more.

LaQuandra scoffed. Who the hell did this uppity, self-righteous bitch think she was to tell *her* that *she* was an enabler, trying to insinuate, once again, that *she* was the problem?

No. The problem was Cassandra-goddamn-Simms.

Not her.

She was a lot of things, but an enabler was not one of them. And she resented Dr. Dangerfield for making such a ridiculous judgment call.

LaQuandra crossed her legs, then shifted in her seat. "Do you know me?" she asked Dr. Dangerfield snottily.

Dr. Dangerfield regarded her for a moment, before finally saying, "I only know what you've allowed me to know."

LaQuandra twisted her lips. "Exactly." She straightened her back and placed a hand up on her hip. "And have we met before?"

Okay. So she wanted confrontation, Dr. Dangerfield resolved, taking in LaQuandra's posturing. Combative. Nothing new. She was used to men and women becoming defensive when confronted with things they didn't want to hear. The truth. It hurt like hell, sometimes. Hell, most times. But the truth could also set you free from self-justifying and self-destructing behaviors, if one was willing to listen.

"Mrs. Lewis," Dr. Dangerfield said calmly. "I'm not your enemy. I'm here to help you rediscover the passion in your marriage—or within yourself."

"*Mmph.* I can't tell," LaQuandra muttered. "Seems like all you've done thus far is point fingers at me. You haven't said *shit* to Isaiah about his goddamn disregard for me and my feelings or his disrespect toward me as his wife."

Krista wanted to roll her eyes up in her head, but instead she kept her face expressionless. She'd only come to today's group session for the entertainment, because—well, quite frankly—she didn't have that problem. She wasn't an enabler. And chasing behind some cheating-ass husband wasn't her life story. So the front-row view was just fine with her. All she needed was a bag of buttered popcorn and a large Pepsi.

"Your husband will have his time in the hot seat—if you will, soon enough," Dr. Dangerfield promised. "But right now. This is about you."

LaQuandra huffed. She was frustrated. And this bitch was pissing her off. "And there lies the problem, ma'am . . ."

Brenda nearly died. *Ooh, no she didn't give her the* ma'am. *Girl, I'm dead!*

LaQuandra kept her stare locked on Dr. Dangerfield as she continued, "The fact that you think this is about me is a real problem for me. No, sweetie. This is about Isaiah."

Dr. Dangerfield smiled. "Yes. It is. And it's also about *you*. Because, believe it or not, Mrs. Lewis, you play a very big role in your marriage and in what you allow to happen to you while in it."

LaQuandra frowned. "So you're telling me that it's my fault that Isaiah runs off and fucks his baby mother? Are you blaming *me* for his ass allowing that bitch to constantly disrespect me?"

"The same way you disrespect her?" Dr. Dangerfield inquired. "Because from where I sit, that's exactly what you've been doing from the moment we met. You've done nothing but call your husband's child's mother out her name. And, quite frankly—"

LaQuandra cut her off. "I treat that bitch the way she's treated me. She's shown me no respect. Ever. So why the hell should I show her any? That whore knew Isaiah was a married man, and yet she kept fucking him, while grinning in my face."

"And you blame her for sleeping with your husband?"

LaQuandra scoffed, her pupils flashing fire at Dr. Dangerfield. "No. I blame *her* for being a whore."

Yes. That's right. When all else failed, blame the other woman. Always. It never failed. Most women would rather place all the responsibility of her relationship discord on the other woman, while there was hardly ever any real culpability for the men who cheated.

Dr. Dangerfield considered her words thoughtfully.

"Tell me, Mrs. Lewis. Was it *you*, or your husband, who sought out Passion Island?"

LaQuandra shifted in her seat. "I did. Why?"

"Only asking for clarity," Dr. Dangerfield said. "So why exactly are you here? Is it for an extended vacation? For the money you're guaranteed at the end of the six weeks? Or is it because your marriage is in serious trouble and you're afraid of losing it?"

LaQuandra huffed. "Honestly, both. We, *I*, needed this getaway. And, yes, my marriage needs help. I thought, maybe, that by coming here, you, this process, would get Isaiah to stop his shit and get him to see that he has a good woman who loves him and wants this marriage."

Dr. Dangerfield nodded. "So you want me to change him? Is that what you're hoping for?"

Actually, that was *exactly* what LaQuandra was hoping for. She needed someone else to get Isaiah to see how much he'd hurt her, how much she loved him, because obviously he wasn't listening to her. She was tired of being second best. Tired of second-guessing herself. Tired of vacillating; one minute wanting to pack his shit and throw him out, the next minute wanting to fight until the death of her to hold on to him. Something had to give.

"And what exactly has your role been in your hot mess of a marriage—your words, not mine?"

LaQuandra frowned. "I've done nothing, except be a good damn wife to him."

"Perhaps," Dr. Dangerfield said thoughtfully. "However, doing nothing is doing something. And if you've done nothing, then your role has been to keep accepting the mess. You've played a role of enabling."

Enabling. There went that word again.

Bitch, bye.

Brenda shifted uncomfortably in her seat. She'd been guilty of that. Enabling. But this wasn't about her. Not yet.

Krista sat quietly. As far as she was concerned, she had a good marriage. Wait. So why exactly was she really here? Oh right, right. The show.

Dr. Dangerfield watched the other two women out of her peripheral vision as she kept her gaze on LaQuandra. She waited in silence. Waited for LaQuandra to continue in her delusional thinking.

"I love Isaiah. And, yes, I've put up with more shit than I probably should. But I don't see that as enabling him. I see that as being a committed wife."

She'd walk through fire for Isaiah. That was the depth of her love for him.

"And I don't see a damn thing wrong with that," she added.

Dr. Dangerfield agreed. "You're right. There's absolutely nothing wrong with being a committed wife, a devoted partner. Those are great gifts to any relationship. But not for the sake of compromising who you are or for what you believe in. And definitely not when it requires you to lose pieces of yourself and keeps you stuck in misery."

LaQuandra swallowed. "Well, this is something that we are just going to have to agree to disagree on. I'm done." She had nothing more to say on the matter. She was not going to wear the title of an enabler. Not today. Not tomorrow. Not ever.

Brenda shifted in her seat again. She remembered that her mother had loved her father so much, more than she loved herself, until she ended up with nothing, giving him every ounce of her love, every piece of her heart until it ended up broken, shattered.

And the bastard still left her—for a much younger, much more willing woman.

Brenda shook the memory. "Now I'll admit—and Lord knows I'm not one for admitting much," she said, "but I have definitely been guilty of enabling Roselle. From his past gambling to his womanizing and anything else in between, I have been his clean-up woman. Always somewhere cleaning up his messes."

"And how has being your husband's clean-up woman made you feel?" Dr. Dangerfield asked.

"Angry," Brenda admitted. "At times homicidal." She laughed. "Some nights I stood over him in bed and watched him sleep, thinking about setting him on fire in his sleep or slicing his throat or smothering him with a pillow." Brenda shook her head. "I came this close"—she showed a small space between her thumb and index finger—"to smothering him. I stood over him, holding that pillow in my hands, ready to suffocate him. But then I thought about my children and what that would do to them. They'd be without a mother and a father. Orphans. No, I couldn't do that to them, no matter how pissed off Roselle made me." Brenda crossed her legs and ran a hand over her left hip. "Besides, I'm too fabulous to be behind bars."

This time LaQuandra laughed. "*Girrrrl*, I know that's right. Because, *trust* . . . if I could get away with putting a bullet in Isaiah's baby mother, I would do it in a heartbeat. But I'm too scared of the consequences."

"Violence isn't the answer," Dr. Dangerfield asserted. "It never is. If a relationship is bringing you more grief than peace, then it is time to reevaluate what your needs are in that relationship, and what your real reasons are for staying. It all comes down to two simple questions," Dr. Dangerfield continued. "How much of yourselves are you investing in your marriages? And what are the returns on your investment? Meaning, are there more positives than negatives? And if there are more negatives than positives, then the next question to ask yourselves is: how much more of yourselves are you willing to compromise before enough is enough?"

Dr. Dangerfield allowed her gaze to meet each of the three women, while the question hovered in the air.

LaQuandra had a blank look on her face.

Brenda regarded the therapist with a questioning look.

And Krista, bless her heart, simply appeared uninterested in anything being said. Because, frankly speaking, these bitches were crazy. All this foolish talk of smothering husbands and killing baby mothers . . . Lord Jesus! They needed lots of prayer, and a good cleansing to purify their murderous souls.

"Krista," Dr. Dangerfield said gently. "I've noticed that for the last half hour or so you've sat here very quiet. Is there something you'd like to add to the discussion?"

Krista shook her head. "No. Not particularly."

Of course not, LaQuandra thought as she rolled her eyes up in her head. *This country-ass bitch thinks her shit doesn't stink. Girl, bye.*

LaQuandra was certain there was a crack in Krista's little happy world, somewhere. And she couldn't wait to bear witness to it all crumbling down around her. But, of course, she wasn't wishing her any ill will. Oh no, never that. She was simply being realistic.

"Aren't marriages supposed to be about compromise?" LaQuandra asked, locking her stare on Dr. Dangerfield.

Dr. Dangerfield nodded. "Oh, absolutely. There always has to be a degree of compromise for any relationship to work. However, there needs to be a balance. When compromising becomes one-sided and you find yourself giving into things that you don't believe in, things that do not sit well with your spirit, then it becomes a problem."

Brenda tooted her lips. "Mmph. I'm always compromising."

"*Girrrl*, welcome to my wondrous world," LaQuandra quipped.

"Then that's seriously pause for concern," Dr. Dangerfield emphasized. "You cannot become so caught up in creating a world that you believe your partners should live in for the sake of forgoing your own dignity and your own self-worth."

"All I need is for Isaiah to grow a pair of balls when it comes to that trifling *bit*—baby mother of his. If she were out of the picture, life would be just duckie."

LaQuandra caught Krista shaking her head, smirking.

"Umm, something funny, Kara?" she questioned.

"It's *Kris . . . ta*," Krista corrected. "And, yes. Sad to say, something is funny—*you*. It sounds to me like you're angry with the wrong people. And seems to me you're blaming the wrong person for your unhappy marriage. That woman is a threat to your marriage because you have allowed her to be."

Scowling, LaQuandra set her jaw tight. "Excuse you?"

"I *saaaaaid* it sounds to me like you're . . ."

"Oh I heard what you said," LaQuandra clarified. "I'm just trying to understand why you're even here, interjecting your opinion, when you obviously believe you have such a wonderful marriage."

Krista shrugged. "Well, sorry to say. I do. I mean. It's not perfect. No marriage is. But I can honestly say it's nowhere near as dysfunctional as yours."

"*Dysfunctional?* Bitch, please. Who the hell are you to call someone dysfunctional?"

Krista scowled. "I didn't say *you* were dysfunctional. I said your *marriage* was. Big difference."

"Bitch," LaQuandra spat, "that fucking weave you're wearing is dysfunctional."

Brenda nearly gagged. *Ohmygod! LaQuandra is really doing the most. But, ooh, I love it.*

Dr. Dangerfield clapped her hands together, and her diamond-encrusted bangles clanked. "Ladies, please. Stop this. Let's exercise a little class and decorum and mutual respect for one another. Please."

Krista grunted. "*Mmph.* Well, you can't expect someone to be respectful when they apparently can't respect themselves. Class is something you either have or you don't. Sorry, hon. Class can't be bought. And it damn sure can't be borrowed."

LaQuandra sneered. "Girl, bye. I have more class in my pinky finger than you'll ever have. I'm an educated black woman and—"

Krista half scoffed, half laughed. "And you still don't respect yourself. Perhaps you should request a refund for all that education because the moment you open your mouth, nothing but ghetto spills out of it."

LaQuandra's eyes narrowed to slits. "Bye, Felicia. All I know is, you had better be glad I've changed my ways, because trust. The old me would hop up from this chair and lay hands on you."

Krista's nose flared. "Sweetie, I'd love to see you try it. I will lay my Bible down and beat your—"

"No, Ice Queen. How about you lay it down to suck a damn dick," LaQuandra snapped. "A good man deserves a damn good dick suck."

"Ladies. Ladies," Dr. Dangerfield calmly said. She wasn't one to raise her voice or yell at a bunch of grown women. "Threats of violence will not be tolerated anywhere on this island. This level of disrespect is *not* acceptable."

"Well . . . and neither is Miss Goody Two-Shoes' opinion of me," LaQuandra snapped. "Like I said, I'm an educated woman. And I don't appreciate some frumpy ole scared-to-suck-her-husband's-dick trick talking to me like I'm trash."

Krista laughed. "Trash is what you are. You're a miserable soul.

And you're still from the hood, hon. Face it, girl. You're a fraud. But it's okay, sweetie. I'm going to pray for you."

"No, *hon*," LaQuandra retorted. "Save your prayers for yourself. You're going to need them more than I do."

"LaQuandra," Dr. Dangerfield interjected. "I believe what I hear Krista saying is that you seem to be blaming everyone else for your unhappiness instead of taking responsibility for it. To be miserable, to be unhappy, to live in chaos, is a choice."

What Dr. Dangerfield said fell on deaf ears, as LaQuandra said, "The only thing I'm unhappy with is Isaiah's baby mother. Like I said before, she's the problem."

Brenda and Krista both gave LaQuandra blank stares.

Dr. Dangerfield sighed inwardly, and then glanced up at the wall clock. Their ninety-minute group session was finally coming to a close. Thank God for small miracles.

"Well, ladies," Dr. Dangerfield said thoughtfully. "I will leave you with two things to consider. The first, if you want change, then start with yourself. And, the second, you and only you alone can decide if your relationship is feeding your soul. Or bleeding it."

Twenty-Three

"What would you say is a major concern in your marriage?" Dr. Dangerfield asked Brenda in her session with her and Roselle. Brenda and Roselle were seated on a white leather loveseat, holding hands—the picture-perfect couple, while Dr. Dangerfield sat in a white leather duchess chair.

All this damn white.

Brenda admired the lavish décor (clearly, a ton of money had been paid to some interior design team), but it needed a pop of color in here, some reds or oranges, something loud to liven it up. As beautiful as white was, it felt so sterile to Brenda. *Doesn't she like anything other than white?* she thought. And then she glanced over at the beautiful pink floral arrangement and then over at the waterfall, with sheets of beautiful blue water splashing endlessly down into a basin filled with shimmering stones, before her gaze caught the red-bottomed soles of Dr. Dangerfield's four-inch, white crystal-spiked heels.

Mmph.

Every so often a mist of lavender-scented air wafted out from some invisible vent, filling the room with a peaceful calm.

Brenda shifted in seat. "Roselle and I have a great marriage for the most part," she stated. She really believed that to be true. "We're very compatible. And I believe for the most part, we not only love one another, we like each other too."

"But . . .?" Dr. Dangerfield asked, waiting. There was always a *but* somewhere lingering at the end of every "he's-so/she's-so wonderful" story.

"But, honestly. I'm tired of his cheating." She let Roselle's hand go, and Dr. Dangerfield watched as Roselle shifted in his seat and then tried to take hold of it again. "If Roselle could learn to keep his thing in his pants, we'd have the perfect marriage."

"Is that so? Define *perfect*," Dr. Dangerfield insisted.

"Well, nothing is ever really perfect, per se," Brenda quickly corrected. "But our marriage would be better. We'd be closer. Our chemistry is already through the roof, but I believe if he wasn't out there cheating all the damn time . . ." Brenda shook her head. She felt herself becoming agitated. "The only thing we ever really fight about is his cheating."

Brenda was simply tired of sharing his dick with other bitches. All she wanted from this Doctor lady was for her to get Roselle to see that he was potentially about to lose her behind his bullshit. Or not.

She—

Wait.

Was that what she really wanted? To leave him? It wasn't like he cheated *allllll* the time. It wasn't like he had a steady sidepiece. And he'd never fucked any of her sisters or friends—well, none that she was aware of.

Still. Was she really willing to give up on her marriage? Did she really want to walk away from everything she and Roselle had built together simply because he liked sampling new pussy on occasion?

She couldn't answer that. And, honestly, she wasn't ready to.

Roselle glanced at his Rolex, a gift from Brenda two Christmases ago. She'd saved all year just to make the extravagant purchase.

Dr. Dangerfield took the couple in for a brief moment, then

landed her gaze on Brenda. "That must be exhausting. Constantly in conflict over your husband's infidelity."

Brenda sighed, and then she shot Roselle a dirty look. "Very. I'm tired of having to confront other women."

"Then why do you feel the need to confront them? They aren't the problem. They aren't the ones disrespecting your marriage."

Dr. Dangerfield glanced over at Roselle. He looked cool, calm, and collected, but inside, he was bracing himself for the blowup. Brenda was definitely going to flip from zero to a hundred. He glanced at the clock. He'd give it fifteen more minutes, before she went off.

"They *are* the problem," Brenda said, shifting again in her seat. "They *know* he's married and they *still* chose to fuck him. So, yes, I confront them." And she'd fought a few, too. Yet Brenda decided the therapist didn't need to know that part.

"How do you know that these women know your husband is married?"

Roselle's eyes met Dr. Dangerfield's. "Because I tell them—all of them. I don't ever mislead them to think that it's ever gonna be more than a lay. Am I wrong for that?"

Dr. Dangerfield cocked her head in question.

"Am I?" Roselle repeated.

"The question should be, are you wrong for cheating on your wife?" she said.

Roselle's eyes stayed firmly on Dr. Dangerfield's, but he was talking to Brenda when he said, very softly, "Of course I am. Dead wrong."

"Are these emotional affairs?" Dr. Dangerfield asked. Emotional affairs were much harder to let go of, and much harder to work through. "Or strictly physical?"

The question was for Roselle, but Brenda was quick to answer.

"Physical. I know for a fact I'm the only one who is ever going to have his heart." She shifted her body to face Roselle. "Correct me if I'm wrong here."

"You right," Roselle admitted. "The only woman I'm ever gonna love is you. I'm loyal to only you, baby. You already know this."

"There's always a reason why people do what they do," Dr. Dangerfield stated. "And men cheat very differently than women and for very different reasons, most times. But speaking of loyalty—because I heard you say that the only woman you are loyal to is your wife. Is that correct?"

Roselle nodded. "No doubt."

Dr. Dangerfield clasped her hands in her lap. "Well, here's the thing about loyalty, Mr. Woods. Loyalty is the foundation of true love. In a relationship, loyal partners aren't thinking just only of themselves; every decision that they make, every behavior that they display is with their partner in mind. Loyal partners are conscious about how their choices will affect their spouses. So they keep their interactions with the opposite sex strictly professional and they exercise appropriate boundary setting. Loyal partners are not allowing themselves to get entangled in a web of lies and deception . . ."

Brenda twisted her lips. "*Mmph.* You better preach."

Roselle frowned. "Hold up. I put my family—my wife *and* our kids, *first*, before all others. Period. I don't give a fuck about them other broads. I fuck up sometimes"—Brenda gave him a hard stare—"okay, okay; most times. But that doesn't mean I love you any less, baby."

Brenda sucked her teeth. She knew Roselle loved her, but she felt like dragging him over the coals nonetheless. "Then why do you keep cheating on me, if you love me so damn much? What is it that those other bitches are giving you that you can't get from *me*—at home?"

Roselle shrugged. "Nothing really." And that was the truth. "I enjoy the chase. Variety. Can I be honest?"

Brenda rolled her eyes. "I thought that was what we were here to do, Roselle."

Roselle shook his head. Then glanced at the clock again. Countdown. Ten minutes or less. "The thought of new pussy excites me."

Brenda snorted. "Nigga, the only pussy that should be exciting you—and keeping you excited—is the one between *my* legs, you yellow motherfucker." She huffed. "'New pussy' excites you, *neeegro*, please. You can kiss my ass with that. How many times have *I* invited *new* pussy into our bed?"

Roselle swallowed. "Plenty."

"And how many times have you invited some new dick into our bed?"

Roselle gave her a look that said, "what the fuck?"

Dr. Dangerfield decided to sit back and see how it all unfolded.

"Is that what you want? Another muhfucka in our bed?"

Brenda gave him a smug look. "Maybe."

Roselle shook his head. "Nah. I'm not tryna hear no maybe shit. Either you do or you don't."

"I said maybe. Is that a problem?"

"You must'a bumped your damn head if you think I'ma be in bed with another muhfucka, letting him smash you."

"Oh really? But it's okay for you to put your dick in whatever wet-hole is willing to open for your nasty-ass. Fuck that, Roselle. If you can fuck new pussy whenever you feel the urge to, then I should be able to go out and catch me some *new* dick whenever I want to."

Roselle's jaw twitched.

"So, what are you suggesting?" Dr. Dangerfield interjected. "An open marriage?"

Brenda glared at Roselle. "Maybe. He knows I am very open-minded. I don't have a problem with him screwing another woman. My problem is, him doing the shit behind my back. And my biggest problem is him running out and fucking some white woman."

Roselle scoffed. "Oh, okay. So all roads lead back to *that*, I see."

"Yes," Brenda snapped. "All roads lead straight to that white bitch. Of all the beautiful black women out here, you had to go out and fuck some skinny *white* bitch."

Roselle met her glare, but said nothing.

"So had she'd been a skinny *black* woman," Dr. Dangerfield probed, "would that had made a difference?"

Brenda inhaled. "Yes," she pushed out. "No. Shit, I don't know. I mean I would have still been angry with his ass, but not livid to the point of putting him out and trying to run him down in my car."

Dr. Dangerfield forced her lashes from blinking. "Excuse me? Am I hearing you correctly? You tried to . . .?"

"Exactly," Roselle stated. "She was way outta line for that."

Brenda scowled. "Outta line my ass, Roselle. At least I didn't bleach and burn your shit, too. I neatly packed your shit and put it out on the curb. You're lucky I didn't run you *and* that bitch down like I wanted to."

"C'mon, Bren," Roselle said calmly. "And fuck up your life? What about our kids? Your salon? I know you were hurt, but damn."

Brenda sighed. "In that moment, I didn't give a fuck." She shook her head. "All I saw was red. Now, I'll admit. I'm glad I didn't get to either one of you, because you're right. I have kids to think about—even if you don't—and a career, and a life outside of you and your cheating."

Dr. Dangerfield pursed her lips. "And what was it about your husband cheating on you with a Caucasian woman that had you so enraged?"

Brenda gave her a hard stare. Black women had been fighting since the beginning of time; fighting to hold on to their men. First, slavery, where their men had been snatched from them, then drugs and prisons, and now—more than ever, they had to worry about their men running off to be with some white woman. She couldn't believe that this obviously educated, seemingly strong, *black* woman was sitting here asking her *that*. Did she not know the plight of . . . She shook her head quickly deciding she wasn't in the mood to educate or enlighten her.

"I watched my father walk out on my mother and his three daughters," Brenda offered, "and I saw what that did to her. A strong *black* woman who held her man down, bore his children, loved him through all of his failures, praised him on every accomplishment, helped put him through grad school—*she* wrote his papers, researched his thesis—while she worked *two* jobs and still made sure his meals were cooked, his clothes were pressed and his house clean. She would come home dog-tired and still she made time to stroke his ego, rub his back, nurse his ailments, *and* sex him down . . ."

"She sounds like an amazing woman," Dr. Dangerfield said thoughtfully.

"She was." Brenda sighed, and then she shook her head, feeling the sting of fresh tears. "She'd never recovered from that level of betrayal. She died broken-hearted. And that bastard still lives and breathes with his precious little white whore."

Roselle reached for Brenda, but she swatted his arm away.

"No. My mother, though not perfect, loved that man. But—guess what? That wasn't enough and the minute he'd had enough, the minute he became bored, he packed his shit and left her. He walked out on me and my sisters for another woman—a *white* woman!" She swiped a fresh string of tears from her cheeks. "So excuse me, motherfucker, if I have an issue with *you* fucking some white bitch!"

"But, baby, I didn't walk out on you for one," Roselle offered softly.

Brenda glared at him, her nose flaring. "The moment you stuck your dick in one, you might as well had."

Twenty-Four

Desire . . .

Coveting, craving—those were things attached to desire.

It was a life force. It was the strong sense of wanting something, needing something, longing for something, even when that which was longed for was not necessarily good for us. And yet many would still indulge themselves. Feed their libidos. Quench their lust. And then . . .

Want more.

It was desire that moved us. It motivated us. And gave us direction. And in that desire, there was purpose, one not always met with meaning.

Yet the yearning, that burning sensation, that thirst for fulfillment, could oftentimes become consuming and overwhelming.

Oh, yes. Desire.

It could be dirty. It could be sinful. It could be as painful as it was pleasurable.

And Dr. Dangerfield knew that, in excess, desire could ultimately become greed. And greed (the pursuit of new desires) was destructive. It was insatiable. It was damaging to any relationship—healthy or not—if not tempered by self-restraint and boundaries. It prevented partners from enjoying one another, fully, wholly, without limits, without shame, without regret.

It was greed that kept partners lying and scheming and cheating on one another. And it was repressed urges that kept men *and* women hiding behind masks, living double lives.

Not all. Many.

Dr. Dangerfield believed that sometimes you had to surrender to your desires. Indulge yourself. With the one you loved, the one you committed yourself to.

What healthy relationships needed was for both parties to be the object of their partner's desires. Sadly, most weren't. Most were distracted by the yearnings for everything else except for what was already standing before them—their partners.

And, today, Dr. Dangerfield planned to explore the innermost desires of the women. If they were ready and able to be honest—*first*, with themselves; and then here—then they could work toward being more open and honest with their husbands about what their sexual needs were. What they desired most.

Dr. Dangerfield didn't believe women should have to sublimate their desire, their pleasure to the pleasures of the men in their lives.

No. A woman's desires were real. They were alive. And they evolved.

Sadly, many women didn't know what they truly desired . . . for themselves.

She took in the three women seated in the four-chair circle. The room was alit with coconut-scented candles. The atmosphere was relaxed, for the moment. But Dr. Dangerfield was no fool. She knew all too well that today's session could evoke defenses and flare tempers. Someone was bound to become judgmental and/or belligerent. Someone always did.

"I wish this island had better cell service," Brenda randomly stated.

Dr. Dangerfield nodded, knowingly. Having a weak signal meant being forced to focus on their partners and their marriages more than making phone calls or connecting on social media. It was by design. The whole point of being on a remote island was to get away from day-to-day stressors and distractions.

LaQuandra laughed. "Hell, I'm glad there's shitty service. That makes it harder for Isaiah's trifling-ass baby mother to reach him."

Brenda laughed along. "Girrrl. I'm so glad I don't have one of *those* to deal with."

"Lucky you," LaQuandra stated flatly. "That bitch irks my soul."

"Ladies," Dr. Dangerfield said gently. "Let's refrain from using the *B*-word, especially when referring to another woman."

LaQuandra rolled her eyes. "Well, that's what she is. But okay."

Dr. Dangerfield forced a smile. She wanted to find something likeable about this woman, but so far the only thing she liked was the silver cuff bracelet on her wrist.

"I'll thank you now for your efforts," Dr. Dangerfield said to LaQuandra. She shifted in her seat, then crossed her right leg over her left. "Today, the focus is on each of you. I want to tap into your desires. Hidden or not. They can be as filthy or as slutty as you want them to be. The purpose here is to get you talking about them, without shame, without guilt, without ridicule. To embrace your sexual desires, own them, without justification."

Dr. Dangerfield glanced around the small circle of women taking in their facial expressions. Krista met her gaze with a blank look on her face, while Brenda and LaQuandra looked eager to share.

"How about we start with you, Mrs. Woods?" she suggested.

Brenda smiled. Good. She couldn't wait to share one of her sexual fantasies. She was in touch with her wants and needs and desires, so sharing was fine with her.

She'd indulged in a ménage à trois, once. She'd offered Roselle another woman in their bed—a sexy Latina with big, bouncy tits and thick hips, who'd done nasty things to the both of them with her tongue.

She wanted more. More tongues. More hands. More fingers.

"I fantasize about being in an orgy," Brenda shared.

"Okay," Dr. Dangerfield said. "Tell us what is happening in this orgy."

Brenda subconsciously licked her lips. "Well. There are about eight to ten men, naked and horny. Their hard dicks, long and thick—and even short fat ones . . ."

LaQuandra cringed inwardly at the idea of a short fat dick trying to enter her. She wouldn't dare let some stumpy-dick man fuck her. Her pussy probably wouldn't get wet, anyway, she mused. Then, again, lies. Right about now, she'd practically beg a stumpy-dick fucker to poke her untouched slit, give her a good teasing, with its head, because that's all it would be—a tease. Shit. Some attention from a hard dick, itty-bitty or not, would be better than nothing at all. She was tired of using her fingers and her dildo.

"One after the other, the men are fucking me, giving it to me real good," Brenda continued, crossing and uncrossing her legs. She felt her body begin to heat as she shared her desire to be the only woman surrounded by men who took turns ravishing her cunt, her mouth, and, maybe, even her ass. Each dick pushing against her inner walls, filling her, testing her, thrusting wildly, hammering inside her until she screamed out.

She would be fucked hard and deep until her body burned and stretched and gushed wet fire, her orgasm white-hot and blinding.

"And then when they're all done taking turns with me," Brenda said. "I lie on my back, my hand between my legs, playing with my raw pussy, while they circle me, jerking their wet, sticky dicks." Brenda licked her lips again. "Simultaneously, they grunt and come, coating me with load after load after load of white, creamy nut—in my face, in my opened mouth, on my breasts, all over my stomach, and over my throbbing pussy. When they are done, I am soaked in cum."

Ooh, I knew I would like this one, Dr. Dangerfield mused as she regarded Brenda's fantasy. "Sounds like what you desire is a *gang*bang. Not an orgy."

Ugh. LaQuandra made a face. *Ooh, this bitch is nasty.* However, she knew she didn't have room to judge after all the random fucking she'd done in her life.

Brenda smiled, then licked over her lips. "Yes. A gangbang."

Krista grunted. "*Mmph.* Why would any decent woman want to be in some filthy group sex mess?"

"What Mrs. Woods seeks isn't group sex," Dr. Dangerfield declared. "Group sex—or as it's typically referred to as, an orgy—is where there are several participants performing a variety of sexual acts while sexual acts are being performed on them as well. There is often sharing or swapping happening between them as well; however, in a gangbang, several people perform sexual acts on only one person, either taking turns or at the same time."

Krista frowned. *What a filthy heathen.* It sounded nasty, but she kept her opinion to herself.

"Thank you for sharing that very sexy scenario with us." Dr. Dangerfield uncrossed her legs, then crossed them at the ankles. "What about you, Mrs. Lewis. Would you like to share with us what you desire, sexually?"

"*Wellllll,*" LaQuandra said, tooting her glossed lips. "Mine isn't quite as kinky as this one's"—she flicked a finger over at Brenda—"but since you've asked. I've never, ever, cheated on Isaiah. And, honestly, I would probably never even consider it if things between us were different. But they aren't . . ." She paused, taking a breath. "Just once, I want to cheat on him. I wanna have sex with a man I don't know, and would never see again. A stranger. I want him to ravish my body, do me in ways Isaiah has never dared."

"So, you want him to watch?" Brenda wanted to know. "Now that would be some sexy shit."

LaQuandra wanted a wild night of uninhibited sex. Just one night of reckless abandon. Maybe she'd feel better. Maybe she'd be able to forgive Isaiah for sneaking off with that trifling bitch, Cassandra.

She shook her head. "Oh, God, no. Isaiah would never go for that."

"So, would you rather he walked in and caught you in the act?" Dr. Dangerfield questioned.

If she were a scandalous bitch, she'd fuck one of his brothers or, maybe, his sixty-five-year-old father. She'd heard he had a big, juicy dick. But she wasn't that kind of woman. Well—okay… not anymore. And, besides, she didn't want to hurt Isaiah like that. Sharing her body with another man was more for her. She wanted validation that she was desirable. She wanted to feel sexy and wanted; something Isaiah had failed to do over the last several months; maybe even longer if she were willing to be completely honest with herself.

"No. I want it to be my own little dirty secret," LaQuandra confessed. "You know, something I can keep to myself. I need to be able to look Isaiah in his face with a smile, knowing I gave someone else a taste of what he thinks, what he *still* believes, is his and his alone."

Dr. Dangerfield understood. "What if I told you that Passion Island is all about delivering the most sensually intimate experiences, and can help you turn that fantasy into a reality? Would you still want to explore it?"

Would she?

Could she?

She'd given up all of her whoring ways once she'd snagged Isaiah. Yes. She'd changed her ways. She'd hung her whore hat up and burned her ho-card, vowing to never let another man touch her body or slide between her thighs as long as she had Isaiah.

But where had that gotten her?

LaQuandra's pulse raced at the possibility. Just once. What could be the harm in that? What Isaiah didn't know wouldn't hurt him. Right?

She pursed her lips, contemplating. The thought fanned a small spark of excitement through her. "Yes," she pushed out. "I'd do it in a heartbeat."

Dr. Dangerfield smiled. "You'll need to think it through, very carefully," she warned. "Because once you step through that door, there's no turning back once the deed is done."

"I know," LaQuandra murmured. "I'm clear. I want it. No"—she shook her head—"I need it in more ways than one." And then she chuckled. "Whew, is it getting hot in here, or is it just me?"

"No, girl," Brenda said. "It's definitely not you. All this talk about fantasies, I'm so ready to get back to my husband." She laughed. "I'm gonna tear his ass up."

Krista couldn't believe her ears. These bitches were scandalous. The point of being here was to strengthen their relationships *not* fantasy-fuck other men behind their husbands' backs, wasn't it? She was too through.

Dr. Dangerfield sensed Krista's apprehensiveness. She smiled over at her.

"Mrs. Evans, why don't you tell us what you desire most?"

Krista straightened her back. Ran a hand through her hair. Then shifted in her seat. "The only thing I want is for Kendall and I to grow closer in Christ."

Krista had attended church sporadically over the years, but a year ago, she'd rejoined church and had decided to live a more Christian-like life. Unfortunately, Kendall hadn't been onboard to turn his life over to Christ, but she was hopeful that one day he would see the light.

Dr. Dangerfield kept her expression neutral. Hadn't she been paying attention? Perhaps she'd misunderstood the question, she reasoned as she offered a hint of a smile.

"I think that's great. But, sexually speaking," Dr. Dangerfield pushed, "is there anything you desire, anything you fantasize about, that your husband isn't aware of?"

Krista shook her head, indicating no.

"*Nothing?*" Brenda probed.

"No," Krista insisted.

LaQuandra grunted. "Krissy, stop lying. We all adults here; let your hair down and keep it real."

Krista frowned. "Um. I don't know what you are implying, but I am keeping it *real.*" She shifted in her seat. "Not to discuss my private life, but I'm *very* pleased sexually."

LaQuandra gave Krista an amused look. "Some of the biggest freaks are hiding up in the church behind a Bible," she said half-jokingly. "I bet you sit up in the pew with the Church Mother."

Krista scowled. "I'm in church for the word; nothing more, nothing less."

"Do you think it's ladylike for a woman to give her man head?" Brenda asked inquisitively. Krista didn't look like the type to swallow, so she was curious to know.

Krista shrugged. "Women can do whatever they want with their men. I only know what *I'm* doing. And that's *not* going down on a man around the clock."

Brenda gave Krista an incredulous look. "*What?* You mean to tell me you don't give your husband head? Ever?"

LaQuandra laughed. "Girl, you know Krissy isn't playing head doctor. She doesn't even swallow. Who you know not sucking her man and *not* swallowing?"

Krista narrowed her eyes. "I'm not going to discuss what I do or *don't* do with my husband."

"Well, do you at least enjoy *getting* head?" Brenda asked.

Krista frowned. "No."

Brenda and LaQuandra both gave her a sorrowful look. She had no idea what she was missing.

"Why?" LaQuandra asked.

Krista felt herself becoming annoyed. Why the hell was she being interrogated, while the therapist sat there and said nothing?

"I don't think that's any of your business," she said in a razor-sharp tone.

LaQuandra grunted. "*Mmph.* You're right. It isn't any of my business. I don't care, anyway, because—truthfully—you sound a bit—no, a whole lot—prudish. No disrespect, hun."

Brenda eyed LaQuandra over the top of her sunglasses. Then tilted her head, just so, and pursed her lips. She was glad she'd said it and it hadn't come from her. She liked Krista, with her ole churchy-acting ass.

Krista looked indignant. Prudish? Oh these nasty bitches had her all kinds of twisted. "Come again, sweetie," she said. "I screw my husband at least three times a week—and most weekends twice in the same damn day. I give him good loving, okay. And, *no*, I don't have to put my mouth on his dick to do it." She pointed over at LaQuandra. "If you enjoy sucking your husband's dick, sweetie, then suck on."

"Yes, honey. I love sucking his dick," LaQuandra admitted. "*And?* Maybe you should learn to love having a dick in your mouth, too. Maybe then you wouldn't be so uptight."

Krista half laughed, half scoffed. "Well, since you're the expert in dick sucking and spicing things up in the bedroom, how about you tell us how that's working out for you, since your husband hasn't screwed *you* in months, remember?" She tilted her head, and waited. LaQuandra wanted to leap out of her seat and punch this pudgy bitch in her fat neck, but she willed herself still in her seat, and simply crossed her legs.

After all, she was a lady.

"Please, ladies," Dr. Dangerfield finally interrupted. "No judging. And let's refrain from abusive language. This is a safe zone, for all of you. And everyone is entitled to her opinions, but that does not give anyone the right to judge or criticize."

LaQuandra huffed. "I wasn't judging her. All I did was state an observation. She *is* uptight."

Krista eyed LaQuandra nastily, and LaQuandra stared back.

Before the two women tore her office up, Dr. Dangerfield stepped in. "Mrs. Evans, you seem offended that Mrs. Lewis would say—or should I say, suggest—that you sound, operative word . . . *prudish*. Would you like to share why that is?"

"Yes, Krista," LaQuandra said sweetly. Too sweetly. Flies were suddenly swarming all around her. "Please share."

"I have nothing more to say." Krista stood to her feet. "You ladies have a good day. I'm done." And with that she walked out, leaving a sudden chill lingering in the air behind her.

Twenty-Five

Who the fuck does that ghetto bitch think she is? Calling *me* prudish?

Bitch, bye.

Krista couldn't believe how angry she'd become over one simple word. But she was. And she now had a pounding headache. Maybe it wasn't so much being called prudish that had bothered her most. No. It was the fact that that bitch, LaQuandra, had tried to be messy. And that was one thing Krista couldn't stand—some messy-ass bitch.

So what if she wasn't some dick-sucking cum-eater, like she was. If LaQuandra wanted to fellate, then so be it. She could suck a dick until her damn jaw broke off. But that didn't mean *she* had to. No. Hell, no! She knew how to satisfy *her* husband. Well, shit. She thought she did. But lately, she wasn't so sure anymore. Still, she wasn't about to do any nasty-ass tongue tricks just to keep him, either.

She slowly exhaled. *Lord, forgive me for calling that heathenish woman all types of bitches. But that's what the hell she is.*

Krista took another deep breath.

I know you know my heart, Lord.

Out of nowhere, a crash of lightning burst across the sky, like a cracking whip, followed by an enormous boom of thunder. Krista thought she felt the earth shake as she angrily stomped her sandaled-feet down the trail that led back toward the villas.

She was still beside herself with annoyance. How dare that hoodrat bitch—Lord forgive her—call *her* prudish? And then have the audacity to suggest she learn to suck dick. Krista didn't need that bitch telling her how to please her man. The bitch couldn't even keep her own man happy.

Prudish, hell . . .

Remembering the time she'd thrown caution to the wind and had given into pleasure brought a smirk to her face. That time on the Carnival cruise ship, Sunshine, two summers ago. 1:30 a.m. They had been at sea. Sailing from St. Thomas to Grand Turk. Up on the sky deck. Her white sundress was raised up over her thick hips, her nude-colored panties (and she'd paid good damn money for the silky item!) torn at the crotch by Kendall's strong powerful hands. She'd gripped the railing and looked up at the darkened sky alit with stars as Kendall slid himself inside of her, and fucked her deep, in slow sensual strokes.

She couldn't believe it. Allowing herself to be fucked out in the open like *that* . . . so vulnerable, so constrained (because she couldn't cry out in fear she'd be heard) and yet so, so damn wet. Wetter than she'd ever been in her entire life.

What had gotten into her that night (besides Kendall's hard dick)?

It'd taken almost four days of cajoling and sweet-talking and damn near pleading for Kendall to finally get her to let him make love to her there, in that very spot, beneath a dome of stars. But she'd finally acquiesced and gave into Kendall's desire. She'd let him have his way with her, his dick thrusting wetly in and out of her body. Ooh, Lord, have mercy on her little slutty soul. Because that was what she'd imagined a slut would do, of what being slutty would be like.

And she'd come quick and hard . . . so, so hard . . . that she nearly passed out.

So LaQuandra could kiss her whole ass. She might not have been as freaky as those two whores, but Krista damn sure wasn't some puritanical lay, either.

Still . . .

Thunder rumbled.

She couldn't believe those bitches back there. Fantasizing about cheating on their husbands. *Mmph.* And that therapist sitting up in there encouraging such salacious behavior like there was nothing wrong with those two heathen-ass hoes entertaining the possibility of lying with another man. Fantasy or not, it was still wrong.

More lightning flashed overhead.

Krista looked up at the swaying coconut palms and then at the darkening sky draped in swollen clouds.

Lord, get me back to the villa before it pours.

A raindrop hit her face, then another. Krista nearly squeaked. Then came the booming sound of thunder. Krista might have been a bit rough around the edges (on occasion), but everyone who knew her knew she was deathly afraid of thunder and lightning.

She picked up her pace as another bolt of lightning struck closer. The raindrops were so big that they thumped heavily on her head. This is nothing but the devil, Krista thought, swiftly walking in the direction toward what she thought were the villas. Lightning continued to fork out above her. And then what started out as drizzle turned into a downpour. The torrential rain had come from out of nowhere. Now she could barely see through the curtain of rain.

The wind whipped fiercely around her, flinging heavy raindrops all over her. More lightning split open the darkened sky and Krista began a run-walk. Her feet started sliding in her sandals, making it difficult for her to move as rain sloshed between her painted toes.

More lightning flashed.

Then came a crackling sound in the distance. A tree had been struck.

Krista's heart raced. Now she wished she hadn't stormed out of the session so hastily. Perhaps she'd been a bit more defensive than was necessary. But she couldn't think about that now. She needed to get to safety before she was electrocuted.

More lightning crackled.

The rain was so thick that she could barely see. Drenched, Krista quickened her pace to nearly a run and stumbled as her right foot slid out of her sandal. She broke her fall with her hands, skinning her palms on the stoned pathway as she fell. Krista rolled, trying to prevent further injuries, and landed in a foot of water. Goddamn it. Now she was a muddy mess.

Pulling herself up from the mud and water, she swiped her wet hair from her face and attempted to slide her sandal back on her foot to only find that it had broken. To add insult to injury, her nipples were painfully hard. *Shit.* She quickly picked up her torn sandal and hurriedly walk-ran with one sandal on.

She wanted desperately to get out of this rain. Up ahead. There it was. She could barely make out the shape of a structure. The rain nearly stung her eyes as she tried to bring the building into focus. Oh. Okay. Up ahead was the villa, she thought. She blinked, straining for a clearer look. Yes, God. Thank you.

Wait.

She blinked through the rain again. She saw only one building—a house-like structure. That wasn't *her* villa.

Ohgod, no, no, no, nooo . . .

Krista realized she had taken the wrong path when she didn't see the villas or the ocean ahead. She needed to go in the opposite direction. She'd been so distracted by her thoughts that she'd somehow managed to go the wrong way.

Nothing but the devil! Goddamn you!

Another burst of lightning struck a nearby tree, splitting it, and causing Krista to duck. The loud *crack* sounded too close for comfort. And Krista was now more frightened of the wildness of the storm than ever. She hadn't come here to die. To be struck down by lightning.

As she neared, she saw what in fact was a cottage of some sort. Its slanted roof was a vibrant mosaic of pinks and blues and greens, and its chimney billowed out a thick cloud of smoke. Sheets of water poured down either sides of the roof like a rushing waterfall.

Something was lit inside, hopefully a fire. Krista needed to warm herself and dry out from the elements. But why was this bungalow out here in the middle of nowhere? And why was there no door?

With one waterlogged sandal in hand and the other on her foot, Krista raced through the door-less frame, without considering who might be inside. All she knew was, she needed out of the storm.

Twenty-Six

Candles illuminated the front part of the house, along the walls, all along the baseboards. Fresh-cut floral arrangements sat atop pedestals, which Krista thought odd. And yet she breathed in the erotic stimuli, nonetheless.

"Hello?" Krista said nervously. "Is anyone here? I don't mean to barge in like this, but I was hoping I could come inside . . ." She walked further inside. "Just until the rain stops."

Krista's wet feet squished over the iridescent aquatic-blue glass-tiled floor as she walked. Her one shoeless foot chilled against the tiles as she moved deeper into the room. The room smelled of scented pineapples and cedar.

"Hello?" she called out again over the rumbling outside. Deeper inside was another room where a fire crackled inside its hearth. Apprehensively, Krista inhaled. She loved the smell. Loved the crackling sounds of burning wood.

"Hell—"

She didn't finish calling out *hello*. She thought she heard what sounded like moans coming from the back part of the house.

"Mmmm . . ."

"Uh. Uh. Uhhh . . ."

Was that grunting?

Krista stopped in her tracks. She held her breath.

More lightning cracked across the sky.

Then came the sounds of more moaning. More grunting.

Krista continued forward as the rain and wind continued to howl outside. The bungalow suddenly filled with a sinful amalgamation of sensual sounds, of grunting and groaning and hissing and moaning, almost as if in surround-sound.

Curiosity got the best of her. And, instead of whirring toward the exit, ready to brave the storm, Krista treaded forward, toward the seductive resonances.

She peered around into the doorway, and breathed in the sweet funk of sex and hot seeds and stained sheets.

Right there, in the center of the last room was where sin greeted her. There was a huge circular platform bed. Its walls covered in mirrors, mere reflections of sweat-slick bodies. Skin slapped against skin and, like tribal drums, the echoing sounds of moaning filled the room.

And then came the lascivious sound of sucking—dick sucking, toe sucking, sucking, sucking . . . and more sucking. High-heels and swaying breasts and bouncing-asses and hard dicks and chiseled nakedness was all around her.

Krista's eyes batted in surprise.

Realization dawned. This was . . . oh, God . . .

A sexy, tanned Latina with heart-shaped lips, big breasts and an even bigger ass was on all fours, her skin shimmering in sweat and glitter lotion. Behind her was a Nigerian hunk, fucking her, pounding her, deeply, while her face was buried between the thighs of a thick-hipped East Indian woman. The East Indian had thick dark lashes and dark hair that fanned out over the white bed sheet. Her breasts were swollen. Her areolas were dark and almost as long and thick as a pinky.

Krista watched on in stunned amazement as another man, with his sun-kissed tan, hovered over the East Indian woman and dipped his head, sucking a nipple into his greedy wet mouth, while lightly pinching her other nipple. The woman mewled out as his engorged cock bounced up and down over her forehead.

His dick was big, shamelessly begging to be stroked. To be sucked. To unleash a thick load into a warm hole, someone's mouth, or slick cunt. Krista fixed her gaze on the thick tendons of his throat. A rivulet of sweat slid down his corded neck as he gyrated his hips in a deep, lazy movement.

Another woman—a Brazilian—took to the same bed, her knees sinking into the plush mattress as she crawled in back of Mr. Sun-Kissed and shoved her face in between his muscled hamstrings. She licked the back of his balls. Sucked them into her mouth. Then she brazenly pulled open the smooth muscled globes of his ass. And she licked him there. Again and again, she licked and licked. And each time her tongue laved him there, stroked over his hole, his dick jerked.

God no. *What kind of nasty shit is going on in here?* Krista pressed a hand to her heart and then clutched at her rain-soaked chest and frowned.

He must be bisexual, Krista thought. Because, in her thinking, no straight man, no *real* man, wanted his ass licked. And he damn sure wasn't letting anyone fuck him in it with fingers, toys, or anything else. But here this manly-looking man was, hunched over letting some woman tongue-fuck him. She was convinced he was down-low and nasty. Sorry. A real man was never letting anyone or anything go anywhere near his ass. Period.

Krista's stomach churned, and all the pineapple chunks she'd consumed earlier in the day burned like acid. But she didn't look away. No, no. She swallowed instead. Still, she knew she should turn away. Knew she should scurry back out the way she'd come. But she couldn't. She didn't want to. And she didn't know if she should be more afraid of the hurricane-like storm outside or frightened of the sensuality and carnal energy that swirled haphazardly around her.

She didn't know if any of them were aware that someone was watching them. If they did, they didn't seem concerned that prying eyes—*her* prying eyes—might be on them.

All she knew was—

"Are you enjoying the view?" came a low, deep voice from behind her, vibrating its way up her spine.

Krista whirled around. Panic hit her square in the chest as she looked up into the searing gaze of a half-naked man, dark chocolate skin sliding over thick muscle, shining from coconut oil. There was an island lilt to his voice, she thought. He was well over six feet, and his body was nearly as wide as the doorframe.

A sleek tattoo of a panther wrapped around the hunk's torso with its head propped up on his right shoulder, its golden-colored eyes staring at her. And he wore a loincloth and loads of hot sensuality. Nothing more.

Krista shivered.

Where had he come from?

He regarded her with a smirk.

"Yes. No. I mean. I-I-I'm drenched," Krista stammered, looking into his eyes. They were beautiful eyes too. Deep, searing brown eyes. He wore his hair in long dreadlocks, tied back into a ponytail that brushed against his lower back, the sides and back of his head neatly faded low.

". . . needed to get out from the rain," Krista offered sheepishly. Once again, she'd been caught . . . this time *spying*. Watching lovers indulge in carnal pleasure.

What in the hell was wrong with her?

Was this some newfound *thing*? Watching, eavesdropping, like some perverted, sex-starved heathen. She'd never been known to do any nasty shit like this. Hell, she didn't even watch porn. She found nothing remotely enticing about watching some staged-fucking. But, oh God, there was nothing scripted here. It was all live and direct and . . .

He smiled, and his brown eyes twinkled at her. And then his gaze latched onto her erect nipples.

"I see."

Yes, he was definitely of Caribbean descent by the accent.

Self-consciously, Krista brought her arms up over her chest and crossed them in a clumsy attempt to hide her protruding nipples. Why hadn't she worn a better bra, one with more padding?

He deliberately licked his lips.

"Would you like to join in?" he asked, gesturing with a hand for Krista to enter the room—the den of wicked sin, if she dared . . . of course not.

Krista shook her head emphatically. "No, no. I-I-I was looking for a restroom, someplace where I can dry myself off . . . until the rain stops."

"Aah, yes," he said over a smile. "The rain. The perfect backdrop for lovemaking." His eyes journeyed over Krista's thick body, taking in the way her sundress clung to her hips like a second skin. Oh, yes, he would fuck her slow and deep until she opened to him, then he would pound her until she clawed his back, the sheets, and cried out his name, begging him to have mercy on her stretched open hole.

And now . . . now Krista felt undressed, naked, stripped down to her flaws.

He licked his lips again. "I'm Soul."

"I-I-I'm," Krista stammered.

"Very *wet*," he said over a grin. "Shall I help you undress . . .?"

Krista blinked. "Absolutely not. I should get—"

More lightning crackled.

"Do you enjoy being made love to?"

"No. I mean, yes. I mean," she said indignantly, "that's none of your business."

"You like watching other people *fuck*, though."

"No," she said crossly.

"It wasn't a question," he stated.

Krista blinked, and the man reveled in hearing the hitch in her breathing. She was more than simply taken aback by his accusation. She was goddamn appalled. And deathly frightened too. What if he tried to take advantage of her? What if they *all* did? Held her hostage here and fucked her through the storm? Fucked her all through the day and night?

What in the hell had she been thinking? Just barging up in here like that. And then she heard the drum of rain beating on the roof and the shudder of the palm trees and she remembered why.

The storm.

She eyed the muscular hunk warily, one eye in the direction toward the door. Could she make a mad dash for it, make her great escape, before he—

"Are your panties wet? And *not* from the rain."

Krista's eyes widened; part shock, part embarrassment.

"I beg your—"

He pressed two very long and very thick fingers to her lips. "Sssh. Say nothing. I bet you're so wet I could stuff all four of my thick fingers inside you."

Her skin flushed, while she fought to control her panicked breathing.

Oh, God, no. *The Lord is my shepherd . . .*

More thunder, more lighting.

The hunk slowly removed his fingers from Krista's quivering mouth. "You're safe here, baby," he said seductively low. "And so is your secret."

Secret?

She had no secrets. Yes, she was wet. Soaked. And, *yes*, her panties were damp. Because her dress was drenched, not for any other reason, thank you very much!

Then, um, why was she standing here shivering and *not* from a chill in the air?

Why were her nipples suddenly aching to be touched?

And, why—for heaven's sake—was there a slow throb between Krista's trembling thighs?

Simple.

Because temptation was all around her.

Because the devil was a damn lie . . .

Twenty-Seven

"Thanks for coming in to see me," Dr. Dangerfield said as she watched LaQuandra settle in the seat across from her.

LaQuandra ran a hand through her braids, and then removed her sunglasses. "Did I have a choice?" she asked, propping her purse up on her lap.

Dr. Dangerfield smiled. It was forced, but still offered nonetheless. The couples were already at the halfway mark of their stay on the island and Dr. Dangerfield had still not been able to find anything she liked about LaQuandra. She wanted to. Tried to. But her shitty attitude made it that more difficult.

She answered in kind, "We always have a choice, Mrs. Lewis. Even when the choices we have aren't the most pleasing."

LaQuandra offered a grunt as her response.

"How are things with you and your husband?"

LaQuandra gripped the straps of her purse. "He still hasn't fucked me, if that's what you're asking."

"I wasn't asking that, per se. I meant, overall, how are things with the two of you? Are you communicating better?"

LaQuandra gave a one-shouldered shrug. "Aside from his one-worded answers, we're not arguing."

"Well, that's a good start. Constant bickering can be damaging to any relationship, especially when hurtful things have been said. Things that can't be taken back once they're said."

LaQuandra said nothing. She shifted in her chair.

"I guess you're wondering why I asked you to come in today?"

"Yeah, the thought crossed my mind. Mind telling me?"

Dr. Dangerfield nodded. "Well, I wanted to talk a little bit more about the lack of intimacy in your marriage."

LaQuandra frowned. "Why you want to talk to *me* about it? Isaiah's the one with the intimacy issues, not me."

"Perhaps," Dr. Dangerfield agreed. "However, the lack of intimacy in your marriage is affecting you, am I right?"

Dr. Dangerfield believed marriage was more than a mere contract. It was a covenant that entailed being not only physically present in the marriage, but emotionally, spiritually, and sexually giving. Sex was an important component of any healthy marriage. To think otherwise was foolish.

LaQuandra swallowed. "Of course it is." She turned her attention toward the sculpture of the naked man, her eyes fixed on its enormous erection. She felt her cunt clutch in want.

"Has he told you he doesn't love you anymore?"

LaQuandra peeled her gaze from the erotic statue and shook her head. "No. Not in so many words. But his actions . . ." She paused, taking a deep breath. She didn't want to get into this, her feelings, today, didn't want to think about them, but this messy bitch was trying to drudge shit up, and now she felt herself on the verge of tears.

She needed a drink.

"What do you think is the cause of him pulling away from you, emotionally?" Dr. Dangerfield asked cautiously. "Do you think he's no longer in love with you?"

LaQuandra scoffed. "Do I look like I have a crystal ball? How should I know? I'm not the relationship expert. Shouldn't you be asking *him* that? I mean, damn, you're the one making over six-figures, I'm sure, to ask stupid-ass questions. So go ask him, because I'm tired of asking, and I'm tired of begging. The shit's exhausting."

LaQuandra felt her chest tighten. She hadn't wanted to consider that to be the case, but the writing was scrawled out all over the walls. And she couldn't deny it—Isaiah wasn't in love with her. Had he ever been?

Dr. Dangerfield ignored LaQuandra's outburst. She knew that her pain ran much deeper than the lack of intimacy in her marriage.

"I want you to tell me how your husband's emotional and sexual neglect makes you feel."

LaQuandra huffed. Hadn't she gone through this already with her in her session with Isaiah some weeks ago? Hadn't she been clear enough, how Isaiah not making love to her made her feel?

Worthless.

Ugly.

Rejected.

Unlovable.

Unwanted.

Abandoned.

Should she go on?

Isaiah not touching her, shutting her out emotionally and physically, made her feel alone. And it took her right back to that dark, ugly place she'd spent her entire life trying to forget.

Home.

Where she'd never felt wanted.

"I imagine you miss your husband. And now that he's robbed you of his touch, of his love, that takes you to a very dark place. And I'm sure that is frightening. And very lonely."

Shockingly, LaQuandra choked back a sob. Dr. Dangerfield had summed it all up in one big, ugly-ass nutshell. She disliked this meddling bitch. Yet the power of Dr. Dangerfield's words seemed to thicken the air around her. For the love of God, she missed him so much. Missed the way he used to look at her. The way they used to fit so good together.

Or maybe she'd simply imagined it all. Maybe they'd always been misfits, a hodgepodge of bullshit and emotional baggage. Maybe they'd been everything she imagined them to be because it was simply what she had wanted to believe, what she *needed* to believe.

Who else would ever love an ugly black bitch, with kinky hair, like her?

She was ugly. Baldheaded. Bucktoothed. Had no ass. She was all tits and big lips.

Her mother had made it her life work to remind her of those flaws. Hurtful words used to admonish her, to hate herself, to despise the color of her own beautiful dark skin.

Growing up, she had to compete with the prettier girls, the lighter-skinned girls, for the attention of boys. She had to fuck them (one, two, sometimes three at a time) to get them to look at her.

Eventually, after a countless number of sex partners—she'd stopped counting after seventy (she'd kept a diary up until she graduated college)—she'd mastered how to mask her pain with meaningless moaning and emotionless orgasms.

Consequently, her mother upgraded her from "ugly, black, baldheaded bitch" to "little black slutty bitch" and then it was "the ugly-bitch with the good pussy" from the boys, who'd pulled their hard dicks out every chance they'd gotten.

Fucking had nothing to do with her libido. It had everything to do with her self-esteem. If her mother belittled her, she fucked. If she had a bad day at school, she sucked dick. If a prettier, more popular girl made a snide comment about her, she fucked. Maybe even the prissy bitch's boyfriend. If she got an A on a progress report or a test, she sucked dick and fucked.

Fucking, fucking, fucking . . .

It was the only time LaQuandra had felt wanted. Momentarily, she'd felt special. Yes, sadly, only when she was lying flat on her back, or down on her knees between a boy's legs, or taking it from the back. So what if they usually had to be smoked out or drunk. They'd still wanted her.

Her.

They'd cheat on their pretty bitches to feel the inside of *her* pussy. Even if it was a late-night creep—out in the woods, in some abandoned building, behind bleachers, in the backseat of some old, beat-up car. Even if they only wanted to smash and dash, they had still wanted a piece of her. She made them feel good. Made them want to do things, nasty things, to her that they wouldn't do to those uptight uppity bitches they'd parade around during daytime hours.

Eventually, she'd learned to love it when they'd talked dirty to her.

"Eat this nut, bitch . . ."

"Suck this dick, ho . . ."

"Take this fat dick, smut . . ."

She'd learned to love being called dirty names. At least she wasn't being called *ugly*.

Freaky bitch.

Nasty ho.

Slut-ass.

However, no matter what they'd called her growing up, there was one thing that she'd taken pride in: the fact that she had good pussy and sucked dick and ate cum like a pro.

Fast-forward, fifteen abortions and dozens of STDs later, LaQuandra snagged the only man who'd made her heart fill with something other than lust. A nineteen-year-old boy from Hempstead, New York, who had a thick, curved dick and the ability to stroke her G-spot over and over and make her squirt, something no other boy—or man—had been able to do.

She was eight years his senior, but he handled her and her body like a grown man.

LaQuandra knew then that she would have to do whatever it took to reel him in before the rest of the thirsty Brick City (Newark, NJ) bitches got their hooks into him.

Isaiah Lewis.

So she spoiled him with the latest footwear and designer digs and fucked him real good every chance she got until she'd finally gotten him to move in with her. And every night, she'd fuck him to sleep, then wake him up with the sweet sounds of her sucking his dick wetly and sloppily. Then she feigned being pregnant. Then faking a miscarriage several months later, after she'd gotten him down to City Hall, where they'd said, "I do."

Deep down, LaQuandra knew she hadn't gotten Isaiah to marry her because he had fallen madly in love with her. No. He'd fallen in love with the pussy and all of the trappings that came along with sexing down a dick-whipped bitch. And now LaQuandra felt her own guilt creeping up inside of her. Their marriage hadn't been built on love. It'd been built on lies. Deceit. And, although, she'd allowed Isaiah a glimpse at a few bones of her past, she'd managed to keep the skeletons in her closet buried beneath the floorboards.

Twenty-Eight

Dr. Dangerfield glanced up at the time in the right-hand corner of her laptop, and shook her head—not surprised that Krista was a no-show for her individual session today. That woman was a walking ball of self-denial and delusions to think her marriage was any less troubled than Brenda's or LaQuandra's. But Dr. Dangerfield wasn't in the habit of forcing anyone to see what he or she refused to see. And she definitely wasn't in the business of chasing anyone down. Either you wanted help. Or you didn't.

Period.

So if Krista wanted to stay in denial, then she'd leave her right there, stuck in it. Hell, it wasn't her marriage on the line. She wasn't the one too blind to see that she wasn't giving her husband all that she could sexually. If she couldn't see that she was missing out on the very best parts of her husband's sexual self, then shame on her.

So fuck Krista Evans—and her no-show ass.

Dr. Dangerfield had no problem putting her time to better use, healthier use; more exciting use. She hurriedly typed in the last line of her treatment note, saved her file. And then shut her laptop just as a knock sounded at the door. She looked up to see the object of her desire standing at the door.

Sin.

"You ready for me?" he asked, allowing the lust he felt for her to pour out into the room.

Dr. Dangerfield smiled, standing to greet him. "I'm always ready . . . for *sin*."

He laughed, walking in and then shutting the door behind him.

"Yeah, baby. That's what I like to hear." And then he was pulling her into his arms, so she landed against the muscled wall of his chest. "So fucking beautiful, so sexy," he said hoarsely. And then he surged forward, taking her mouth with his, hungrily and greedily. Their mouths melted hot, their tongues dancing wetly around the others.

She groaned into his mouth as her hands roamed over his hard body. Suddenly desperate to have nothing between them, they tore at each other's clothing until their clothes went flying—his shirt this way, her dress that way, her bra smacking against the door, his pants hitting the wall—until his delicious dick was between them, sandwiched tightly against her belly.

She stood in her heels as they continued their kiss, his mouth moving hotly over hers, the plushness of her soft breasts, even the turgid points of her now-hard nipples, searing his flesh. Dr. Dangerfield released a delicious sigh because those *lips*, that *mouth*. Oh God, as if she weren't already on the verge of creaming her thong—there went his tongue again.

And he'd only been inside her office all of two minutes.

Dr. Dangerfield leaned further into his kiss, melting and sighing in sweet surrender, giving in to Sin. He licked delicately over her plump bottom lip, nipping lightly with his teeth, then licking over it again until he was back inside her mouth.

She met his tongue with the tip of hers, brushing softly over it, until Sin nearly groaned aloud. God, she tasted so sweet, so feminine. Sin's dick roared to life.

Dr. Dangerfield straddled him and then quickly fit him to her heated opening and without hesitation, she slid down and engulfed him in one motion, deeply into her body. Wet fire.

"Fuck," he groaned. "Pussy so wet."

"For you," she said. She needed this. Needed him.

Sin's strong hands slid to her ass, cupping her there as she rose up, her pussy gliding wetly up over his shaft to the head of his dick. Dr. Dangerfield sucked in her breath until she was nearly light-headed. And then she slid back down, taking all of him all over again, to the balls, her ass coming to rest on his lap.

Thick, nine inches of sin, that's what he was. He felt so big inside her, but Dr. Dangerfield reveled in the tightness, her body welcoming the sweet agony of her stretching cunt.

"Oh, yes," she pushed out, finally, over a breath as he palmed her breasts and then put his mouth to one nipple, sucking ravenously.

Dr. Dangerfield's swollen pussy clutched, squeezing him as she rhythmically galloped up and down the length of him.

"Goddamn, baby," Sin hissed. He loved the way, like Nairobia, she wasn't afraid of the dick. She didn't run from it. Hell nah. She rode it. And owned it. Made the dick hers every-and-any-time they were together.

And Sin loved that shit.

Dr. Dangerfield rose up slowly, inch by inch until she clutched only the head of his dick, using her muscles to suck him there as she slowly twirled her hips, rocking her body over the crown of his dick.

She paused for a moment, staring at him. His eyes glittered as he stared into hers. She was bad as fuck. The kind of woman he could love—maybe—if he were the loving a one-woman kind of guy. He loved pussy and pleasing it—lots of it—more than he believed he could ever love a woman.

"Let me fuck you." The words rumbled gruffly from somewhere deep in his chest. "Balls deep, baby. Let me bury this dick inside your guts."

"Oh Sin!"

His erotic words heated over her, splintering more need through her body, pushing her that closer toward release; her entire body bowed and then spasmed. And then her juices were gushing out around him, soaking him, his balls, and the leather sofa beneath them.

"Now, this pussy is all mine," he breathed, cupping her by the ass and then rising to his feet, his dick still impaled inside her body. He gripped her ass and then slammed her up and down on this dick, pushing himself up and into her, faster, harder, stroking over her G-spot until Dr. Dangerfield was crying out his name.

"Oh Sin, Oh Sin, Oh Sin . . ."

He carried her over to his, thrusting up into her with each step until he bent at the knees and set her ass on the edge of the desk, sweeping everything off her work space, knocking the contents to the floor.

He lifted her legs and parted them up over his shoulders, but then he flipped one of her heels off and sucked her toes into his mouth.

And Dr. Dangerfield cried out and arched upward, her legs shaking spasmodically.

"Play with yourself," he rasped over a mouthful of toes. And so she did, her hand going between them, her index and middle fingers going to her clit.

"Oh," she breathed out, her head lolling backward as her eyes slowly rolled to the back of her head.

Sin licked the sole of her foot, then sucked its heel into his mouth, his dick moving swiftly in and out of Dr. Dangerfield as he bathed her foot with his mouth and tongue.

"Oh, oh, ohhhh," she mewled.

Finally, he released her foot from his mouth and leaned in for her lips again, gently sucking them into his mouth, before sweeping his tongue back inside. They stayed this way for a while, kissing, him stroking her until Sin finally withdrew, enjoying the sensuous slide from her body. Her pussy was good. Not as good as Nairobia's, but still—very, very, goddamn good. He slammed forward and began thrusting into her slippery heat, hard and deep. Faster. Harder.

"Oh, fuck," he gritted out.

Dr. Dangerfield's eyes rolled back in her head again. She'd never felt anything so goddam good in her life. Sin—oh, God, yes. There was nothing like sinning for him.

Sin.

Yes, yes, yes . . .

"Oh God, Sin, don't stop. Keep fucking me . . . *mmm* . . . yes, just like this."

"I got you, baby," he rasped out as he pounded into her, the force of his thrusts causing her breasts to jiggle enticingly, her nipples so hard and beaded that his mouth watered.

He leaned in and sucked one of her nipples into his hot mouth.

"Aah," Dr. Dangerfield moaned. And then razor-sharp need splintered through her as he bit down into her turgid peak. Her orgasm swelled around the width of his dick.

"Oh, Sin," she whispered, his name nearly a groan.

"Yeah, baby," he murmured, grabbing her hips, "give me all that pussy." His thrusts deepened, quickened. "Aah, fuck . . . nut all over this dick . . ."

"*Uh, uh* . . . come with me," she cried out, her voice nearly pleading.

Sparring tongues.

Sloshing juices.

Damp skin slapping.

Sin's body sizzled inside her raw, creamy pussy. He wanted to stay right here, inside her wet, juicy heat, but he knew better.

He groaned.

Then reluctantly, begrudgingly, he pulled out of her body, and frantically grabbed hold of his wet dick and stroked himself, his body violently jerking as he shot his hot load all over the front of her, covering her clit and the seam of her pussy.

"Ah, ah, ah . . ." His body jerked one last time as more nut spurted out of him. Then he rubbed his sticky dick over her glistening sex, smearing his nut into her skin, before sliding back inside her body. He stayed that way, staring at her, peering into her soul until Dr. Dangerfield closed her eyes, shutting him out of that part of her.

Sin smiled. He'd already seen what he needed to see. Unfettered desire. He leaned in and kissed her until his dick went limp and wetly slipped out of her still quivering cunt.

Twenty-Nine

Dirty Talk . . .

It was the art of seducing a lover with arousing words.

Flirty.

Filthy.

Sexy.

Used to build sexual tension.

To keep him/her thinking about you, about the promise of what was to come.

To illicit toe-curling orgasms.

Sultry whispers.

Deep soulful tones.

It could be subtle. Indirect. Or brazenly direct.

Text messages. Telephone calls.

Letters and notes . . .

Or in person.

The idea was to play on words, to tantalize.

Yes, dirty talk. It wasn't what you said, but *how* you said it that stoked the libido.

And today Dr. Dangerfield had enlisted the help of Nairobia (the queen of seduction) to help her get the couples' sexual juices flowing.

Roselle, Isaiah, and Kendall were seated in white leather chairs.

All three men were donned in white. Loosely fitted drawstring linen pants, unbuttoned linen shirts. And they were barefoot.

Waiting . . .

Dr. Dangerfield thought the contrast of the white against their bronzed, dark-chocolate, and cocoa-brown (in that order) skin was beautiful. They looked handsome, especially Kendall—with his smooth, bald head.

For a split-second, she imagined her tongue gliding down the center of his head and nearly swooned. She almost allowed herself to get swept up in the imagery, but Asiahn singing in the background about role-playing quickly brought her back to this very moment.

"I can be whoever you need . . . we role-play . . ."

And that's exactly what Brenda, LaQuandra, and Krista would be doing.

Role-playing.

Dr. Dangerfield and Nairobia had spent the last two hours coaching the women on the art of dirty talk. No surprise, Brenda and LaQuandra already had it mastered.

But Krista?

Krista, Krista, Krista . . .

She—Dr. Dangerfield shook her head—was a hot mess. Krista was just too tightly wound to let go. She didn't appreciate dirty talk in the bedroom—initiated or not. It wasn't in her repertoire to talk dirty. She was okay with a little "give me that wet pussy" this and a little "ride this dick, baby" that, but nothing more. And definitely no *B*-words or using the *C*-word. There was nothing sexy about being called a bitch or that *other* word. It felt dirty and disrespectful and degrading.

The three women were in the back getting dressed, getting primed, and ready to turn their men on. They were tasked with choosing an outfit, something sexy, provided to them by the island's Passion Collection.

Red—the color of fire and passion and desire—would be worn.

Dusk was upon them.

The ocean rolled in back of them.

The candles were lit.

The music was playing low.

Now all they needed were the women.

Dr. Dangerfield was anxious to see what they'd chosen to wear to represent them—their sexy, seductive—selves.

Sevdaliza's "Sirens of the Caspian" began to play. And, in dramatic Nairobia-style, she was the first to step through the archway. Breathtaking. Standing. Cascading in diamonds. Hands on hips. Legs spread apart. The silhouette of her sculpted body showed through her diamond-encrusted mesh gown.

In back of her, stood Brenda—her thighs and breasts on display in a red hip-hugging dress. In back of Brenda was LaQuandra. She'd chosen a red skintight silk halter-top gown, with one very long slanted split that stopped at the center of her pussy. A diamond choker dressed her slender neck.

Although she wasn't in the mood to talk dirty to Isaiah's ass, she wanted the bastard to see and hear what he could be getting. Besides, she was more than happy to play dress-up for a night and wear expensive gowns and exquisite jewels.

Last, but not least, was Krista in a red . . . *pantsuit.*

Where was the seduction in that?

Nairobia had exhausted precious breath trying to coax the sexual sloth (what she called men and women who were uninspiring and uncreative in the sheets) into something a bit more revealing. But Krista had been insistent. She wanted the pantsuit. But she'd begrudgingly agreed to ditch the blouse and wear a red bustier in place of it—a first for her. And now she was standing here uncomfortable, feeling exposed and sinful.

This whole island was nothing but the devil's playground.

All this red, all this sexual music, all this naked flesh, all this—

Dr. Dangerfield nearly dropped to her knees and cried out to the heavens when she spotted Krista. She stared on instead.

"Krissy is," LaQuandra whispered in back of Brenda, "dressed like she's on her way to a J.C. Penney catalog photo shoot."

Brenda shushed her, biting back a laugh. Poor Krista. The suit was *cute*. But it didn't scream, *take me!* If anything, it cried, *free Willy!*

Roselle and Isaiah and Kendall latched their gazes on Nairobia.

"Goddamn," Isaiah hissed, admiring his wet dream.

Nairobia seductively sauntered down the catwalk-like ramp, pressing a perfectly manicured hand over her earpiece. "Good evening, my loves," she said, addressing the three men, "I give you your wives,"—she spread open her arms—"Brenda, LaQuandra, and Krista. And tonight they will seduce you, not in deeds, my darlings, but with words. So sit back and prepare yourself for a night of dirty talk . . ."

Kendall's cyes widened, surprise registering over his face. Krista and dirty talk just didn't fit in the same sentence. Oh I gotta see this shit, he thought as he looked on.

Brenda, always ready for a turn-up, shimmied her shoulders, causing her breasts to shake, as she walked.

"Yeah, baby," Roselle said, a fist pumping in the air. "Do that shit. My baby, sexy as fuck."

Brenda slid her tongue out of her mouth, and then when she reached Roselle's chair, she stood in front of him. A hand on her hip, she struck her best seductive pose.

LaQuandra followed suit, two-stepping her non-rhythmic-having ass, down the narrow walkway. Isaiah had to admit, LaQuandra looked good. Maybe it was the lighting, or the way the makeup artist painted her face; either way, he was impressed.

The minute she reached Isaiah, she did as she'd been instructed—the way they'd rehearsed in the back—and stopped, both hands on her hips, legs spread, her thigh peeping out from her split. She tried not to look at Isaiah. But he looked good in all white. Lord, this bastard . . .

And then came Krista, clumsily, making her way toward Kendall in a pair of four-inch heels. They were way too high for her and the strap over her foot was cutting into her skin. Her damn foot was swollen. But she'd push through it, she told herself. Just like she'd push through this ridiculous stage show.

Dirty talk. *Mmp.* This whole experience was taking her out of her comfort zone.

Kendall smiled at her the second she reached him. He winked at her.

"You look good, baby," he said.

Krista rolled her eyes, but—in spite of herself, she smiled.

Even Dr. Dangerfield felt her lips curving into a smile of her own as she watched on.

"Now, my darlings," Nairobia coached. "Lean forward and grab the arms of your husbands' chairs. Then look him in his eyes . . ."

The three women did, their arms capturing their respective men, boxing them in.

"Now look him in the eyes," Nairobia said saucily, "and tell him you love him."

Brenda and Krista repeated the words with ease.

LaQuandra, however, swallowed. She did love Isaiah, but the way he'd been treating her, he didn't deserve to hear it. He stared at her, smirking.

"You know you love me," he said cockily.

She rolled her eyes. "Fuck you, Isaiah, okay."

"Yeah, talk dirty, Quandra," he said over another smirk.

"Eat my ass," she snapped.

Isaiah laughed. That was some shit his son's mother would say. "You been drinking?"

"Yeah, and? I had a few nips. Why?"

He shook his head. "Figures. Your drunk-ass needs—"

"Now, *mijn liefdes*," Nairobia said, cutting Isaiah off, "lean into your husbands' ears and whisper, 'I want you.' Let him know how badly you can't wait to make love to him. Tell him how you can't wait to love all over *zijn lul*—his dick. How you want to lick it. Tease the head and then suck him deep . . ."

"You know I'm not into this kinda shit," Brenda said flatly.

"I know, baby," Kendall said softly. "But do it for me. Let me hear you talk dirty."

Nairobia noticed Krista's hesitation and eased her way over toward her and Kendall.

She sauntered in back of Kendall's chair, her erotic scent sweeping around them. Nairobia glided her hands over Kendall's shoulders and then slowly down his arms, leaning over him, his smooth head nestled in the center of her bosom.

Her mic now off, Nairobia pressed her cheek against Kendall's, eyeing Krista. "Love your man with your words, my darling. Get into his thoughts. Tell him how good he makes your *kut* feel . . ."

Krista frowned.

"Your pussy, my darling. Tell this fine chocolate man how good he feels inside of you." Nairobia gave Krista a hard stare. "Tell him."

Krista caught the way Kendall was looking at her, all lusty-eyed and she wasn't sure if it was because of this freaky-bitch or if he'd already had that look in his eyes before Nairobia had come over here, brushing her titties all over her man.

Krista leaned in, her lips flush to Kendall's other ear, and said, "I love the way you touch me. I love the way you stroke me . . ."

"Damn, baby," he murmured.

"I can't wait to have you tonight," Krista pushed out, determined to not let this bitch upstage her.

"*You* are good love," Nairobia whispered in Kendall's other ear. And then she urged Krista to tell him how wet he made her, how she loved when he stroked her deep. The sound of Nairobia's sultry voice had Kendall's head spinning, his thoughts now swimming in images of *her* licking over his balls and then sliding her tongue in his ass.

Nairobia pulled back, her fingertips lightly grazing over Kendall's bald head, then down the back of his neck, then over his shoulder. "Tell your husband how good he feels on your tongue, how good he tastes in your mouth."

"I-I . . ." Krista's face flushed, shame washing over her. She couldn't. She'd never *tasted* him. A nut in her mouth—oh God no. And—hell, his dick brushing over her tongue wasn't a favorite of hers—had this bitch not been briefed?

"C'mere, baby," Kendall said, pulling Krista onto his lap, rescuing her from further embarrassment. Truth was, he appreciated Krista's gesture. It needed work—lots of it, but still, she'd tried. And that was all that mattered.

A sly smile eased over Nairobia's glossed lips. Her work with Krista was done. She was a helpless sap. "*Deze teef is een waardeloos lay*," Nairobia murmured.

Kendall grinned, turned on even more by Nairobia's dialect, thinking she'd said something utterly sexy, before sauntering off, when what she'd said was: "this bitch is a worthless lay."

Mic back on, Nairobia said, "Tell your husbands what you can't wait to do to him tonight. Say it slow and sultry. To him, my loves, you want him to stretch himself into your heat . . ."

Roselle grinned as Brenda's lips brushed against his earlobe, her breath warming his skin. "I want you so badly, baby," she cooed. "I can't wait to suck your dick and feel your nut bust all in my mouth." She moaned. Then lapped her tongue over his ear. "Me and my wet kitty can't wait for you to make slow, sweet love to us . . ."

"Keep talking that nasty shit, baby," Roselle responded as his dick swelled in his pants. "You gonna fuck around 'n' have me fuck you right now. All that sweet, juicy ass in that skimpy-ass dress. Got my dick brick, baby."

"Mmm, you make my pussy so wet," Brenda murmured, slowly winding her hips to the music that played in the background. Two Feet sang about twisted love.

"Sinking . . . sinking love . . . sinking . . ."

Yes, she was that type of girl. The one to get down and dirty with her man, for her man, and over her man; Brenda would kill a bitch and she'd kill him, too.

"Your dick feels so good inside of me," she whispered. And then she nipped Roselle's ear with her teeth.

A few feet away, Isaiah sat with his arms folded. He wanted to stay in the moment, but LaQuandra's mouth and bullshit made it difficult for him. And, as he sat here, all he kept wondering was why the hell he was really here—on this island. Was his marriage really worth saving?

"I wanna suck your dick tonight," LaQuandra stated in as sexy of a voice as she could muster given the circumstances. "It's time you fuck me, Isaiah." She pulled back and looked Isaiah in the eyes, so that he knew just how serious she was. "I need you to *fuck* me."

Isaiah blinked, LaQuandra's face was mere inches from his. "We not here for that, Quandra," he said nonchalantly. "We're here for other shit—to fix this marriage. Remember?"

"And how the hell is that working out for us so far, huh, Isaiah?"

LaQuandra felt herself beginning to shake from the inside out. She struggled to stay on script, but between the four shots of Tequila, her hormones, and thoughts of that bitch Cassandra creeping up in her head, she couldn't help herself—no, she really didn't want to—so she grabbed Isaiah's face and dug her fingertips into his jaws and said, "Does that ghetto bitch suck your dick the way I do? Has she ever fucked you to sleep, like me?"

And then she mushed his face back.

"What the fuck?" he snapped.

"No, tell me," she insisted. "Is that trashy bitch sucking your dick, huh, Isaiah?"

This time, she spoke over the music, loud enough for everyone else to hear.

Dr. Dangerfield looked over at the couple.

"Tell me, Isaiah! Is that bitch's pussy as wet and juicy as mine?"

"Chill, Quandra," Isaiah said calmly, but he was boiling inside. "You asking shit that isn't a part of the program."

"Fuck a program, motherfucker! I'm standing here pretending with your ass, feeling like some stupid, thirsty-ass bitch. I'ma boss-bitch, nigga! If you want that trashy bitch, then you can go be with her. I'm sick of this shit."

Isaiah scowled, allowing her to see how pissed her tirade made him.

"Bitch, you crazy as fuck." Isaiah jumped up from his chair and pushed LaQuandra out of his way, causing her to stumble. "I'm out."

If LaQuandra wanted all eyes on her, she now had them.

Six sets of eyes, all watching, waiting . . .

As she picked herself up from off the floor.

Thirty

Krista glanced over at Kendall, who was lightly snoring. He hadn't stirred since his head hit the pillow and he'd fallen asleep. He was sleeping soundly. Peacefully. But Krista spent a terrible night tossing and turning.

Her mind racing, her thoughts consuming her, Krista couldn't shake the feeling gnawing at the pit of her soul. She couldn't quite put a finger on it, but something felt . . . *off.*

Different.

Or maybe it felt too *good.*

Either way, she was beginning to think coming here was a mistake—a very, very big one. There was way too much temptation here. Too much sin surrounded her, surrounded them. All this sexual energy that hovered in the atmosphere wasn't good. Too much of anything never was.

Krista rose quietly from the bed, careful not to wake Kendall. She sighed, stretching her sore muscles, and then stumbled over to one of the dressers and opened the top drawer, pulling out a nightgown—a powder-blue one with pink roses dotted all over it. She slipped it over her naked body. And then she retied the black silk scarf she'd wrapped around her head last night to hold her hair in place back into a neat bow.

She shuffled to the bathroom, padded thumps of her feet muffled into the thick carpet, to relieve herself. She washed her hands, still feeling Kendall's heavy erection between her legs. Then she returned to bed, glancing at the window as the first light of morning softly illuminated the room.

Krista's gaze then lingered over Kendall's body. His back stretched wide, his large hand clutching the sheets, the top sheet covering his ass and legs. She thanked God for him. Every waking moment, she gave the glory to Him—for blessing her life, for blessing her marriage.

Krista crawled back into bed.

Girl, stop this damn foolishness, Krista mentally scolded. *That bitch is only an illusion, a fantasy. Kendall's ass isn't thinking about some damn porn star whore.*

Mmph. She knew Kendall loved her. Knew he was devoted to her. Yes, she'd done well for herself. She'd snatched herself one prize of a man. Honest. Hardworking. Good provider. Good lover. Faithful.

She'd prayed for a man like him. And God had saw fit to grace her and He had come right on time.

He always did.

They'd met at Liberty State Park in Jersey City. She'd been there for her church's thirtieth annual family day picnic. He'd been there, over on the other side of the massive park, for his family's thirtieth (a sign right there) family reunion. He'd bumped into her as she was struggling to drag a large cart packed with aluminum pans of food. Kendall had been headed to the parking lot to grab the two bags of ice he'd forgotten in his truck, but he'd stopped and asked Krista if she'd needed some help.

Of course she did.

And, yes, she'd sized him up. He was tall enough. Handsome enough. And he seemed harmful enough. So she accepted his offer.

Forgetting about the melting ice in the backseat of his SUV,

Kendall took the handle of her cart from her and pulled it with ease, eyeing Krista out of his peripheral, catching the swell of her breasts hidden beneath her I LIVE & LOVE FOR THE LORD T-shirt and the curve of her hips, that she'd tried to hide under an ankle-length skirt—some farm girl shit that reminded him of something worn on that old-ass television show *Little House on The Prairie* his grandmother—rest her soul—had loved watching.

Still, Kendall had thought Krista was cute. A bit homely, but underneath her plain-Jane look, he saw her beauty. And he'd told her so, right there at the park, while she'd graciously fixed him a hefty plate of a little bit of this and little bit of that—a thank you gesture for helping her with her cart.

And then he'd boldly asked her for her number—right there in front of Pastor Hurtson, of all people, with his prying, judging eyes taking it all in. However, Krista didn't dare give out her number to a *stranger*, no matter how fine said stranger was, or how sexily said stranger's jeans had hung from his hips—loosely fitted, but still fitted enough to show he was handsomely endowed.

Not that size had mattered. Well, okay, it *did* matter. Sometimes. Okay, hell, most times. But Krista hadn't had sex in nearly three months. She'd been on a hundred-and-eighty-day cleanse—a self-imposed detox from hard dick. And, although, she'd secretly been horny, she'd had no intentions of breaking her pledge of celibacy—not until she'd married a God-fearing, church-going man.

But there had been something about the way that Kendall had looked at her when he'd asked for number. He had looked at her. Right at *her*. With those intense brown eyes, he stared, taking her in, waiting for her response.

And in that moment, she'd felt her inner walls clench—and she knew *he* was the one she'd been praying for. Even he hadn't stepped inside of a church in ages.

Still, Krista had done what any good Christian woman would have done while Pastor eyed you like a hawk. She'd coyly taken his instead. And then she had held on to it for months, before curiosity and boredom and a relentless throb between her thighs, along with her sister Latrice's insistence that she was going to end up being an old maid with a dry-rotted crotch if she didn't find herself a good man with some good dick to *shake the dust loose* from her *cooch.*

So she'd called Kendall. Asked him if he'd like to see her.

Sure he did. An hour later, he'd picked her up and they'd caught that new Denzel Washington movie, the one she'd really hadn't wanted to see but ended up enjoying after all. And Kendall had been gentlemanly afterward; too damn much so. But she'd liked his calm disposition and quiet strength and the fact that he made her feel special so much that she couldn't wait to see him again.

Three dates later, Krista had invited Kendall inside her panties.

And he'd fucked her and made her forget all about some silly-ass rule of waiting, holding out on sex until some church pimp swept her off her feet.

No, Kendall, had already done that.

Six months later, he married her.

Yes, yes, yes—God, yes—Krista had a damn good man.

And she loved Kendall for that.

She hadn't really considered herself an insecure woman, but somehow—she'd found herself questioning herself, questioning her looks, questioning her body.

Was she really enough woman for Kendall after all these years of marriage?

Oh, God. She couldn't believe she was asking herself that. But she'd caught the way Kendall had gazed at Nairobia last night.

Bitch.

Slut.

Whore.

She'd never caught him before, gazing at another woman. Of course she knew he *looked.* All men did. But, last night, she'd caught him, and there'd been a glimmer of something—a smoldering heat—in Kendall's eyes that she didn't recall ever seeing before.

Sure, Kendall desired her sexually. Krista couldn't pretend otherwise. He'd proven that the moment they'd stepped inside the villa last night. He'd made love to her, ravished her. Dicked her down, the way she loved it.

Tenderly.

Lovingly.

Passionately.

"Tell me how good this dick is, baby . . . tell me how good this dick makes you feel . . ." he'd murmured, urging her on with every deep stroke of his dick.

"Yes, Kendall, baby, yes . . . it's so good. Oh sweet God, yes . . ."

And then when he'd emptied himself inside her, he'd lain there a long while, still inside her, as his breaths calmed, kissing her—her lips, her neck, her shoulders, smoothing his hands down her arms and then down her sides, telling her how beautiful she was, how much he loved her.

But was it really *her* that had had him so turned on? Or was it that bitch who'd had her damn titties all up on her man, feeling all up on him?

Krista hadn't appreciated that shit. She didn't need that bitch telling her how to talk to her man—her husband. *She* knew Kendall had good dick and that he was *good-loving*—and, shit, so did he. God forgive me, Krista thought, shaking her head. It was too early in the morning for all this heavy cursing.

Still . . . that *bitch!*

"Your pussy, my darling. Tell this fine chocolate man how good he feels inside of you." Krista *tsk*ed. Kendall knew how good he felt inside of her; Krista didn't need to tell him that. When *he* felt it every time they made love.

And yet, when she'd glanced down into Kendall's lap—while Nairobia was fawning all over him, Krista had seen his dick print. Rigid. Full. Ready.

His dick had been harder than it had been in years.

And now Krista was up, way before the crack of dawn, thinking, remembering . . .

The poor chunky church-girl with the dreadful plaited hair, the deacon's daughter with the overbite and the overly religious mother.

"You dirty heathen! You give praise. You give thanks. You give your life over to God. But you don't ever give yourself over to sin. You don't ever give a boy your body. You don't let him touch you there, lick you there, or stick you there. Ever. Or so help me, I will beat you dead . . ."

Those had been Krista's mother's harsh words to her—the whip-like anger of her tone slashing into her, when she'd walked in and caught her youngest child sharing her first kiss with thirteen-year-old Charlie Benson, while he was on top of her eleven-year-old body—her ruffled church dress up over her hips—grinding himself on her, over her white and pink-flowered panties, causing a friction between her legs that had magically caused heat to bloom in the pit of her belly, then spread out through her body, stretching to the tips of her toes.

"I will not raise a whore in my home. Strip!"

"No, momma. Please. I promise it won't ever happen again."

"Naked. Now."

"Momma, please . . ."

Slap.

"I will not give Satan the glory! I will not have some nasty heathen

in my home. I will cut out your crotch before I allow you to sin in my home. Strip!"

"No, momma. Please."

"Krista Nicole Blandberry. You do as I say . . ."

Slap!

And so eleven-year-old Krista did. She'd removed her clothes with trembling hands, her knees nearly knocking, and raised her arms high up over her head.

And then . . .

Gave into the lashings.

Determined not to go there, not to let those bad memories eat away at her, Krista shoved those thoughts solidly from her mind and propped herself on her elbow, content to watch while Kendall slept. She did that sometimes. Watched him sleep. She admittedly loved to watch him wake up, his eyes all dreamy, fogged with sleep and a half-smile on his face, before leaning in and kissing her on her lips, his morning breath clinging to hers.

She didn't have to be a whore to get him. And she didn't need to be a whore to keep him. All she had to do was keep him fucked. Her wet pussy kept him satisfied.

Krista smiled at that knowing, and then after a few more moments of staring, Krista reached her finger out to trace the sharp lines of his jaw. She followed it down and around and then over Kendall's lips, enjoying the feel of him beneath her fingertips.

Wasn't that what that bitch had urged the day out on the beach?

"*. . . Ladies, reach out and touch your men. Caress his face. Allow a finger to trace the curve of his lips. Let it linger there for a bit . . .*"

Kendall groaned, and then his lids fluttered and his eyes opened, immediately finding her gaze.

"Mornin'," he rasped, his voice groggy. "What time is it?"

Krista shrugged. "I don't know." She craned her neck and glanced over at the clock on the nightstand behind her. "Almost six."

Kendall inched closer and planted one of his morning kisses on her lips. Krista eyed him. And he sleepily made a face, feigning a frown. "What?"—Kendall cupped a hand over his mouth—"I know it's not my morning breath. I know how much you love it."

He pressed another kiss to her lips.

"Am I enough woman for you?" Krista asked in a quiet voice. "And don't lie to me."

Kendall studied her face, a raised brow, her stare intense; Krista burned her gaze into him. Shit. Where the hell was she going with this? He was too tired for a long talk, or interrogation. All he wanted to do was fall back to sleep.

He'd deal with this some other time—in counseling, with Dr. Dangerfield.

Not now.

"Of course you are, baby," he said softly, pulling her into his arms. Reluctantly, Krista reached for the covers around them and pulled them up over her as she snuggled against his side, curving her body into the hollow of his shoulder.

Kendall sighed, kissing the top of her head, and then he closed his eyes, wrapping his leg over hers, his morning hard-on pressing thickly against her flesh.

Krista sucked in her breath at how good he felt there, against her skin—all warm and heavy. Heat washed through her veins, and slowly she melted into Kendall's embrace.

Shit. Kendall wasn't going anywhere. That porn star bitch didn't have anything on her. She'd just been overly sensitive, acting paranoid over nothing.

Krista closed her eyes, and finally she relaxed and fell into sleep with him.

Thirty-One

"Girl," Brenda said, reaching over and grabbing LaQuandra's hand, "we haven't really had a chance to talk, since"—she tilted her head and tooted her lips—"your meltdown the other night. How you been making out?"

Brenda had invited LaQuandra and Krista to have a light lunch on the beach with her over cocktails, while the men had their session with Dr. Dangerfield. Krista had decided not to come—surprise, surprise. Which was probably for the best since Brenda wanted LaQuandra to speak freely about how she'd shown her naturally flat-ass on stage in front of everyone.

Brenda still couldn't believe Isaiah had knocked her to the floor. Lord, had that been Roselle—she would have beat his ass down with the heel of her shoe. But, then again, she wouldn't have made a spectacle of herself the way LaQuandra had. Ooh, she was ratchet. *Mmph. I wonder what that baby mother she's so jealous over looks like.*

LaQuandra gasped. Was this bitch trying to be low-key messy, because she damn sure didn't think the nosey heifer really cared one way or another about her *or* her damn man?

Nosey bitches stayed doing the most.

And then she frowned. "What meltdown?"

"Girl, don't play coy with me," Brenda said. "You know what meltdown I'm talking about. The one you had on stage the other night."

As Brenda spoke, LaQuandra's mouth dropped open, and she now sat gaping at Brenda. The gall of this bitch! Still, LaQuandra reached for her mimosa, took a quick swig, and then said, "Girl, you call that a meltdown? Ugh. Not hardly," she said dismissively. She stared at the other two flutes of champagne she'd ordered, before looking back at Brenda.

Brenda squeezed LaQuandra's hand. "Oh, hon, it's okay. Trust me. We've all been there, making a fool of ourselves over our men."

LaQuandra blinked, pulling her hand away.

"You know like I know," Brenda reassured her. "Love makes us do some crazy shit sometimes."

LaQuandra couldn't deny that truth. And she'd paid for it dearly when she and Isaiah had gotten back to the villa that night and the door had shut and locked behind them.

"Bitch, is you fuckin' crazy, huh?" Isaiah had hissed, snatching LaQuandra by the throat. He didn't want to put his hands on her, but she'd asked for it. Isaiah had tried to kill her, choking her nearly unconscious with one hand wrapped around her neck. "You ever put your motherfuckin' hands on me out in public again like that, and I'll beat your ass to sleep."

Tears had sprung from LaQuandra's eyes, blurring her vision as she had tried to claw his hands off of her, but the harder she tried to fight him off of her, the tighter his grip became around her neck. She'd seen it in his eyes, that wild, dark dangerous look of a man who'd been pushed too far. And she believed he would kill her, then dump her lifeless body in the ocean. All she kept thinking was, "God, not here. Let me get back to the States—away from all this damn water—before he kills me."

Isaiah must have seen the fear in her eyes, but he'd let her neck go and then she crumbled to the floor, gasping.

"Stupid bitch," he'd spat, before storming out of their villa.

That night LaQuandra had barely slept. She tried to convince herself that Isaiah's violent outburst had been unwarranted, that he was dead wrong for attacking her like that, but she'd known she'd gone too far. And she had to admit to herself that Isaiah had let her get away with a whole lot more than any other man would have probably done. But, shit, she'd put up with a whole lot more of Isaiah's shit than the average bitch would.

Still, she'd known she'd fucked up the moment she'd grabbed his face and dug her nails into his cheeks. That bitch Cassandra was winning. The thought of her completely losing Isaiah to his ratchet-ass BM made her sick to her stomach.

And she was scared of that possibility.

LaQuandra blinked Brenda in as her voice pulled her from out of her reverie. "You know I'm not judging you, girl," Brenda added. "I didn't want to say anything in front of Krista . . ."

LaQuandra rolled her eyes, but she was glad Brenda had used her discretion and waited for a time when Krista wasn't in the midst. That self-righteous bitch would do nothing but judge her.

Brenda reached up and shoved a lock of hair behind her ear, then rubbed her hands together. "So what's the tea, girl? Did your husband whoop that ass? Because I know I would have, if I'd been him. No man I know would have ever taken what you did lightly. I mean, it's fucked up how he pushed you to the floor. Now I didn't agree with that. I don't subscribe to a man beating on his woman in the streets. But, b-b-b*aaa*by, behind closed doors, your ass would have gotten handed to you on a stick. You a bold bitch, girl, to go in on your man like that out in public."

The only good thing about Brenda's long-winded diatribe was that it had given LaQuandra a chance to gulp back the rest of her Mimosa and conjure a reply that would, hopefully, shut her up.

LaQuandra's throat threatened to close up, but she managed, "He didn't push me. I tripped. And Isaiah doesn't *beat* my ass. Trust."

Oh. Brenda tilted her head and rapidly batted her mink lashes.

Now she was certain what she had seen. But, okay, if LaQuandra wanted to go there with her, who was she to tell her otherwise? It was her truth. Her story.

Who was she to try to rewrite it the way she'd seen it?

Brenda looked out toward the ocean for a bit, and allowed LaQuandra a moment to sit in her delusions while she sipped her drink. She knew she had her own problems, but, shit, Brenda was more than happy to have them rather than to have those that LaQuandra was faced with. A man cheating on you *and* beating your ass was way too much drama.

It needed to be one or the other. Not both.

Brenda brought her gaze back to LaQuandra; she wanted to change the subject to something a bit more light-hearted, but she couldn't let go of the question that nagged at her. Brenda knew it was none of her business, but she was nosey. So instead, she dug deeper into the matter, to the question that suddenly became more pressing to her.

"You really think he's still sleeping with his son's mother?"

Dread crowded LaQuandra's chest. "I know he is. I just can't prove it."

Brenda shook her head. "What are you gonna do?"

LaQuandra drained the other two flutes before setting them back down. And then she gave her head a tilt.

What *was* she going to do? Good question. She hadn't quite figured that part out, yet. But she knew without a doubt what she *wasn't* going to do.

LaQuandra's gaze hardened. "I'm not letting that bitch have my man."

"Good luck, sweetie," clung to Brenda's tongue. But she gave LaQuandra a half-smile instead, reaching over and putting her hand over hers.

Thirty-Two

"So tell me," Dr. Dangerfield started as she crossed her legs. "How are things going for the two of you?"

Krista's body stiffened. She wasn't sure she wanted to be here today. This was actually her first session with Kendall. And it was a week ago today that she'd brushed off her individual session with Dr. Dangerfield. Oh, well. She didn't need any one-on-one time with this woman—not like the damaged ones—*LaQuandra*—Krista believed. Her marriage wasn't troubled like the others, yet she still felt a bit on edge.

Kendall half-smiled. "It's going—"

Krista shot him a look, cutting him off. "Exactly what is that supposed to mean, Kendall?"

"C'mon, baby. Don't get defensive. All it means is that we're here taking in everything. If you had let me finish, you would have heard me say it was going good."

Oh.

Krista shifted in her seat.

Dr. Dangerfield crossed her legs at the ankles, and said, "Mrs. Evans. Why don't you tell me what's going through your mind at this very minute."

Krista rubbed her left forearm, then pulled imaginary lint from her shirt, before looking up at Dr. Dangerfield. "I'm wondering why I am really here. Why *we* are here?"

"I see," Dr. Dangerfield said. "Well, the purpose of being here is to help you and your husband to strengthen your bond through love and understanding and acceptance."

"I know all that," Krista stated. "But that's not Kendall and my issue. We have a strong marriage"—again, she glanced over at Kendall—"at least I hope we do."

And then Krista's gaze locked on Dr. Dangerfield's. "I don't cheat. And Kendall isn't cheating on me." She looked over at Kendall again, this time for substantiation. He couldn't, he wasn't ready to, answer that, so he reached over for her hand and she took that as validation. "So, what really is the problem?"

"I don't doubt you and your husband love one another," Dr. Dangerfield said as she opened a folder that she'd held in her lap since Krista and Kendall had walked into her office. "Do you remember the night you and your husband were in The Garden playing the couple's game?"

Krista shifted in her seat again. "Of course I do. Why?"

"Well, it was evident that although you know a lot about your husband, there were still things about him that you obviously didn't know."

Krista cut her eyes over at Kendall, then fixed her gaze back on Dr. Dangerfield.

"Like the fact that he wanted you to swallow him during oral sex," Dr. Dangerfield said, glancing down at her notes, "and that he preferred making love to you from the back rather than missionary . . ."

Krista felt her face heat. "Is there a point to all of this?" she asked. Yes. She was on the defense and she didn't really know why.

Dr. Dangerfield offered her a smile. "The point is, real intimacy comes when genuine connections are made, when compromise can be made and partners can be sexually transparent and honest with one another."

Krista frowned. "So are you trying to tell me that Kendall is keeping secrets from me, other than the fact that he likes to choke his chicken behind my back and has some idea that I should swallow his sperm?"

Dr. Dangerfield felt the urge to laugh in her face. "No, no, that's not what I'm proposing," she clarified instead. "But what I am suggesting, however, is that based on the questions you'd gotten wrong, it would seem that your husband has been keeping parts of who he is sexually from you. A partner should know that his or her partner enjoys masturbation, or what their favorite sexual positions might be."

Krista scoffed. "So because I didn't know that Kendall likes to play with himself, that means our marriage is in trouble?"

Dr. Dangerfield paused a beat, then said, "Tell me this, Mrs. Evans. After game night, did you talk to your husband at any time once you returned to your villa about any of his answers?"

"No," Krista stated.

"Well, why not?"

"Because honestly, I didn't feel like talking about it. If Kendall wants to play with himself—even though I give him sex three-to-four times a week, then let him. But what I do want to know is"—she turned to Kendall—"when are you doing this?"

Kendall shrugged. "Mostly when I'm home alone. But there are times when I masturbate when you're either asleep or I'm in the shower."

Krista grimaced. "So you're addicted to masturbating?"

Kendall shook his head. "No, baby. Nothing like that."

Krista raised a brow. "Then what is it?"

"I enjoy it," he said.

Krista scowled. "Well, what or *who* are you thinking about when you're doing it?"

Shit. He should have known that question was coming. He wasn't about to confess to her that he watched porn. The type that most men would never publicly admit to—let alone tell his wife. So a lie was better than the truth.

"I'm not really thinking of anything, most times, when—"

"Oh come off of it, Kendall," Krista interrupted. "Don't insult me. You are not going to sit here and tell me that your dick just gets hard and you're not thinking of something or *some*one."

Kendall shifted in his seat. Of course he thought of something—having his prostate milked. But he wasn't going to tell her that—not right now. Not after seeing how she was already acting about him masturbating.

Krista gave him a blank stare. Then blinked. And before he could answer her, she said, "What kind of man likes to play with a dick when he has a wife who screws him whenever he wants sex?"

Kendall frowned. The kind of man who isn't getting all of his sexual needs met from his wife, he wanted to say. "It's mine. Why can't I masturbate if I want? It's a part of me. Most times I just milk it. Tease myself. Most times I fantasize about you doing things you don't normally do with me in bed," he added.

Krista scoffed. "Ugh. I don't even want to know. Not right now."

Kendall looked over at Dr. Dangerfield and she took that as her cue to step in. "Mrs. Evans, when a man or woman who is partnered masturbates, it's not always a reflection on the other partner, nor does it have to do with not having a pleasingly healthy sex life."

"Oh, I know it's not because of *me*," Krista said indignantly. "So let me stop you right there." She shifted her attention back to Kendall. "So again, Kendall, what kind of man is playing with himself, like it's some hobby?"

"C'mon, Kris. Stop. I masturbate because, one—it feels good;

two, it helps relieve stress; and, three, because sometimes I'm too horny to want to wait until you get home to have sex."

Krista grunted. "So you *fuck* yourself?"

Kendall let out a frustrated sigh. "No. I stroke myself."

Dr. Dangerfield jumped in. "Mrs. Evans, masturbation isn't some antisocially deviant behavior. Frequency of sex in a marriage has little connection to the frequency of when a partner masturbates. In fact, there are plenty of couples that have extremely healthy sex lives who still enjoy pleasuring themselves. Self-pleasuring—masturbation—is a healthy part of our humanness. Exploring one's own body is a healthy part of our sexuality.

"And there are many married men and women who enjoy sex with their partners, while still enjoying pleasuring themselves. It doesn't mean that there is anything wrong with their partners or with their relationship/marriage. In fact, masturbation allows a person to stay in touch with their own bodies and their own sexual needs and desires. Self-exploration brings about self-discovery. For men, masturbation can help them learn ways to control their orgasms, while women can learn how to have orgasms more easily. Simply put, Mrs. Evans, good sex begets more good sex."

Krista turned her lips up. "I would have rather not known that my husband likes playing with his dick."

Kendall cringed. "Wait a minute, Kris, what exactly are you trying to imply here?"

"I don't know. Why don't you tell me, Kendall? You're the one who likes having a dick in his hand."

"Not a dick," he snapped. "*My* dick. It's a big difference."

Krista snorted. "*Mmph.* It's still a dick, no matter how you look at it."

Kendall responded by giving his head a little shake, as if he couldn't have possibly heard Krista right. He stared at Krista, and then shook his head again in disbelief.

"You're joking, right?" Kendall asked.

"Do you see me laughing," Krista said.

Dr. Dangerfield felt like screaming out, "Stroke it! Finger it! Get yourself off. Masturbation is good for the soul!" But, instead, she uncrossed her legs and then shifted in her seat and said, "Self-love is a beautiful thing. It can be empowering to explore one's own body."

Krista just crossed her arms over her chest and rolled her eyes.

"Judging by your facial expression," Dr. Dangerfield said. "I take it you don't masturbate?"

"No. I absolutely do not," Krista said incredulously. "I wipe it. I clean it. I don't need to play with it."

"Oh, I see. So tell me, Mrs. Evans," Dr. Dangerfield continued. "Do you not love your body?"

Krista huffed. "Of course I do."

"Then why not *love* it in every way?"

"I have a husband for that," Krista stated.

Dr. Dangerfield nodded. "So then what is it about self-stimulation that you find so appalling?"

Krista stared at her, then folded her arms. "Lust is a sin. And masturbation goes against God, His ways, His word, *and* His purpose for how a married couple should relate to one another in their union as husband and wife. Period."

"It doesn't have to be," Dr. Dangerfield challenged. "Not when it's in the context of a marriage. Not when a wife arouses her husband, or when a husband arouses her . . ."

"I'm not going to debate this," Krista said, annoyance coursing through her. "Kendall should be able to say no to his lustful thoughts. If he turned to Christ and gave his life to our Savior, he wouldn't allow temptation to control him. He wouldn't be pulling out his dick or having the need to masturbate."

Kendall just blinked, sighed. He was really beginning to think he was fighting a losing battle. Krista was sounding more and more like a certified whack-job.

Dr. Dangerfield felt like hopping from her seat and smacking Krista upside the head with her folder. "Mrs. Evans, can you tell me where in the Bible it states masturbation is a sin? There is a whole lot more emphasis on adultery, wouldn't you say? There is absolutely nothing wrong with a married man or woman enjoying both their partner's sexuality while continuing to enjoy their own."

Krista blinked. Ooh, this bitch really wants to go there with me, she thought. The Bible spoke explicitly about sexuality and sinful lust, so why was this ho trying to go there? And before Krista could give it to her real good with scripture from the book of Matthew, Dr. Dangerfield continued, "Although I do understand that sex and sexuality have intrinsic moral implications for many, there is nothing inherently wrong with a man or woman touching themselves to experience pleasure. And masturbation is not always immoral. Clearly, if Mr. Evans is fantasizing about another woman, then biblically speaking, it can be said he is violating his vows."

Truthfully, Dr. Dangerfield didn't whole-heartedly subscribe to the notion of fantasizing being sinful, but from a religious standpoint, she knew how to talk the talk when she needed to. Still, she revered in fantasy. Believed fantasizing was healthy. That it could enhance a couple's sex life. And—yes, she was probably going to hell in a gasoline hand basket. But she'd go well fucked, and sexually liberated.

Krista turned her attention to Kendall. "Are *you*, Kendall? Fantasizing about other women when you're masturbating? Sinning with your dick in your hand?"

Kendall swallowed, but he kept his eyes on Krista's. Of course I am. "No." The lie was better than the truth for now.

Krista raised a brow, skepticism now etching her face. "Are you watching porn?"

Yeah—anything with ass play. "No."

Krista shifted her stare to Dr. Dangerfield. "Like I said, if Kendall wants to play with his dick, let him. No. I don't like knowing that he has urges to pleasure himself, but I am not going to leave him for it. *Unless* he's playing with his dick because he really wants a dick?"

"What the *fu*—" Kendall stopped himself from going off, but just that quick, Krista had his blood boiling. "My dick is the only dick I have any interest in touching. Period. So whatever crazy notions you have stirring around in your head, get rid of them." He pinned Krista with a hard stare. "You hear me?"

Krista shrugged. "I'm only saying . . ."

"Krista, you're not saying shit, okay," Kendall snapped. He rarely ever cursed at his wife. But goddammit, she was crossing the goddamn line. He blew out a frustrated breath. "Damn, Kris. I love you. But shit."

"Kendall," Krista said. "Like I said earlier. It's your dick. Do with it what you want."

Dr. Dangerfield glanced at the time. She would have loved to continue the session, but she was drained. Krista had worked her last damn nerve. And now what she needed was a stiff drink and a hard dick to relax her. But it would be none of that. She needed to detoxify and prepare for tonight's festivities. The couples were being invited to a night of hot, steamy adult fun.

"Okay, our time is almost up," Dr. Dangerfield announced. "But before we end, I want to give the two of you a homework assignment." She looked between Krista and Kendall, and then right back at Krista. "Mr. Evans, the next time you have the urge to masturbate, I would like for you to invite your wife to join you.

And, Mrs. Evans, I would like for you to sit back and watch your husband as he pleasures himself. Are you okay with that, Mr. Evans?"

No. That was his private time—*alone*. And *no*—fuck no, he didn't want to share it with Krista's ass. "Sure," he lied.

"Great. And you, Mrs. Evans, do you think you can do that?"

Krista shrugged. "Maybe." She was still brooding over Kendall's narrow-minded remark. So that was how he really saw her. Narrow-minded.

Mmph.

Dr. Dangerfield offered a smile. "Set the mood. Candles. Music. Allow yourself to simply watch for at least fifteen minutes"—she glanced over at Kendall—"Provided you can last *that* long," she said slyly.

"Rising to the occasion won't be my problem," Kendall said.

Krista shot him a look, but said nothing.

Dr. Dangerfield nodded. "Then, Mr. Evans, I would like for you to invite your wife over to you and allow her to finish stroking you off to an orgasm. No intercourse, however; just your wife stroking you, loving you with her hands. Mrs. Evans, I want you to stay in the moment, focus on pleasuring your husband. Bring him to a happy ending."

With instructions doled out, Dr. Dangerfield shook the couple's hands, then sent them on their way, while the nagging voice in the back of her head kept saying, "Krista Evans is going to lose her man to another woman . . ."

Because what one woman wouldn't do, another always would.

Dr. Dangerfield knew that reality all too well.

Thirty-Three

An oasis of sensuality hidden behind thick mahogany doors awaited the three couples as they climbed out of the chauffeured-driven stretch Bentley. Earlier in the evening, the couples had been told by Dr. Dangerfield in almost a seductive whisper to, "Dress sexy—or wear nothing at all."

Club Passion was where discreet, horny couples teetering on sexual boredom and a craving for something salacious came to toss their inhibitions to the wind, releasing their inner freaks without judgment, and without care. It was where carnal desires were fulfilled. And the four-floor exclusive club—each floor more scandalous, more licentious, than the next—owned by the same woman who not only owned the island, but owned another adult club back in the States as well—was the only one of its kind here in the South Pacific.

The main floor was available to all who entered. The remaining floors required key-coded membership cards for access. And the only way someone gained admittance inside the club was either by way of special invitation or you had to have a membership. And membership came with a hefty price. But the men and women who participated in the couple's retreat were always granted a special invite to indulge their desires during their stay on the remote island—on the main level, of course.

And always at their own risk.

The big red sign over the door read: LOSE YOURSELF TO PASSION

And on either side of the huge doors stood two of the most beautifully sculpted men Brenda and LaQuandra had ever laid eyes on. They both looked of Polynesian descent. Probably Hawaiian, LaQuandra thought as she nearly choked on her drool.

Brenda seductively licked her lips.

And, Krista, well . . . she seemed unfazed by the doormen's exquisite physiques. She seemed more fixated on the skimpy outfits Brenda and LaQuandra had decided to stuff themselves into.

Brenda had her breasts nearly spilling out of an extremely short wrap dress that revealed the edges of her big, fluffy ass cheeks. *Curvy* wasn't the word that best described her. For a thick woman, she was well proportioned and stacked in all the right places. And Brenda loved every dangerous curve on her body. She exuded confidence and sex appeal—lots of it.

Yet, Krista fought to keep a scowl from forming as she watched Brenda walk in front of her, her ass shaking every which way. Her thick shapely legs seemingly more elongated in a pair of seven-inch fuck-me pumps.

Krista wondered if the tramp had on panties.

Mmph. Probably not . . .

Next, Krista's gaze swept over LaQuandra. And this heifer had the gall to wear a skintight black dress with a cutout back and a pair of sexy black six-inch, open-toed heels. Her flat ass didn't look so flat, and Krista thought she might be wearing silicone butt pads. She couldn't blame her, though, if LaQuandra were wearing padding in her underwear.

Every woman deserved to have an ass they could be proud of. Right?

Still . . .

Krista couldn't believe Brenda and LaQuandra would come out dressed like two hoochies on the ho-stroll. Hadn't they been told to dress sexy, not whorish. Whatever. She wasn't in the business of judging folks, so if they liked it, she loved it.

She glanced down at her outfit—a white linen skirt, white silk blouse with matching linen jacket. She normally liked to wear her blazers buttoned, but tonight she'd decided to wear it unbuttoned to show the ruffles in her blouse.

And then Krista stole a glance down at her white peep-toe pumps. The three-inch heels were already starting to hurt her feet, but she'd suffer through it for a few hours. She hadn't been to a nightclub in years. And she hadn't had a drink in about four years. And the only dance she knew was the Electric Slide, so unless they played the Electric Boogie or the Cupid Shuffle, she'd be holding up the wall with a Pepsi in her hand, sipping through a straw.

Of course, Kendall looked handsome in his white linen pants and white linen dress shirt. The pants hung just right over his white loafers. Krista couldn't help but grin, knowing they were dressed to the nines. She was still peeved about what had been said in their session, but not enough to allow it to ruin their evening.

"Girrrrrl," LaQuandra drawled out as she leaned in to Brenda. "Why in the world is Krissy . . .?"

"Who?" Brenda asked, giving her a confused look.

"The church lady in back of us."

"Oh"—Brenda chuckled—"you mean, Krista?"

"Yeah, *her*," LaQuandra stage-whispered, and then she quickly glanced over her shoulder to make sure she wasn't in earshot. "Tell me why is she dressed like she's going to a woman's day program?"

Brenda nearly doubled over in laughter. "Girl, stop. You are so wrong for that."

LaQuandra shrugged. "But am I right? All she needs is the hat and gloves."

"Girl, stop. I think she looks cute in her patent leathers." Brenda opted to not say anything more than that. She decided LaQuandra was the messy one, so she'd let her messy-ass be messy by her damn self.

LaQuandra grunted. "Uh-huh. She's dressed like she's ready for communion."

"Girl, be nice. Let her dress how she wants to dress," Brenda said. And then she shifted the conversation back to the chiseled hunks standing up at the top of the stairs. "If the men in this club look anything like those two up there, I'm gonna need a change of drawz."

LaQuandra laughed.

Isaiah and Roselle scowled at the chiseled men with the wide shoulders and muscled chests and rippling abs.

What the fuck? Roselle thought as he sized up the two hunks standing up at the top of the stairs. *I hope this club isn't packed with a buncha half-naked niggas. I wanna see some sexy bitches with lots of ass and tits.*

Instinctively—with the exception of Isaiah, Roselle eased up alongside Brenda and grabbed her hand, while Kendall reached out and took Krista's hand. Both men, clearly marking their territory as they walked up the red-carpeted steps leading up into the club.

Krista smiled, as her hand got lost in Kendall's as he led her up the stairs. She didn't need to gaze at another man, when she had all the man she needed right here beside her.

LaQuandra didn't seem to notice that the other husbands had taken their wives' hands. She seemed more focused on the two gladiator-built men standing guard at the entrance of the club.

On either side of the two hunks appeared two equally stunning women, wearing exquisite diamond necklaces and bedazzled pasties and matching G-strings. And they wore elaborate ostrich-feathered headdresses atop their heads.

As the couples ascended the stairs, LaQuandra felt her knees buckle as she took a long look at the massive bulges tucked behind each doorman's loincloth. She cursed under her breath—at Isaiah, at them, at herself. She blamed Isaiah for the state of her aching loins. She blamed the two manly delights in her view for doing nothing to alleviate the agony that suffused her entire cunt. And she blamed herself for being in this predicament in the first damn place.

Upon entrance through the double doors, the couples were greeted with the sounds of erotic music. Each woman was handed a colorful mask encrusted with Swarovski crystals (the *real* jeweled masks were for card-carrying members), while the three men were handed simple black Zorro-style masks.

"Indulge your desires," a bejeweled masked woman said, her curvy body wrapped in a nude-like bodysuit covered in sparkling Austrian crystals. Her lips were shellacked to perfection in tangerine. "A night of decadence awaits you."

Thirty-Four

Byzantine Time Machine's "Adventure in Istanbul" greeted the couples as they stepped inside the extravagant club. Hips seductively swung. Breast swayed. Pelvises thrust. Bellies rolled. Arms rhythmically moved up over dancers' heads.

"What in the . . .?"

Raw lust.

Hot sensuality.

Animalistic heat.

The club dripped of sex.

Candle tray dancers, wearing beaded veils, seductively danced as they carried burning wax candles on fourteen-inch, flat round trays on top of their heads, their flames dancing above their heads.

Huge go-go cages sat atop massive speakers, displaying the most succulent pieces of pelvis thrusting eye-candy—women in mesh mini-dresses. Their muscled counterparts were either wearing leather G-strings or leather briefs with a zipper over thick bulges, the ridges in their abdomens tightening as their bodies sensually moved.

Flames shot up from the floor.

Beautiful bodies moved slow and nasty.

Four women—with round, plump ass cheeks were bent at the waist, their hands wrapped all the way around their ankles, their faces looking down onto the crowd—were up on a glass ledge that was eye-level for onlookers, making their asses bounce in sync to the music.

Krista's mouth dropped open.

Nude sculptures of men and women in various sexual positions were strategically placed around the club. In the center of the dance floor was a larger-than-life penis adorned with two humongous balls carved out of the world's finest dark chocolate, spilling rivulets of mouthwatering white chocolate lava from its dickhead.

Naked women covered in chocolate stood in its enormous basin of melted white chocolate, their hands sensually gliding up and down their bodies.

LaQuandra nearly licked her lips at the sight. All she saw was dick, balls, and hot creamy cum, even if it were only an illusion. She found herself fantasizing, imagining herself licking over those huge balls, their chocolate melting all over her tongue.

She swallowed.

Nairobia had once seen the same chocolate sculpture at a nightclub in Vegas and had thought it sexy. She wanted one for her own club.

"Girrrrl, this is. *Evvvvvvery*thing," LaQuandra said to Brenda.

"Honey, yes. It. Is," Brenda agreed, her knees dipped a bit. And then her shoulders slowly moved up and down.

Red lights splashed over the crowd, while body-painted women hung upside down in the air from invisible wires seductively winding their hips as if they were literally having sex on the ceiling.

"*Yasssss*," Brenda said, snapping her fingers. "They are giving me my whole life up in here. C'mon, baby." She grabbed Roselle's arm, dragging him onto the dance floor, where she shimmied and gyrated her own pelvis. A hairsbreadth away from him, she moved in closer and then bumped and grinded into Roselle's pelvis until his dick grew hard. Then she slowly turned and pressed her ass into him.

"That's right, baby," he murmured in her ear over the music. "Give me that shit."

Dancing all slutty, Krista thought, placing a hand up over the 14kt white gold cross that hung from her neck. This was blasphemous.

"Baby, you wanna dance?" Kendall asked, knowing damn well the answer would be no. More like, *hell no*. Krista shot him a look, and he simply smiled, head tilted, palms out, shoulders slowly bouncing.

"You know this kind of circus isn't my cup of tea," she said over the music, and yet she couldn't stop staring. She had never seen anything like this. Such, such filth, such freakiness, such sin—all up under one roof.

Kendall wrapped an arm around her, fighting to keep his own eyes from bouncing all over the place. There were so many beautiful women—naked, half-naked, body-painted—that he was having a hard time staying focused. He pressed a kiss to the side of Krista's head. "I know, baby. We can leave in a few. If you want?"

She craned her neck and eyed him, and then raised a brow. "Is that what you want?"

Hell no. Kendall wanted to stay and get sucked into all the sexual energy swarming around him. He wanted to find a dark corner, pull out his dick and fuck.

"Yeah, baby," he said, pulling her into him so that her back was to him. He wrapped an arm snugly around her waist. "Whatever you want."

Krista folded her arms, her lips turned down in disgust; her eyes now glued on four bare-chested men, with skin the color of black licorice, grinding their massive bodies into a reddish-brown woman; her arms were up over her head, her eyes closed in pure ecstasy as each man's hands and body heat engulfed.

"I'm going to walk around," Isaiah stated over the music to LaQuandra.

"Bye," she said. And then she shuffled off toward the dance floor. She didn't even bother to ask him if he wanted to dance because she knew the motherfucker would turn her down. She didn't come here to stand around like some wallflower. So fuck him.

She threw an arm up in the air and then moved to the beat. Her lips tooted, her head going from side to side. She plucked a drink from off the tray of a passing cocktail waiter, wearing nothing but his shiny dark skin and a loincloth.

She dipped real low, careful to not splash a drop of her drink, then rolled back up. She may not have had a porn star ass, but LaQuandra Lewis knew how to work the middle. And so she did.

Isaiah grabbed a drink from a passing waitress wearing a G-string and pasties. Her smooth body glittered, and he kept his eye on her swaying ass as she strutted by.

"You sure you don't wanna dance, baby?" Kendall asked Krista again.

Krista shook her head, her gaze floating back over at Brenda and Roselle. Ooh, the nasty skank had her dress practically up over her hips. All Krista saw was thigh and her whole ass cheek.

I knew that nasty-bitch didn't have on any drawz . . . mmph.

Kendall wasn't the greatest dancer, but he had a few good moves and the music was doing something to him. Besides, he had hoped to get on the dance floor to get a closer look at the woman in the gold six-inch stilettos, with the big ass and heavy breasts. Her rich dark skin was the color of silt. Her eyes were shadowed in gold, so were her plump lips. Her arms were adorned in elaborate gold and ruby bangles. In each hand, she worked a tambourine.

She mewled out as her body moved, almost as if she were being possessed. Isaiah felt his dick stir, so he pressed himself into Krista and did a slow grind, his eyes locked on the woman who commanded almost everyone's attention.

"You okay, babe," Kendall asked, leaning in and then kissing her on the cheek.

Krista nodded, shook her head, then nodded again. Hell, she didn't know if she was okay or not. She covered a hand over her face, but slyly peeked through her fingers. She couldn't watch, but she didn't want *not* to watch. There was a lot of debauchery going on, and she couldn't wait to get on the phone with her sister Latrice to fill her in on all the hot fuckery.

Kendall looked over at the winding glass staircase to the right of him, and then his eyes landed up on the second floor. Standing at an elaborate gold railing—in a long, white roman-style gown—was Dr. Dangerfield looking down into the crowd. Kendall blinked. He thought his eyes were deceiving him, but they weren't. Her nearly see-through gown took him by surprise. Goddamn, he thought. That body.

Standing beside Dr. Dangerfield was a masked woman in a sheer gown more provocative than hers. The woman was practically drenched in diamonds. The two women shared an exchange of words, and then the masked-woman laughed.

Kendall caught Dr. Dangerfield's eye and then quickly shifted his attention back to the dance floor, back to the dark chocolate beauty with the tambourines and the big juicy booty. When he glanced up again. Dr. Dangerfield and the masked woman—who he suspected was Nairobia—were both gone.

Forty minutes later, LaQuandra was rocking back and forth on the heels of her bare-feet. "Owww! Yes!" She'd finished off her fifth cocktail; her shoes were off, the straps dangling from one hand. Oh yes. She was feeling good. And she didn't give a damn that one of her toenails had cut open her fishnet stocking and now she had one red-painted big toe hanging out. Yes, she was drunk. But she wasn't sloppy with it.

"Owwww!" She glanced around the dance floor in search of Isaiah, but he'd disappeared from LaQuandra's view. He was over on the other end of the massive club entranced by four exotic-looking women who had him snared, rhythmically moving around him in a slow seductive circle. He stood there, bopping his head, gripping the sweaty neck of an ice-cold Fijian beer. He grinned when each woman took turns brushing a hand over his crotch, teasing him.

The sounds of cracking whips and sensual moans suddenly seeped out from the hidden speakers out over Nato's "Gonwa." And then came the *pop-pop-pop* sounds of asses being slapped, followed by tribal calls.

When the lights dimmed, bodies glowed with tribal markings. The club was drenched in ethnic sounds. The bass thumped. Deep tribal jungle music controlled the sway of hips. Suddenly, a long wall slid open and the dance floor swelled with naked men and women who had somehow managed to find a way to brazenly fuck each other on the dance floor.

"Oh this is too goddamn much," Krista hissed. "Get me the hell out of here, Kendall." Before Kendall could say a word, Krista was nearly tripping over her feet, her cunt violently clutching, as she dashed toward the door.

Thirty-Five

"Are you enjoying your stay on the island?" asked the six-four, very lean-muscled man the following morning. He was part West Indian, part Polynesian, wearing a smile over his kissable lips as he looked up at Brenda. His strong hands moved rhythmically up and down and around her left calve.

God yes.

Oooh, he was sexy, sexy, sexy—that was the only word that came to Brenda's muddled mind as she watched his muscled tattooed arms flex as he skillfully slid his—firm, strong, and oh so very warm—hands up a little higher, up over her knees and then back down to her ankle, where they lingered for a bit, kneading.

God, all she needed was for him to suck each of her toes into his mouth.

Brenda moaned. "Yes. Every. Single. Moment of it." She sexily eyed him over the rim of her shades. He was too young for her, but he was delicious to look at. *Lawd, forgive me. This boy can't be no more than twenty*, she thought, feeling her cunt flutter as his hands moved to her right calf, working the peppermint massage oil into her flesh.

Up, down . . . all around.

God yes.

His hands were heavenly. It had to be the three Passion Punch drinks she'd drunk so far that had heat swirling around in her belly.

"How old are you?" Brenda asked Mr. Sexy Tattoo.

"Twenty-four," he stated proudly. "Real grown." He flashed her a sexy smile. Lord, this man-child even had one deep dimple in his left cheek. And then he had the nerve to lick his lips.

LaQuandra fought back a yawn as she eavesdropped. She'd tossed and turned practically the whole night last night. But she didn't want to think about it—or the reason why. So she glanced over from her own massage chair, where she, too, was relishing in the sensations shimmering up her legs as the hands of a brown-skinned man with Chinese-looking eyes and a headful of curly dark-brown hair massaged peppermint lotion into her calves.

LaQuandra cocked her head, pulling her shades down to the edge of her nose and then eyeing Mr. Sexy Tattoos, before locking her stare on Brenda's.

"Not grown enough," she muttered.

Brenda reluctantly agreed. "But, baaaaby. If only I were single and twenty years younger," she stated as if the young hunk wasn't at her feet hearing her. Her eyes were glued to the muscles in his neck. In the center of his neck was a set of lips—red and wet, with a cherry between those lips—directly over his Adam's apple. Brenda licked over her own lips, imagining herself sucking him there, on his neck, over those sexy red-tatted lips, licking over that red cherry inked over his Adam's apple.

Mr. Sexy Tattoo swallowed and Brenda watched that cherry move up and down, her mouth growing wet. "Lawd! Girl, stop this shit," Brenda mentally scolded herself. She shook her lusty thoughts from her head.

The three women had been whisked off to other side of the island for a day of pampering in the sun, before they would need to return to the other side of the island for their next group session. And then later tonight, they'd been invited to dine with Dr.

Dangerfield. Shockingly, even Krista had been looking forward to a spa day.

So far, they'd had their manicures, were now wrapping up their pedicures, and soon they would be stretched out under a cabana getting massages but masseuses. It'd been years since Krista had a professional massage. She was long overdue. And, surprisingly, looking forward to getting one.

Brenda leaned her head back and snapped her fingers as The Weeknd's "Valerie" played in the background. She stretched open her toes, loving the feel of Sexy Tattoo's hands. His fingers swiftly slipped through each of her toes, tugging them lightly one by one. Brenda slyly opened her legs a little wider, so that he could see she hadn't worn any panties. And then she smiled when his eyes looked up. If she were out here alone, she'd be tempted to formerly introduce him to Kitty. She leaned her head back, instead, and closed her eyes, allowing him to enjoy the view.

LaQuandra glanced over at Krista, who had her head back, her eyes closed behind a pair of dark shades, while a shirtless, gray-eyed, bronzed-skin hunk pulled her right foot out of the foot bath and began scrubbing it with a foot file.

LaQuandra's gaze stopped at his chest, and she couldn't help but admire the bulging muscles of both arms and his upper chest. There was a smattering of curly hair in the hollow and then a fine line of hair trailing down to his navel. Before LaQuandra allowed her booze-soaked mind to wonder what was behind the drawstring of his white pants, she jerked her gaze back up and over at Krista.

"Krissy, you all right over there?" LaQuandra asked.

Krista cringed inwardly the moment LaQuandra opened her mouth and spoke. "It's Krista," she said, refusing to open her eyes or look over at the ole horse-faced troll. Krista shook her head. *This ghetto bitch works my last nerve.*

God, forgive me . . .

"Oops," LaQuandra said. "I like *Krissy* better, though. I mean, with you being all *Christian* and all."

Krista rolled her eyeballs behind her lids. "Yes. I'm Christian. And I love the Lord. Perhaps you should try it. Maybe your blessings—"

"Don't worry about my blessings, boo. It's all good over here."

Krista sighed. "Then perhaps you shouldn't be worried about me and focus on all of *your* blessings."

Brenda shot both women a hard stare. "Let's play nice, ladies." She couldn't understand why LaQuandra liked antagonizing Krista. Let her be.

"Oh I *am* nice," Krista said. Her lids fluttered opened, then she finally turned her head and looked over at LaQuandra as she pushed her shades down to the tip of her nose. "But if I need to forget my religion for a moment, I will." She stared at LaQuandra a bit longer than she wanted, then pushed her sunglasses back up over her eyes, and stared down at the smooth-faced man as he placed her foot back in the bath and then pulled out her other foot and began scrubbing it.

Krista nearly moaned out as he handled her callouses. She didn't have the most attractive feet—they were wide and flat and her toes looked like thick little sausages, but she loved keeping them pampered.

LaQuandra laughed. "Krissy, you a mess. Let me find out you're a fake Christian."

Brenda opened her eyes and looked over at the two women. "Krista, girl, don't pay LaQuandra's ass no mind. You know she's special, right?"

Krista shrugged. "She adds no value to my life, so trust me. I'm not paying her messy-ass any mind."

LaQuandra laughed again. "Girl, bye. Messy isn't me. You need a drink to relax."

"And you obviously need a hard dick," Krista snapped. *Lord, forgive me. This bitch is tryna take me there.*

"Ooh, girl, you got me there," LaQuandra said sarcastically. "I confess—I need some dick." Three weeks on this island and Isaiah had still not fucked her. She glanced down at Mr. Curly Hair who pretended to be more focused on polishing her right pinky toe than paying attention to her. "Isaiah and I haven't been intimate in months. But guess what? At least I can be honest about it. I'm transparent, boo. Can you say the same?"

Krista scoffed. "I have nothing to hide, sweetie. I have a good man. And I'm not the one being deprived of—"

Brenda's head jerked over at LaQuandra. "Wait a minute," she said, cutting Krista off. "Did I hear you right, girl? You haven't had a dick-down in *months?*"

LaQuandra reached for her drink, then took a long sip. She swished the potent fruity elixir around in her mouth, allowing it to soak her tongue, before she slowly swallowed.

And then she finally answered, "It feels like years."

Brenda's mouth dropped open in surprise. "*Girrrrrl*, say it ain't so." She shook her head. "Ohmygod. I wish Roselle would try some shit like that with me. His ass would be put out. No damn way I'ma have a husband, laying up in the same bed with me, and his ass isn't putting it down in them sheets."

LaQuandra sighed, and then took another sip of her drink, only this time the concoction felt too thick to swallow. She spat it back into her glass, then set it back down in its holder. "Well, welcome to my world. Now enough about me and my honey-hole." LaQuandra looked back over at Krista. "Back to you, Krissy. How about you tell us, why you ran up outta the club the other night?"

"No—no, sweetie." Krista turned her head in LaQuandra's

direction again, peering at her over the rim of her shades. "How about *you* tell us who your husband's *screwing*, since he isn't screwing *you.*"

Brenda nearly choked on her tongue.

Work, bitch, work!

Thirty-Six

Krista couldn't stop looking. No matter how many times she dragged her stare away, her eyes landed right back on Nairobia perched on the lap of a caramel-coated man with a neatly trimmed goatee and a beautiful bald head. He'd been on the plane ride over—one of the flight attendants, but Krista couldn't remember his name. Darn. It was going to annoy her that she couldn't remember it.

But she remembered that handsomely rugged face. She never forgot a face, even if she couldn't remember a name. And now she sat here wondering why she'd taken this particular seat. Why hadn't she chosen the seat on the other side of the table? No, no. Everything happened for a reason. Had she'd not taken this chair, Kendall would have been sitting here instead, ensnared by temptation in a see-through dress and heels. It was in this chair, from this vantage point, that Krista could see *her*—salaciously luring her prey into her web of seduction.

Nairobia stroked the bald man's head while conversing with him and . . . Sin (of course Krista would never forget a name like that when that was all she was surrounded by.) Sin. He sat on the same love seat next to the other man. What in the world was his name?

Saint. Yes, yes. That was it.

Saint.

But there was nothing saintly about the way he was caressing the side of Nairobia's right breast over the flimsy fabric of her tangerine gown. And there was nothing saintly about the way he was nibbling on her neck. Krista shuddered. The porn-star whore was holding court right out in the open—well, partially open, since she was the only one able to see them—without a care in the world.

The couples were dining on seaweed salad, oysters, caviar, shrimp, lobster tails, calamari, coconut chicken, and curried pork. Then various fish dishes followed. And while everyone else made sounds of delight over their chattering as they ate their meals, Krista's gaze was riveted back to the scene playing right in front of her eyes. Saint now had Nairobia's left breast out, rolling her nipple between his fingers, while Sin's hand slowly eased up the slit of her gown.

The shameless hussy was turning the star-lit evening out on the roofed platform, overlooking the ocean, into her own sexual playground. Nairobia threw her head back when Sin's hand reached between her legs, and he cupped her there, his fingers finding her clit. Krista watched on as his hand moved methodically beneath Nairobia's gown, and then she jerked her eyes away.

Dr. Dangerfield caught the direction of Krista's roaming eye, and smiled over the rim of her martini glass, before taking a sip.

"Mrs. Evans," Dr. Dangerfield said, "how's your meal?"

Krista cast her a quick look. "Fine. Everything's good." And it was, if only she could focus on her plate instead of Nairobia. She was over there, partially hidden, in the throes of passion as Sin fingered her and Saint caressed her exposed breasts—together, bringing her to orgasm, while the rest of the couples engaged in laughter and chatter.

Krista's gaze drifted back over to the devil in heels and her two playmates.

Sin's hand appeared from beneath Nairobia's dress, and then his fingers were in his mouth, before sharing them with her.

Krista suddenly felt flush.

Nairobia said something, and both men laughed. And then Sin reached over and smoothed his hand up and down her leg while Saint's hands were now loosely clasped around her hips. It was obvious she held both men's attention, even after they'd fondled and fingered her. And judging by the way they were both enthralled by her, she'd probably have them both in her bed later in the evening—for a long night of fucking.

Krista frowned at the thought, but quickly averted her eyes back to her dinner plate when Nairobia's gaze caught hers and she licked over her lips.

Krista reached for her napkin and then covered her mouth and coughed.

"Babe, you okay?" Kendall asked, giving her a concerned look.

Krista reached for the glass of water that had been set in front of her and took several large gulps. She dabbed her napkin at the corners of her mouth. "Yes, yes. I'm fine." She placed a hand to her chest. Then cleared her throat. "Something caught in my throat." This time she took a slower, smaller sip.

"Krissy, you all right over there," LaQuandra asked in between bites of her swordfish. All she needed was a basket of Red Lobster's cheddar bay biscuits and she'd be in heaven. "Why you over there all quiet?"

Krista ignored her.

LaQuandra laughed.

"Girl, leave Krista alone," Brenda said, reaching over and wiping the corners of Roselle's mouth with her thumb. "Krista, you know I got your back, girl."

Krista offered her a smile. "Thanks." And then her eyes went to

Kendall as he ate one smoked oyster after the other. "Since when you like oysters?" she asked. All the years they'd been together, she'd never known him to (or seen him) eat a molluscan shellfish.

Kendall shrugged. "Felt like trying something different. You know. Step outside my comfort zone for a change. Wanna try it?"

Krista blinked. His snide comment hadn't gone unnoticed. And yet she wondered if he were talking about trying an oyster or hanging upside down from a ceiling.

Kendall speared a smoked oyster and then reached over and offered it to her. Krista looked at his fork before opening her mouth. Kendall slid the fork into her mouth, and Krista nearly gagged as she chewed the mollusk.

She coughed into her napkin, discreetly spitting it out, before excusing herself to use the restroom, but not before glancing over to find Nairobia and her two conquests gone. Clearly, the skank's propensity for threesomes would include those two.

"I'll be right back," Krista quickly said, standing to her feet.

Kendall nodded, and then looked up at the servers who returned to the table with yet another platter. And more drinks. Everyone was intoxicated enough; more rounds would more than likely seal their fates of having to crawl out of here, Kendall mused as he accepted another glass.

"It is almost time for dessert, no?"

Kendall blinked in the beautiful sight of Nairobia, and he found himself nearly speechless, as she stood before him in her form-fitting gown. Beneath the light, filmy fabric, Nairobia wore a bejeweled thong.

All chatter ceased.

"You are all enjoying yourselves, no?"

Everyone agreed; the women over smiles, the men over grins, their eyes dancing up and down the curves of her body, fantasizing, lusting, wanting.

"Good." With drink in hand, Nairobia called, "A toast." She paused, glancing down at Kendall. "Wait. Where is your . . . lovely wife?"

"Restroom," Kendall said sheepishly.

"I wait for her, no?"

Kendall shook his head. "No. You're good."

"Krissy's ass ain't drinking, anyway," LaQuandra stage-whispered over at Brenda.

"Girl, stop," Brenda said, biting back a laugh. "Behave."

"Very well," Nairobia said. And then she lifted her glittering crystal glass. "To passion, and the heated pleasures that it brings."

"To passion," everyone said, raising their drinks. LaQuandra rolled her eyes at Isaiah as she downed her drink. He shook his head. Drunk-ass, he thought as he decided not to monitor her drinking. As long as she didn't try to start her shit, Isaiah was fine with her stumbling around, making a fool of herself.

Nairobia's eyes landed on Kendall. "I will entertain you while your wife freshens up, no?"

"Uh, sure," he stammered, trying to keep his gaze from peering at her jeweled crotch. He shifted in his chair as Nairobia smiled at him, pulling out Krista's now empty chair and sliding her voluptuous ass onto its seat.

"Um, excuse us, ladies and gentlemen," Brenda said as she rose from her chair. "My man and I have a date down on the beach." She shimmied her shoulders. "So if you all don't mind. We're out. C'mon, baby."

Roselle hopped up from his seat. "You ain't gotta tell me twice." He gave Isaiah a fist bump, then put his fist to his chest at Kendall, who did the same.

"Their fire still runs hot for each other," Nairobia said as she eyed Roselle. She circled the rim of her glass with one delicate finger and Kendall found himself wondering what her finger would taste like in his mouth.

He quickly shook the thought. And then chuckled. "Yeah. They can't seem to keep their hands off of one another."

Dr. Dangerfield smiled. And then she stood as well. "Nairobia . . . lady"—she glanced over at LaQuandra—"and gentlemen, it's been a long night. I am retiring. Mr. Evans . . . give Ms. Evans my regards when she returns."

He nodded. "Will do."

Nairobia held up her glass. "Good night, my darling. You'll find gifts waiting for you at your villa when you arrive." A sly smile eased over her lips. "Enjoy."

Dr. Dangerfield caught the glint of mischief in her eyes and smiled. "Oh, I'm sure I will." She said her goodbyes, then sauntered off, leaving LaQuandra, Isaiah, and Kendall in the company of Nairobia.

"Isaiah, you wanna go down to the beach?" LaQuandra asked sweetly. The moon was bright, the stars were twinkling overhead, and the alcohol flowing through her veins was pooling between her legs. And her pussy was soaked in heated need.

Isaiah gave her a look, and then frowned. "Nah. I'm good right here."

"You sure?" she asked with pleading eyes.

Isaiah felt Nairobia's gaze on him, and then solemnly shook his head. He sighed. "A'ight. C'mon." He gulped back his drink, then stood. He decided LaQuandra could suck him off while he fantasized about having his dick balls-deep inside Nairobia.

It was the least she could do—for being such a whiny, nagging bitch.

LaQuandra reached over for Dr. Dangerfield's glass and then drained the rest of what was left of her drink, before giving Nairobia and Kendall a two-finger wave. "Nite-nite," she said. And then she followed Isaiah toward the winding stairs that descended down to the beach.

"There is no love in his eyes for her," Nairobia stated once they were no longer in earshot. "She has drained him, empty."

"Wow," Kendall said as he regarded her. God. She was fine, he thought. And Kendall felt like a horny adolescent boy sitting here with a hard-on. "What do you see when you look at Krista and me?"

Nairobia regarded him thoughtfully. "I see a man full of sexual energy, a man full of passion and hot need . . ."

Kendall blushed. "And my wife, Krista?"

Nairobia feigned a yawn. "She's a bore, my darling. She will never surrender to your desires, or her own."

Kendall didn't know if he should laugh or shrink in his seat at her honest assessment. "Is there hope? For any of us?"

Nairobia's gray eyes bore into him. "There is hope for those who believe in what they have, my love." And then with a lazy grin, Nairobia dipped her forefinger into her glass and stirred her drink, then sucked it between her lips, causing Kendall to nearly groan.

"Do you believe, my darling?" Nairobia asked.

Kendall gave a slight shrug. He didn't know what to believe anymore. "Sometimes," he said. Damn. The drinks. He hadn't really meant to say that. Or had he?

Nairobia licked over her lips. "Good loving does not exist in your life, no?"

"I-I, well . . ."

Kendall attempted to rise to his feet when he spotted Krista walking in, but stopped himself. "I was wondering what happened to you. We were just talking about you," he said as he quickly sat back in his chair.

"Oh?" *I seriously doubt that.* "Is that so," Krista said as she walked around the table to him, looking around. "Where'd everyone go?" She'd been gone no more than ten minutes, if that, and somehow Nairobia had managed to clear out the whole rooftop, leaving Kendall in her clutches. Krista pulled out the chair beside him and sat.

"Down on the beach," Kendall answered, wrapping an arm loosely around the back of her chair. He scooted his chair up a bit, just in case Krista felt compelled to cut an eye down into his lap.

Krista looked over at Nairobia, and fought to keep a sneer from forming over her face as she took in her cleavage on open display, enticing anyone who dared to look. "Thanks for entertaining my husband while I was gone." She leaned into Kendall—a bit possessively, and then flashed her a slight smile.

"My pleasure," Nairobia said seductively. "I live for pleasing, my darling."

"Oh. I am sure you do," Krista said snidely. "Now what was it the two of you were talking about? Me?"

"Baby, she wanted to know how long we'd been married," Kendall lied, before taking his glass and draining it. "And if we had any children."

Krista felt the pounding of her heart in her chest. What was this bitch up to? "Yes. Happily married. And, hopefully, a baby or two within the next year or so." They'd been trying for four years with no luck. And Kendall had given up hope after the fourth false-pregnancy test. But Krista's faith had told her to hold fast for a baby would soon be hers.

Nairobia's heart-shaped lips curled into a grin. "Happiness, my darling, is sometimes an illusion." She slipped off one heel, then stretched her bare foot toward Kendall's leg.

Nairobia made contact with Kendall's inner thigh, just above his left knee. Kendall coughed, his body tensing, but he didn't give her away, just cast her a gaze as his arm went around Krista's shoulder.

Krista's brow rose. "Meaning?"

Kendall's lips parted. And then his breaths came quick as Nairobia's foot inched closer and closer to his dick. He squeezed Krista's shoulder. And Krista took that to mean for her to play nice.

"No, Ken," she said. "I want to know what she meant by that?"

Higher, higher . . .

Ah, yes. Right there.

Nairobia's foot made contact. Hard and thick, bulging. Kendall's breath caught, causing his chest to go still.

Nairobia grinned. "Tell me, my darling," she said to Krista as she rubbed the ball of her foot along the length of Kendall's bulge. She licked over her lips when his dick pulsed beneath her foot. "Have you ever wished you could step outside of yourself—for a night . . .?"

Nairobia pressed deeper into Kendall's dick, causing it to throb harder in response, the crown dampening with pre-cum. Her nipples tightened, and she shamelessly arched her back and allowed her breasts to protrude further out.

Even as Kendall's eyes glazed over with lust, he felt his lids going heavy. "Ah, shit," he wanted to groan out as he fought the tingling sensation Nairobia's foot rub caused over his linen pants. Now he wished he'd worn a pair of baggy shorts and a pair of boxer briefs instead of his silk boxers. Nairobia stroked Kendall from base to head

". . . and allow temptation to guide your desires?" And then she spoke in her native tongue. "*Om te geven in plezier . . .?*"

Krista gave her a blank look.

"To give into pleasure, my love?"

Krista scoffed. "Um, absolutely not. I do not find pleasure in sin."

Kendall felt himself going lightheaded, his free hand gripping the side of his chair.

"Then you, my darling, have truly not lived," Nairobia said, lowering her foot and slipping her heel back on. Nairobia feigned another yawn, though she'd now grown thoroughly bored to tears by Krista's presence. She rose. The universe held no promise of seduction for the two of them.

"I will leave the two of you to the rest of your evening."

And, as quickly as she'd appeared, Nairobia vanished.

"The devil is busy," Krista said, her heart nearly pounding in her ears.

Kendall let out a long breath, then filled his lungs with air. "C'mon, babe, why don't we go roll around on the sand?" He leaned into her and nibbled on her neck.

Krista twisted in her chair. "Mm. No. I'm not rolling around down on no beach. I don't want sand in this weave, or getting stuck all up in my ass."

Kendall shook his head, his hard dick quickly deflating.

Thirty-Seven

Dr. Dangerfield had been greeted by Nairobia's mysterious gift—Sin, Saint and Soul—the moment she stepped inside her villa.

Her breath caught.

Her cunt grew wet from the sight of the three sex gods standing in the middle of the room, naked, playing with their dicks, waiting on her with smiles on their faces.

She'd been with Sin more times than his brother Saint. But she'd never had the pleasure of being with Soul. And yet here she was with all three.

Their glorious erections (thick chocolate cylinders etched with veins) hers, all for the taking—to be sucked and fucked.

Saint's mouth brushed across the column of her neck, and Dr. Dangerfield bent her head to one side to welcome his lips as each kiss caused her skin to heat.

He slipped a hand between her thighs and found her clit, already slippery with want, the hardened nub throbbing with need. He pressed on it, and Dr. Dangerfield gasped—from the pressure, from Soul in back of her, on his knees, spreading open her ass and licking her there.

"Is her pussy wet?" Sin asked as his hands closed over her breasts. He leaned in, flicking his tongue over one chocolate nipple.

"Let me find out for you," Saint said and then he dipped a finger into her naked pussy, stroking upward, twice, three times, through her wetness. "Ah, yeah. That shit wet."

Dr. Dangerfield moaned, her body thrumming with a slow burning fire that only a hard fucking could extinguish.

Soul nipped at each of her ass cheeks, then slapped them, making her ass jiggle, the sting causing a bubble of aching need to stretch inside her.

"Fuck me," she whispered frantically.

No one spoke.

Instead, she was being flipped over to her stomach, having a pair of pillows shoved under her. Grabbing her hips, Saint was the first to thrust deep inside her.

Dr. Dangerfield gasped and her pussy grew unimaginably wetter as Soul greeted her lips with his long, ten-and-a-half-inch dick.

He slid his dick over her lips, then swung it like a bat, slapping it across her face, her lips. Dr. Dangerfield gazed at it.

"Stick out your wet tongue," Soul urged. And she did, allowing him to slap the rigid shaft down on her tongue. Spit splattered with each slap.

"Look up at me," he said.

Dr. Dangerfield's eyes fluttered up as Soul finally slid his dick over her tongue and into her waiting mouth toward the back of her throat, stopping when her lips rested not even halfway up its length.

She grunted as Saint pummeled inside of her, his balls slapping against her ass with each greedy thrust.

"Man, shit. This pussy good," Saint said, more to himself than anyone else. Several pumps later, he was pulling out of her quaking body, and Sin was sinking his dick into her cunt in place of Saint's.

Dr. Dangerfield's moans and spit gurgled over and around Soul's dick.

"Yeah, suck this dick, baby," Soul murmured; his throaty voice spurring her on to suck him deeper, wetter, swallowing him down her neck.

Dr. Dangerfield felt herself going faint as Soul's dick clogged her airway. "Ahh, ahh, ahh."

"Yeah, gag on that shit, baby."

Eyes filled with tears, she breathed through her nose and focused on loosening the muscles in her throat, letting Soul fuck her there as much as possible without gagging, without choking to death.

"Ah fuck, yeah," he muttered. "She got some good neck. Ah, shit . . ."

"Let me get some of that wet mouth," Saint said, holding his hard, beautiful shaft at the base as he moved in.

Sin groaned in back of Dr. Dangerfield as she arched her back and melted around his thrust. Pound, pound, pound—oh God, yes, yes, yes. Harder. Harder. Harder.

"Ahh, ahh, ahh," she grunted as saliva splashed out from her mouth. Then her mouth was being stretched wide—two huge, mushroom-sized heads between her lips.

Saint and Soul feeding her mouth; the sweet, salty mixture of their precum gathered on their tips and she suckled, edging out more of their cock juice.

Dr. Dangerfield raised her gaze as she sucked them both. And then she cried out over their dicks as Sin's dick bumped her cervix. She gasped and mewled with every lunge inside her lush body.

"Yeah, Sin," Saint rasped. "You hitting that shit. Beat them guts up, bruh."

"This pussy so fucking . . . wet," Sin breathed out. And then he groaned as her walls tightened around him. He felt the base of his spine tingling and his balls tightening. He knew he wouldn't be able to hold out much longer if he kept stroking her, so he pulled out.

"Nooo," Dr. Dangerfield cried. "More dick. Please. Give me more."

Nothing more needed to be said. Her wish was their command.

With her mouth full of two dicks at a time, they took turns fucking her mouth, her pussy, their strong hands grabbing her by the waist, their balls slapping wildly into her ass.

One after the other, they stretched her. Fucked into every part of her pussy until her vision blurred and all she could see through her watery eyes were white lights.

In and out, in and out . . .

Switch.

In and out, in and out . . .

Switch.

In and out, in and out . . .

Switch.

One hard dick after the other was being pulled out to be only replaced with another, lunging in, sinking deeply into every space of her core.

Dr. Dangerfield moaned, her cunt clutching wildly, each stroke making her pussy juicier than the stroke before.

More wet gurgling sounds burst from the back of her throat.

"*God*daaamn," Saint hissed. "She's sucking the shit out these dicks."

Soul grunted in agreement. He'd always heard the good ole doctor was a freak. He'd be back for another round for sure—but alone.

He wanted this fine, freaky-bitch all to himself.

They fucked her until the wee hours of the morning, ravishing Dr. Dangerfield's cunt, her mouth, giving her the most exquisite pleasure imaginable.

"Ah, God, yes."

Click, click, click.

Her wet pussy squishes.

Click, click, click.

Her wet mouth squishes.

The sounds become a sensual melody over the sweet hum of Dr. Dangerfield's moaning. She is plummeting over the edge, coming, coming, coming . . .

Shrieking in ecstasy.

Mewling in bliss.

Now Dr. Dangerfield was being flipped on her back.

More thrusting. More pounding. More deep fucking, primal grunts and low groans snatched the air around them. Each man's orgasm spun out of their bodies, bursting through swollen dick-heads, splashing out in thick ropes of white cream.

And then they took turns licking over her pussy, sinking their mouths where each one's dick had been, their individual tongues swirling in hot, rhythmic circles on her engorged clit.

Dr. Dangerfield whimpered helplessly as more pleasure spiraled through her and instinctively, she thrust upward into their alternating mouths, basking in the sensations that ebbed and flowed through her body.

Her pussy surged with fresh juices, even after having just come—for the third time.

"Oh yes, oh yes," she murmured. "Lick my pussy. Bite my clit . . . *oooh*, yes . . ."

Saint, Sin, and Soul licked and kissed over her body. Three male mouths on her flesh one at a time. Dr. Dangerfield shut her eyes, drank in the pleasure, felt it pulsating through her pussy.

And then cried out.

Thirty-Eight

Investment . . .

The giving of one's self to a relationship.

It required honesty and respect.

It required time, energy, and emotion.

It required letting go of ego and pride.

It required attention and affection.

And, most importantly, it required *effort*.

Partners needed to put something into the relationship in order to get something out of it. And in doing so, it created the possibility of long-term sustainability—the weathering of life storms, together, with purpose and passion.

Dr. Dangerfield saw more too often than not many couples who were simply staying in relationships with men and women who they saw no *real* future with just for the sake of not being alone. They were staying in marriages that were lacking in trust, intimacy, openness, and *love*. Expecting something for nothing. Expecting change when they weren't willing to change. Expecting respect when they themselves were not willing to give respect.

Yes, investing in any relationship came with risk and a certain level of vulnerability. But the more couples put into their relationships (and in their partners), the greater were the returns.

So the question always remained: Was the relationship an asset or an endless debt? Bad investments, even in relationships, never ended with a happy return.

"Mr. Lewis, how are things going with you and your wife?" Dr. Dangerfield asked, not expecting love and light at the end of the proverbial rainbow. But the couple was due for their next session together and she wanted to know how many Excedrin she'd need to pack in her bag the day of.

Isaiah shrugged. "It's a'ight. I guess. Quandra's Quandra." He tilted his head and raised a brow. "Need I say more?"

Dr. Dangerfield gave him a sympathetic look. Not because she felt sorry for him. No. She held no pity toward him, or for him. Fact of the matter was, Isaiah was responsible for his own misery. And he'd sit in it, drown in it, and—more likely than not, die in it—unless he did something different. But. There was always a *but.*

Isaiah seemed unmotivated. And he seemed to be attracted to drama—some men were. From all outward appearances, Isaiah was unmoved and unbothered by the fact that his marriage was rapidly deteriorating. And Dr. Dangerfield wanted to know if his aloofness was a defense mechanism or did he simply not give a damn.

"Do you want your marriage, Mr. Lewis?" Dr. Dangerfield asked.

Isaiah leaned forward in his seat, fixing her with a hard stare. "If I say no?"

It was on the tip of Dr. Dangerfield's tongue to congratulate him for getting the hell out of it, if he didn't want to be chained to his miserable state or to the likes of his wife anymore. But that wouldn't have been professional of her, so she settled on, "Is that what you're telling me?"

Isaiah shook his head. "Nah. That's not what I'm saying." He pushed out a curse. "Shit. I don't know if I do or don't. All I know is, shit has to change." His voice took on a more purposeful tone, and he leaned back, surveying Dr. Dangerfield with appraising eyes. "Tell me, Doc. You married?"

Dr. Dangerfield regarded him, mulled over his question. She didn't typically self-disclose too much about herself with clients, but it was an appropriate question. And so she said, "No. Divorced."

"You left him?" Isaiah asked.

Dr. Dangerfield shook her head. "No. We left each other." And no she had no interest in expounding on that tidbit. They'd simply outgrown one another. Outside of sex, they'd had no real common ground. He'd wanted to gamble and trick his money away on luxury cars, slot machines, strippers, and cocaine.

And the husband before Taylor had been blessed with big beautiful balls and a long tongue. But he'd been cursed with an itty-bitty dick. And he came quickly. Yet that hadn't stopped him from fucking half of Venice Beach, then coming home and bringing her gonorrhea.

She'd divorced him—quick, fast, and in a hurry, taking with her the summer home in Hawaii, along with three hundred-thousand dollars as part of her divorce settlement.

"Sometimes couples outgrow one another. Sometimes they fall out of love with one another. And other times, the blueprint of their life plan has changed and the person they'd thought they'd wanted to build a life with is no longer who they thought they were. I say all that to say, people change. Relationships change. Needs and wants and desires change. But most couples won't talk honestly about it. Or they're afraid of letting go."

"So the question is, Mr. Lewis, how invested are you in your marriage at this very moment? Because right now is all that really matters."

Isaiah shrugged. "Right now . . ." He let out a sigh. "It's whatever. If Quandra stays, she stays. If not, I'm cool with that too."

Dr. Dangerfield regarded him thoughtfully. "I see. So at this moment, you have very little investment in your marriage or in trying to fix what's broken."

Isaiah shook his head. "Man, listen. I'm tired; feel me? You don't know what I have to put up with. Shit's draining."

"I can only imagine. Still, it is all by your choice," Dr. Dangerfield pointed out. "We always have a choice in what we allow in our lives."

"It's not always that cut-and-dry," he stated.

"You don't love her, do you?" Roselle asked bluntly as he stared at Isaiah. He couldn't relate to not wanting his wife. He wanted Brenda. He loved her. And he wanted his marriage. Fuck whatever hoes he fucked in between time. Bottom line, he wasn't leaving her crazy ass.

Isaiah was caught off guard by Roselle's question. And yet he felt compelled to be straight-up with him. "No, I don't. I mean. I care about her. We've been through a lot of shit together. But . . . *fuck*."

"*But* what?" Dr. Dangerfield asked.

Isaiah shook his head, more in disbelief than anything else. He was surprised at himself for openly admitting as much as he'd already shared. Most times he just pushed his thoughts to the back of his mind and drowned his feelings in work and bottles of brew, or Hennessy—or any other dark liquor that would give him the buzz he needed to cope.

"Like I said. I'm tired." And that was the truth. He was tired of LaQuandra. Tired of Cassandra. Tired, tired, tired—of both of those crazy bitches.

"Then it's time you reevaluate your situation," Dr. Dangerfield said softly. "And make some changes. Being unhappy is unfair to you. And it's unfair to your wife. Being miserable isn't what marriage is about."

Isaiah shook his head solemnly. She was right. But shit. He had too much time and money tied up in his marriage. They'd recently bought a new home, a bigger home—one he knew would never be filled with more kids. Something he wanted. He knew LaQuandra wouldn't want to sell their home and she definitely wouldn't move out, so he'd have to be okay with practically giving it to her. And he wasn't.

"It's obvious," Dr. Dangerfield stated, "that there's no real emotional investment in your marriage. Staying and being miserable only depletes the remaining balance of your emotional reserve."

Isaiah *tsked*. "Man, listen. The bank is broke. I'm drained. I have nothing left to give."

"Damn, bruh," Roselle said, shaking his head. "That's fucked."

Isaiah simply nodded. There wasn't anything else to add to that. All around, he knew he was in a fucked-up situation.

"Mr. Lewis, if there is anything else you'd like to share, the floor is still yours."

He shook his head. "Nah, I'm good."

"I'm available to you," she offered. "Anytime you need to talk, to sort things out, you can reach out to me." He nodded, appreciatively. And then Dr. Dangerfield moved on to Roselle.

"Mr. Woods, I know you've been very vocal about how much you love your wife . . ."

"No doubt," Roselle said over a smile. "That's my baby."

Dr. Dangerfield offered a slight smile of her own. "But do you love her enough to give up your cheating? Every time you engage in a one-night stand—and your wife catches you or learns about it—you are taking away from the marriage; you are robbing your wife."

Roselle gave her a questioning look.

"You are stealing hope for her marriage away from her. You're taking marital investments and laying them down in bed with another woman. Every time you cheat, you steal from her, Mr. Woods." Dr. Dangerfield kept her tone even, nonthreatening, nonjudgmental, and almost soothing.

Roselle cringed inwardly. He didn't like the way that sounded.

"I don't cheat on Brenda to hurt her. Shit. Most times, I don't expect to get caught."

"And yet you still do," Dr. Dangerfield stated.

Roselle frowned but didn't deny it. And he didn't interrupt her.

"There are cracks in your marriage, Mr. Woods. Even if you can't see them, they exist. And each time you cheat, you are chipping away at the foundation of your marriage. It's only a matter of time before it—your marriage—starts to crumble."

Roselle shifted in his seat. "Nah. We good. Brenda ain't leaving me. Ever."

"I didn't say she would," Dr. Dangerfield said. "All I'm stating is the obvious. And yet you still haven't answered the question."

Dr. Dangerfield caught Kendall's eyes on her. He'd found himself staring at her. Staring through her. There was something about her that reminded him of Persia. Maybe it was the short, pixie-style haircut. Or maybe it was the way she subconsciously licked over her perfectly glossed lips that made him think of Persia's hot, wet tongue on his dick, his balls—and fuck yeah—in his ass. And the thought was not only making him horny, but it was making his dick painfully hard as well.

Shit.

"What was the question again?" Roselle asked.

Dr. Dangerfield crossed her legs at her ankles. "I asked if you loved your wife enough to give up your womanizing ways? But now I'm asking if you are more invested in cheating than you are in your marriage?"

Damn.

Roselle couldn't say he could give it up. But he didn't want to say he wouldn't either. So he settled for somewhere in the middle. "I can only try."

And Dr. Dangerfield took that to mean he'd stick his dick in the next wet hole made available to him—just like on the beach, and on the plane ride. Yes. She knew all about those indiscretions. Nothing happened here that she wasn't privy to.

"Trying is a start," is all she offered. And then her attention moved on to Kendall.

"Mr. Evans, are you okay? You seem a bit preoccupied today."

Kendall stretched out his legs and ran his palms down along the inside of his thighs as he stretched. He shifted into the plush leather cushion of his chair.

Yeah. I'm horny. I want my prostate stroked, so I can bust a good nut.

He and Krista still had not completed Dr. Dangerfield's masturbation assignment, because he hadn't been in the mood to. And Krista hadn't shown much enthusiasm nor interest in the idea.

"Yeah, I'm good. All is well."

Dr. Dangerfield gave him a doubtful look.

Kendall kept his eyes locked on hers. And then he asked, "When is our next couples' session?"

Thirty-Nine

Brenda felt sexy sitting at the bar as she sipped on her second drink, Wet Heat—a mixture of coconut rum, Dark rum, pineapple juice, jalapeño slices, and a splash of coconut cream shaken and then served chilled in a half-shelled coconut.

She'd decided to have a drink down on the beach and watch the water, drink in its tranquility, while she waited for Roselle to shower and get dress. She knew it would take his slow-ass close to an hour to get ready, so here she sat—in a short white dress, her ample cleavage nearly spilling out, while the cutout back revealed her smooth, tanned skin—swaying to the sounds of H.E.R as she sang about not having enough practice in love, not wanting to play games.

Brenda didn't have that problem though. She knew how to love. And she loved hard. Maybe too hard sometimes, perhaps a bit obsessively at times.

Still, she loved.

And she loved Roselle. She loved his touch. The way he held her, kissed her, licked her, teased her; the way he made love to her and fucked her all in the same strokes. Roselle knew how to make her pussy cream and squirt simultaneously.

Yes. He was a gifted lover.

But he was also a pain-in-the-ass too, but he was hers.

And, no, he wasn't perfect, but he'd always been perfect enough for her, even with his wandering eye and bouncing dick and whore-mongering ways. He was still the only man for her.

Brenda licked over her lips. She found herself thinking about Roselle's dick. *Beauty*—yes, God. It wasn't enormous, but it was nowhere near small—it was exceptionally way above average. It was heavenly bliss. It was eight-plus inches of thick, golden-brown goodness that stroked into her core and reminded her of why she'd stolen Roselle from her ex-best friend in the first place.

Did she have any regrets?

Hell no. She'd had her eyes on him, first, that night at Club Scandal. But Trinity had gotten to him first. Given him her number. Fucked him. Then cuffed him.

And then instead of keeping her mouth shut, all Trinity did was brag about how fine he was, how freaky he was. About how good the dick was, how Roselle had made her toes curl every time he licked over her clit with his long tongue.

Yes, Brenda had hated—a little at first. But then she'd seen the way he'd look at her any time she came around with heat and hunger in his eyes. And, yes, she'd wanted some of him. She'd been bold enough to tell him so. And bold enough to suck his dick and swallow his babies, while he fingered her pussy, outside of Trinity's apartment complex.

Weeks later, they were fucking on the low. She'd become his sidepiece. And, okay, so she'd thought that that would be enough. And for a while, it had been.

But, after a year of having his raw dick coating the inside of her walls, Brenda had been determined to have him for herself. So she waited, schemed, and kept him satiated with stress-free sex.

Oh yes, Brenda had been a scandalous bitch, smiling in her good friend's face, while fucking her man. Everything Trinity wasn't willing to do, with him and to him, Brenda had been more than willing to step in and indulge him.

The dick had been too good not to.

And though she'd prayed for it, she never pressured him into leaving Trinity. He'd done it on his own, in his own time. He'd left Trinity for *her*. And then he'd put a ring on it.

Two kids and eleven years later, and Roselle was still coming home to *her*.

So, no—fuck no—there were no regrets. Trinity had never been a real friend, any-damn-way. Besides, that lame-ass bitch hadn't deserved him. She didn't know how to handle a man like Roselle. And she damn sure didn't deserve to birth his curly-haired babies. No. Brenda had deserved him. But wait for it. She knew she deserved everything else that came along with having him.

And she was fine with that. Most times.

Brenda knew she was a whore. A whore who rode her man, any time, any place. Bitches had better get on board or have her man snatched up by the next freak lying in wait, like she'd been.

H.E.R's "Facts" played and Brenda rocked her shoulders. She pursed her cherry-glossed lips. Call her dick-dumb. Call her crazy. She didn't give a goddamn. But a bitch would never call her sexually repressed, or lonely.

She slowly sipped through her straw, allowing the concoction's sweet heat to wet her tongue and pool through her veins. One more and she was for certain she'd be tumbling off the barstool. Yes. She was feeling herself. Thick in all the right places, she was a bad bitch—and she knew it.

And she felt like being naughty. She thought to guzzle her drink, then head back to her villa in hopes to find Roselle naked. In her mind's eyes, she saw herself dropping to her knees, nuzzling his groin and feeling his dick, wrapping a hand around the thick base of his growing erection, before licking the crown of his dick and drawing him deep into her hungry, wet mouth.

Yes. That was what she'd do, she decided, sucking down the rest of her drink through her straw. She slid off her stool and, somehow, managed to stand on wobbly legs. She ran a hand through her shoulder-length hair, tucking the strands behind her ears and then shouldered her purse.

"Leaving already?" said a voice so richly baritone that Brenda nearly swooned. Or was that from the effects of the liquor? Brenda's skin prickled with nerves as she turned and found herself looking up into the face of Sin. Lord, she didn't remember him being this fine when she'd first seen him on the plane—or when he'd slyly winked at her on the beach. But—damn him—up close and personal, his body mere inches from hers, towering over her, he was a massive ball of sexual energy.

For a moment, Brenda simply stared up at him, trying to swallow down the air that had caught in the back of her throat. And then Sin slid his muscled body onto the stool next to her and grinned.

"I hoped I'd see you again," he said simply, sounding cool and confident, like a man who knew what he wanted and knew how to take it.

One of Brenda's eyebrows lifted, and she cocked her head to the side. "Is that so?" she said softly.

"No doubt, baby."

Baby. The word slipped from his lips and slid over her like warm honey—thick and sweet. When the bartender stopped in front of him, he ordered a double-shot of Remy. And then he looked at her. "She'll have another of whatever she's been drinking."

"Oh, no—please, no," Brenda quickly said. "I can't—I shouldn't."

Sin's lips curved up into a devilish grin. "But you will. If you want to."

"No. I have to get going."

Sin took her in. "One drink, baby. Live a little. A little sin . . ." He paused. And then he scanned her body with his eyes, slowly, seductively, licking over those beautiful chocolate-brown lips, "every now and then, never hurt anyone."

Brenda felt herself flush. Or maybe it was the two drinks she'd already had. She glanced down at her watch, then up at him.

Sin.

How apropos.

She sinned every day. Yet, she stood debating, trying to talk herself out of one more drink with a dangerously fine man with a name like Sin.

Without even touching her, Sin seduced her.

Robbed her of the will to resist.

Him.

His challenge.

Why was he taunting her? But, more importantly than that, why was she aching, wanting, and suddenly feeling wet.

Damn him.

But shit. He was scrumptiously sexy. Oh hell. Brenda slid back onto her barstool. So much for the delicious dick-suck she'd planned in her head with her down on her knees between Roselle's muscular thighs.

"One drink," she said firmly. "I've already had two too many."

"One drink is all you'll need," he said smoothly.

This time she smiled, and he grinned. And then his long thick fingers reached out and touched her cheek. Brenda blinked, but she didn't jerk her head away, not even as his finger trailed to the corner of her mouth. No. She should have, but she didn't. Instead her breath hitched and her lips parted the barest of centimeters in response.

Sin stared at her, his brown eyes sizzling her with purpose.

He leaned into her. "I've been wondering what you taste like," he murmured. His lips flush to her ear, a teasing hot-breath brushed her skin.

Brenda swallowed, then licked her lips. She didn't know what to say to that, but she knew she needed to say something. So she stated the obvious. "As flattered as I am, I'm a married woman."

Sin cocked his head slightly to the right, and Brenda swore she saw the dirty mind behind those smoldering eyes. "And I still wanna stick my tongue deep inside you and lick out your soul."

Lord God—sweet Jesus.

Suddenly, she felt heat everywhere. Scorching her skin. Searing her cunt. Burning the tip of her clit. Brenda felt her mouth go dry, but her pussy grow wetter.

If she weren't here, on this island—with Roselle, she'd invite him to taste her pussy. He could lick the inside of her uterus, then suck out her ovaries if he'd wanted.

This was so inappropriate. She knew this. And yet she still wanted to indulge him, to engage him.

The bartender returned with their drinks setting them on the bar in front of them, and Brenda quickly grabbed hers, thankful to have something to squelch her growing desire, to drown the rising heat in her belly.

"Where's your husband?" Sin asked in a swift change of subject.

Who?

Brenda gave him a questioning stare.

Sin grinned and chuckled lightly. "Your husband, baby. Where is he?"

Oh. Him.

"Getting dressed."

"Cool. You happy with him?"

Brenda nodded. "Yes. Very. He's good to me."

Sin's eyes twinkled. "Does he dick your body down, handle them curves with long, deep thrusts?"

Brenda raised her head in surprise, at his bluntness, at her body's response to it—*him*. She took a long sip of her drink. "Yes," she admitted. And then she smiled. "You're trouble."

Sin dissolved into laughter, his head going back, the cords of muscle in his neck bulging, before turning to take her in. "I'm Sin, remember? I'm supposed to be." There went those brown eyes again, intensely staring at her. "But I'm good trouble, baby. The kind you look forward to sinning for."

Brenda felt her body shake.

"You ever cheat on him?"

"On who? My husband?" Brenda asked, surprised he'd ask her that.

She shifted in her seat and then looked down at the napkin under her drink. She played with the ends, her expression pensive, as if deciding whether or not she wanted to tell him. The truth.

"Yes," she admitted softly, her gaze locking on his. Brenda saw the flickers of interest and hunger in his eyes, and it heated her body. She licked her lips. And Sin grinned.

"I wanna fuck you."

"I . . . I," Brenda stammered.

"One night," Sin said, "that's all I need—one night to bury myself so deep in your guts that you'll still feel me pulsing inside of you weeks later."

Brenda's fingers gripped her drink, pressing into the coconut's shell as she pressed her thighs shut, her cunt pulsing to the sound of those four words—"I wanna fuck you"—*yes, yes . . . fuck me, Daddy . . .*

"My God. You are so tempting," she muttered. "And trust me, if I—"

"Hey, baby."

Both Brenda and Sin whirled around to see Roselle heading across the bar toward them. Sin couldn't be sure, but he thought he heard Brenda utter a curse under her breath.

Roselle dropped a kiss on Brenda's lips, then stood between her and Sin as he extended his hand. "Roselle, man."

Sin took his hand. "Sin."

Roselle ginned. "And I bet you live up to your name, man."

Sin laughed. "I confess. My moral compass is faulty."

Brenda blushed and caught Roselle's curious stare out of the corner of her eye.

Roselle checked his watch. "Well, thanks for keeping my beautiful wife company. But we gotta head out." He looked over at Brenda. "You ready, baby?"

"Yes. Let me just finish my drink." And then Brenda's lips were wrapped around the tip of her straw and she was quickly siphoning out her drink until all that was left was an empty coconut shell.

Sin smiled. "Was it good?"

"Very," Brenda said as she slid off her barstool. "Thanks for the drink," she said, eyeing Sin, while trying to not look down into his crotch. "And the conversation."

Sin smiled. And Brenda caught something shimmering in his eyes—lust.

"The two of you enjoy the rest of your evening."

"No doubt," Roselle said, giving Sin a fist-bump. "Don't hurt 'em out here, playboy."

Sin laughed again. "What's the fun in that?"

Roselle let out a laugh of his own. "Right, right." And then he draped an arm over Brenda's shoulder, pulling her body into his. He kissed her on top of her head. And then, as they walked away, he said, "You wanna fuck him, don't you?"

Forty

"What is it that you want from me, Kendall, huh?" Krista blew out a frustrated breath. Things between the two had become tense over the last several days. Krista couldn't understand why all of sudden, Kendall was becoming more sexually demanding. Expecting her to do shit he *knew* she didn't like doing. Like once again, rubbing his thumb over the seam of her ass three nights ago, while he'd had her bent over the bed, brushing over her sweet spot from the back.

And then, *uh*—Krista felt herself becoming annoyed all over again just thinking about it—but, last night she'd wanted to have sex. But Kendall didn't. He'd claimed he wasn't in the mood. Since when? He'd not once ever denied her sex—nor had she ever denied him. And yet last night, he'd managed to refuse her physical intimacy. He'd flat-out told her that he wanted some head—from his wife. That he wanted her to sit her ass up on his face while she sucked him off. She hadn't wanted to, but, yes, she did it—69'd with him. But he'd gotten frustrated, demanding she got off of him, claiming he didn't like how she was sucking his dick; that he could tell she wasn't really into it. And that had turned him off.

After all these years of marriage, his ass wanted to have a sexual revelation of sorts. Calling her out on her sexual performance. Really?

Krista blamed Kendall's newfound attitude on this island, these sessions, and being around that porn star bitch—that, that . . . sexual defiant.

Nairobia-what's-her-face.

"I've been a good wife; haven't I?" Krista pressed.

"Yes, baby," Kendall said honestly. "Most definitely. You're a good woman, Kris. And I love you for that."

Krista cringed inwardly. She thought she heard a *but* coming. So she braced herself. There was simply no other way to say it. Kendall had been dancing around the truth for long enough. And, quite frankly, he was tired. Tired of not having his sexual needs met. Tired of denying himself certain pleasures that he really only wanted from his wife, but had to seek outside his marriage.

And the fucked-up thing was, Kendall felt no real regret for his cheating. He'd never want to hurt his wife. Still . . .

Not being halfway truthful about his desires was hurting him more.

"I love you, Krista," Kendall said again, "and—"

"You already said that, Kendall," Krista pointed out, cutting him off.

"Mrs. Evans," Dr. Dangerfield said gently, "why don't you give your husband a chance to finish? The purpose of all of this is to allow for the two of you to express your wants and needs and desires without harsh judgments in hopes that it will bring the two of you closer."

Krista frowned. How dare this bitch. Like she didn't know all this already. "Well, then he needs to stop all this pussyfooting around and say what's on his mind, because if you're trying to imply that I don't listen to *my* husband, you are sadly misinformed."

Oh? You don't say.

Dr. Dangerfield offered Krista a smile, one that hadn't quite met her eyes. "Yes. I'm sure you do listen to him." *When it suits you.* "But now I would like for you to *hear* him as well. And I'd like for you to try to hear him out without becoming defensive. Do you think you can do that?"

Krista stared at Dr. Dangerfield trying to understand why she was sitting here talking to her as if she were some insolent child.

"I don't get defensive," Krista snapped.

"Perhaps you are not always aware of it," Dr. Dangerfield suggested. "Sometimes it's not necessarily in our words or voice tones, but in those nonverbal cues that give off defensive energy. Body language speaks volumes, Mrs. Evans."

Krista fixed her eyes on Dr. Dangerfield, fighting the urge to roll them up in her head.

Kendall slowly shook his head, shifting his chair, so that he could face her. He needed to be mindful of his choice of words. He reached for Krista's hand, then gently stroked his thumb over it. "As I was saying, baby. I love you. And I enjoy being inside of you when we're making love."

Krista stared at him. "But . . .?"

Kendall swallowed. The moment of truth was upon him. The door had been opened. He either walked through it or let it close.

So he said, "But I'm not always satisfied. Sometimes I want more. Sometimes I need more."

Krista's mouth gaped open and her gaze turned incredulous as she stared back at him as if to determine whether he was serious. But Kendall returned her gaze unflinchingly, his eyes telling her he was serious as a hurricane.

"Are you kidding me?" she shouted, snatching her hand from his. "How exactly are you *not* satisfied, huh, Kendall?"

"Sexually." Kendall kept his voice calm, and his gaze firmly set on Krista's.

Krista scoffed. "Oh really? The one night I don't suck your damn dick to your liking, and all of a sudden, you're not satisfied. Really, Kendall?"

Kendall shook his head. "Giving me—your man—head should be something you enjoy, Kris, because you know it pleases me. But—no, you'd rather put minimal effort into it. Anything I ever ask of you is always faced with resistance. Always. So no. I'm not satisfied, Krista. Most times than not."

Krista blinked.

Had she heard him right?

That sometimes he wanted more when she had sex with him regularly; even when she didn't feel like it. Why? Because that was one of her wifely duties, to keep her man well fucked. What was so *basic* about that? Mmph. And he sat here and had the audacity to tell her that he wasn't *satisfied*.

Krista's eyes narrowed as she absorbed his words. Shock crested, then quickly morphed into anger. She felt like exploding, spewing out a string of expletives. Loud, colorful language to light his ass up good, but Krista wasn't about to let the devil have his way with her tongue.

Krista caught the eye of Dr. Dangerfield, and then disgust painted over her face. "Is that why you'd gotten so mad at me for not letting you shove your fingers into my ass?"

Kendall sighed. "It was a thumb, Krista. Not fingers."

Krista huffed. "Same damn difference."

"And I didn't get mad because of that," Kendall corrected. "I got mad because of your attitude about sex. Anything I want to do sexually with you is a problem for you. If I want to give you oral sex, you complain about it. If I want to pull open your beautiful ass and look inside it, you have a problem with it. If I want to kiss you there, you think it's dirty."

Krista felt the vein in the center of her forehead pulse. "Oh Kendall, get over yourself. Excuse me for not wanting you down between my legs snacking on my privates all damn night. If you want to lick me there, then lick me there and then be done with it. And, as far as my ass is concerned, I don't want you sticking your fingers—oh excuse me, your thumb—in my ass. Period. Or your damn tongue."

Kendall let out a frustrated breath. "For Christ's sake, Krista. But ever since you've gotten involved in the church again, you've changed."

Krista snarled, "Oh don't you dare blame my getting saved on this bullshit, Kendall. I can love the Lord and love you too—and I do."

Kendall shook his head. "Then love *me*, Krista—all of me. And let me do the same."

"I do you love you, Kendall," Krista snapped. "But if you think I am going to stop loving my relationship with the Lord too, then you have another thing coming."

Kendall sighed. "That's not what I'm asking of you, Krista. You're my damn wife. If I want to go down on you, let me. If I want to lick over your ass, let me. Damn. I love everything about you. All I'm asking is for you to be a little more open-minded; that's it. I'm simply asking you to be more adventurous sexually with me, to open your mind a little more. I wanna explore new things with you, Kris."

"So ass licking is your new thing now, huh, Kendall?"

Kendall pinned her with an intense stare. "Yes, Krista. I wanna lick your ass, sometimes. Damn."

Krista grunted. "First fingers and a tongue, then you'll be wanting to stick your damn dick in it. No. There will never be any ass play going on in bed with me. Ever. So what other bitch's ass have you been licking on, huh, Kendall?"

Kendall frowned. "Are you hearing yourself right now, Krista, huh?"

Dr. Dangerfield finally decided to interject. "Mrs. Evans, anal play—"

"*No*," Krista snapped, putting a finger up, stopping Dr. Dangerfield. "This is between me and *my* husband. I don't need your interference. You've done enough meddling in my damn life." Bitch.

Dr. Dangerfield kindly swept a hand out, giving Krista the floor.

"We're here, Krista, because *we* need help."

"No," she countered. "*You* need help, Kendall, if you think I'm about to let you do a bunch of freaky shit to me."

Kendall gave her an incredulous look. "And what is so freaky about me wanting to make love to my wife in every way imaginable, huh, Krista?"

"I'm not having no man sticking his fingers in my ass. Period. Husband or not."

Kendall sighed again, and then he shook his head solemnly. "Baby, the fact that you can't even see how rigid you are is sad. The fact that you don't think you need any help is what's even sadder." Kendall gave her a pained look. "Anything that you deem inappropriate or that doesn't fit into your narrow-minded world, you somehow manage to turn it into something negative. I masturbate. And I'm going to continue to masturbate—even after I sex you down. I wanna tongue you in every part of your body when I'm making love to you. Why? Because I love you, Krista, and it turns *me* on. And you should wanna keep me turned on. *Me*, Krista. Not some stranger in the streets. And yet you seem to have a problem with *that?*"

Krista's jaw clenched. She felt like slapping the shit out of him. But she quickly composed herself and said as she stood, "If you want some freak-ass whore, then go be with one."

Kendall gently grabbed her arm. "Again, you're missing the point. I don't want a *whore* out in the streets, Kris. What I want is for *my* wife to be my whore."

Krista felt herself shaking with fury. "Well, I hate to be the one to break it to you, Kendall. But I'm not that wife." She yanked her arm from his grasp. "I'm done here."

Dr. Dangerfield called out to her, "Mrs. Evans. Please. Don't storm out. Let's explore this further."

Krista shot her a furious glare. "How about *you* explore your own shit, instead of trying to destroy people's marriages."

Kendall remained in his seat and watched in disbelief as Krista stormed out of the office. A few seconds ticked by before Kendall peeled his eyes from the now shut door.

He looked over at Dr. Dangerfield and then said, "Now what?"

Forty-One

He was lying through his teeth. Then again, she had been too. They were both liars. But that wasn't the point. The point was, LaQuandra knew he was lying, and all she wanted was for Isaiah to man-up, and finally admit that he was fucking *that bitch.*

"Just say it, Isaiah," LaQuandra insisted. "I know you've been screwing Cassandra."

Isaiah sighed. This bitch just wouldn't let up. "You bugging, Quandra. Damn. Let it go. You hear me?" He pinned her with a hard stare and then shook his head. "I told you I'm not thinking about Cass, and you still wanna be on this dumb shit."

This was the couple's fourth session with Dr. Dangerfield, and Isaiah had yet to admit to his cheating with his child's mother. And he had no intentions of doing so.

But LaQuandra was insistent and she had no intents of letting it go. But that didn't matter because Isaiah's answer was still—and always would be—*no*, *no*, *no*, and *no.*

"Stop lying, Isaiah. I know you still fucking that crazy bitch."

The pot calling the kettle . . .

Dr. Dangerfield shifted in her seat, pushing her decorative glasses up over the bridge of her nose. She didn't know what was more draining: Krista's rigid views on sex or LaQuandra's ghetto-ass ramblings about her husband's sexual proclivities—real or imagined—with his child's mother.

And between the two of them, Dr. Dangerfield felt like she was in Hell's Kitchen.

Isaiah sighed. This shit was so draining. Toxic. And he was slowly beginning to reach the end of his rope before he snapped.

Dr. Dangerfield caught the way Isaiah's jaw tightened, and yet he kept his eyes fixed on LaQuandra, not once shifting them when he denied her allegations.

Dr. Dangerfield wasn't completely convinced that he was being truthful, but his credibility wasn't for her to decide.

"Well, I want you to take a lie detector test," LaQuandra stated firmly.

Isaiah gave her an incredulous look. "A *what?*"

"You heard me," she snapped. "If you aren't sleeping with that whore, then prove it. Take the test."

"Man, fuck outta here," Isaiah said angrily. "I'm not taking that shit. You take one."

LaQuandra blinked. "And what the hell would I need to take one for, huh, Isaiah?"

"So we can see how many lies you've told, since you wanna be on lie patrol."

LaQuandra frowned. "Motherfucker, I'm not the one fucking that slutty-bitch, you are!"

"Fuck outta here." Isaiah snorted as he stared at her. "And I keep telling you 'bout calling her out her name."

Anger seized LaQuandra. She jerked around in her seat and faced Isaiah, trying to keep her temper in check. "But you let that bitch disrespect me. Fuck you, Isaiah!"

"Mr. and Mrs. Lewis," Dr. Dangerfield interjected. "Let's take a moment to calm down. Dirty fighting accomplishes nothing."

She paused, and then calmly stated, "It is very clear that this is a very painful topic for you, Mrs. Lewis. And I understand your hurt. Believe me. I do. But from where I am sitting, this seems to be an issue that will have no clear resolution." She looked at Isaiah. "Mr. Lewis, you insist that there is no romantic or sexual involvement between you and your son's mother, is that correct?"

Isaiah shifted in his seat. "Yeah. I already said that."

LaQuandra sucked her teeth, and then rolled her eyes. "Yeah, right."

Dr. Dangerfield turned her attention to LaQuandra. "And you, Mrs. Lewis, are insistent that there is something going on between the two."

"Because there is," LaQuandra spat. "I'm not stupid."

"Then why the fuck are you still with me, huh, Quandra?" Isaiah growled, pinning her with a burning stare. "Since you already have it all figured out in that fucked-up head of yours that I'm still fucking Cass, then why the fuck are you still in my face, huh? Riddle me that shit."

LaQuandra scoffed. She had no immediate answer for that, and yet she managed to push out, "Don't try to play head games with me, Isaiah. Admit the shit, so we can move on from it."

Isaiah snorted. "Yeah, okay. We'll never move on from this shit, Quandra. And you know it. Anything that has to do with my son's mother is always gonna be a problem with you and you know it."

"Mrs. Lewis, have you asked your husband's—Miss Simms, right out if she's sexually involved with your husband?"

LaQuandra made a face. "For what? The thot has told me in so many words that she's still screwing him; even as we were boarding the plane that bitch couldn't wait to let it be known that she had her ass spread out over his face the night he dropped his son off."

Isaiah sucked his teeth. "Man, fuck outta here. That's bullshit. I was nowhere near her ass." *Just her pussy.* He shook his head. "She be sayin' shit just to fuck with you."

LaQuandra tilted her head and twisted her lips

Dr. Dangerfield decided it was time to put this dead horse down once and for all. She was exhausted from LaQuandra's obsession with this Cassandra woman, and she wanted to get it all out in the open once and for all.

So . . .

LaQuandra's nose flared. "You need to check her, and let that bitch know her place."

Dr. Dangerfield cleared her throat. "Mrs. Lewis, say—for argument's sake, that Mr. Lewis did admit to his indiscretions with his son's mother, then what? What does that do for you? And how does that knowing then affect your marriage?"

LaQuandra blinked. She hadn't really considered that Isaiah might actually confess his sins, nor had she considered what might happen if he did.

"I just wanna know."

"And then what?" Dr. Dangerfield pushed gently.

LaQuandra slumped in her seat, slowly shaking her head. She honestly didn't know. "I just want the truth. That's it."

Isaiah huffed. "Damn, Quandra. I already told you the truth. And you still don't believe me."

"And why should I, Isaiah, when you've lied to my face before about fucking her? And then months later, that bitch comes banging on my door with an infant in her arms, telling me to say hi to my new stepson. And the only reason you couldn't lie your way outta that shit is because the baby looked exactly like *you*."

LaQuandra turned from him, shifting in her seat so that her back was twisted toward him, fighting back tears she'd sworn she wouldn't shed.

Dr. Dangerfield wanted to muster up an ounce of sympathy for the woman, but she didn't have it in her. "There are a lot of resentments here. And your wife is still hurting from the betrayal, Mr. Lewis."

Isaiah glanced over at LaQuandra. "I didn't sleep with Cass or make lil' Isaiah to hurt you, Quandra," he said softly. "But I am sorry that it did."

LaQuandra closed her eyes, and took several deep breaths. This was the first time that she'd heard Isaiah apologize to her and it sounded sincere.

"Mrs. Lewis, can you look at your husband, please?" Dr. Dangerfield asked.

LaQuandra turned in her chair and looked at him, her eyes narrowed slits of fury.

"Little Isaiah is my heart, Quandra. And I don't regret ever having him."

"I know he is, Isaiah," LaQuandra admitted. "And you know how much I love him too. But I can't help still seeing her in him. A life that you and her created, one that I wasn't a part of."

"I know," Isaiah said. "Don't you think I wanted kids with you, huh, Quandra? Don't you think I wanted to build a family with you? But it didn't happen for us."

A pain shot through LaQuandra's chest and she almost choked on its intensity. She couldn't lose him to her lies, to her own betrayal. So she would never tell him about the many feigned pregnancies and miscarriages.

She just couldn't.

"I know you did," was all she managed to say.

"Mr. Lewis, do you think you can set healthier boundaries when it comes to your son's mother, calling her out when she disrespects your wife?"

LaQuandra eyed him. And waited.

Isaiah hesitated. This counseling shit was too stressful and too much fucking work. He sighed. "I'll do better," he offered.

LaQuandra relaxed in her chair, somewhat satisfied. But not enough to let go of her nagging suspicions, and so she pressed Isaiah again. "Are you fucking her, Isaiah? And don't lie."

"No. I'm not," Isaiah firmly stated.

LaQuandra eyed him suspiciously. "Then why aren't you fucking me?"

"Because I'm tired, Quandra. I'm tired of the bickering. I'm tired of the back and forth between you and Cass. I'm tired of being in the middle of drama and bullshit. You and Cass are fucking drama queens. And, keeping shit straight-up with you, Quandra—I'm tired of both of you crazy bitches."

"And I still don't believe you," LaQuandra said.

Isaiah shrugged. "Then I don't know what else to tell you."

"There are always three sides to every story," Dr. Dangerfield said. "There's his truth, your truth, and the real truth somewhere in the middle. So, Mrs. Lewis, to help you to decide which truth you wish to believe, I have two options for you." She waved a hand out over toward the other side of her office. "Over there is a lie detector, for which both of you will be required to take?"

LaQuandra rapidly blinked. "Excuse me? I'm not the one who—"

Dr. Dangerfield cut her off. "You want transparency, you want truths, then there's your chance for it. But your husband deserves the same."

Isaiah stretched back in his seat, arms folded with a smirk on his face. "Yeah, I'm kinda diggin' that."

LaQuandra rolled her eyes. "And the other option?"

Dr. Dangerfield smiled. "Glad you asked." She pressed a button, and then a wall slowly slid open revealing a large screen. "I have had the pleasure—and I use that word loosely—to speak candidly with Miss Simms."

Oh shit. Isaiah felt the blood draining from his face.

"Oh, Lord," LaQuandra groaned, feeling her pulse racing. "And what did that ratchet *bit*—she have to say? Did she admit to it?"

"You can find out for yourself," Dr. Dangerfield said. "Miss Simms has agreed to a call-in, and she's already on standby. So what will it be? The lie detector test or the conference call?"

Isaiah's mind was already made up. Cassandra's ass was too unpredictable and impulsive, but he also knew she wouldn't put him on blast unless he gave her reason to.

"I want the lie detector," he said.

LaQuandra raised a suspicious brow. *Oh, now this motherfucker wants to take the test. He must not want me to hear what that bitch has to say. Nigga, puhleeeze!*

"No. Call her," LaQuandra said. "I wanna hear what she has to say." She shot a nasty look over at Isaiah. "So we can clear the air once and for all."

Isaiah kept a straight face, but he was smiling inwardly. And then he prayed like hell that Cassandra stayed on script.

"Mr. Lewis, are you okay with this?"

Isaiah shrugged. "I guess."

"Very well then," Dr. Dangerfield said. And then she pressed another button, bringing the screen to life.

"Day'Asia, where the fuck is you going," blared out through the speakers, "leaving up outta here looking like some cheap whore? Day'Asia? Don't do me, bitch; you hear me talking to you!"

Isaiah cringed.

LaQuandra twisted her lips.

"Miss Simms? Hello? Hello?"

"I hear you, damn! I'm going to see Clitina."

"Nigga-coon, *boom!* Oh no the hell you not! You ain't going up to no gawtdamn prison dressed like no skank to see a skank. And you ain't smuggling no more drugs up there for that triflin' bitch, either. Both you whores are sickening. That bitch halfway retarded smoking anything that come from outta that rotted stank-hole of—"

"Mommy, Fuquan hit me."

"I did not, fucker!"

"Goddamn you, Fuquan. Don't have me break my fist in your mouth. You know I got that therapist bitch about to call me about Isaiah's *fahver*. Now don't do me. Go take your ass up to your room."

"Hello? Hello? Miss Simms?" Dr. Dangerfield called out again.

LaQuandra grunted, while Isaiah shook his head.

And then finally up on the screen appeared Cassandra Simms. With her thick, long lashes, almond-shaped eyes and flawless smooth butterscotch complexion, she was clearly not what Dr. Dangerfield had envisioned. In each of her ears was a large diamond stud.

"Hello? Miss Simms?"

"Yes, it is," Cassandra said, swinging her long Nicki Minaj-esque ponytail over her shoulder. "How may I help you?" She leaned forward, her face mere inches from the screen and then she leaned back, and waved. "Hey, baby daddy. Isaiah, come in here and say hi to ya *fahver*. He on camera with his mule-faced wife."

LaQuandra's jaw tightened, but she'd made it up in her mind that she wouldn't let this bitch get to her, not in front of the therapist.

Seconds later, a very handsome teenaged boy appeared, the spitting image of Isaiah. "What's good, Dad?" he said, and then he smiled, flashing perfectly white teeth and one deep dimple in his left cheek. "When you coming home?"

Isaiah smiled, and it was the first time Dr. Dangerfield saw his eyes light up since she'd been working with him.

"What's good, lil' man. I'll be home soon."

"Bet," his son said. "Make sure you come scoop me up."

"No doubt, man. I got you."

The teenaged boy threw up deuces and then leaned in and kissed Cassandra on the cheek. And then he was gone.

Cassandra smiled. "My baby so fine. And thank gawd he gotta big dingaling like his *fahver*."

Isaiah grinned. And LaQuandra swung a hand at him, hitting him in his chest.

"Miss Simms, I would like to thank you for—"

"Joshua, bring me my Bumblebees. The Chanels. And hurry up. Quandra's ugly-ass is hurting my eyes."

LaQuandra sat up in her seat, hand on hip. "*Bit—*" She caught herself. She huffed. "Can we please get on with this?"

"Miss Simms, please. May I have your attention?"

"Did you transfer them coins into my account?" Cassandra asked. "Because you know my time is money."

"Yes," Dr. Dangerfield said. "As agreed upon, five-thousand dollars has been successfully wired into your account."

LaQuandra blinked. *This money-hungry bitch.*

Cassandra smacked her glossed lips, reaching for her sunglasses. "Then you have my attention." She slid the designer shades on her face. "Now how can I help you?"

"As you see, we have Mr. and Mrs. Lewis here. And—"

"Yes. I sure do. I see my baby *fahver* and his ugly wife."

LaQuandra clenched her teeth and glared over at Isaiah, who sat leaning forward with his head down and his hands clasped. *This goddamn coward! Pussy-ass bitch*, LaQuandra thought.

"Miss Simms, please try to be respectful."

"Oh, I am being respectful. I've been good to LaQuandra. I ain't hop on that ass and beat her edges out in a minute. But she due for a new ass-stomp 'cause I know she still talking slick about me."

"Bitch, I don't say shit about your ghetto-ass," LaQuandra snapped. "But you stay talking shit about me!"

Cassandra smiled. "You see, Miss Therapist. I told you. She lucky I'm in a good mood today, so I'ma keep it classy. But, anyway, back to the Bobblehead you got in your office. Admit it, Quandra. You hate me because I gave Isaiah what you couldn't."

"No, bitch. I hate you because you're a whore."

Cassandra laughed. "But I ain't the one with my name engraved in a permanent chair down at the clinic, sugah-boo. You are."

Isaiah looked up.

LaQuandra swallowed. And then she shot a look over at Dr. Dangerfield. "Are you gonna ask this bitch, or what?"

"Nigga-coon, boom! Ask me what, bitch? Am I sucking Isaiah's dingaling? Am I letting him get all up in this sweet cootie-coo? Is he licking this juicy ass?"

Fuck. Isaiah held his breath.

"Yes, bitch!" LaQuandra shouted. "Is Isaiah still fucking you?"

A pre-teenaged boy with a gun drawn on one side of his face and a middle finger on the other side suddenly appeared behind Cassandra with both his middle fingers up.

"And if he is," Cassandra taunted, "what you gonna do, huh, sugah-boo, come beat my ass?" She laughed again. "I'd like to see you try. Are you—" She craned her neck, and swung her fist at the boy behind her. "Fuquan, you little big-dick fucker, get the fuck from behind me before I punch your goddamn eye sockets in! Don't do me."

He ran off laughing.

Cassandra sighed. "These ratchet-ass kids about to have me get ghetto up in here. I don't know where these motherfuckers come from." She took a deep breath. "I need to get down to The Crack House for some get-right 'n' shake these hips to get this mind right, before I end up in jail."

Dr. Dangerfield shifted in her chair. "Miss Simms, focus. Please. I promise we only need a moment of your time. So I'll get right to it. Are you and Mr. Lewis romantically or physically involved?"

"Focus? Nigga-coon, *boom!* Don't do me, Miss Lady. If Quandra wanna know if I'm fuckin' the skin off my baby *fahver's* dingaling, then let her ask me."

"Fair enough," Dr. Dangerfield said, ignoring the woman's hostility.

LaQuandra sucked her teeth. "Cassandra, don't play games. I already did. Now are you fucking him or not?"

Cassandra lifted up her sunglasses and peered into the screen. "LaQuandra, if I tell ya ugly-ass *no*, is you gonna believe me? And if I say *yes*, are you gonna leave him?"

LaQuandra blinked, and before she could answer, Cassandra was already speaking for her. "Of course you not gonna believe me. So why is we really here? Is your freaky-ass tryna invite me to a threesome? And you ain't leaving him, either. You wanna know why, Quandra? Because you scared I'ma move him up in here. You scared I'ma unlock these tubes 'n' give him another baby. And I still might—just because I can. And you can't."

LaQuandra felt her heart stop.

"Yo, what the fuck!" Isaiah snapped. "Damn! Both you bitches need to stop this dumb shit. Quandra, Cass ain't going nowhere because I gotta son with her. But if you wanna be on your bullshit 'n' wanna bounce, then bounce. But if you staying, then you need to stop talking shit about her, stop obsessing about shit. Damn."

Cassandra grunted. "Mmph. Let that coon know, boo."

"Yo, that shit goes for you too, Cass. You need to fall back on your bullshit. Stop slick-talking 'n' disrespecting LaQuandra. She's my wife. And you need to respect that shit. The only thing that matters to me is my son. Period. So both of you bitches need to figure it the fuck out."

Isaiah hopped up from his seat. "I'm out."

Cassandra and LaQuandra both blinked.

Dr. Dangerfield glanced at the time. She needed a drink. "Well, ladies. Time's up. Miss Simms, thanks for your time."

Forty-Two

The fresh scent of wet pussy perfumed the air, as Nairobia and Dr. Dangerfield lay curled beneath rumpled sheets watching the footage of Krista sitting in The Garden by the lagoon reading her Bible.

"Just look at her," Dr. Dangerfield said over a sigh.

Nairobia rolled her eyes as she cupped Dr. Dangerfield's breast, and then teasingly circled her nipple with her finger. Watching Krista was making her cunt go dry.

"What a dry little muffin," Nairobia drawled out. "Is there hope for her?"

Dr. Dangerfield let out a soft moan. Like Nairobia, she believed her sexuality, like many of her clients', wasn't neatly wrapped in a box. It was layered. Fluid. She didn't believe sexual expression was fixed or static. No. Sexuality was a matter of uncovering, discovering, one's own desires.

Nairobia pinched her nipple.

"Uh . . . *mmm*," Dr. Dangerfield moaned out. "There is . . . *uhh* . . ." She moaned again when Nairobia's hand slinked its way down over the curve of her hip, slowly finding its way between her legs. "No hope today. But maybe . . . tomorrow."

"Shameful," Nairobia said, her hand sliding over the front of Dr. Dangerfield's cunt. Her legs parted and Nairobia's fingertips pressed over her clit.

Dr. Dangerfield heard the desperate sound of her own whimper as Nairobia teased her there. And then she sucked in a gasp when Nairobia slid a finger inside her.

"Oh, yes," she said, her voice raw. She sucked in a gasp as her body clenched tightly around Nairobia's finger.

They'd spent the better part of the morning in Dr. Dangerfield's private suite, behind the sliding wall, watching the surveillance footage of the couples, particularly Krista, from over the last two weeks.

Borrrrring.

Dr. Dangerfield switched to another monitor and Nairobia licked over her lips at the sight of Kendall's impressive cock. Dr. Dangerfield zoomed in on it.

"He makes my pussy wet," she muttered as Nairobia continued dipping her fingers in and out of her body.

"No, my darling, your cunt is wet for more good cock, for more good fucking." Nairobia momentarily pulled her fingers from Dr. Dangerfield's swollen sex and then she reached over and pressed a button on the bottom of a remote.

The wall slowly slid open, and . . .

He was there, in the opened space—six-foot-four of chiseled, milk chocolate goodness, one of Nairobia's many boy-toys.

Josiah.

He worked at Nairobia's adult club in New York, The Pleasure Zone, having moved up the ranks from bartender to her dutiful assistant. And he'd come to the island at her request—to assist her in any-and-every way imaginable. Nairobia's wishes were always his command. He loved her pussy. Loved the way it spoke to him; the way it wetly sucked and slurped his dick. He loved Nairobia, loved pleasing her. He didn't consider himself her sex slave. But his dick, his body, was hers to do with whatever she desired. There was nothing he wouldn't do for her. And he'd share everything he was with whomever she wanted him to.

Dr. Dangerfield admired and appreciated his undying loyalty to her.

Nairobia's hypnotic effect on men never ceased to amaze her.

Josiah licked his lips.

And Dr. Dangerfield took mental snapshots of the ropes of muscle in his long legs, before latching her eyes onto his glorious, reddish-brown dick. Every muscle in his sleek torso bunched as his gaze flicked over their naked bodies. No longer interested in the likes of Krista, Dr. Dangerfield reached over for the remote and paused the footage. And then her gaze slid back down Josiah's body, her mouth watering at the sight of the thick, meaty dick that hung between his thighs, her pussy suddenly pulsing at the earlier memory of him deep inside her, stroking her still-slick walls.

Mmm, yes . . .

Dr. Dangerfield swallowed her drool. Then purred low in the back of her throat, widening her legs, her hips now thrusting upward as Nairobia's fingers spread open her wet folds, then wickedly slid in and out of her. Pleasure seeped into her blood, traveling through her body. And then Nairobia kissed her, her warm, sensual mouth working exquisitely over hers, coaxing her tongue to dance around hers.

Dr. Dangerfield groaned into the kiss, as Nairobia's lips moved sweetly over hers, stealing her breath. She couldn't breathe because Nairobia didn't let her. So she arched into the slick heat Nairobia's diving fingers were causing inside of her. And when she scissored her fingers, stretching open her sweet, pink center, Dr. Dangerfield cried out.

"*Ja*, *Ja*, my darling. Squeeze my fingers with your wet *kut*. Flood them with your nectar."

Nairobia's impassioned words sliced through her. Dr. Dangerfield shut her eyes and gave into the liquid pleasure. A moan built deep in her chest, caught in her throat, until it spiraled out in a sound of sweet agony. Oh, God, yes—yes, yes, yes.

Dr. Dangerfield cried out as her orgasm bolted out of her in a rush of molten lava.

Her body shook, the aftershocks of her orgasm still rippling through her core. Slowly, her lids fluttered open, and her hazy-eyed gaze locked onto Josiah's, dark hunger flashing across his handsome face, as he stood there, watching, longing; stroking his swelling dick in his hand.

Dr. Dangerfield's pussy clenched, her walls throbbed, at the carnal hunger she saw in his eyes. Nairobia saw it too. "Come, my love," she said as she summoned Josiah with wet, sticky fingers to come to them. "Feast on her juices, then feed her weeping *kut* with your big, hungry dick."

Another jolt of heat blazed through Dr. Dangerfield at the erotic sound of Nairobia's words. Everything about her was mesmeric.

Erogenous.

Lethal.

Nairobia had an uncanny way of pulling out the darkest side of others, bringing them pleasure while coaxing out their most erotic desires.

Nairobia brushed Dr. Dangerfield's lower lip with her cunt-soaked fingers, and she slid her tongue out, flicking it over them. Nairobia pressed her fingers between her lips, and Dr. Dangerfield suckled, savoring the taste of her pussy.

She shuddered as Josiah made his way over to them. His gait was smooth, every motion fluid as he moved like a starving panther, sleek and purposeful.

Nairobia scooted over as Josiah climbed up on the bed, the plush mattress absorbing the weight of him. She leaned over and kissed Dr. Dangerfield, offering her more tongue, before pulling back and then kissing Josiah, her tongue now searching the inside of his mouth, until she finally pulled free from his greedy lips.

"Fuck her deep, my love," Nairobia urged, sliding off the bed and then onto her feet.

Josiah grinned. "Anything for you."

"Wait. You're not staying—for more fun?" Dr. Dangerfield asked over a moan as Josiah leaned down and pressed his mouth between her breasts.

Nairobia flicked her gaze momentarily over at the monitor, Krista's stilled image in the center of the screen, then she tore her eyes away to land them on Dr. Dangerfield.

"I will go to her."

"Uh, mmm—*who?*"

Dr. Dangerfield arched into Josiah, seeking more of his mouth. And so he gave her more, kissing and sucking and licking a line down to her belly.

She moaned as his lips made their way over her mound. He kissed her there, nuzzled deeper, inhaling her scent as he stroked his fingers through her velvety folds.

A ragged moan tore from her throat as he swiped his mouth from her slit to her clit. He sucked lightly on it, before licking downward again.

"The sloth," Nairobia answered as she inched up behind Josiah and slid a finger along the crack of his ass. "I will go to her." Her finger slid back and forth over Josiah's hole, and then she was reaching over and sliding that same finger into Dr. Dangerfield's mouth.

"While he fucks you good, my . . ."

Dr. Dangerfield sucked Nairobia's finger into her mouth as Josiah, with teeth and tongue, nipped at the swollen nub, grazing it, scraping her with exquisite pleasure. Suddenly, everything around Dr. Dangerfield blurred, and the sound around her muffled as Josiah's tongue slid inside her, fucking her in slow, sensual strokes, tasting her from the inside out.

When she was finally able to blink through the haze, Nairobia was gone, and Josiah was steadily stroking her with his fingers and tongue, lapping hungrily at her pussy.

"I'm coming, I'm . . . com . . . *ing* . . . oh God—yes . . ."

Dr. Dangerfield's legs closed against his head, anchoring him in place, filling his mouth with her wet honey.

Forty-Three

Krista stared at the huge gift basket sitting on the oval glass table, where it'd been collecting dust for the last four weeks. A frown formed over her face as she stood in the living room of her villa with a hand on her hip, wondering why she hadn't tossed it out already.

Dildos of varying sizes and thickness. Clit wands. Vibrating beads. Cock rings. Butt plugs. Edible undies. Gels. Creams. Flavored oils. And lubes. Thanks—but no goddamn thanks. This was way too much kinky-shit in one place.

She'd never been into sex toys. Hell, she didn't even masturbate. And on those rare moments when she climbed on top of Kendall and rode him, she didn't even touch her clit or squeeze her own breasts or lick over her nipples.

That was what Kendall was for.

And she dared not *ever*—she plucked *Good Pussy* from the back slit of the gold cellophane wrapping—read *this* shit. But that didn't stop Krista from flipping the book over and staring at the face of its author. *Just look at her. Looking like some damn call girl.* She was nearly naked. Practically covered in diamonds. Her hands crossed over her breasts. Sprawled out on a white mink rug in a very sexually suggestive position—her beautiful legs spread open, the puffy print of her sex on display beneath a diamond-encrusted thong.

Good Pussy.

More like a community hole, Krista mused as she grunted, letting the hardcover book *clunk* down onto the table. She was so over all of this shit. All this sexual energy swirling around her was too much for her. The devil was everywhere. And this island was nothing but its dirty little playground.

Krista missed her church family. She needed more than just reading scriptures from the Good Book. She needed her soul feed with a good sermon, with a little praise and worship. She needed to be surrounded by church saints, not a bunch of damn sinners.

Shaking her head, Krista scooped up the basket of filth, but before she could make her way to toss it and its contents into the trash, there was a knock at the door. Krista froze, dismay coursing through her veins as she knew Kendall wouldn't be knocking since he had a key. So who the heck was it?

She could ignore the door, but the knocking was incessant. Krista sighed, setting the basket back down on the coffee table. It had to be Brenda, because she knew that ghetto-bitch, LaQuandra, wouldn't dare be at her door. She wasn't in the mood for company. But maybe it was housekeeping, she mused as she went to the door. Taking a deep breath, she opened it. Blinking in shock, Krista took in the fact that it wasn't housekeeping. But as she stared wordlessly at the woman standing before her, she suddenly wished that it had been LaQuandra instead.

Krista blinked again, suddenly feeling dirty and unkempt. "Can I help you?" she said, her voice coated with disdain. She tried not to inhale the sweetness of her scent.

"No, my darling. You can't. I'm here to help *you*," Nairobia said sweetly. "May I come in?"

"Hell no! You may not," Krista heard herself saying as she stared at Nairobia, dressed in some sheer pink gown—long, flowy, fitted waist, plunging neckline—that once again left nothing to the imagination.

Krista caught the dark prints of Nairobia's peaked nipples and quickly shifted her eyes. The tramp had no shame. She wanted to slam the door in her face. Tell this slutty bitch how she really felt about *her* and her wicked island. But she wasn't going to give her the satisfaction. For she knew the devil was a damn lie.

Krista stepped back, motioning for her to come inside.

Nairobia grinned. She made the church frump nervous. Without invitation, she took a seat on the love seat. And then Nairobia patted the empty space beside her, ignoring the indignation on Krista's face. "Come, my love. Sit. Let us get better acquainted."

Krista folded her arms. "No. I'm perfectly fine standing."

Nairobia offered her a smile. "You do not like Passion Island, no?"

Krista shrugged. "No—yes. I mean, it's a beautiful island. But . . ." Krista shook her head. "This island is not for me."

"You wish to leave, no?"

Krista shifted her weight again, and the look of contempt in her eyes did not go unnoticed. "Yes. I'm ready to get home."

Nairobia nodded, knowingly. "My loins ache for you, my darling," she said as she ran a hand through her hair. Women like Krista might have found Nairobia repulsive because of the fact that she proudly wore her sexuality like a second skin. But Nairobia found women like Krista just as revolting. A bunch of frigid, prudish bitches who lived their lives sexually repressed, simply because they were too afraid of letting go, too fearful of giving into their deepest desires.

Krista scowled. "Excuse *you?*"

"Your enslavement, my darling. It aches my loins knowing you are so trapped, sexually, my darling."

Krista blinked.

"Yes, my love. My *kut* weeps for you. It aches for your liberation."

Krista gave her a quizzical look, one that Nairobia purposefully ignored. She glanced over at the basket on the table. "You do not like my gifts, no?"

"The basket was thoughtful," Krista said, shifting her weight from one flat foot to the other. "But it's not for me?"

Nairobia gave Krista an amused look. "Why not, my darling? Do you not enjoy the hum of a vibrator rolling over your clit, or wetly wedged inside your *kut*, humming along your walls?"

Krista swallowed. "I just don't like them."

"Shame, my love. Do you not touch yourself?"

Krista frowned. "That's none of your damn business," she said indignantly. "Now why exactly are you here?"

Nairobia's gaze roamed over Krista. She was nothing exciting to look at. Her cunt did not clutch from the sight of her. "You are only good pussy because your husband tells you so, no?"

Krista's brow rose. "I beg your pardon?"

Nairobia stood to her feet, untying the knot around her waist.

Krista blinked. "W-w-what are you—"

"You are not good pussy, my love," Nairobia continued as she opened her gown and allowed the flimsy material to flutter to the floor. "And you are, sadly, my darling, not good loving. You are simply wet walls." Nairobia walked over to the gift basket and pulled out one of her favorites from her toy collection. She tore open the box and quickly pulled the toy out of its package. Then she wielded the ten-inch-long vibrating dong at Krista, who stood in shock as Nairobia reached inside the basket again and then pulled out her trademarked lube, Sweet Pleasure.

Krista felt the blood draining from her face. "Get out," she said in a stricken voice. And yet she didn't move to show her to the door. She couldn't. Her feet were stuck in place.

Nairobia widened her stance. "You are just a shell, my darling. An empty vessel for your husband to plant his seeds in; that is all, my love."

Krista's eyes widened in disbelief, a mixture of alarm and an unexplainable amount of fascination flowing through her veins, as Nairobia squirted lube over the silicone phallus, using her hand to slather the gel up and down its shaft and then over its head.

"The essence of sexuality, my darling, is in the giving and receiving of sexual pleasures between two lovers," Nairobia continued, pressing the multi-speed vibrator on a random setting. She slid the dildo between her legs. Krista's gaze followed Nairobia's hand as she slid the dildo over her clit and then slid it back and forth over the opening of her slit.

Krista's mouth opened to say something, but she clamped it shut when Nairobia said, "And you will lose your husband to another. You will lose him to not only good pussy, but to good loving and unforgettable fucking, my darling . . ."

Nairobia kept her eyes trained on Krista. "You are not unforgettable, my darling. Your *kut* is not unforgettable."

This brazen bitch! Krista felt violated. How dare she disrespect her? Wait. Had Kendall said something to her? Had Dr. Dangerfield? Krista nervously shifted her gaze from Nairobia's hand to the floor to the front door and then back to the low hum between Nairobia's thighs.

"Loving your *kut*, my darling, is loving yourself," Nairobia said huskily. Her hips sensually moved as she pressed the head of the dildo into the mouth of her pussy. "You cannot love you, without loving it." Nairobia dipped at the knees, pushing inch after inch of her dildo inside her. "Mmm . . . *ooh* . . . your *kut* . . . *uh* . . . is happiest when you feed it. When you allow it to be free. Do you not want to free your pussy, my love?"

And then the dildo was gone. Wetly sucked into Nairobia's body, humming on a high speed.

Krista's heart pumped fiercely, but she was too numbed by shock to feel the anger that her mind told her she should feel. Her face drained as realization dawned. What if Kendall walked in and found this whore fucking herself in the middle of their living room?

She couldn't let that happen. She remembered all too well that look he'd had in his eyes for her. "I need you to leave," Krista said in a panicked tone. "Now. Or I will call security." And yet she didn't make a start toward the door.

Nairobia tossed her head back and laughed. "This is my island, darling." And then she pinned her with a look, her gray eyes shimmering pools of heated lust as she pulled the dildo from her cunt and then slowly licked over it.

Krista blinked.

"I will leave you with the scent of my pussy, my love. And the memory of these last words: You are a lazy lay. Selfish in your deeds." Nairobia swirled her tongue over the top of the phallus's head. And then she sucked it into her mouth before her pink tongue laved over her lips. "Your handsome husband, so virile, so hungry, needs a whole woman, my darling. A *sensual* woman, a *sexual* woman, a woman comfortable in her sexuality, a woman fearlessly willing to embrace her desires—one who knows how to embrace her strength and her femininity, while still allowing him to be a man. That woman is *not* you, my darling."

Nairobia shamelessly laid the cum-slick dildo on the table next to the basket.

Krista frowned.

Nairobia bent at the knees and scooped up her gown, sliding her arms through its sleeves. She sauntered toward the door. "And, my darling," Nairobia said over her shoulder, "know this: someone else will give your husband what you are too afraid to give. Pleasure."

Forty-Four

Fuck.

No motherfucking Wi-Fi service again.

Isaiah tossed his phone.

He was drunk. And he was horny. And he wanted to bust a nut. But he wasn't going to lie on this pullout sofa bed another moment longer playing with his dick without being able to watch porn. Something he'd been doing in the wee hours of the night—well, most late nights whenever his Wi-Fi connected—since arriving on the island.

But, tonight, this motherfucking island and its whack-ass tower were fucking up his flow.

He couldn't just close his eyes and masturbate. He tried it. But his mind wandered. And then his dick would go from rock-hard to semi-hard to near flaccid. So then he would tug at his soft dick, shaking and pulling at it to get it to rise to the occasion. The shit was pissing him off. His sac was full of nut that he needed rubbed out.

So he forced himself to try to think of something, like Cassandra—fucking her in that big ass of hers. The way she felt. The way his dick felt inside of it. The way she came around his dick—out of her ass while her pussy squirted.

Isaiah squeezed his eyes shut tightly. And concentrated.

Yeah. That was usually enough to get him off. But—*fuck*. Not tonight. Not after he'd snuck back over to Club Passion earlier tonight. Although he didn't participate in any of the fuck-tivities, he'd watched some serous girl-on-girl shit pop off on the dance floor. Being in the club again, surrounded by all them sexy-ass broads—naked and horny; watching motherfuckers fuck all around him while on the dance floor—he now found it hard to keep his fantasizing focused on Cassandra's freak-ass.

He needed something more.

Wet pussy.

He could still smell it. It had clung thickly in the air in the club by the end of the night, and now he wanted some. But *not* from LaQuandra. He wasn't putting his dick in her—again, until he knew what he wanted from her.

He let out a frustrated sigh. *Shit.* What was the real point in that? By not fucking her—his wife, what was he proving? And in the end, what was the benefit of not fucking *her* when he had readily available pussy in reach?

Fuck if he knew. All he knew was, he had a hard dick, and needed some pussy.

Isaiah lightly pinched his right nipple while slowly massaging the head of his dick.

Wake up, little big man. Damn. Let me get this nut out.

Frustrated, Isaiah kicked the sheet off of him, and then bent one leg at the knee. He scrunched his face up and then he saw it. The Butterfly. Its colorful wings stretched out across the bare ass of the mocha-skinned beauty he'd seen a while back dancing up on the stage. Damn, she had a big, juicy ass.

"Yeah, there you go," he muttered. "All that big ass." Slowly, his dick began to swell as he stroked himself. "Uh, yeah, baby. Bend over 'n' let me stick this fat, hairy dick in you," he whispered. Isaiah hock-spit into his hand and then used it as lubricant to stroke himself, his palm slipping wetly over his now swollen dickhead.

He frantically fisted his dick, his lids sliding shut as he grunted and ground his ass down into the mattress as his hips moved in sync with his hand movement.

"So fucking horny," he rasped.

Isaiah's balls swelled. He was finally on the verge of spilling out his orgasm. Eyes shut tight, in his mind's eye, he saw that elaborate butterfly fluttering as Mocha's ass bounced back on his dick.

"Aah. Shit . . ."

Isaiah sensed something in the room and his hooded lids slowly lifted. "Aah, *sh*—what the fuck . . .?"

LaQuandra was staring down at him. Naked, the moonlight illuminated her shiny, dark skin. She shimmered.

"I don't know who the fuck you're thinking about," she said tersely. "But you're not wasting that nut tonight." And then the weight of her body sank into the mattress beside him.

"Yo, what the fuck is you doing?"

LaQuandra climbed up on top of him. "You fucking me tonight, nigga."

"Nah. Go 'head. Damn."

"I'm not asking you." LaQuandra slid down his body.

"I'm not beat," he said, the resolute sound of his tone defying his throbbing dick as she snatched his hand away from his dick and licked up the back of his shaft, before flicking her tongue over the head.

And though his mouth said *no*, his hands delved into her hair, holding her between his legs as he guided her to his hard dick.

He gritted his teeth as the wet heat from LaQuandra's mouth engulfed him. She sucked over his head, suckling and nursing there, before licking his balls, running a thumb up the length of his dick. And then she drew her tongue up the back of his dick again.

Isaiah hissed in burning need, forgetting his mantra of not wanting her, of not fucking her.

LaQuandra's tongue cradled his dick. She needed this—him, his dick. Hunger seared her entire body as she took Isaiah to the back of her throat, then eased out with a wet suction so strong that Isaiah's toes curled.

LaQuandra dug her fingernails into his thighs as Isaiah fisted his hand in her braids, and fucked himself into her mouth.

No, this motherfucker wasn't coming into her mouth—not tonight. Her pussy. It had to be there. *She* wanted it there. His dick, his nut . . . buried deep inside her.

She struggled against the tight grip of his hands, holding her head like a basketball as he thrust in and out of her mouth, each time his dick going deeper, deeper, until she had him lodged down into her neck.

Abruptly, she pulled back and all that could be heard was a loud pop when his dick left her mouth. Her pussy clenched for the long, heavy length of him.

Isaiah growled in frustration. "Fuck."

LaQuandra licked his balls again, and then she eased back up his body, her wet pussy dragging over his shaft, then resting over his dickhead.

She leaned in and kissed him.

For a second, Isaiah struggled against the kiss, but LaQuandra persisted, devouring him. Reluctantly, his mouth parted and LaQuandra's tongue swept the roof of his mouth, before dancing around his tongue. He tasted of Jack Daniel's and beer. And LaQuandra groaned inside his mouth. The blood heating through her veins now pooling between her legs caused her cunt to quiver.

"You fucking me tonight, Isaiah."

"Go 'head, Quandra. Damn. I told you I'm not tryna fuck you."

LaQuandra sucked on his earlobe. "I'm not asking. I'm your wife, and this dick is mine. So close your eyes and keep thinking about whatever bitch you thinking about. But tonight, this dick is going in my pussy."

When her hand drifted down his abdomen and she reached for his dick, Isaiah pushed out a groan. She rubbed over the heavy weight of it, and then circled her fingers around it.

"C'mon, Quan—"

"I miss this big dick, Isaiah," she stated huskily, cutting him off with another kiss. "My lonely pussy misses you." She licked the side of his neck. "You like that?" she asked, all coy and needy, as she roughly stroked his length.

LaQuandra inched up and directed his dick into her body, and sank down, taking him deep. Her head fell back in delicious wonder.

Oh, oh, oh . . . it had been so, so fucking long since she'd felt him inside of her. Her breath released in a shuddering gasp. Rising and falling over him, LaQuandra rocked her hips with each downward motion, grinding her clit against him.

"Oh, oh, oh, oh," she chanted. Her eyes opened and when they did, they fell on Isaiah, his body gone rigid. "Don't you want this? Tell me how much you need this pussy?"

"Nah," Isaiah muttered, trying to push her off, push her down to his groin. "Suck my dick, so I can nut in your throat."

"*Suck my dick so I can nut . . .*" The words sliced into LaQuandra, and suddenly something inside of her snapped. And she felt it. The tears, hot and angry, sliding down her face.

Slap.

"You fucking bastard! Fuck you, Isaiah," she snapped. She slapped him again.

Isaiah grabbed her hand. "Yo, chill with the fucking hands."

LaQuandra struggled against him, trying to break free from his grasp. "Am I that goddamn black and ugly to you, huh, Isaiah, that I'm only good enough to suck your fucking dick?"

They tussled and his dick slipped out of her wet pussy. And then she landed on her back, pinned down into the mattress.

"Get the fuck off me," LaQuandra spat. "I'm goddamn sick of you hurting me, Isaiah! If you want that bitch, go be with her. I'm done fighting to keep you. I'm done fighting you. I'm done fighting her. You win, Isaiah. That bitch wins. Just go fucking be with her."

She squirmed in his grip. "Get off . . . *me*. Or I'll scream."

"Not until you calm the fuck down," he rasped, suddenly feeling the effects of the alcohol flowing through his veins draining from his system.

All he'd wanted to do was bust a nut in peace. Not deal with this shit, this bitch.

He had both her wrists snagged in one big-handed grip up over her head.

"I don't want to hurt you," he admitted in a gravelly voice.

LaQuandra stopped fighting, stopped trying to get free from his grasp, and seconds later, his grip on her wrists loosened, slightly.

"I swear, Quandra, I never wanted to hurt you."

"Then why do you, huh, Isaiah? Do you hate me that much? Do I repulse you so much that you can't even stand to fuck me, huh?" LaQuandra sobbed. "I love you, Isaiah! And I know I can't make you love me back. But why won't you just let *me* love you, huh? Why?" She wailed. "All I want is you—*you* motherfucker!"

Isaiah cringed. He turned his head, unable to bear looking into her eyes. All he saw swimming in her tears was pain.

It, surprisingly, bothered him seeing her so hurt, so fragile. The fucked-up thing was, he really didn't know what he wanted. Didn't know if he wanted this marriage, or if he wanted a divorce. But what he did know was, he felt like shit seeing LaQuandra like this. So broken.

This wasn't her. Emotional. So vulnerable. Or maybe it was and he hadn't ever noticed.

"C'mon, Quandra. Don't cry. Damn."

"Am I that fucking ugly to you, huh, Isaiah? Is all you see when you look at me is some ugly, black barren bitch?"

He slowly shook his head. "That's not what I see," he said softly. And he meant it. What he saw was a fiercely independent woman. He saw a woman who loved ferociously hard.

Yeah, she was broken—but shit, who wasn't?

More tears splashed from LaQuandra's eyes. "I'm sorry for not being enough woman for you. Sorry I can't give you b-b-b*aaaaaa*bies." She felt so empty and alone. She felt like she was dying inside—or maybe she was already dead. And the ugly, scarred shell of her existence was all she had left.

LaQuandra's eyes flooded with more tears as she stared into the eyes of the man she loved. Ached for. And through her hurt, she felt her body still melting for him.

"That bitch—Cassandra . . ." her voice cracked. "She can have you."

She went limp beneath him. Skin to skin, nothing but heat between them, something in Isaiah's chest tightened. He could feel her heartbeat. Feel her body trembling beneath him. Fuck. He wasn't built for this emotional shit.

It was fucking with him, nearly breaking him.

Isaiah's lids grew heavy, his nostrils flared.

His dick was hard and throbbing.

So he did the only thing he could. He nudged LaQuandra's thighs wide, and then, without a word, he plunged into her with a quick force that had them both gasping.

Slowly, he pumped at her tightness, his movements growing fast and furious the more her body opened to him, the more her need for him swept through her, heating his blood and making him ache to give her a new brand of passion.

LaQuandra moaned and wrapped her legs around his waist,

squeezing him as he drove into her body, her pussy contracting and sucking him in further, milking him.

Isaiah's dark brown eyes grew darker as he rhythmically fucked into LaQuandra's body. Between gnashed teeth, he hissed. "I'm sick of you crazy fucking bitches. Is this what you want, huh?" He slammed his dick back in and out, stabbing LaQuandra's pussy, deep and hard.

"Oh God, *yes, yes, yes.* Fuck me," LaQuandra whimpered, tears still spilling from her eyes. "Beat my pussy up . . . *uh, uh, uh* . . ."

Isaiah's hand went around LaQuandra's neck—a new sensation that quickly sent her over a blissful cliff—and he lightly choked her as he pounded in and out of her body.

LaQuandra's eyes rolled up in her head.

So, so Alpha male.

Domineering.

Isaiah took control of her body, her pussy, and LaQuandra yielded, sweetly, clawing at the sheets. And then she cupped him by the ass and dug her nails into his muscled flesh.

Another sob ripped from LaQuandra's chest. She raked her nails along Isaiah's back, breaking skin, marking what was hers. Her breaths were coming in short, rapid spurts. Her orgasm was—

"You fucking crazy . . . bitches," Isaiah muttered, biting into LaQuandra's neck. "I fucking hate you, *ahhh*, shit . . ." He tightened his grip around her neck. And then clamped his mouth around her right nipple. He bit down. And then teased the sensitive bud with the flat of his tongue, before biting down on it again.

LaQuandra mewled. Thrashed. Her pussy clamped around Isaiah's dick as he groaned around her nipple. He shifted forward, shifting the angle of penetration.

"Oh, motherfucker. Yes, yes, yes . . ."

LaQuandra felt herself falling, falling, falling; her orgasm flooding the walls of her pelvis; she felt it swelling hot in her belly, rising, rising, rising.

Isaiah's dick slashed into her cunt, fucked out her juices.

LaQuandra's eyes rolled around in her head. "Oh yes, oh yes, oh yes. Fuck me, you dirty bastard. Fuck me. *Aaah . . . uhh . . . mmm!*"

She met his thrusts with greedy, licentious thrusts of her own. Her pleasure built. And when Isaiah kissed her, in rough, hungry need, LaQuandra croaked out another sob as she came around him. The mattress bounced. The springs squeaked. Isaiah let go of her neck and grunted, quickly pulling himself out of her quivering pussy. He choked back a yell as heavy ropes of cum shot through his dick, scorching over LaQuandra's pussy, lapping at her clit, then splattering over her trembling belly.

Dazed, he took his still-hard dick and slathered his seed into her flesh and then he plunged back inside her and pumped and pumped and pumped, until another heated ribbon of cum splashed deep into the basin of her pussy.

Over and over, Isaiah pumped himself until his throbbing dick was spent, but empty . . .

He stayed there, still. In the moment, inside her, enjoying the satiny clutch of her.

Until LaQuandra stopped sobbing, until she stopped clinging onto him, until his dick finally slipped out of her still shuddering body.

Forty-Five

"Have you ever cheated on me?"

The question caught Brenda off guard. In the eleven years that they'd been married, not once had Roselle ever asked her that.

So why now?

Oh yes. Because Dr. Dangerfield sat here in her all-fucking-white talking about emotional transparency, revealing one's inner self, being completely honest and vulnerable in one's feelings. Sharing those things that prevented closeness in a relationship.

Which definitely was not a problem, as far as Brenda was concerned, in her marriage. She and Roselle were very close. And they were not ever lacking in intimacy—or passion.

Yes, she'd cheated on Roselle—a few times. But she'd never been caught. She'd never given him reason to ask, to doubt, or to suspect. So her answer—the only answer—was no. And that was what Roselle should have heard coming from her mouth, and yet Brenda looked him in the eyes and said, "I should be allowed one night to fuck whoever I want after all the bitches you've run your dick in. Don't you think?"

Roselle frowned. What the fuck? "Is that a yes?"

"No, Roselle. It's a question."

Mm. Defensive, Dr. Dangerfield mused. She clasped her hands

in her lap. "Mr. Woods, is there a reason why you're asking your wife about infidelity? Has something come up that has you now asking if she's ever been unfaithful?"

Roselle shifted in his seat. "Nah. I'm only asking. I mean, sitting here listening to you talk about being transparent kinda got me wondering; you know." He looked over at Brenda. "Keep shit a hunnid, Bren. You ever let another muhfucka get up in them guts?"

Brenda matched his stare. She didn't blink nor flinch when she said, "No."

Roselle narrowed his eyes, skepticism now coloring his face. He raised a brow. More cynicism bubbled to the surface, but he knew he had no legitimate reason—other than being a selfish bastard—to doubt her answer or feel any type of way about it if she had ever cheated.

"So you've never given another muhfucka head or let him eat you out? Because eating is still cheating, feel me?"

Roselle caught Dr. Dangerfield's eyes and smirked.

Brenda rolled her eyes up in her head, shaking her head.

To lie or not to lie? That was never a question. It was a necessity.

"No, Roselle," Brenda said. "I haven't

Brenda felt Dr. Dangerfield's piercing stare on her and so she kept her own eyes on Roselle in fear Dr. Dangerfield might see the truth.

Roselle let out a sigh of relief. Something was happening to him. He couldn't put it into words, but he'd been feeling sort of . . . different the last few days.

"Look, baby," he started. "If you have, I couldn't blame you. And I wouldn't hold it against you; feel me? 'Cause on some real shit, I know I've hurt you, Bren. And I know I've broken hella promises over the years to not cheat."

"And still you did," Brenda said, annoyance slowly coursing

through her tone. Talking about Roselle's infidelities always had a way of agitating her, and his most recent transgression with that white bitch was still a fresh wound for her. "Time and time again," she added, "one lie, one broken promise, after another."

"I know, baby," Roselle said apologetically. "And I'm really sorry for that. For real this time, baby. Hurting you has never been my intentions."

"And why should I believe your apologies this time, huh, Roselle, when I've heard them over and over?"

"Because this time I'm apologizing not because I have to, Bren, but because I need to. I want to. All the other times, I just told you what I thought you wanted to hear and what I thought I needed to say, knowing damn well—the first chance I got, the first piece of willing ass—I was gonna cheat on you. So this time, Bren. I really mean it."

The sincerity in his tone chilled her.

Wait . . .

Brenda blinked.

"Roselle, what the hell is going on here, huh? Are you dying?"

Roselle chuckled. "Nah, nah, baby. I'm good."

"Is some bitch pregnant?"

Roselle frowned. "Hell nah. I've never fucked any of them hoes raw, Bren. Damn. Give me more credit than that."

Brenda frowned. "Then what the hell is going on? You're scaring me right now."

Roselle shrugged. "I don't know, Bren. This island, all these sessions . . . you."

"What about *me*?"

" I love you."

"I know you do. And I love you."

Dr. Dangerfield fought to keep from rolling her eyes.

"So what is really going on here, Roselle? You're night dying. You don't have some bitch pregnant, but you're sitting here—"

Roselle closed his eyes, and sighed. "I'ma fuck-up, baby. And yet you still love me—even when I've been at my worst." He opened his eyes, and then reached for Brenda's hand. "You've been the best thing that has ever happened to me, Bren. And I've done nothing but shit on you with other women. You don't deserve that. Sometimes I don't think I deserve you, baby. But I love you with everything in me; however, it doesn't always feel like it's enough; feel me? So I sex you down the way I do because I feel that's all I have to give."

Brenda just stared at him. What was he looking for? Forgiveness? Understanding? Confessions? Finally she blinked, taking him in. Seeing the pain in Roselle's eyes, something she'd never seen before, almost made her want to fall to her knees and declare her own indiscretions. But how could she ever tell him that she allowed his cheating, accepted it, because sometimes she felt as if it was what she deserved. How could she ever admit to sleeping with his brother?

Renaldo.

God—she couldn't even remember if it had been good.

It was only once. One night of despair, fueled by yet another night of Roselle missing in action—filled with tears and a few shots of Jack Daniel's—and one thing had led to another. Before she knew it, her skirt was up, her panties yanked to the side, and Renaldo was dicking her down—raw.

Twenty minutes later, his thick, sticky dick was being stuffed back inside his boxers, his designer jeans were being zipped, and—along with the promise of taking their dirty deed to the grave—he was walking out the door, back to his family.

To this day, Brenda was still haunted by what she'd done. And every time she had to look into the eyes of her beautiful eight-year-old daughter, she was reminded of that sordid night, wondering if Roselle was her daughter's father or not.

So, yes, she put up with his cheating. Not because she wanted to, but because she had to. Her own guilt wouldn't allow her not to.

"I don't wanna keep cheating on you," Roselle said, "but I can't promise you that I won't." His eyes were bleak, his face filled with a pain she'd never seen before.

Brenda's heart pounded wildly in her chest. Was he about to ask her for a divorce? No, no. She hadn't come way out here for Roselle to have some epiphany, some dame "come to Jesus" moment. She wanted her marriage. And she wanted him—the good, the bad and the ugly. Because the naked truth was, she wasn't that goddamn good. She'd done some wrong. And that was her cross to bear.

"I'm not leaving you, if that's what you're thinking," Brenda said.

Roselle sighed, and then slowly shook his head. "Maybe you should, Bren. It would serve me right. From the rip, I needed you to make it clear that I was lucky to have you, that you wouldn't give me a second chance if I ever cheated on you once we got married. But instead, you kept taking me back. You kept letting me cheat on you, Bren. Sometimes I resent you for that."

What the fuck was going on here? Roselle couldn't believe he was admitting this to her. But here he was. He wasn't blaming Brenda for his cheating ways, but she'd made it easy for him to keep doing it, as did all of the other women in his past.

Brenda blinked. "*Ex*cuse me? How the hell are you resenting *me*, huh, Roselle?"

"Baby, don't you see, every time I cheat on you, I do it because I can. The moment you were down to creep with me when I was with Trinity, you made it okay."

Brenda frowned. "Well, it's not. And it hasn't been."

"Can you tell me, Mrs. Woods," Dr. Dangerfield asked, "what made it okay for your husband to cheat on his ex with you?"

Brenda's mouth parted, but then she closed it. What was she to say to that?

"Because *I'm* his wife," she finally stated. "*She* wasn't."

Oh, okay. Dr. Dangerfield took in her words. "So infidelity is acceptable as long as the persons involved aren't married. So had he been married to his ex, would that have changed anything? Would it have stopped you from being with him?"

"Um no—I mean, yes." Brenda shook her head. "I don't know. I wanted him."

"And now you have him," Dr. Dangerfield stated, "with all of his mess."

Brenda swallowed. "But he's my mess."

Dr. Dangerfield offered her a smile. "That he is."

Brenda tilted her head, giving Dr. Dangerfield a smug look that said, "Ooh, you tried it, boo." But then she remembered the session with Dr. Dangerfield on enabling, and she sighed, glancing over at her husband. "You're right, Roselle. I should have left you the first time you'd cheated on me. And the second and third, and fourth, and twentieth time you stuck your dick in another woman. But I didn't. And I probably never will. You wanna know why, Roselle?" Brenda felt herself becoming emotional. "Because I refuse to give up on *you*—on us. I refuse to break up our home and have our children not having both their parents with them, under the same roof." Like my sisters and me.

Roselle lifted Brenda's hand to his lips and kissed it.

"Baby, that's all I needed to hear. And I promise you this: I'm ready to step up and be the man you need me to be. I'm ready to invest more of myself into our marriage"—he glanced over at Dr. Dangerfield and then back at Brenda—"and to be more committed to you."

Dr. Dangerfield dragged her tongue over the front of her teeth. She didn't believe him. Not one word, not one damn bit. No cheater just *stopped* cheating or changed his behavior—just like *that*. No, this sneaky bastard was up to something. Dr. Dangerfield was sure of it. But she wasn't going to push. Today.

Mmph. I wonder what his wife would say if she knew he'd already fucked two other women since being here on the island, Dr. Dangerfield thought as she wrote in her notes. "So what happens next?" she asked the couple.

Brenda hesitated, raking her hand through her hair. "I honestly don't know." Biting her lip, she looked over at Roselle. "Are you asking for a divorce?"

Roselle drew in a breath, and his chest expanded. Where in the hell did she get that notion? Hell, sometimes she got on his last fucking nerve with her bullshit. But he loved her. And since being here on the island, he realized no other woman would ever put up with his shit the way Brenda had.

"Nah, baby. I don't want a divorce," Roselle said as a bell dinged, alerting them that their time was up. "I think we should try an open marriage."

Forty-Six

Instead of having his thoughts on his wife's whereabouts, Kendall had spent the early part of his morning on his phone, emailing back and forth with Persia, while Krista was "out for a walk." It had been his first real opportunity to log into his emails in almost a week. So he'd eagerly gone through his work and personal email accounts first, before logging into his private AOL account. He had eight new emails, but there was only one that he'd been most interested in.

The one from PassionPainPleasure.

Persia had sent him an email, along with an attachment, several days ago, of her sucking her fiancé's long, thick dick, telling Kendall how much she wished she could wedge her tongue in the crack of his ass, and then tongue him good.

Kendall couldn't think of dude's name, but he was one lucky bastard, he thought, to have a freaky woman like Persia in his life. Like him, Persia only cheated because her man wasn't open to some of the things she liked doing sexually.

The corners of his mouth quirked in a half-smile as Kendall replayed the email message in his head: MY WET MOUTH, SO HUNGRY FOR A SWEET NUT, the email message had said, followed by a smiley face. ENJOY! THIS MOUTH WILL BE WAITING WHEN YOU GET BACK!

Kendall's dick had instantly gotten brick-hard from reading the email and then opening the attachment and watching Persia's luscious lips glide up and down over her lover's long dick, making it disappear deep into her mouth. Balls deep, nose pressed into his groin, Persia had damn near sucked the cartilage out of her fiancé's dick and the promise of giving Kendall that same mouth work had him pulling out his own dick and then taking a picture of it from his cell and sending it to her, before jerking out a thick, hot nut.

His orgasm had come fast and he exploded all over himself, his body shaking as the climax ripped through him. It had been a good nut.

Yet, that had been almost an hour ago, and Kendall's dick was still hard.

He was still horny.

So with Krista still nowhere in sight, Kendall played with his dick again, his mind on the sexy Scorpio with the wet nasty tongue and deep wet pussy who had no sexual hang-ups about freaking with him. The woman who loved being fucked doggy-style and having her asshole licked and finger-fucked.

"I'm team ass-licker," was what she'd told him in her initial email correspondence to him two years ago. And, so far, she'd stayed true to her word, sucking his dick, licking his balls, tonguing his ass, stroking his prostate—with no prompting, no hassles. And she did it because she loved it.

"Damn, Persia," Kendall muttered as he thought about her. She loved a man nutting in her pussy, then licking his nut out of her body, and then kissing her. That kind of shit turned Kendall on.

His dick throbbed as he imagined his tongue inside Persia's ass—and hers inside his. And Persia loved to kiss him afterward, the scent of pussy and dick and ass on their tongues as they swirled around the other's.

That shit was a big turn-on.

Kendall groaned.

His mind drifted to Nairobia, to her role in his favorite porn, *Ass Lickers*; to the day she'd sat across from him, her foot easing up his leg. She was breathtaking. Goddess-like. Almost too real to be real. And yet she was as real as the air Kendall breathed.

So feminine.

So sensual.

So sexual.

What man would be able to resist her?

A better man than him, for sure.

Kendall's hand languidly slid up and down the shaft of his dick as precum streamed from the tip. He milked himself as he slowly fucked his fist. Another shining bead of excitement welled from the crown and then slid down to the edge of his hand.

Kendall cupped his balls with his free hand, gently massaging himself there. His sac was so full and tender. Wetting two fingers with his spit, he smeared his spit over his balls, imagining it was Persia's tongue, Nairobia's tongue.

"I wanna fuck," he muttered. "Mmm . . . aah, shit . . ." His hips rotated down into the mattress. Another swelling of precum was right below the crown. He knew if he didn't stop, he'd explode. His orgasm was right there, on the edge.

But he kept stroking, slow and deep. He shifted upward, bending one leg at the knee. With his other hand, Kendall took his index and middle fingers and lightly brushed over his perineum, that area of skin between his balls and ass. He stroked over it with his fingertips, pressing down over it every so often.

Kendall's dick grew harder.

He removed his hand from his perineum and then stopped pleasuring himself. He needed a moment to keep himself from ejaculating. It was sweet torture, teasing himself like this.

He glanced over at the clock on the nightstand, and then groaned. *I need to hurry and bust this nut*, Kendall thought. *Krista should be back soon.* She'd already been gone for over an hour.

Kendall reached for the water-based lube he'd snuck from the gift basket a few weeks back. Shit. Krista wasn't going to use it, so he decided to put it to good use—at least a few times, while he was here. Why the fuck did Krista have to be so goddamn rigid? How could he want his marriage so much, but still feel the need to seek pleasure outside of it?

Kendall sighed as he flipped open the cap and then squirted a glob on his two fingers. He prided himself on being a selfless lover, but Krista—Kendall sighed and shook his head. Thinking about it was making his dick go soft. He'd been guilty of holding on to hope that Krista would one day become more open-minded and sexually adventurous. But he realized, now since their stay here, that he was being a damn fool. There was no hope for Krista. She was a fucking lost cause.

Kendall sighed again. He wasn't miserable. He wasn't unhappy. But—shit, life was too short to be sexually unfilled. But was that enough, a reason, to leave?

Kendall squeezed his semi-erect dick at the base, and then slowly slid his hand up and down his shaft until it became rigid again. He reached further beneath his balls, his wet fingers pressing on his hole. "Aah, fuck . . ." He pressed the tip in. Stroking his dick faster, he pushed his fingers in further, curling them up toward his abdomen.

Practice. That's what it had taken for Kendall to be able to find his P-spot—that fleshy, walnut-sized ball hiding behind the wall of his anus—without much effort, like now, the pad of his fingers on the round bulb of tissue.

"Ah. Uh . . . oh shit," he groaned, deepening the hand strokes on his dick as he rhythmically massaged his prostate. The base of Kendall's spine tingled. His balls tightened. A keening moan burst from Kendall's chest as the muscles in his lower stomach tightened.

Eyes shut tight, Kendall's torso lifted as heat speared through him and his orgasm burst out of his dick. His body jerked as he squeezed out the remainder of his nut. He flopped back on the bed, eyes still closed, breathing heavily. Slowly, he pulled his finger from his ass. And then—

"Oh. My. God."

To Kendall's shock, Krista stood in the doorway, a hand over her mouth, her eyes wide. She looked furious—and hurt.

"Krista," Kendall said as he scrambled out of the bed, his sticky dick swinging like a pendulum as he attempted to go to her.

"Don't!" she shouted. "You dirty down-low motherfucker! Don't come anywhere near me with your shitty-ass fingers."

"Kris, baby. It's not what you think."

Krista looked flustered as if she had no idea what to say to that. But then she quickly found her voice. "Oh I saw it with my own two eyes, Kendall! You with a goddamn finger shoved up your ass, fucking yourself."

"Let me explain, Kris."

She shook her head, taking a deep breath to compose herself, to try to wrap her mind around what'd she'd just walked in on. "No. You can't explain shit, Kendall. Are you gay?"

Kendall frowned. "Hell no."

Krista sneered. "And yet I walk in on you with your fingers in your ass. That looks a whole lot gay to me."

"Look, I'm not gay, all right? If you'd just let me explain."

Krista blinked. There was nothing Kendall was going to say to make her see it any other way than what she'd seen. "I want you to pack your shit and get out!"

Kendall gave her an incredulous look. "Get out? Are you serious, Krista? And go where?"

"I don't care, Kendall. I want you and your ass-fucking ways out of my face!"

Kendall's jaw tightened. And when he didn't move fast enough, Krista started grabbing things off the dresser and throwing them at him.

"Get out! You hear me, Kendall, get out!"

"Kris, baby. I'm telling you. It's not what you think."

"No. Kendall. I don't want to hear shit about why you had your finger in your ass. So either you leave or I will." She stepped back and folded her arms tightly over her breasts, trying not to look down at his dick or his damn hand—the hand with the finger he'd used, moments ago, to poke around in his ass with.

He shook his head. Yes, he was embarrassed that she'd walked in on him like that. But there was also a strange part of him that suddenly felt relieved. Still, he didn't like the look of disgust in Krista's eyes as she stared at him.

Kendall stalked over toward the dresser and then yanked open a drawer. He pulled out a pair of basketball shorts and pulled them on, then slipped on a *Passion Island* T-shirt.

He looked at Krista. She looked like she was on the verge of tears.

"Baby, I promise you, it's not what you think. I'm not gay."

She sneered. "Oh you're not?"

"No, Kris. I'm not."

Krista grunted. "So you just have gay tendencies then."

Kendall scowled. "Hell no."

"It wasn't a question," she said, her nose flaring as she watched him grab a few things from out of drawers and then stuff them into a bag. He had no idea where he would go for the night, but if Krista wanted space, he'd give it to her.

Krista met his eyes, held them as if she were seeing him through a different set of eyes. In her stare, he saw a set of eyes full of terror and disappointment and hurt.

For a moment, he just stood there.

Krista swallowed the thick knot in the back of her throat. Then she pushed out, "I will *not* share my bed—or my life—with some down-low homosexual," she said, her voice low but trembling with anger. "Or some man who likes fingers in his ass."

Her words stabbed at Kendall, but he didn't feel like arguing with her. And he didn't feel like trying to change her mind. Yet a part of him knew he should say something, anything. He debated how to respond to her comments, then decided that now wasn't the time. He knew better than anyone that once Krista had something in her head—it was fact. No matter how distorted it may be.

And being truthful, he really didn't give a damn. He knew he should. But he didn't. He was tired. And, surprisingly, relieved.

Krista stepped to the side and allowed Kendall to pass by. Then she followed behind him. The last thing he heard her say, before the door slammed shut in back of him was, "I want a fucking divorce!"

Forty-Seven

Dr. Dangerfield ran her fingers through her hair, trying to process all she'd been told by Kendall while at the same time keeping her panties on. She wanted to give him some pussy. Fuck his embarrassment away. She wanted to empty out his balls, come all over his dick, then wash him with her tongue. But instead, she remained poised and professional as she sat on the sofa across from him; her nipples tightening beneath her lace and silk-clad breasts as he spoke.

There was a quiet sexiness about Kendall that made her inner walls clench with want. She felt her cunt juice trickling out of her body, dewing around the folds of her swelling sex. The erotic imagery of him pleasuring himself played vividly in her mind's eye as he shared bits and pieces of what had transpired between him and Krista.

Although he hadn't shared much in any of the group sessions, Kendall surprisingly felt comfortable with Dr. Dangerfield. So when she pressed him as to why his wife would question his sexuality, he felt compelled to confess to her, believing she'd hold no judgment in her eyes toward him.

And she hadn't.

Still, he would have never expected to be here. In her office, confessing.

When he'd left the villa, he'd walked aimlessly for nearly twenty minutes before he finally landed at her office, shouldering his duffle bag. Now he sat here kicking himself, thinking if only he'd gotten up from the bed after the first nut. He wouldn't be in this mess. Krista wouldn't have caught him with his hand in the proverbial cookie jar—or in this case, his finger in his ass.

And he'd still be hiding his desires from her, while living his secret sex life.

"Shit," he muttered, but the word was low and without malice.

Dr. Dangerfield gave Kendall a look, one she hoped appeared to be full of compassion and not lust, even if she wanted to leap from her seat and kiss him hungrily.

Kendall's eyes shifted to the naked sculpture and then back to her.

"What do you see when you look at that statue?" she asked.

Kendall glanced at it again, this time really seeing it and said, "Freedom."

Dr. Dangerfield smiled. "There's nothing like having the freedom to step into your own sexual truths, to be sexually liberated. Repression and silence can slowly kill a relationship. But now that you've been found out, sort to speak, hopefully your wife will see things clearer after a day or so, and give you an opportunity to explain. I can help facilitate the process in a couples' session. Perhaps help her understand that there is nothing remotely gay about a heterosexual man enjoying anal play . . ."

She caught herself looking at Kendall's hands, wondering which finger it'd been probing his ass. God—if she could have been a fly on the wall. She couldn't wait to get to her surveillance room to roll back the camera.

She swallowed the drool pooling inside her mouth.

"She says she's filing for a divorce," he added. "And thinks I'm gay—or as she said, 'some down-low homosexual.'"

That silly bitch, Dr. Dangerfield thought. How could she part her lips to call this six-foot-one hunk of sexy man *gay*? Then want to divorce him? *Dumb bitch has a freak for a man and she doesn't know what to do with him. Well . . . good riddance to the lazy-fuck.*

"That is unfortunate," was all she said.

"The crazy thing is," Kendall continued. "I wish I could rewind the clock and this morning never happened." Kendall looked nostalgically sad. "I love my wife. But . . ."

"But?" Dr. Dangerfield gently prodded.

Kendall sighed. "I wanted to believe Krista and I had a good sexual connection because of the amount of sex we have—*had*. But I couldn't bring myself to share with her my interest in . . ." He shook his head, not wanting to finish the words.

"Anal play," Dr. Dangerfield answered for him.

Kendall nodded. "Yeah."

Dr. Dangerfield understood. "And now . . . here you sit."

Kendall slowly nodded his head. "Yeah. Here I sit." He pushed out a breath. "And I'm the one who convinced Krista to come on this trip, practically begged her, selling her the idea that coming here would enhance our love life, bring us closer sexually. Now look at us." He laughed at the irony of it all and lowered his eyelids to hide his chocolate-brown eyes.

Dr. Dangerfield's clit throbbed and she pressed her thighs together, crossing her legs at her ankles. "I always stress the importance of couples being able to talk openly about sex—all kinds of sex. About urges, curiosities, and dark desires. Because when partners cannot openly and comfortably share their sexual wants/needs, then they will ultimately find a way to find it—and get it—elsewhere."

Dr. Dangerfield kept her eyes on Kendall, and when he looked away from her, she knew he'd already found what he needed in someone else.

"Do you love her?"

Kendall gave her a confused look. "Who? My wife?"

Dr. Dangerfield tilted her head. "No. The woman who indulges your sexual urges and fulfills your desires."

Kendall swallowed. "I respect her. And enjoy her." He shook his head. "But, no, I don't love her. I'm in deep like, I guess you can say." He sighed again. "What I have with her is what I would have loved to have with Krista."

"Maybe you still can," Dr. Dangerfield stated. "Maybe your wife will be willing to work in her own therapy to address the roadblocks to uncovering her own sexuality."

Kendall gave her a *yeah-right* look. "*Krista?* You think?"

"If your wife *did* have a change of heart, would staying in your marriage with her make you happy?"

Kendall considered her for a moment and then shook his head. "Maybe not."

Dr. Dangerfield tilted her head and raised a questioning brow.

"Well, no," he amended. "Not sexually." He sighed. "Maybe I should have been more forthcoming about my desires."

"Then why didn't you?"

He shrugged. "Don't know. I guess I was being selfish."

"In truth, Mr. Evans, we know why we choose to not disclose certain things about ourselves to those we care about."

"Yeah. You're right. So honestly speaking, I didn't tell her because I didn't want her judging me, or staring at me with contempt in her eyes. I was afraid to scare her, to disappoint her. I didn't want the woman I loved to look at me differently because I enjoy having my prostate stimulated."

"I understand. Sadly, partners who don't allow room for new sexual experiences or who aren't willing to embrace the idea that being sexually adventurous—or, if you will, a bit freaky—in the bedroom can be an exciting thing will sometimes end up missing out on the best parts of their partner's sexuality. True sexual intimacy requires partners to trust, explore, and indulge in each other's desires—within what is comfortably reasonable, of course."

Kendall grunted. "Krista isn't—wasn't comfortable with much of anything." He shook his head. "How can anyone stay so stuck and be okay with it?"

Dr. Dangerfield removed her glasses, propping them up on the crown of her head. "I wish there was an easy answer to that. There are a myriad of reasons why someone may be unable or unwilling to express their natural sexuality. Traumas. Upbringing. Cultural views. Religious beliefs. The beautiful thing is, sexual behavior is not constant. It can change. When someone is ready to change. Hopefully, your wife will be open to counseling."

Kendall shrugged. "You know, Doc. At this point, I've given up on hope. Krista's said some things that just can't be unsaid. If a divorce is what she wants, then so be it. I'm tired." Kendall glanced at his watch. He'd been sitting here for nearly two hours. "I guess I should get going."

But Dr. Dangerfield wasn't ready to see him go. She wanted to know more about his penchant for ass play, wanted to know more about the woman who indulged his desires.

"No, no," she quickly said. "No rush. Please. Stay as long as you want."

Forty-Eight

Nairobia wet her lips, the pink tip of her tongue darting out. Kendall nearly groaned as he remembered that tongue in her porn movie, *Ass Lickers*. The way it had slid over her male lover's asshole, before it laved over his balls. The memory of how the cameras zoomed in on her beautiful pussy; the way it flared each time she licked him there was still etched in Kendall's brain.

And now he sat here wondering what it would be like having his dick surrounded by her sweet lips (the ones on her face, first—and then the ones between her thighs) and then how it would feel coming down her throat.

He imagined her pussy and neck were both like heated velvet; so smooth, and so damn silky. Liquid heat, he imagined them both to be.

He licked over his lips—part nerves, part desire—at the sight of Nairobia's nipples. He wanted to reach out and grip her breasts, lean over and lick their stiffened tips. The imagery alone caused heat to coil in his testicles. He would surely come on himself—something he hadn't done since he was twelve, thirteen—if he didn't get a hold of himself.

His dick began to swell, his balls heating and filling as Nairobia's nipples distended, a lurid sight causing him to grow weak in his resolve. He looked from them to her transfixed gaze, then back.

This was un-fucking-believable.

Here—with Nairobia Jansen. Alone. With a hard, throbbing dick.

Dr. Dangerfield had summoned Kendall to The Chambers—an opulent circular structure, with vaulted ceilings and a retractable roof. Inside, it held numerous rooms, used mostly for interviews—for a special session without his wife.

Kendall had been surprised to walk in to find Nairobia waiting on him, instead of Dr. Dangerfield. He didn't question the whys of this encounter. All he knew was, he was glad to be sitting here.

Kendall felt his pulse quicken as Nairobia stood to her feet and then prowled around the table to him; a touch, a caress, a finger danced up the back of his neck and then over his bald head. She leaned over and wrapped her arms around his chest. And then in his ear, she whispered, "Your wife is a fool, no?"

"She's a good woman," Kendall said softly. Still, he felt the need to defend her. He loved her, still, despite all of the recent things she'd said, thought, about him.

"But she is not good loving. Her *kut*, my love, is fuckable, but it is not unforgettable."

Nairobia's delicate finger traced over Kendall's lips. His mouth slightly parted. And then her finger was gone.

"Good woman or not, my darling, your wife isn't top-of-the-line fucking and she never will be . . ."

Kendall swallowed, his throat working overtime to handle his over-salivating glands.

"I image *je lul proeven zoals zoete melkchocolade*," Nairobia said seductively, telling him she imagined his dick tasting like sweet milk chocolate. And then Nairobia smiled. "I will allow you to explore your sexual desires, to release the inhibitions your wife denies you. Would you like that, my darling?"

Hell fucking yeah, he wanted it. And yet Kendall gave her a perplexed look. Was she really saying, asking—

"You want to be wrapped in my heat, no? To drink in my womanhood, to say you have been given pleasure by me, the dick-riding goddess, no?"

The sultriness in her tone made Kendall's toes curl. He clenched his fist. There was no breathing. Kendall's lungs begged for oxygen, but he couldn't think straight enough to inhale for fear he'd breathe in more of her, and then explode inside of his boxers.

Kendall nodded as he swallowed again. And then he let out a nervous chuckle. "Is this for real, a joke?"

Nairobia's lips curled into a slow grin. "Is your cock hard for me?"

Kendall pulled in his bottom lip and then glanced down into his lap, before crooking his neck and looking up at her, his dark gaze now heated by lust.

"What you think?"

"Then this is real," she said sweetly, as she lifted herself from Kendall's back. Nairobia moved so that she was now standing in front of him, so that he could see her as she slid a hand in between the slit of her sheer dress.

Kendall's dick jumped.

"Listen to my *kut*, my darling." Her finger clicked wetly as she teased herself there. *Clickety-click-click-click* . . . "It sings to you, my love. Can you hear its melody, so wet, so slick . . .?"

Kendall's dick pulsed. Again and again and again until it became painfully hard trapped beneath underwear and khaki shorts.

He clenched and unclenched his fists, and groaned inwardly, hissing out a curse.

Shit.

Tension sparked the air around them as Nairobia's hips thrust hungrily, filling his head with her seductive scent.

"Hear that," she rasped, her accent purposefully thick and heated. "My wet *kut* is alive and ready to suck you into my womb."

Kendall was transfixed by her—this mesmerizing sex goddess

thrumming with self-pleasure and with want for him. He could hear her fingers wetly clicking between her thighs; God, she sounded fucking juicy—so slick, so ready.

Then she withdrew those slender fingers to her mouth, her eyelids sliding closed as she sucked clean her cream. And then they were gone—those fingers, dipping in her cunt again. Another dip, another suck. Then twice more, before prowling around Kendall again.

She folded her body over his again, her breasts pressed over his shirt, against the muscles of his back. "My arousal thickens for you, my *kut* aches for you."

Nairobia's gray-eyed gaze lifted and she looked right into the mirrored-wall, before kissing a line down Kendall's jaw, her heated breaths coming in intoxicating bursts. Her tongue flicked over his fleshy earlobe, and then she sucked it between her teeth.

Kendall groaned. He couldn't believe this, this right here—with Nairobia, was happening . . . to *him*.

Nairobia licked and then swirled her tongue around the shell of his ear.

"A man like you deserves unforgettable *kut*, my darling. He deserves unforgettable pleasure."

Kendall couldn't dispute her on that. It was what he'd wanted with Krista. It was what he'd been aching for from her, his wife. Sadly, to no avail. Kendall wanted—

"I will lick over your cock and balls; make love to you with my mouth, lips, tongue and hands, sucking out your thick, sweet milk. I will lick where your wife has refused. You want my tongue caressing you there, over your musky manhole, no?"

Kendall flexed his fingers back and forth. Goddamn this shit. He wanted to touch her. Taste her. Fuck her. And yet he sat here fighting for control.

Kendall sputtered, "I-I . . . damn—I wish I could. Shit. But I'm still married . . ."

"And unfulfilled," Nairobia said.

Kendall shook his head. "I want to, but—"

"She's leaving you," Nairobia reminded him. "No?"

"It's over, Kendall . . ."

Kendall stammered, "I-I'm . . ."

"A good man, a loving man. A man who should not go unsatisfied."

Kendall nodded, the truth resonating through him. "You're right. But—"

"She does not deserve you; her *kut* has not earned good loving, my darling."

Kendall inhaled, breathing in her sweet, intoxicating aroma—the scent of heated arousal and perfume. She was breaking his resolve.

Nairobia's lips slid to the corner of Kendall's mouth, and then she kissed him there, softly, purposefully, every so often her eyes flickering over at the mirror.

"You want to dive into me, no? Sink deep inside me? *U wilt uw grote lange lul glijd in me . . .?*"

Kendall had no idea she was asking him if he wanted to slide his big, long dick inside of her, if he wanted to fuck himself inside her body, her soul. And yet his dick managed to throb in response.

Yes, he wanted to fuck her. To fuck away thoughts of Krista, to pound out the sting of her words as they still rung in his ears. *"I will not stay married to an undercover faggot! I want a divorce . . ."*

Nairobia craned her neck, and again, her eyes fluttered over at that mirrored wall. Her lips curved into a sly grin and then her tongue slowly, sensually, slid over her top lip.

Her pussy did not burn hot for Kendall, but it warmed at the promise of being a pleasure to him; it grew wetter at the knowing that she would bring him to orgasm. Her cunt juiced knowing what (and who) stood on the other side of that mirror.

Watching.

Forty-Nine

Eyes narrowed, Krista gasped as she felt blood draining from her face.

Kendall.

With, with . . . Nairobia.

She stood here, unsteady on her feet, yet unable to look away from the sight of them. Krista thought she'd seen Kendall's body tense, his muscles tightening as that brazen bitch tried to entice him with her sexual wiles, as she preyed, stalked around him with her amazing tits, touching and rubbing and hovering over him.

Krista winced when Nairobia pressed her breasts against Kendall's back and then wrapped an arm across his chest, whispering in his ear again.

She was certain that Kendall would refuse Nairobia's advances. She hoped, had stood here and prayed, that Kendall would resist the seductive wiles of that—God, she wished she knew what was being said inside that room. Audio, that's what she needed—but then she saw it, desire. The hunger on Kendall's face was undeniable, unmistakable. And she knew then . . . he wanted that bitch. And Nairobia was going to find a way to exploit the heat burning in his eyes.

It took all Krista's willpower to keep from banging on the two-way mirror. It took every ounce of her stubborn, Christian will to keep from taking her fist and swinging it upside Dr. Dangerfield's flawlessly smooth forehead.

Yes, she'd told Kendall she was leaving him and, quite frankly, she was more certain now than ever before that it was the right decision. And yet she was disappointed and disillusioned that Kendall chose to be in that room with that enchanting slut instead of scouring the island looking for her, to at least try to talk her out of leaving him.

Krista was beside herself with hurt. She couldn't believe what she was seeing, behind the glass, on the other side of that very wall where Kendall was engaging in dirty, filthy—

"Please know you are welcome to leave at any time," Dr. Dangerfield said, extending an arm toward the door. "No one is keeping you here, Mrs. Evans."

Nausea churned in her stomach. Still, Krista did not move. Defiantly, her gaze stayed locked on Kendall, her feet rooted in place. She didn't want to look, but she couldn't tear her eyes away.

Instead, he'd easily given into temptation, defiling their wedding vows more than he had already done by fingering his ass.

"You did say you were leaving him once you returned to the States, did you not?" Dr. Dangerfield asked as she looked on, her pussy juices pooling in the lining of her panties. "Or has that changed?"

Krista's stare hardened. "No. It's over." She shook her head and took a breath, fighting back a surge of tears she hadn't expected. "Kendall has proven he isn't the man I thought he was." She tore her eyes from the window—just for a second—and glared at Dr. Dangerfield. "I hope you're satisfied with yourself for ruining my life and destroying a relatively happy marriage."

"I'm sorry you feel I am the cause of the current state of your marriage," Dr. Dangerfield said thoughtfully. And she was regretful. Not for anything that she'd done or said, she regretted that Krista couldn't step into the light and give into temptation, to allow her deepest, darkest desires to be uncovered. She'd wanted to see Krista step outside of herself and become more open. But, since day one, she'd been too rigid and too damn stubborn to get out of her own damn way. So, this mess was all on Krista.

Dr. Dangerfield wasn't about to take blame or responsibility for the state of the Evanses' marriage. All she did was shine light on what was already beneath the surface.

"It is never satisfying knowing that a couple's truths are what has torn them apart."

Krista gave her an incredulous look. "And exactly what truths are you speaking of?"

Dr. Dangerfield offered a slight smile. "That your husband wants more than what you've been willing to share with him."

Krista scoffed. "What he wants, a finger in his ass, is unnatural for a man—a straight man, that is."

"Mrs. Evans, it's unfortunate that you believe that to be true. Anal stimulation isn't just a gay man's desire. It saddens me to know that you are willing to let a good man go, all because you can't get out of your own way. Your husband is a heterosexual man with a very healthy sex drive. The fact that he's comfortable enough in his masculinity to know what it is that he enjoys makes him that more manly. His sexuality shouldn't be in question."

Krista's hand curled into a fist. "A man wanting his ass licked, fingered, or fucked, is where I draw the line. Period."

"And yet here you stand," Dr. Dangerfield stated. "Watching your husband . . . "

Nairobia whispered something in Kendall's ear. Seconds later, he was rising from his seat. And then Nairobia took his hands and placed them to her breasts. Kendall cupped her there, and then Nairobia's mouth was beside his ear. And her hand was sliding over the front of his shorts, kneading his dick.

Kendall glanced down at Nairobia's hand, then back at her. Nairobia spread her legs as Kendall slid his palm inside the slit of her dress, and then over the curve of her ass.

Krista swallowed, not sure if she should look away or run for the door.

"How does seeing this make you feel?"

Krista shot her a murderous look. "How do you think it makes *me* feel?" Her voice was icy. "My husband is about to let some nasty bitch do God knows what to him, and I'm watching it all unfold. So you tell me, Doctor, how do you think I should feel?"

"I'm sure I could prattle off a list of adjectives for you," Dr. Dangerfield said calmly. "But I'd prefer to hear them in your words."

Krista's nose flared. "I'm not sharing shit with you."

"I understand how you might be feeling, Mrs. Evans."

"Oh you have no idea how I'm feeling right now." *Bitch.*

"You can always stop it," Dr. Dangerfield suggested. "You have the power to go in there and take *her* place. You can let go of your pride and selfish ego and go to your husband. You can give into your husband's sexual needs and allow him to pleasure you in ways you've never imagined. The choice is yours, Mrs. Evans."

Krista shook her head, her jaw clenching. "I want no part of anything going on in that room. If Kendall wants to desecrate our marriage vows with immoral sex, if he wants to bite into forbidden fruit, then let him."

"Tell me, Mrs. Evans, what are you so afraid of?"

Krista scoffed. "I fear no evil."

Dr. Dangerfield tilted her head. Gave Krista a half-amused look. "And yet you are afraid of letting go, afraid of embracing your inner freak."

"I am not—"

"Oh yes you are," Dr. Dangerfield interjected. "You are more of a freak than you will ever admit. And your newfound penchant for voyeurism proves that."

Krista blinked, shock draining the blood from her face.

"You love watching the pleasure of others. Even now. Admit it. Watching Nairobia with your husband has, oddly, turned you on, hasn't it? And that frightens you, doesn't it?"

Krista shook her head. "No."

"You're afraid of standing in your own truth. When you had your ear pressed to the bathroom door, eavesdropping on Mr. Woods fucking LaLani, you felt it. The heat, didn't you?"

Krista blinked. "I-I . . ."

"Scrambled back to your seat with the walls of your vagina pulsing."

Embarrassment washed over Krista's face. "I-I—"

"Found yourself dangerously aroused when you found shelter from the storm and walked in on an orgy. You stayed. You watched."

Krista felt her knees buckling. "I did no such thing. I only stayed until the lighting stopped."

"And yet you left there wet—and not from the storm. It's okay. Admit it, Mrs. Evans. Voyeurism is one of erotica's many sexual pleasures."

"Lies. Sexual intercourse should only be within the confines of a God or—"

"Let me stop you right there," Dr. Dangerfield said, putting a finger up. "Do not go scripture on me. Scripture never says what a married couple can or can't do sexually. What it does say is that you should both faithfully submit to one another—*any*thing you do in the context of your marriage is not immoral. Last I checked, you and your husband were of one flesh; isn't that what the Bible says? So do not go there with me. Satan tempts the flesh when it is being denied."

Krista blinked. She opened her mouth with the intent of reciting a verse out of either Hebrew or Corinthians, but Dr. Dangerfield shut her down.

"Being a saved woman, a Born-Again Christian—or whatever it is you are calling yourself, does not mean that you close your mind to pleasing your spouse. You can be both. A Christian woman serving the Lord *and* a sexually liberated woman pleasing her husband." Dr. Dangerfield tilted her head. "Shall I reference to the King James Version for you?"

Krista's mouth curved into a frown. "Don't you dare stand here and try to twist scriptures for your sick perversions. I've been nothing but a good wife to Kendall. And I have kept him well sexed. And if that hasn't been enough for him, then sadly, I am not the woman for him."

Dr. Dangerfield gave her a look, one filled with pity. "But you could be, Mrs. Evans. You have the ability to become everything that your husband needs—and still be you, Krista the good wife, Krista the churchgoer."

"Are you criticizing me?"

Dr. Dangerfield glanced down at her clenched fist. "If that's how you take it . . ." She paused, shaking her head. "It's too bad you haven't been an open-minded lover, where pleasing your husband is concerned. Now, you're here—on the outside looking in, stuck in what I am sure is your own version of hell."

"Bitch, how dare you judge me," Krista spat. "Ungodly sex is wrong. It is a grievous sin. And I will not bend on that."

"No, Mrs. Evans. What has been a grievous *sin*—as you call it, is your unwillingness to open your heart and mind to new sexual experiences—with your husband. Yes, God allows you the freedom to set boundaries and decide what is right and wrong in the context of your marriage. But, Mrs. Evans, the fact that you find everything wrong is, quite frankly, disturbing. And, sadly, it is your narrow-minded ideology about sex and religion that will have you leaving this island alone."

Krista breathed in. Once, twice. She needed to gather herself, her thoughts. She needed to maintain her composure, to at least give some illusion that Dr. Dangerfield hadn't completely destroyed her with nothing more than her words.

Slap.

Krista heard it in her head. In her mind's eye, Krista saw the palm of her hand going across Dr. Dangerfield's face. Oh how she wanted to slap her. She clenched her hands into two tight fists. Then opened them, stretching out her fingers.

"I can't wait to get the hell off this island and away from the likes of you," Krista managed to say despite her gritted teeth.

Dr. Dangerfield smiled. "Then you should get packing." She walked to the door and then swung it open. "Arrangements will be made to get you back to your uneventful life. I'll keep you in my prayers."

Fifty

Guilt . . .

It was a belaboring feeling. Guilt occurred when someone violated his or her own moral code or standards of behavior (cheating, lying, stealing, purposefully hurting someone). It enslaved you. Weighed you down. It victimized relationships.

And Dr. Dangerfield oftentimes likened the potentially destructive emotion to cancer. If not dealt with, if not cut out, it could slowly spread through other parts of a relationship. It slowly eroded seemingly trusting relationships. Ate away at the core of one's own psyche and opened the door to self-destructive, self-sabotaging behaviors.

And, no matter how many times you tried to ignore it, no matter how many times you tried to deny it, no how many times you tried to will it away—over time, guilt had a way of rearing its ugly head and coming back to haunt you.

So it was no surprise to Dr. Dangerfield that Brenda sat across from her in her office confessing her greatest transgression—fucking her husband's brother.

"I don't know what to do," Brenda croaked out over a sob.

How about tell him the truth, bitch?

"I believe you do," Dr. Dangerfield said gently.

Brenda shook her head. "But at what costs?"

Bitch, you should have thought about that before you spread open your legs and let your husband's brother fuck you raw.

"Unfortunately, deception comes with a price," Dr. Dangerfield said.

"I know." Brenda sighed. "I just don't want this guilt eating away at me. I thought about taking some of Roselle's hair, or his toothbrush, and sending it in for DNA testing."

"It wouldn't be legally binding, however. But it would be strictly for your peace of mind. Still, it wouldn't absolve you of your infidelity."

Brenda felt a headache coming on. "I didn't say it would. I'm not looking for a pardon. I know what I did was wrong."

"There are other forms of testing that can be done, such as sibling DNA testing," Dr. Dangerfield offered, "of your son to determine if they were both fathered by the same man. Your son—he *is* your husband's?"

Brenda frowned. "Of course he is," she said incredulously. "I'm not that damn scandalous."

Oh?

Dr. Dangerfield just stared. Allowed several seconds to tick by, and then said, "The truth will affect many lives."

"I know. That's why I can't tell him." Brenda swiped a tear from her eye. "But sometimes I feel like I'm suffocating because I don't."

"Don't you think he deserves to know?"

Brenda looked pensively at Dr. Dangerfield, biting the inside of her bottom lip.

"Only if he's not the father," she admitted. "Not about what I did—or with who."

Dr. Dangerfield nodded, knowingly. Brenda was a selfish bitch, like Roselle. The two of them were cut from the same cloth. They deserved each other. And there was a special place in hell reserved for scandalous bitches like her.

"And what of your daughter?" Dr. Dangerfield asked. "If your husband turns out not to be her father, how do you think that will impact her? Him?"

Brenda cringed inwardly. She didn't want to envision what it would do to either of them. Roselle would be destroyed for sure. He loved Ariel more than he loved the air he breathed. Probably even more than he loved *her*. And poor Ariel—God, her precious little world would be turned upside down. Roselle was her everything. She couldn't snatch that away from her.

The thought made Brenda sick to her stomach.

"I know I should have never slept with Renaldo. That night was the worst mistake of my life."

"I'm sure," Dr. Dangerfield stated. "So now what?"

Brenda pushed out a long breath. "I honestly don't know. I came here hoping you'd somehow help me feel better."

Oh so this ho is looking for penance?

Bitch, bye.

Well, she'd come to the wrong place. She had better take her ass to a confessional. Dr. Dangerfield wasn't in the business of giving out sympathy.

Brenda used the tissue she'd been gripping tightly in her hand to dab at her eyes. "You know, talk me out of telling Roselle." She blew her nose. "Or at least tell me that it was okay to take this secret to my grave."

Dr. Dangerfield closed Brenda's file. "Mrs. Woods, I can't tell you what to do—or not to do. But I can, however, suggest you consider how the choices you make will affect the others around you. I suggest you weigh out the consequences. There's no getting around the fact that someone will be hurt. The damage has already been done. Now it's simply a matter of thought and action. So the question comes back to you. What do *you* think is the right thing to do?"

Brenda considered Dr. Dangerfield's words thoughtfully. And for the briefest moment, she saw herself coming clean to Roselle. Sure, he'd be infuriated, at first. But he'd come around, eventually. Hadn't he already said he wouldn't hold it against her if she had cheated on him?

Roselle wouldn't want to tear apart their home. Sure, he might beat her ass and then go jump on his brother, but he wouldn't take what they'd done to him out on Ariel.

No. Roselle would forgive her, in time.

And he wouldn't love his daughter any less.

Or wouldn't he?

"Do you think your husband is your daughter's father?"

Brenda nodded. "I do. Most times. But then I see her when she's with her cousins, and I see the resemblance and then I start to doubt myself all over again. Ariel looks like both of them to me."

Dr. Dangerfield uncrossed her legs and then shifted in her seat. "Well, you did sleep with brothers."

Wringing her hands, Brenda swallowed back the sting of truth. "I know. I'm reminded of that tidbit every day." Her voice, though short, was also apologetic. "Every time I look at my daughter, I am reminded of what I did, wondering when someone might come along and—"

Brenda didn't want to think about it, or talk about it, anymore. The thought of doing what was right by not hurting those she loved was exhausting.

"Renaldo and I swore to never tell a soul of that night—ever. I know he wouldn't go against his word. It's his bond."

"How noble of him," Dr. Dangerfield said. Her words felt sarcastic, but Brenda chose to ignore them.

"So then what's your fear?"

Brenda shrugged. "I don't know. I just wanna let go of this guilt. That's it."

"Then you'll need to get honest. And then forgive yourself."

"Do you think Roland—?"

"Renaldo."

"Ah, yes, Renaldo. Do you think he suspects Ariel might be his?"

Brenda's heart thundered in her chest. She looked mortified. "God, no. All she is to him is his spoiled little niece. But even if the thought ever crossed his mind, it would be a fleeting one. He loves her deeply. And he loves his brother, so he would never want to hurt either of them. And he definitely wouldn't want to destroy his marriage behind some nagging suspicion."

Dr. Dangerfield nodded. "Then I guess you have your answer."

Brenda sighed, then stood as the timer dinged. "Yes. I guess you're right. I guess I just needed to finally let it out, holding on to it was killing me."

"Sometimes talking is all someone needs."

Brenda reached for my Kleenex, then wiped her eyes one last time. "You're right. I will not shed another tear over this. What's done is done. I can't change it. Everything in me says Ariel is Roselle's and *that* is what I have to go with."

Dr. Dangerfield rose from her seat and extended her hand. "All the best to you, Mrs. Woods."

Brenda shook her hand, and then pulled her into a warm hug, before kissing her on the cheek. "You're some kind of special, Doc. Thank you for everything."

Shocked by the gesture, Dr. Dangerfield stepped into the embrace, then quickly pulled away from her. "It's been a pleasure working with you. Let me know how life in an open marriage works out for you and Mr. Woods."

Yes. Brenda had agreed to an open marriage—on a trial basis. She knew it was Roselle's way of being able to fuck other bitches, but she'd laid down a few ground rules: one, she chose who he fucked; two, she got to fuck who she wanted as long as Roselle watched; three, Roselle wasn't allowed any extracurricular pussy unless he asked for it—and was given her permission.

Dr. Dangerfield had thought the rules unrealistic, and suspected the arrangement wouldn't last long. She believed they both had a skewed view of what an open marriage entailed. Open marriages weren't about open permission to cheat, which was the case of non-monogamous couples like Brenda and Roselle. Having a healthy polyamorous marriage required a true understanding of its meaning. And neither seemed to understand that it required lots of trust, clear agreements, and an abundance of open communication.

Brenda didn't trust Roselle. But she saw the idea of an open marriage as a way of taking control of her marriage and monitoring Roselle's cheating in a way that didn't consume her.

Dr. Dangerfield believed Brenda's new vision for her marriage was more of a concession to her own guilt and in a desperate response to Roselle's pathological cheating than anything else. She had cautioned them both to tread carefully.

Roselle's request for an open marriage was for selfish reasons, not because he was invested into the art of love, passion, and openness but because it afforded him an open-ended invitation to new pussy.

And, although there was an allure in openly allowing room for a partner to be sexual with someone other than their partner, knowing this couple, Dr. Dangerfield predicted nothing but disaster for Brenda and Roselle.

But only time would tell.

"It should be interesting," Brenda said, slicing into Dr. Dangerfield's reverie.

Dr. Dangerfield offered a smile. "Well, then enjoy the journey."

She eyed Brenda. And just as she made her way toward the door, Brenda turned back and asked, "Do you think I'm a messy bitch for not telling him?"

Dr. Dangerfield gave her a questioning look.

"About—you know, sleeping with his brother?"

"Mrs. Woods, I think you are a woman doing what she feels she needs to do. And that is your cross to bear. The question is, do you see yourself as messy?"

Brenda ran a hand through her hair. "I do. But—oh well."

Dr. Dangerfield's lips pursed ever so lightly. "Then stay true to who you are."

Fifty-One

"I'm not gay."

Krista shrugged as she stared blankly at the man she loved. "I don't know that."

Kendall frowned. "Well, I'm telling you. I'm *not*. And I'm not some DL cat living a double life, either."

"Your actions speak otherwise." Krista fought to keep the bite out of her tone. She was still angry, still hurt, still shocked. But she was no longer homicidal—thanks to prayer. However, she found herself struggling to keep from jumping up and smacking his face, punching him in his mouth, his chest, upside his head. She wanted to fight him for lying to her, for embarrassing her, for deceiving her.

She stared at him, through him. "If I'm not mistaken, I'd asked you a few years back if you wanted to get fucked in your ass and you'd told me *no*. Remember that?"

Kendall's brows furrowed. He hadn't remembered that. Well, vaguely, he did.

Oh so now he wanted to play stupid. Krista sucked her teeth. "You came home and told me some bullshit story about some man down at the barbershop liking his ass fingered—and I specifically asked you if you had anything you wanted to tell me."

Kendall swallowed.

Damn. She remembered that. Just like a woman. Remembering every-damn-thing. He said nothing, and Krista took that to mean he had nothing to say. But the truth was, if he admitted to remembering the conversation, it would more than likely turn into an argument. He hadn't come here for that.

"All I ever wanted," she continued, "was for us to have an honest relationship, to grow closer in spirit; that's it, Kendall."

Kendall gave her a pained look. "I wanted that too, Krista. I did. But . . ." He sighed.

Krista's jaw twitched. "But *what?*"

Kendall sucked in his breath. "You never made it easy, Kris. You were so judgmental and—"

Krista's nose flared. "Bullshit! Do *not* make this about me. You should have been man enough to tell me you liked it in the ass. You owed me that, Kendall. The goddamn truth."

He tensed, his gaze focusing intently on her. "You're right. I should have told you. I should have been man enough to tell you about my secret desires. That I loved my ass licked—by a *woman*. That I loved the feeling of having my prostate massaged, milked—by a *woman*. But I didn't—I couldn't. And I apologize for that, Kris. I knew how adamantly opposed you were to the idea. And getting a divorce was the last thing I wanted. So, no, Kris, I wasn't going to confess my sexual desires with you. Because I didn't want to lose you."

Krista felt tears swimming somewhere in the back of her eyeballs, and so she blinked several times to ward them back. She wasn't going to shed one goddamn tear in front of this, this . . . freaky-ass bastard!

Krista shook her head solemnly. "You knew I wasn't signing up for none of that nasty shit. You knew this!"

Kendall sighed. He'd come to the villa to apologize and hopefully figure out a way to salvage his marriage, but as he sat here looking at his wife, he realized the naked truth—they were simply too opposite. They were not like-minded. Hell, maybe they'd never been compatible, sexually speaking.

He glanced around the living room. Over on the end table sat her Bible. And he realized in this very moment that it no longer mattered to him what she thought. He was no longer that invested in her thoughts of him. He knew he didn't want to spend the rest of his life depriving himself of pleasure simply because Krista wouldn't accept it.

And he didn't expect her to. She was who she was. And he was who he was. He understood that his sexual tastes and appetite had evolved, whereas his wife's hadn't. Sad as it was, Kendall was finally able to accept it.

"You're right, Kris. I did know. And I know now that withholding that part of who I am from you wasn't fair to either of us. Truth is, I want more sexually than you are willing, able, to give. Being here has helped me accept who I am as a sexual being, as a heterosexual man. There is nothing wrong with my desires. And I'm no longer going to be embarrassed or be made to feel ashamed about them. I'd done both for long enough. I enjoyed making love to you, Krista, because you were my wife and I loved you. But I always felt lonely in my desires for something more."

"You selfish-bastard," Krista hissed over gritted teeth.

Kendall cringed. He had been selfish, for good cause, he believed. But he knew that he'd been wrong for doing so.

"Maybe if you went to church and gave your life over to Christ, we could work through this," Krista offered. "You know, you could repent your sins and let Reverend Lynch pray those sexual demons out of you."

Kendall gave her an incredulous look. "I don't need an exorcism.

And I have no interest in participating in any organized religion. What I desire sexually is not a sin, maybe to you. But I'm good."

Then he paused, still staring at her, his eyes oddly sympathetic. "I want you to be happy, Krista. You're a good woman. If you want a divorce, I won't fight you on it. Whatever you want, it's yours. I'm not looking to beef with you, or make your life difficult. But, trust me, baby. My sexual wants and desires have nothing to do with this."

Tears pricked Krista's eyelids. "You have some other bitch, is that it, Kendall?" She shot up from her seat, slamming a hand up on her hip. "Which one of those filthy whores been licking your ass, since we've been here, huh? That slutty therapist-bitch, or that nasty Nairobia-bitch. I saw you with her. Did you fuck her? Did you let that scuzzy whore stick you in your ass?"

Kendall sighed, shaking his head. "All I ever wanted, Krista, is for you to open your mind, be more adventurous—with *me*, for *me*," he said, ignoring her questions. No. They hadn't fucked. But—for fuck's sake—he had wanted to. Badly. But Nairobia had had him so turned on by all of her promises of licking his balls and bathing his hole with her tongue and sucking his dick deep into her pussy that he'd shot his load the moment she stroked his dick in her hand.

"All I ever wanted was for you and I to explore our freaky sides together," Kendall continued. "Sex between us was supposed to get better over time, be more fun, more exciting. But it wasn't. It was the same ole thing. Yes, we had lots of sex, but that's all it was. Sex. Nothing exciting. All I ever wanted was to help you find your inner slut, baby. But I know that isn't possible. So whatever it is that is stopping you from doing that is what has come between us. Not my desires. But your rigid mindset when it comes to pleasing your man and allowing your man to please you."

"Fuck you, Kendall," she yelled. "You are not going to blame me for your freaky homosexual acts. No, motherfucker! So just get the fuck out!" She stomped over toward the door and swung it open.

Kendall inhaled, then pushed out a frustrated breath. He stared at Krista for a moment and then moved toward the door. A part of him wanted to wrap his arms around her, but his pride and ego wouldn't allow it.

So he walked out.

"If you want a finger in your ass or some slutty bitch to fuck you in it, then go be with her," she shouted in back of him. "I'll have all of your shit packed by the—"

Mortified, Krista stopped herself midsentence. There stood LaQuandra and Brenda down below, their mouths ajar, their eyes wide with surprise and speculation. The last thing Krista wanted was for those two scandalous bitches to be witness to any of her personal business.

Brenda managed to close her mouth long enough to lick over her lips, before taking Kendall in with a new-found appreciation in spite of the embarrassed look on his face as he descended the stairs.

LaQuandra, however, tilted her head and give Krista a look that said, "*Bitch. I knew it,*" just as Krista slammed the door in their faces.

She hadn't slept in spite of taking two sleeping pills, and now she was barely functioning after two cups of coffee—black, no sugar.

For most of the night, Krista had paced, wondering how she had gotten to this point, to this aching realization that her marriage was over.

She tried to tell herself this would all be okay. That going home without Kendall was okay. That losing her marriage would be okay. But it wasn't. None of it was.

And yet the frightening image of Kendall with a finger in his ass kept playing over and over in her head, like that of a horror movie. His words—that he loved a finger in his ass, that he loved a woman licking over his hole, rang in her ears.

Krista loved him. God knew she did. But not enough to accept that he liked being fingered. *There.* Playing in his ass like some baboon. Like, like . . . some damn—

Ugh.

She was sick with grief, with hurt. She couldn't stop the image from playing in her head. Krista wished she had a reset button, but she didn't. And that despicable image was there—haunting her. His hard dick, his finger in his ass, him jerking himself off while fucking himself—it was all too much for her.

And Krista didn't give a hot goddamn about Kendall's ramblings about being straight or Dr. Dangerfield's previous rhetoric on the sexual benefits of prostate stimulation for a man. As far as she was concerned, Kendall was suspect. And that bitch had managed to ruin her marriage; filling Kendall's head up with all those freak-nasty ideas and cosigning this ass play shit. Then turning him against her, making her out to be the problem.

There was nothing normal about a man wanting things pushed in his ass—finger or not. A straight man's pleasure wasn't coming from his ass.

No, no. No man, no husband, of hers would be fingering himself. Ever. And she couldn't stay with a man who did. His ass-fingering and ass-licking behaviors were unacceptable.

And Krista knew herself. She knew she'd never be able to trust Kendall. She'd always be watching, searching, waiting to catch him.

And that hurt her most. Knowing this.

How had she missed it—the signs?

That he—

Krista croaked out a sob as she packed her suitcase, haphazardly tossing her belongings inside.

Her husband was gay or bi—or whatever.

Over the noisy, raw sobs that racked her body, Krista clutched her chest. It hurt just thinking about it, trying to make sense out of it. She'd finally been able to call her sister, Latrice, late last night and she'd confided in her all that she'd experienced while here on the island, including what she'd witnessed the morning she walked in on Kendall.

"And then . . . and t-t-then he d-d-didn't even have the decency to try to beg for my forgiveness. All he said was, 'I'm sorry you had to walk in on that.' What the hell, Latrice?"

"Aww, sweetie. I'm so sorry you had to walk in on that." Latrice sighed. "You know how much I love Kendall," she had said. "But that man is gay, hon, and now you know. Now you can go on with your life, girl. At least you didn't have to catch him in some dirty motel room fucking some bitch with a dick, like I'd caught Herbie. I think I would have rather caught him with a finger in his ass than that shit . . ."

Krista had cried, hard, not wanting to hear anything more about Herbie and his propensity for transsexuals. It wasn't natural.

And neither was a man stroking his prostate—code for fucking himself!

Her strong king, her lover, her black man . . . a, a, a . . . *homosexual*. Okay, okay—maybe he wasn't a homosexual. But he was suspect. And the possibility of him engaging in something more than fingering himself was real for Krista—at least in her own mind.

Like Herbie, Kendall didn't look like he was—*gay*. He didn't act it. Not that that meant anything. But the possibility would linger in the forefront of her mind, at first. Then it would somehow (through prayer—lots and lots of prayer) find its way to the back corners of her mind, perhaps. Prayerfully.

But she'd still be suspicious. Cautious. And distrusting.

More tears slid down Krista's face. She felt deceived.

"Maybe he's down low," Latrice had offered over Krista's wailing. "Maybe he goes both ways."

"I don't know what to believe anymore. This whole situation is a mess."

"Men like that are just confused, Krista." Latrice had *tsked*. "Makes no damn sense. But if you love him enough to—"

"Love him enough to *what*, stay?"

"Well, yes."

Unless he gave his life over to Christ and repented, unless he allowed Reverend Lynch to help him overcome his deviant behavior, she'd always be looking at him sideways, wondering what man—or woman—he was out there letting screw him in the ass.

Krista sniffled. "I can't—I won't—live like that. Ever."

Latrice grunted. "Good for you. He and Herbie can sword fight while I help you pack your shit when you get back to the States," was the last thing she'd heard, before falling to her knees and crying her eyes out.

When Krista had finally managed to pull herself together, she'd prayed most of the night, asking her Lord for strength, and then she prayed for Kendall, asking her Father to rid him of his filthy sins.

Afterward, she'd read the Bible—and yet, even in scripture, she'd found no solace. Krista knew her God was a forgiving one. Shit. Someone needed to be.

Because she wasn't, and she doubted she ever would be. She'd have to pray extra hard on that.

"Fuck you, Kendall!" she yelled again, slamming her last suitcase shut, then slinging it off the bed. Krista looked up at the ceiling. "Why God? Have I not been a faithful, devoted saint to Your word?"

Her vision blurred by anger and tears. She was relieved to be leaving all this wickedness behind. The remaining couples still had a few more days left on the island, but somehow the rule of not leaving the island without one's spouse had been lifted. Seemed like Dr. Dangerfield and that bitch Nairobia were all too eager to get rid of her. Of course, she wouldn't return to the States on the private aircraft. No. Arrangements had finally been made this morning for her to be ferried over to Tahiti, then catch a commercial flight on Air Tahiti to Los Angeles, and then a connecting flight back to New Jersey.

The extensive layovers, although they felt spiteful, were fine with her. Krista knew she wouldn't have had the stomach to be on the same flight back home with Kendall, knowing their life together was over, especially knowing that LaQuandra and Brenda had heard her tirade.

Krista sighed. And then she swallowed, hard, as she admitted inwardly that she would have rather not known that her husband was a goddamn queer.

Dr. Dangerfield had been right about one thing. Couples would leave this island different in some way, that nothing would be the same for any of them.

Her whole world had been turned upside, her heart crushed, her dreams shattered.

Passion Island had done nothing but destroy her marriage and her faith in a man she'd given her body and heart to. And now Krista wished more than ever that she'd never stepped foot on this remote tropical island, where new-found intimacy and reignited passion had been promised.

It had all been one big-ass lie.

From the moment she'd stepped on this beautifully lush island, she knew it was nothing but the devil's playground. And, now, she was going to sue Dr. Dangerfield and that slutty-bitch, Nairobia Jansen, for destroying her marriage.

Fifty-Two

Resentment . . .

It was poisonous. It was a haphazardly toxic emotion that showed itself in many guises. It built over time and slowly eroded relationships. It siphoned out the intimacy in marriages and caused partners to emotionally withdraw. Left them detached. It magnified flaws. Kept the past present. And, like anger and guilt, if not dealt with, it ate away at you and drained you of your emotional resources.

And Dr. Dangerfield believed that couples needed partners who were willing to hear one another out and work through issues—together—without blame, without hostility, without vengefulness. It wasn't about falling out of love (it never was)—no, it was about communication, it was about not letting resentments fester and take over relationships.

Over the years, she found that so many of her patients, clients, were in relationships with people who didn't want to—or refused to, or weren't able to—hear them out. They were oftentimes unwilling (or perhaps unable) to make agreements and hold honest conversations that weren't hurtful or blaming about what they needed, expected, or hoped for.

Sadly, there were things in relationships that sometimes needed to be changed, to be forgiven, and—yes, renegotiated. But when that wasn't able to happen, Dr. Dangerfield believed that couples would then need to rethink being in that relationship.

Leaving a relationship was never easy, even one submerged in lies and deception.

Still, something had to change for something to change.

"I still can't believe this shit," Isaiah said glumly. His head was still reeling from LaQuandra's unexpectedly shocking admission to having a slew of abortions to faking her pregnancies to feigning miscarriages and not being able to have kids.

The night they'd finished making love, she'd uncovered her soul to him over blood-curdling sobs, begging him to forgive her. She'd told him it was killing her, holding on to the lie.

Isaiah had been stunned into silence. And then his anger had gotten the best of him and he'd cursed her out, smacked the shit out of her, and came so very close to breaking open her face.

All this time, he'd been secretly resenting her for not giving him a child, beating himself up thinking that—just maybe—he was, that the drama with his son's mother might be—the cause of LaQuandra's inability to carry a child to full term.

And then the lying bitch hit him over the head with that shit.

LaQuandra was a grimy bitch. He'd heard that sordid tidbit when he'd first started smashing her, but he'd stupidly ignored the street news. She had been good to him, caring and giving. And she'd always given him good pussy.

Good pussy was the root of all fucking evil. It kept a dumb motherfucker believing in a lie. It kept them going back for another dose no matter how fucked up the bitch was attached to it.

That was what Isaiah believed.

"You should work on forgiving her," Dr. Dangerfield said.

Isaiah frowned. "Excuse me?"

"Forgive your wife, Mr. Lewis. Whether you stay or not, make a conscious choice to not hold on to your resentments. Do not let your anger have power over you, or your marriage. It will weigh you down. Keep you from moving on with your life, or in your relationships with other women. Was your wife wrong for withholding that type of information? Perhaps. I am not here to decide. But I am certain she had her reasons—"

Isaiah snorted. "Yeah, because she's a trifling, lying bitch."

"And I am sure you have told your share of lies as well."

Isaiah scowled. "I have never lied to her about no crazy shit. But she fucking took her lies to a whole other level."

"A lie is a lie no matter how it's told."

Isaiah stared at Dr. Dangerfield, his jaw clenching.

"Lies, infidelities—they hurt people, and ruin relationships. As audacious as it is for someone to be completely honest in the beginning of any relationship, it also takes a level of courage to finally come clean."

Isaiah dragged a hand down over his face and then pushed out a breath. "I know. But I feel so fucking betrayed."

Dr. Dangerfield nodded, knowingly. "And no one is saying your feelings aren't valid. They are. That level of betrayal hurts. It cuts deeply. But you can't change nor control the past. But you can learn from it—or not. You can either live in it, or work through it. But it will take time. And practice. And lots of patience."

Isaiah lowered his head and covered his face in his hands, taking deep, steadying breaths. And they sat in the quiet. Aside from the cascading waterfall and the faint tick of the clock, Isaiah welcomed the silence. He needed to quiet the noises in his head.

He needed a moment to think, not talk.

He didn't know what the fuck to do—well, he did know.

Isaiah sighed. Then finally looked up at Dr. Dangerfield. "I wanted more kids—I still do. But now I know that shit won't ever happen—not with LaQuandra's lying ass."

"You love her," Dr. Dangerfield said softly.

It wasn't a question, and yet Isaiah wasn't sure whom she was speaking of.

Isaiah's dark brows drew together. "Who?"

"Your son's mother."

Isaiah shook his head. Out of respect for Dr. Dangerfield, Isaiah wasn't going to answer her with a lie. "No. Not *her*. I love her *puss*—the sex. It's always been about the sex with Cass." He laughed. "Fuck. I thought I did at one time. You know. Love her. Hell, I wanted to. But trying to love Cassandra is like trying to hug a cactus. You have to get through all the prickly needles before you can get to the inside of her. That shit is too much work. And loving her means loving all the drama that comes with her."

Dr. Dangerfield smiled at his analogy. "Almost like the drama with your wife. But is there a difference?"

Isaiah shook his head solemnly. "Yeah, Doc. And that right there is the fucked-up part. I love Quandra." He pushed out a breath. "I'm not *in* love with her—I don't think I ever was, but I love her for always having my back, no matter what."

"Then there is hope," Dr. Dangerfield offered. "And room for forgiveness."

Isaiah *tsked*. "Maybe." The word sounded hopeful, but his tone was very *whatever*.

"In time," Dr. Dangerfield said as the bell chimed. "Even in our darkest moments," she continued as she rose to her feet, "miracles happen. Hope blooms. Forgiveness heals wounds. And we find ourselves shedding layers of the past and opening ourselves to new possibilities. And then, when we least expect it, we find ourselves surrounded by a love we never knew possible. Because, Mr. Lewis, the universe always has the last say."

"That may be true. But I'm not tryna hold my breath for it," Isaiah said as he stood.

Dr. Dangerfield offered a slight smile. "Be well, Mr. Lewis. Don't let your wife's past destroy your present—or your future. You are a man deserving of love and understanding. And so is your wife. If not with one another, then with someone else."

Isaiah bit his lip. And when Dr. Dangerfield offered him her hand to shake, he took it, pulling her into a tight embrace. Shocking himself—and her.

After a bit of hesitation, he stepped back from her.

"I never thought I'd say this, but this therapy shit wasn't half bad. Thank you for giving me clarity over these last few weeks, and for helping me make a decision about my marriage."

Dr. Dangerfield gave Isaiah a perplexed look. "Oh? And what is that?"

"I need to stop fucking with Cass, period. And set some new boundaries."

Dr. Dangerfield nodded. "That's a very big start. And what of your wife?"

Isaiah shrugged. "I haven't gotten that part figured out yet." Then he winked at her. "Baby steps, Doc. Baby steps."

Dr. Dangerfield bit back a smile. "Change is always good, even in the smallest of doses." She walked him to the door, and then opened it. "Take care, Mr. Lewis."

"You too, Doc." Isaiah took her in one last time, then leaned in and kissed her on the cheek. "I'ma never forget you, or my time on this island. Believe that."

Dr. Dangerfield smiled as she watched him stride out of her office and then down the hall, his demeanor rugged, his swag hood. She shut the door behind her, then touched the spot where he'd kissed her. She pressed her thighs together, her pussy near orgasm at the thought of getting back to her villa and rolling back the cameras and watching him fuck the shit out of LaQuandra.

Oh, God—yes. Dr. Gretchen Dangerfield loved her work on Passion Island.

And she was already anticipating the next cycle of dysfunctional couples in search of truth and light and long-lost passion.

And she'd welcome the drama, the lies, and their dirty, dark secrets with baited breath. She always did.

And she always would.

Epilogue

SIX MONTHS LATER . . .

Sexual energy crackled around them. It was a tangible aura that thickened the air and warmed over Brenda's skin. Her hair was sexily mussed and her lips were deliciously swollen from the kisses and from having them wrapped around hard dick. Two dicks.

Roselle's and—

God, what was this fine motherfucker's name?

Or had he even shared his name?

Brenda was too inebriated from lust and from the four cosmopolitans she'd drunk to even remember.

Or should his name have mattered?

Probably not.

Roselle preferred their sexual mates to remain nameless, anonymous—and not from the same area or state as them. It was the only way he would allow her the pleasure of having two—or three (and one time four)—men in the same bed with her.

And so she expected, required the same, when it came to the other woman who shared her husband's dick with her.

Of course these were amendments made to her original checklist of tenets when Roselle had first suggested an open marriage.

Thus far, it had been working. The parameters set had been respected.

But this one—"Oh, God . . ." Brenda gasped and started to come. She wanted to break the rules, just this once, and keep him in her contacts.

They were enjoying their seven-day, all-expense-paid trip to the French Riviera, and Brenda knew she wouldn't see this delectable man again. She wanted to—God, knew she did—and, yes, most likely, behind Roselle's back.

He wasn't as long as Roselle, but he was dangerously thicker. His beer-can thick dick was no more than six-and-a-half or seven inches, but the stretch of her pussy around his shaft burned in exquisite pleasure as he stroked inside of her.

Ooh.

He was so thick.

So heavy.

So good.

So, so, so delicious.

And she was so fucking wet.

"That's right, baby," Roselle said in a husky voice as he bent and sucked her nipple between his teeth. He gave it a sharp nip and then slid his hand down over her quivering belly and then to her engorged clit.

Brenda gasped, and the flush of pleasure radiated over her skin.

"Yeah, he's fucking my sweet baby's pussy," Roselle murmured as he stroked her clit as Beer Can Dick held her legs open, his palms flat on the inside of her thighs, as his dick scraped over her walls, causing heat to curl in her veins and dart through her body.

Brenda moaned. And then she cried out when Roselle pinched the wet nub.

"Is her pussy good, man?" Roselle asked low and husky.

Beer Can Dick moaned appreciatively. "Shit, yeah."

"You got her shit so wet. Fuck her hard, man."

"Oh, God, yes. Fuck me, fuck me," Brenda panted helplessly.

Roselle's eyes darkened as he watched the wet glide of Beer Can Dick's shaft go in and out of Brenda's cunt.

He probed deep, not necessarily scraping the mouth of her cervix, but deep enough to send a spasm of ecstasy ricocheting through Brenda's body. Brenda furrowed the back of her head deeper into the pillow as she arched her body up into the heat, absorbing the weight of each thrust, melting, melting, melting . . .

"You like that, baby?" Roselle rasped, looking down at Brenda through a lust-lidded gaze that sent shivers through her. He stared at Brenda with stark approval in his eyes as her eyes rolled up in the back of her head in response to the rhythmic pounding in and out of her body. And just when she was on the cusp of another orgasm, Beer Can Dick pulled from her body, causing her to whimper in protest as her pussy clutched around the emptiness.

Roselle grinned as he finally pulled his dick out of his boxers, holding it in his hand. "You ready for this dick in your mouth, baby?" he murmured. "Me and my man gonna fuck the shit outta you. You want that, baby?"

Brenda nodded wordlessly, winding her hips into the mattress, thrusting her pelvis upward in greedy need.

The plum-sized head of Beer Can's dick nudged her opening just as Roselle cupped her jaw in his hands. Brenda cried out as Beer Can Dick surged forward, spearing her open in one wide stroke. But her cries were quickly silenced as Roselle forced her mouth open and slid his dick to the back of her throat.

Beer Can Dick stretched and plundered her cunt as Roselle stretched open her mouth, fucking into her throat, both men matching the other's thrusts, bringing her to tears, to orgasm, to indescribable pleasure.

Oh, God, yes . . .

Brenda croaked out another moan. Her lids fluttered before her gaze locked with Roselle's. She loved him.

"You ready for this cream?" Roselle rasped. "Uh, uh . . . you want this nut on your face?"

Brenda moaned over his dick, and her wet mouth splashed out drool and spit.

She yelled hoarsely as Roselle tore his dick from her throat and began fisting his shaft in long, rapid strokes. As the first splatter hit her face, she felt the hot spurt of cum splash onto her breasts as Roselle swung his dick side to side, like a watering hose.

Beer Can Dick groaned as he freed himself from Brenda's wet clutch, tearing off his condom, and then quickly stroking himself.

Roselle groaned. He shot more of his hot cream onto her burning flesh, just as Beer Can's nut shot out from his dick, his release spurting out onto her stomach and then over her swollen sex. It ran down into the seam of her pussy and slithered down into the crack of her ass.

Roselle leaned down and planted a long, passionate kiss on her lips. Then whispered, "Happy Anniversary, baby."

Brenda smiled and then murmured, "Happy Anniversary. I love you."

Roselle leaned over her body and slid his hand over cum-soaked pussy. "I love you, too, baby." He smeared Beer Can Dick's cum over her clit and then dipped two fingers into her wet, juicy hole.

Brenda gasped.

Passion Island had brought her and Roselle closer, made their connection much deeper. No, they weren't perfect. But they were perfect for each other. She'd decided that she didn't need to know if their eight-year-old daughter was his or not. Roselle thought he was and he loved her in a way that only a father could. So, yes, he was her father. And Brenda's heart told her so.

Roselle's curled fingers found her spot.

"Oh, oh, oh, oh . . ." Brenda slid her hands up her belly and to her breasts. She plumped them up and out with her palms and then flicked her tongue out, licking over her skin for Roselle's nut. Her body shuddered. Her cunt clutched Roselle's working fingers.

"That's right, baby . . . come for me," he whispered.

Surprisingly, he hadn't been caught cheating since they'd returned home from the retreat. In fact, he'd told her he no longer had the desire to cheat, especially now.

And she wanted to believe him. For the first time in a long time, maybe she finally would.

Brenda closed her eyes.

And mewled, clawing at the sheets.

Oh God, she was coming and coming and coming. And falling in love with Roselle all over again in a way she hadn't known possible. This was what Passion Island had taught her, this was what she'd desired, needed—unfurled sinfully dark, forbidden desires.

"*Heeeey*, baby *fahver*. Isaiah told me you finally left that ole goat-faced *bit*—"

Isaiah frowned, swerving his car into the nearest parking space. "Yo, what the fuck I tell you about your mouth, huh, Cass?"

Yeah, it was true. Isaiah had left LaQuandra. Well, sort of. He'd moved out at least. But he was over there nearly every other day at her request, moving something, painting something, or putting something together because she was too cheap to hire someone else to do it.

Nevertheless, the night before leaving Passion Island, he'd decided that they both needed space. Him to sort through everything she'd told him. And her to—well, shit, work on her attitude and self-esteem. He refused to stay in a marriage with a nagging, insecure, loud-mouthed-ass woman. Period.

Cassandra sucked her teeth. "Nigga-coon, *boom!* Eat the inside of my ass, Isaiah. I do what I want with this mouth. Bring that ole big juicy dingaling over here 'n' let me remind you of what it do."

He sighed, glancing at his watch. Nearly three p.m. He only had ten minutes to get inside the building. "Fuck outta here, Cass, with that dumb shit. I told you I'm good on that." And he meant it. He hadn't sexed Cassandra since he returned from the couple's retreat.

He knew he needed to keep the peace with her to keep her spiteful-ass from trying to drag him back into court for more child support. But he was no longer going to do it with his dick. Fucking her only fueled more drama. And Isaiah was officially done with the bullshit.

Cassandra grunted. "*Mmph.* I'm just glad you realized exactly how trifling that *bit*—LaQuandra is. I don't know why you ever stuck your dingdong in that rotted troll doll anyway."

Isaiah sighed again. "The same reason you let me stick my shit in yours—because it was good."

He heard her pop her lips. "Uh-huh. But I bet that wildebeest can't make it pop on that dingaling the way I do. She never deserved you, sugah-boo." And then she grunted. "All that dingaling gone to waste inside that nasty nut-trap."

Isaiah shut off the engine. "Yo, I ain't tryna hear all that shit right now, Cass. Why can't I get ahold of Isaiah?"

"Because I took his phone," she said nastily. "That lil' fucker wanna be up all night on the phone talkin' to them nasty lil' bitches he got suckin' on his wee-wee, then come up in here bringing home Cs and Ds on his report card. No sir. Not up in here. So, no gawt-damn phone and no more late-night ho-patrols lookin' for nasty-ass tricks to pump his dingaling in, until he gets them grades up."

Isaiah shook his head. "I'll talk to him."

Cassandra grunted. "Mm-hmm. You better. And you better tell him that the only two holes he better be sticking his dingaling in, is an ass or a mouth. And he better be double wrapping, too. I don't want his horny-ass bringin' no gawtdamn babies up in here or no diseases 'cause if he do, I'ma stomp on his balls. It's bad enough Day'Asia got another nasty-ass drip leaking from that sewer tank."

Isaiah cringed and then glanced at the time again. "Look, I gotta go. I'll be there around six to pick lil' Isaiah up. Tell him to be ready."

"I mean it, Isaiah, you better talk—"

He disconnected the call. He'd heard enough. He had more important things to do rather than listen to the ratchet-ass ramblings of Cassandra Simms.

He removed his keys and quickly hopped out the car, slamming the door shut and then activating the alarm.

LaQuandra rolled her eyes the minute she saw him trotting across the parking lot toward the building. She was annoyed that he couldn't pick her up and drive her to the appointment. Driving two cars made no goddamn sense. And then he'd had her sitting in the waiting room for over twenty minutes, feeling abandoned and alone.

He was probably on the phone talking to that—

She stopped herself. Nope. She wasn't going to let that trashy-ass whore's name roll out of her mouth. Not today. Hell—not most days.

She was getting better at not doing it, especially now. In the grand scheme of things, Cassandra was a very insignificant thing, because that's what she was—a *thing*.

She had a lot to look forward to. The best thing she'd ever done was to confess her past to Isaiah. Yeah, she'd hurt him—he was still hurt. But she knew at some point he'd have to get over it. She was wrong. She'd already admitted that. And she'd apologized over and over again. And she'd keep apologizing and trying to make it up to him until he found it in his heart to forgive her, or not.

LaQuandra swallowed. She loved him. And she didn't want to

let go. But she'd promised herself that she'd give him three more months to be angry with her. And then he would need to either shit or get off the proverbial pot.

She absent-mindedly twisted her wedding band around her finger, pulling it up to her swollen knuckle, then pushing it back down.

And then she nibbled on a fingernail. Her nerves were rattled *and* she was starving.

God, she could eat a horse. All she did these days was graze. And right now she had a taste for sardines and olives.

LaQuandra's mouth watered, but her stomach clenched.

Isaiah walked in frowning, but then he looked over in her direction and his lips curved upward, giving a hint of a smile that resembled more of a smirk than anything else.

Within minutes, they were being called to the back.

LaQuandra assumed her regular position, while Isaiah sat in a chair beside her.

"How are you feeling?" the thirtysomething woman asked.

LaQuandra shrugged, then rubbed her grumbling stomach. "Okay, I guess. I don't sleep much. And I'm constantly hungry."

She felt her eyes prick with tears. "And I'm so emotional."

The woman smiled.

And Isaiah shook his head. He wasn't sure if he wanted to move back in with her moody, bitchy-ass. But he knew he didn't want to live with regrets, either. There was a part of him that knew he didn't want to throw in the towel on his marriage unless he was absolutely sure he'd done his part.

And he hadn't.

Yeah, she lied to him—in the worst way. But . . .

"Would you like to hear the baby's heartbeat?"

LaQuandra bit back a sob as she nodded her head. "Yes."

"No doubt."

The obstetrician smiled and then applied a cool gel to her abdomen. LaQuandra's chest tightened. And she held her breath. Every appointment for the last five months had been like this, her holding her breath. Now she was nearing her third trimester and she was still a ball of nerves.

This life inside of her was a miracle—her miracle. One she'd conceived on Passion Island, the night she'd confessed to Isaiah. Though it was a blessing, she was so afraid of anything happening to her unborn child. She'd lied so many times about being pregnant and had feigned countless miscarriages that she was afraid she'd reap what she sowed for deceiving Isaiah and for spreading those horrible lies out into the universe.

She didn't want her deception to somehow manifest itself into a curse.

The doctor moved the wand over LaQuandra's swollen belly and . . .

Whoosh, whoosh . . . whoosh, whoosh . . .

There it was. Her son's little beating heart. The sound of love and hope and second chances filled the room.

"His heartbeat is very strong and healthy," the doctor said.

More tears filled LaQuandra's eyes.

It was only then that her lungs expanded and she was able to breathe in, then exhale.

Isaiah reached for her hand, and stared at her with those dark-chocolate orbs of his that seemingly sparkled with the promise of, perhaps, forgiveness.

Something he knew he needed to do before his son was born. He didn't want to witness the birth of his seed coming into the world harboring ill feelings toward LaQuandra.

She'd hurt him with the truth, but somehow he saw this pregnancy as redemption.

Isaiah heard Dr. Dangerfield's voice, *"Even in our darkest moments, miracles happen . . ."*

A smile eased over his lips. Dr. Dangerfield had been right. Hope truly did bloom.

Isaiah squeezed LaQuandra's hand even tighter. And then he cupped her cheek and placed a gentle kiss on her lips, and then he pulled away, taking his lips with him, the kiss over almost as soon as it started.

But it was a start.

Baby steps.

A blisteringly gush of wind whipped around Krista's legs and blew up her coat as she bit into her bottom lip pensively.

"If you want your husband back, then go to him. Fight for him . . ."

Those were the words that swirled around in her head as her foot landed on the last step of Kendall's new townhome. The door swung open just as she reached out to press the doorbell. A blast of warm air greeting her along with . . .

"Krista?"

"Hell—*oh*." Krista looked from Kendall to the five-foot, eight-inch woman with the cocoa-brown skin and cute spiked haircut, then back at Kendall, this time with questioning eyes.

Kendall drank in the sight of her. She looked different. Thinner. Despite so many months slipping by, he . . . she—

"Persia, Krista—my *soon* to be ex-wife."

Ouch. Krista felt the sting of those words and cringed.

"Oh," Persia said. She and Kendall had been seeing more of each other, more openly, over the last several months. "Hi."

Krista forced a smile.

Kendall leaned in and kissed Persia on the cheek. "Thanks for stopping by. Talk, soon?"

A surge of jealous anger jolted her. And yet Krista knew she had no right to her feelings. After all, she'd pushed him out. Hadn't she? And, obviously, straight into another woman's arms.

Persia smiled, reaching for his hand. "Of course." And then she flicked a glance at Krista. "Nice meeting you."

With a raised brow, Krista sent her a cold stare and stepped back, allowing her to walk by. Krista waited for the disgustingly pretty, doe-eyed bitch to flounce her bouncy-ass to her Jaguar and then slide behind the wheel, before bringing her attention back to Kendall.

"I guess I should have called, first?"

Kendall shrugged his left shoulder. "Probably," he said, as he leaned against the doorframe, blocking the doorway. "What brings you by?"

God, Krista missed him so much. She'd say anything—do anything, just to have him one last time.

Persia blew her horn, and Kendall smiled. And Krista saw something strangely unfamiliar flicker in his eyes, something . . . *primitive*. Or maybe she was simply imagining it.

Still, she had to know, "Is she one of your ass lickers?"

Kendall resisted the urge to laugh hysterically. But he frowned instead. "Look, Krista. What does that—?"

"I'm sorry," she quickly said. "I'm not here to fight. Can I come in? Please?"

"For what?"

"Please." Krista heard the pleading in her voice, and wondered if Kendall had heard it too. "Please," she said again, now unconcerned about how it sounded.

He sighed, then stepped back, allowing her enough space between them to get through the door, her body mere inches from his as she crossed over the threshold.

She stepped inside the living room, glancing around the place.

It was tastefully decorated in a masculine yet modern kind of way. Several candles sat on a tray burned on top of a large rectangular, leather ottoman.

Kendall closed the door. "So what brings you by?"

"I-I-I wanted to see you—you know, before our divorce hearing."

Kendall's brow rose. "For?"

"To say I'm sorry, Kendall." She fidgeted with the ends of her coat's belt, wrapped tightly around her waist. She choked back a sob. And then cursed inwardly. She'd promised herself on the ride over that she wouldn't break down. That she wouldn't come off broken and needy—although she was.

Broken.

Needy.

She'd thought the separation and pending divorce would be easy; that she could walk away from her marriage and move on with her life, without him. But it wasn't and she couldn't.

"Look, Kris—"

"I'm in therapy," she blurted out. "Working on my, um, issues. Dr. Dangerfield referred me to a—"

Kendall blinked, somewhat shocked by this revelation. "I thought you didn't like her."

"I didn't." Krista shook her head. "I mean. I thought I didn't. But I swallowed my pride and broke down and asked her for help. It wasn't her I disliked. I realized it was *me* I detested. I blamed her and that whole trip for what happened between us, when all the while she was right, you were right. I—*my* thinking—was the problem. And I came here to thank you."

Kendall gave her a confused look. "For what?"

"For helping me see that. Had we not gone to that island for that couples retreat, I would still be living in denial, still stuck in that crazy way of thinking. And I would have never gotten the help I need." Krista pushed out a breath. "I mean. I'm still struggling, still trying to wrap my mind around sexuality and desires and trying to tap into what my own sexual desires might be. After years of it being ingrained in me of how a woman—a Christian woman should behave sexually . . ."

Krista stopped herself. She didn't want to rehash her upbringing with Kendall—the way her mother shamed her into thinking being sexual was dirty, that it was a sin to have desires. She didn't want to relive, at this moment, the memories of her abuse at the hands of her mother—of being tied down or, most times, held down, and her genitalia being whipped raw by the back of a hairbrush or a wooden spoon for exploring her own body.

"Look, Krista," Kendall said. "I'm happy for you; really, I am. But, why do you think I need to hear all this now; we've been separated for nearly six months. Why now?"

Krista winced. She felt her window of opportunity slipping through her fingers by the second.

"Can you ever forgive me?" She fastened a desperate gaze on him. "I'm still trying to forgive me. But I pray every day and with therapy, I'm getting better at forgiving myself."

She bit her lip.

"Krista, there's nothing to forgive. I guess we both hurt each other in some way."

Father, give me strength . . .

"If you want your husband back, then fight for him . . ."

"I-I—um. Can I use your bathroom?"

Kendall gave her a strange look, then shrugged. "Yeah. Down the hall on the left."

Krista quickly spun on her heel, nearly breaking her ankle as she tripped over her feet to make her way down the hall.

Kendall stared in part amusement and part puzzlement, wondering why she would come here now, looking for forgiveness. He decided he wasn't going to put any energy into trying to figure it out. In another week, they'd be divorced.

And then he could finally get on with his life.

Krista stood nervously before the mirror in Kendall's large bathroom.

She unfastened her coat, and then let the big, burly fabric drop to the floor.

Her breath caught.

And then her heart stopped.

She couldn't believe she was doing this.

She stared at her reflection, taking in the strange woman who stared back at her. Twenty pounds lighter donned in a pair of black pumps and a black bustier that made her heavy breasts look like two ripe, juicy cantaloupes, ready for the plucking.

And then there was the garter belt—Dear Lord—and the skimpy red-laced panties that she'd worn beneath her coat.

Krista covered a hand over her mouth and shook her head.

This was silly—God, what was she doing?

Playing dress-up.

Role-playing, pretending to be something she knew nothing about.

She didn't want her life to be a façade. She didn't want to live in a make-believe world. No. Krista wanted a life that allowed her to be something she'd never been. She wanted to live in a world that allowed her to shed her old skin without shame or guilt.

Over the last several months, all she'd lived in was a world filled with regret and lots of remorse.

No. Krista didn't want that life.

All she wanted was a do-over.

God . . . Krista gripped the edge of the vanity and shook her head. What if she failed at getting it right—*this* time?

Hell, she could barely walk in the pricey, clearance-marked heels she'd found at Nordstrom Rack. But here she was, standing in five-inches of pure desperation.

She wanted her marriage. She'd been missing everything she and Kendall ever shared. All she wanted was her husband back. She missed him, his laugh, his light snoring, his kisses, his touch.

Oh, God, and, and . . . that magnificent dick.

That good loving.

That, that, unforgettable . . . *fucking*.

She wanted it all—*him*.

Kendall.

This was what her therapist had been suggesting, encouraging in the last several therapy sessions. Taking risk. Throwing caution to the wind without overthinking it. She'd even had Krista reading erotica, and so she'd been ODing on the likes of Allison Hobbs and Zane and Risqué, transporting her mind to erotic places she'd never imagined existed. She'd even downloaded a few of Nairobia's porn movies. God, that whore was such a sex goddess. She had a way of making some of the kinkiest sex look so damn sexy.

It had her curious. Had her imagining, wondering.

Yet, she was still a work in progress. Lord knew she had a long road ahead of her. But therapy was helping her, healing her. Reading erotica was helping her too. Opening her to new possibilities.

Slowly, Krista was learning to embrace her sexuality, her sensuality, and her femininity, all while staying steadfast in her religious beliefs. However, it was, admittedly, still a struggle. One Krista was determined to overcome.

Dr. Dangerfield had once told her that she could be a Christian woman and *still* be a freak for the man she loved. And she wanted to be.

Krista glanced at herself one last time. "Well, here goes nothing." And then she opened the door. And flicked off the light.

When she returned, Kendall was still standing in the same spot, as still as a statue, waiting. He blinked several times trying to make sure his eyes weren't playing some cruel trick on him.

"Damn," was all Kendall finally managed to say as he stared at her, wondering who this woman was, and where she'd come from. He was nearly undone by the sight of her. And the thought of her sweet pussy hidden behind that patch of silk made his dick suddenly hard, forcing him to shove his hands down into the front pockets of his jeans to hide his growing bulge.

Krista found herself holding her breath as she waited for his response. She felt a moment of panic set in. An infinite amount of time passed by before she forced herself to breathe out through her nose. And when he still hadn't moved or said anything, Krista's knees nearly buckled.

"I screwed up, Kendall. I really, really did. And I am so, so, regretful for shutting you out. For shaming you and trying to *emasculate* you—my therapist's words." She took a breath. "I don't want a divorce, Kendall. I want my husband back. I want *you*—only you." Krista swallowed the lump forming in her throat. She felt as if she were about to be sick. She couldn't bear the thought of baring her soul to him to only be rejected in turn.

But it would serve her right.

"I should have listened to you. I should have been more open to hearing you, Kendall. I don't want to be on the sidelines, watching another woman take what should be mine. *You* beside me, inside of me, on top of me, in back of me—wherever you wanna be. So, Kendall, I stand here, half-naked, offering you me—the best and worst parts of everything I am. The broken and glued and very flawed parts of me. There is so much more to sex than I ever allowed myself to know. I know that now. Therapy has shown me that. All I'm asking . . . is for another chance."

Yes, this whole ordeal had forced her to take a look at herself, and to learn humility.

For the first time in Krista's life, she felt bold. Powerful. And, finally, in control of what she wanted—her marriage, her husband and lover.

Kendall stared at her, his heart nearly jumping from his chest. He'd resolved himself to the fact that it was over between them; that he could—

He cursed under his breath.

He was standing here with a hard, throbbing dick, his balls already tightening from need. And here Krista stood in his living room looking so incredibly sexy, so vulnerable, and so fucking foreign to him. She elicited a burning desire to fuck her in one stroke and then make love to her the next. Truth was, he still loved her.

Kendall watched her with sultry eyes, and a tortured groan welled in his chest and stuck there. What was a future ex-husband to do?

What was he to say?

Nothing.

He thought he had wanted the divorce up until this very moment.

Krista stalked over toward him, no longer able to stand the space between them.

"Kris—"

"No," she said huskily, cutting him off as she slid her hand over the front of his fly. "Let me have this—*you*, even if it's one last time."

Before she lost her nerve and bolted for the door, Krista quickly unbuttoned and unzipped his pants and then impatiently yanked them down, along with his boxers, over his hips as she sank to her knees. Kendall's hard dick sprung upward and Krista's mouth watered, anticipating the taste of him, the feel of his hard throbbing flesh over her tongue. She flicked her tongue over the head, and then drank it into her mouth, sucking gently as she pulled him in deeper.

His musky scent, so familiar, so intoxicating, engulfed her. Krista breathed it in like a favorite cologne before stretching her mouth wider around him (she'd been practicing on bananas and most recently a dildo) and she started to suck in long, lascivious pulls. To the back of her throat and then out again to the very tip before taking him back.

"*Aah*, fuck," Kendall hissed. She quickened her speed, rewinding back everything she'd read in those novels and had watched in those videos. A shudder rolled over her body as Kendall's dick brushed the back of her throat, causing her nipples to tighten.

Krista felt a surge of wetness between her legs and moaned over Kendall's dick.

Unable to bear another second of this blissful torture, Kendall pulled Krista up from her knees, her mouth reluctantly releasing the suction on his dick. And, in one big scoop, Krista was up off her feet and in Kendall's arms being carried over to the leather sectional.

He gently laid her on her back. Covered his mouth with hers. And kissed her deeply as he yanked her panties to the side. And then he peppered her skin with warm kisses, along her neck, down her shoulder, down her belly. And then, and then—oh God, yes.

Right there—over her clit.

Krista closed her eyes as tears of hope and promise streamed down her face. She didn't know if she could ever lick Kendall in his ass, but she'd try it—once. Yes, yes, the new version of who she wanted to be would try anything once with him.

Suddenly, Kendall's hands slid to her ass, and he squeezed as his lips wrapped over her clit. She gasped. And then she felt his tongue, swimming inside of her.

Krista cried out as he licked, sucked and then thrust his tongue back into her pussy.

Fire singed over her skin the moment his fingertip pressed into her asshole.

"Ohgodohgodohgod—please . . ." she murmured as her nails dug into the leather.

His finger slipped in.

And, for the very first time, Krista surrendered, and gave herself over to the magic of Kendall's touch.

About the Author

Cairo is the author of *Prison Snatch*; *The Pleasure Zone*; *Dirty Heat*; *Between the Sheets*; *Ruthless: Deep Throat Diva 3*; *Retribution: Deep Throat Diva 2*; *Slippery When Wet*; *The Stud Palace*; *Big Booty*; *Man Swappers*; *Kitty-Kitty, Bang-Bang*; *Deep Throat Diva*; *Daddy Long Stroke*; *The Man Handler*; and *The Kat Trap*. His travels to Egypt are what inspired his pen name.